Available in December 2009
from Mills & Boon® Intrigue

SOLDIER CAGED

He prayed the kiss would tell him what he needed to know...

And it did. Her mouth tasted the same as he'd remembered. Rich and inviting and unique to Sophia. But what was she doing here, in a bunker? Tipping his head, he changed the angle of contact, changed everything he'd thought was true.

Sophia Rhodes *was* here. And he was holding her.

Desperate to satisfy his craving, he slid one hand down her body, pulling her hips towards him. It seemed that time had reversed itself. They were back in the past together. Only this time he wasn't leaving in the morning. This time he'd keep her captive in his bed for days.

When he began to unbutton her shirt, she stiffened.

She pressed a finger to her lips. "Someone's coming!" She looked wildly around. "I've got to hide."

He didn't question her. The panic in her voice and on her face was enough to tell him she was in grave danger.

SEDUCING THE MERCENARY

"We have a deal, Emma," he said very quietly. "Don't we?"

She studied the hard planes of his face, marvelling at how different he'd looked in those few moments he dropped his guard. He could be lying, a brilliant sociopath manipulating her, working up her empathy, sucking her in with charismatic charm. Or it could be the truth.

Either way, she was trapped. The only way out was to see this mission through, knowing that any mis-step might cost her life.

"Yes," she said softly, placing her hand in his, "we have a deal."

First published in Great Britain 2009
Harlequin Mills & Boon Limited,
Eton House, 18-24 Paradise Road, Richmond, Surrey TW9 1SR

Soldier Caged © Ruth Glick 2008
Seducing the Mercenary © Loreth Beswetherick 2007

ISBN: 978 0 263 87344 3

46-1209

Harlequin Mills & Boon policy is to use papers that are natural, renewable and recyclable products and made from wood grown in sustainable forests. The logging and manufacturing processes conform to the legal environmental regulations of the country of origin.

Printed and bound in Spain
by Litografia Rosés S.A., Barcelona

SOLDIER CAGED
BY
REBECCA YORK

SEDUCING THE MERCENARY
BY
LORETH ANNE WHITE

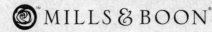

™ MILLS & BOON®

SOLDIER CAGED

BY
REBECCA YORK

Award-winning, bestselling novelist **Ruth Glick**, who writes as **Rebecca York**, is the author of more than one hundred books, including her popular 43 Light Street series for Mills & Boon® Intrigue. Ruth says she has the best job in the world. Not only does she get paid for telling stories, she's also the author of twelve cookbooks. Ruth and her husband, Norman, travel frequently, researching locales for her novels and searching out new dishes for her cookbooks.

To Norman, who always watches out for me.

Chapter One

Jonah Baker heard the chatter of a Kalashnikov, then another weapon returning fire. The sound was familiar in the craggy brown hills of a country where warlords ran rampant over the land, fighting each other for prestige and territory.

The sun played over the top of his helmet, and sweat crawled down his back under his flak jacket. For a man who'd grown up in… Grown up in…

He struggled to remember the place where he'd spent his childhood. He had to have come from *somewhere*. But he couldn't bring it into focus. Not the town. Not his house. Panic tightened his chest. Then he reminded himself that the past wasn't important right now. He had to focus on this village. These people.

They knew who had come here to harvest the viscous fluid from the immature poppy plants, then ship the darkened, slightly sticky mass called opium to middlemen.

He caught a flicker of movement to his right, but it was only a woman peering out from the doorway of her stone house.

Her whole body was hidden by a burka—a blue robe with a face screen that allowed her to view only a narrow slice of the world. But he saw her small hand clutching the wooden door frame. In her other hand she held a metal box with a crank. She let go of the woodwork and began to turn the crank. As she did, music started playing. It sounded foreign and exotic, something the men might dance to on a village feast day or at a wedding celebration. It should have been pleasant, but it sent shivers along his spine.

"Stop," he said, wanting to clamp his hands over his ears. "I mean you no harm," he added.

The woman eased back into the shadows beyond the doorway, but the tune kept grating at him until he strode away, scanning the street for trouble.

A few houses away, a group of men with dark beards, loose-fitting shirts, and colorful turbans stepped into view and stood facing the American soldiers. Some of them had lined, weather-worn faces that made them look as if they were in their seventies. But he suspected they were decades younger. Life in…

Again his mind drew a blank. And then it came to him. He was in Afghanistan. Tramping through the back of beyond, where there were no passable roads. Trying to cut off the source of funding for the Taliban.

"We won't punish you. We just want to know who harvested the opium," Lieutenant Calley said.

Calley?

Wasn't he someone from another conflict, decades ago?

"Damn," he muttered.

"Quiet. Don't interrupt," Calley ordered.

Jonah's head swung toward the man. "You don't give the orders. I'm the major. You're the lieutenant."

"But I'm better at the language. That's why I'm handling the questioning."

Jonah focused on the scene. Everything seemed normal. But something bad was going to happen. He felt it all the way to the marrow of his bones.

The villager doing the talking took a step back, his eyes darting away for a moment. "We don't know the men who came for the opium," he insisted.

"But you watched them work."

Somehow Jonah could understand perfectly what the guy was saying.

"There were a lot of them. They said they would kill us if we interfered."

"Uh-huh," Calley muttered.

Jonah saw him reach for his gun. "Don't!"

"I know how to get them to talk." Calley pulled out his sidearm and shot the old man.

A sick feeling rose in Jonah's throat. "What the hell are you doing?"

"Defending myself."

"No. You started it." Jonah backed away in horror. "Stop. Stop," he kept pleading, but Calley had gone mad.

He saw the woman in the doorway clutch her chest and fall. Red blood spread across her blue burka as she lay on the ground.

A bullet slammed into his thigh and he went down. Then another one caught him in the arm.

Horror swirled through his mind, through his soul. He was still screaming "No" when his eyes opened and he found himself lying on a narrow bed in a darkened room.

Sweat drenched his skin and the T-shirt and briefs he was wearing. The bedclothes were tangled around him. Dim light filtered in under the crack at the bottom of the door.

He'd awakened from a nightmare—about Afghanistan. His last assignment.

He pressed the heels of his hands against his eyes.

No, he corrected himself immediately. That wasn't his last assignment.

The dream was so vivid, that it had seemed like reality. But he knew he had made it up. It wasn't real. Lieutenant Calley was a soldier from Vietnam, notorious for having ordered the mass murder of innocent villagers. That was how he had ended up in a nightmare about the massacre of a village in the Afghan hills.

Or was there something real about the dream—and his mind had twisted the facts? Like the lieutenant's name.

He moved his arm and found it was sore, as though he'd suffered a recent injury. Fumbling beside the bed, he found a table and a lamp attached to the wall. He switched on the lamp, then sat blinking in the sudden light.

When his vision cleared, he looked at the upper part of his right arm and saw a round red scar from a recent bullet wound.

Like in the dream.

And what about his leg?

Quickly he pulled the covers aside and found another scar on his right thigh. Just where he'd been hit in the nightmare village.

So where was he now?

Was this a prison? An asylum?

Once again, panic gripped his throat and he pushed himself off the bed because he needed to get away from the place where the dream had grabbed him.

When he stood up, pain shot through his injured thigh. He caught his breath, adjusted the weight on the leg, then staggered to the door.

To his vast relief, when he turned the knob, the door opened.

Thank God. At least he wasn't locked in. He stared down a long corridor, lit only by dim emergency lights. Like those in his room, the walls were of cinder block painted an institutional green. And the lights were spaced about every fifteen feet, leaving pools of darkness between them.

If he had to guess, he'd say it was night, and they'd turned the lights down because most people were sleeping. Or maybe that was the norm in this place.

He closed the door and leaned against it, trying to bring the recent past into focus.

He felt a wave of relief when details came zinging back to him. He'd been in Thailand. *That* was his last assignment.

Images flooded his mind. Beautiful gold-and-red temples. Fifteen-foot-high statues of Buddha. Lotus blossoms. Peaked roofs so different from the architecture of any other country he had visited. A wide river where fantailed outboard motorboats zipped past each other. Streets clogged with cars and trucks and little three-wheeled open-air cabs with a driver on something like a motorcycle in the front and a bench seat in the back for the passengers.

He'd taken those cabs. And he'd ridden on an elephant, feeling as though he was going to fall off the bench seat swaying on top of the lumbering beast.

Yeah, Thailand. But what was he doing there?

Once he had the name of the country and remembered some of the things he'd seen and done, the answer supplied itself. He'd been working security for a diplomatic mission to Bangkok. The diplomats wanted to see the ancient capital of Ayutthaya, burned by the Burmese two hundred years ago. The stone buildings were still standing, like ghosts of their former selves.

But while the party was away from the city, they got word that bird flu had broken out in the area. A deadly airborne strain. And the only sure way to avoid getting infected was to go underground—into a secret bunker.

As news of the epidemic had spread, panicked citizens had attacked them, trying to get to safety. That's where he'd gotten shot, defending the diplomats. He remembered that very clearly now.

He closed his eyes for a moment, trying to come up with more details. They evaded him.

But he knew he'd made it to safety.

In the bunker?

A secret bunker in Thailand?

Yeah, the U.S. government had dug them for the king at various locations around the country. Or that was the story. What else would they be for?

He looked around the little room. It was maybe seven by ten feet, just big enough for a single bed, a night table bolted to the wall and a small chest of drawers. Besides the door to the hall, there were two others. When he checked them, he found a shallow closet where uniform pants and shirts hung. Not his usual uniform. These were navy blue.

The bunker uniform?

He had some vague memory of having someone strip off his clothing, then take him through a special biological decontamination area. When he came out and dried off, he was issued all new clothing.

He kept moving along the wall and found that the other door led to a small bathroom. Switching on the light, he looked around and saw a toilet, sink and narrow shower stall.

On the shelf over the sink were toiletries, including a tube of toothpaste that was half used up. How long had he been here?

A time frame came to him. Three weeks. He'd been here healing and waiting out the epidemic.

They'd separated the security detail from the diplomats. He remembered that now. And Dr. Montgomery was in charge of this section of the bunker.

So the story about Afghanistan was something he'd made up, a dream. Or had that happened, too, farther back in his past?

He ran a shaky hand over his face, as though that would clear his mind. It didn't help. But at least he could use logic. If he'd been part of a village massacre in Afghanistan, he'd hardly be the choice for a diplomatic mission. Probably he'd be in the brig instead.

Maybe he could ask Dr. Montgomery about that. The name brought back vague memories of being in the doctor's office. Not for medical treatment. The man was a psychologist or something like that, and he was supposed to be helping Jonah cope with post-traumatic stress.

Except that Jonah didn't trust the guy, even when he kept saying what sounded like the right things.

So did that make Jonah Baker paranoid?

He leaned over the sink, staring at his reflection in the mirror. At least he recognized the man who stared back, although he got the impression from the lean look of his face that he'd lost some weight in the past few weeks.

Picking up the glass from the shelf above the sink, he filled it from the tap and took several swallows of cold water. Then he turned off the bathroom light and went back to the twin bed, where he straightened the covers again, tucking in the bottom corners with military precision.

The pillow was half off the bed, and he saw something that had been under it. A pill.

What the hell was a pill doing there?

Wait a minute. It was something he was supposed to take. Only it had made his head fuzzy. So when the sergeant had given it to him, he'd pretended to swallow it. Then he'd spat it out and tucked it under his pillow.

But what was he thinking? He couldn't leave it there. With a dart of panic, he grabbed it and flushed it down the toilet. Climbing back under the covers, he turned off the bedside lamp and tried to go back to sleep. Instead he lay there staring into the darkness, unanswered questions swirling in his mind.

As he listened to the sound of his own breathing, a noise riveted his attention.

Focusing intently, he thought he heard the knob turn. Then the door opened just far enough for someone to slip into the room before it closed again. Someone who assumed Jonah Baker was sleeping and they could sneak around without him being the wiser. So what the hell was the intruder up to?

Too bad Jonah hadn't checked the quarters for a weapon. He had nothing but his hands—and surprise—to defend himself. For the moment, all he could do was remain very still, feigning sleep. He heard the sound of harsh breathing.

So the guy was nervous.

Was he planning to shoot the sleeping man? No. He could have done that already. So maybe he had a knife? That would certainly attract less attention.

When the assailant came softly across the floor, Jonah forced himself to stay where he was. He'd been shot recently, so he wasn't exactly in top fighting form. But in the dim light, this guy looked small, and maybe Jonah could take him.

As a hand reached out, Jonah made his move—springing up and grabbing the outstretched arm, twisting it over and back.

The guy tried to cry out, but Jonah clamped a hand across the man's mouth, pulling him back against his own body.

"Call for help and I'll kill you," he rasped.

Still holding the arm in a grip that would dislocate the guy's shoulder if he moved the wrong way, Jonah slid his other hand downward, searching for weapons.

He didn't find a knife or a gun.

Instead his hand closed over a woman's breast.

Chapter Two

"Jonah, don't."

She spoke as though she knew him well, and the mingling of fear and determination in her voice was like a punch in the gut.

"You're hurting my arm. Let me go."

He eased up a little, but he didn't loosen his hold on her. "Who are you? What are you doing here?"

In the darkness, he heard her swallow hard. "I'm Sophia. Sophia Rhodes."

He hadn't expected to hear a name he recognized. But the effect was that of a baseball bat to the chest, knocking the breath from his lungs.

A few minutes ago, he had remembered nothing about his early life. But the mention of her name sent a bolt of lightning through his brain. The lightning crashed through a mental barrier, releasing a dam of memories into his mind. Not just memories. Vivid physical sensations.

He remembered a night in her bed. A night of passionate kisses and touches. And then two bodies joined in ecstasy and desperation. A night that had branded him for life.

He summoned the breath to speak and managed to gasp, "You can't be."

"I am," she answered, her tone almost as breathy as his, making him wonder if the same memories had flashed through her consciousness and affected her the same way.

Shock made his muscles go weak, and his hold on her loosened. With a small sound, she pulled away.

"It's me," she said. "See for yourself."

Bending down, she turned on the light above the bedside table, and he thought with one corner of his mind that she knew just where to find the switch. He blinked, fighting the sudden brightness as he struggled to focus on her.

She was dressed in a uniform identical to the ones that hung in the closet. Only she had added a cap with a visor. When she pulled the cap off, a cloud of glorious wheat-colored hair fell around her shoulders.

His hand remembered the feel of that hair. Unable to stop himself, he reached out, running his fingers through the wavy strands, letting them tangle in the softness.

In the dark he had assumed she was a man. Now he was confounded that he could have made such a mistake.

Her large blue eyes searched his face, then slid lower—over his almost naked body.

Earlier he'd felt at a disadvantage, lying in bed waiting for some guy to assault him. Now the sensation was multiplied as he stood facing Sophia. But he held his ground, taking in the details of her. She still had the same delicate features. The little turned-up nose that he had found so enchanting. The bee-stung lips. The high cheekbones. The creamy skin that burned when she tried to get a tan.

Too bad he couldn't see the mark that might confirm her identity—the little brown imperfection high up on her right thigh, just below her butt. With an effort, he pulled his mind away from that spot and studied her face again.

She'd been nineteen and back from her first year at a posh eastern college when they'd made love. He had been a couple of years older—because he'd been kept back early in his school career when he'd had trouble learning to read. Then there'd been the year he'd bummed around before he'd let an army recruiter convince him that serving his country was his ticket out of a dead-end life like his mom and dad's.

This woman was definitely older than the girl he remembered. Probably about ten years older. But maturity hadn't made her less appealing to him. There was wisdom in her eyes now. Or was it calculation? He hated to think of her in those terms. In his memory she'd been the goddess who'd starred in the most satisfying and yet the most gut-wrenching night of his life.

But maybe she wasn't Sophia Rhodes. How could it be? How could she have found him? More to the point, how could she have gotten into this bunker in Thailand?

He hated standing in front of her wearing only a pair of revealing briefs when she was fully dressed.

Taking the chance on turning his back, he walked to the closet and grabbed a pair of uniform pants off a hanger. Then he pulled them on, wincing as he lifted his right leg and shoved it into the pants.

While he performed the simple task, his mind was racing. Who was she, really? What if someone had found a woman who looked like Sophia Rhodes, used plastic surgery to make her into an exact double and sent her to him?

And why go to all that trouble to fool Major Jonah Baker?

After zipping the fly, he turned back to her.

"You hurt your leg," she whispered.

"I'll live."

"What happened?"

"I got shot when…" He stopped as warring images clashed

inside his head. "When we were running for the bunker," he finished, watching her face.

She looked concerned for him. But why not? If someone had sent Sophia Rhodes or her double to get information from him, of course she'd act concerned. She'd want him to think she was on his side—whatever that meant.

So was she an enemy agent?

He didn't want to believe that scenario—or anything else bad of her. But, under the circumstances, bad was more likely than good.

His throat was so tight he couldn't speak at the moment. Struggling to conquer his wildly swinging emotions, he studied her face, trying not to react to his memories of the woman or the surge of need that rushed through him. Not just physical need. Something much more profound and much more dangerous.

Ruthlessly, he stiffened his resolve, although he hoped that didn't show on his face.

But he knew he must be alert for any lies she was planning to tell him. "How could you be here? Have you been here the whole time, or did you slip into the bunker somehow?"

She ignored the questions and simply said, "I came to help you."

"Came to Thailand?"

She made a strangled sound. "That's where they said you are?"

"What do you mean? It's not what they *said*. It's true."

Even as he mouthed the denial, he felt a worm of doubt slithering down his spine. He had pictures in his mind of Thailand. Temples. Elephants. An ancient ruined city. Vendors lining the streets.

But sometimes it felt as though he was watching a Power Point presentation as he brought up each scene in his memory.

She must have read the expression on his face. "It's okay. Don't worry about where we are."

"I have to worry about it," he ground out. "It's my job."

"I understand," she answered much too quickly.

He matched her reaction time. "Do you?"

"Yes," she whispered, reaching out her hands and gently clasping his arms. He might have wrenched away. Instead, he went very still. Dragging in a breath, he caught the scent of honey and herbs. His memory didn't associate that combination with her. When he'd known her before, she'd smelled of lemon.

He ordered himself to stop focusing on her fragrance.

Through parched lips, he said, "If you're Sophia Rhodes, tell me something we would both remember."

His heart was pounding as he waited for her to mention the night they'd spent together. Instead she said, "Do you remember Mrs. Watson?"

As he scrambled to bring the name into context, she went on.

"The Latin teacher. We used to say her boobs hung down so low that her belt held them up."

At the image, he couldn't keep a bark of a laugh from escaping. He hadn't remembered that on his own, but now it zinged back to him.

"She'd walk around the room, and you wouldn't know who she was going to call on for a translation of Caesar's *Gallic Wars*. I used to do the homework and translate the chapters every night. But you hated the assignments. You used a pony. You remember?"

Ah, the cheat book. He remembered it well. "Yeah."

"But there were certain words—like *corn* instead of *grain*—that would give you away. If you used the wrong word—the one in the pony—you'd get an F for the day."

"Yeah," he said again. Just an hour ago, his early life had been a big fat blank, but now he remembered hating Latin class. He'd be sitting there across the room from the big clock on the wall. Every time a minute passed, the big hand would move and make a clicking sound. And he'd watch it, praying that it would move around to the time for the bell to ring before the old witch called on him. Sometimes she was in the mood to torture him. And sometimes she let him alone. He'd never known from day to day which it would be.

"Why did you take Latin," she asked, "if you didn't want to do the work?"

"I don't know," he answered, feeling an inward stab. That was a lie. He'd taken it because Sophia was in the class.

To change the subject, he demanded, "Tell me something else."

Partly he was testing her, and partly he was testing himself. Because when she spoke, she brought scenes and people back to him.

"You and Roger Berg and Kevin Drake used to sit at table twenty-two in the cafeteria. All of you wore black T-shirts and faded jeans with holes in the knees. And you'd decide which guys could sit with you. But they had to be tough enough. Didn't Tony Swazey steal a GPS from a car to prove he was up to your standards? Only the cops caught him and he ended up in reform school?"

"I never told Tony Swazey to steal anything!"

"But he did it to prove that he was good enough to sit with you."

"Not my fault."

She caught her breath, and he wondered what she was thinking.

"What?" he asked, watching her closely.

She swallowed. "You know he's dead?"

Jonah's stomach clenched. "Yeah. He was in a helicopter crash in Iraq."

"Yes."

Another memory. That one from after he'd left… He wanted to ask her the name of the town where they'd gone to school, but he didn't want to give that much away.

She was speaking again. "You remember the drama club production of *Bye Bye Birdy?* You were Birdy and I was one of the screaming girls who idolized you."

Yeah, he remembered that. The part had been perfect for him.

Sophia had deliberately dragged his mind away from the death of Tony Swazey. But he was tired of playing the game by the rules she'd set up. Or maybe he was tired of her talking about the time when he'd been unsure of himself with her. He wanted to leap past that period in his life to something a lot more satisfactory. But he wasn't going to be the one to bring up that night.

"Stop talking about the high-school scene," he growled. "Tell me something about us."

He saw her swallow again.

"Okay. We liked each other. We used to watch each other across the room and in the halls. My girlfriends used to tease me about you. But neither one of us had the guts to cross that gap—until that night."

"That night," he repeated, relieved that she'd finally brought it out into the open. "Go on."

"I went to that bar to meet—"

"A guy named Kip Weld," he finished the sentence for her. "Only he never showed up. And I stopped some ratty-looking moron from hitting on you."

She kept her gaze steady. "Actually, I was lying. I was there to meet *you*. I made up the Kip Weld story."

He stared at her, thunderstruck.

It flashed into his mind that the time for lying had passed—about that night and about what was happening now. He had to know if she spoke the truth.

Reaching out, he cupped his hands over her shoulders. Her blue eyes went wide as he drew her close, swaying her body against his.

He stopped looking into her eyes as he lowered his mouth to

hers. Moving slowly, he wrapped his arms around her so that he flattened her breasts against his chest.

He cursed the uniform shirt and bra that denied him the intimate contact he craved.

Still, the pressure went straight from his chest to his groin. He clung to her as a whirlwind of sensations swamped him. The brush of her corn-silk hair against his cheek. The way her body pressed to his. The enveloping honey-spice scent.

Too dizzy to stand on his own, he took a step back, bringing her with him as he braced his hips against the wall. The earth was tilting under his feet, and he fought to anchor himself.

She swayed, her arms reaching up to circle his neck.

He moved his lips against hers, brushing, sliding, settling. His tongue stroked along the seam, asking her to open for him.

Without hesitation, she did, and he played with the line of her teeth, then dipped farther into her warmth, tasting her fully, completely.

It wasn't pure lust that motivated him, although that was certainly part of it. He had been holding his breath, praying that the kiss would tell him what he needed to know—about her and about himself.

And it did—as far as her identity was concerned. Her mouth had the same taste he had remembered on so many lonely nights. Rich and inviting and unique to Sophia.

She made a small sound that zinged along his nerve endings. He needed more, so much more. Tipping his head first one way and then the other, he changed the angle of contact, changed everything that he had thought was true.

He hadn't believed that Sophia Rhodes could be in this place. At this time.

But it was her. Holding her and touching her confirmed that on a very basic level.

One part of his mind was amazed that they had gone from interrogation to intimacy in seconds. But why should he be surprised? He had made love with her on one mind-blowing night, and for ten years, he had wanted more.

Desperate to satisfy his craving for erotic contact with her, he slid one hand down her body, pulling her hips against his erection, sorry now that he had put on his pants.

She moaned, moving against him, telling him she was as frustrated as he was by the layers of clothing that separated his skin from hers.

He was trembling as he slipped a hand between them, cupping one of her breasts, then stroking his fingers across the hardened crest.

"Oh!" she exclaimed, the word going directly into his greedy mouth.

It seemed that time had stood still or reversed itself. They were back in the past together. Only this time he wasn't leaving in the morning. This time he would keep her captive in his bed for days.

She was his. Totally his. He knew that without a sliver of doubt.

When he began to unbutton her shirt, she eased far enough away to give him access. Dipping his head, he buried his face in the valley between her breasts, and she cupped her hands around the back of his head.

Then, all at once, she stiffened. When she pushed against his shoulder, he blinked.

"You don't want—?"

She pressed a finger against her lips. "Someone's coming."

His senses had contracted to a narrow focus—the woman in his arms. Now they expanded again, and he heard footsteps coming down the hall.

She looked wildly around. "I've got to hide."

He didn't question her. The panic in her voice and on her face was enough to tell him she was in grave danger. And it sounded as if they had only seconds to get her to safety.

He dragged her across the room. Turning off the light, he threw the covers aside as he pushed her onto the bed, then came down on top of her, lying facedown, and pulled the covers up. Then he lay still, pretending that he was the only occupant of the room.

The door opened, and he tried to look like a man who was sleeping.

Jonah's back was to the door, but through slitted eyes, he saw the play of a flashlight on the wall. When it shifted to his body, he felt Sophia stiffen and knew she saw it too.

He tensed, readying himself to leap out of bed and assault whoever had invaded his space.

Chapter Three

As Sophia waited to find out what would happen, contingency plans raced through her head.

Centuries dragged by as the guard—it had to be one of the guards—inspected the room and lingered in the doorway. What if he found her here? How was she going to explain what she was doing in Jonah's room? In his bed, no less.

She'd had a cover story. Now it seemed ridiculous that she could be here as part of an oversight team to make sure Montgomery was doing his job. But that was the best she had.

To conquer her fear, she tried to focus on Jonah. The physical sensations would have swamped her, if she didn't have something else to worry about. She could feel Jonah's chest through her uniform shirt. Feel his broad shoulders and his hard thighs.

He was giving a good imitation of a man sleeping, his breath deep and even. But she knew from the tension in his arms and shoulders that he was ready to spring up if the guard came closer.

Long seconds ticked by. Finally the invader backed up and closed the door, and she heard footsteps continue down the hall.

She let out the breath she'd been holding, then pressed a hand against Jonah's shoulder. "You're crushing me."

"Sorry." He rolled to the side, keeping his arm across her middle. "You know who that was?"

"The guards here make random checks. Don't you remember seeing any of them before?"

He made a frustrated sound. "No."

"You're having trouble with your memory?"

Instead of giving her a straight answer, he asked, "Why do you think so?"

She wasn't sure how to respond. She didn't want to alarm him any more than she had to. Not yet. But she knew saying too much or too little could get them both killed.

Before she decided how much to tell him, he asked another question—this one more direct. "Are we in Thailand?"

His voice was full of urgency. But the only answer she could give him was, "I can't tell you."

His hand tightened on her waist. "Can't or won't?"

"It's not a good idea."

"Why the hell not?"

"Because it's better if they think you believe what they told you."

He muttered a curse.

To give him another focus and because she needed to know the answer, she asked, "What do you remember about the days just before you came here?"

He rolled to his back and pulled his arm away, and she breathed a small sigh, relieved that they were no longer lying quite so intimately. The contact made it hard to think. Still, in the narrow bed, there was no way to get much distance from him.

In the dark, she reached into her pocket, then slid her hand down beside the bed, her knuckles hitting one of the slats.

"What was that?"

"My arm slipped off the bed."

In the darkness, she could see only Jonah's profile, but she remembered how he had looked at her a few minutes ago. The image merged and shifted, overlaid with her memories of him.

Ten years ago he'd worn his dark hair a little too long. Now, of course, it was much shorter. Probably it had been military length, but it had grown out in the weeks he'd been here. His eyes were the same. Those dark eyes that she'd always thought could see right into her head. The blade of a nose. The strong jaw. The lean hips.

She pulled her mind back from below his waist and focused on his profile.

It looked as though he was staring up into the darkness. Finally, he said, "You're really Sophia."

She breathed out a small sigh. At least they'd gotten that far. "Yes."

"What are you doing here?"

"I already answered that. I came to help you."

"Help me do what?"

"Stay alive."

He made a small sound in his throat. "How?"

She came back to a previous question, approaching it in a different way. "You said you were in Thailand. What were you doing there?"

"I was part of a security detail guarding diplomats. They went on a sightseeing trip to some ruins. We were supposed to come back to Bangkok by boat, but we got caught in a bird-flu epidemic."

"And how did you end up in this place? What is it?"

"A former fallout shelter built for the king. But it's sealed, so it keeps us safe from the flu."

A clever story. Very realistic, she thought. *So how did I get in?* She kept that question to herself because she didn't want to end up supplying an answer.

"So you remember Thailand." She dragged in a breath and let it out slowly. "But what about Afghanistan?"

He turned toward her, his voice suddenly harsh. "How do you know about that?"

She clenched her fist, her nails digging into her palm. She'd been briefed, but she wasn't sure how much to tell him. Or what information would make him trust her and what would make him sure that she was the enemy. Despite the passionate kiss, she knew he had to be worried about that. And she could only go so far with reassuring him.

"Tell me what you remember about Afghanistan," she demanded, pushing him a little.

"I'm not sure how accurate it is. I dreamed about it. It can't be real, though. I mean, in the dream, Lieutenant Calley was one of the men with me. And he was in the Vietnam War, wasn't he?"

"Yes. But that doesn't make the dream totally wrong."

"Great! Thanks."

Ignoring the sarcasm in his voice, she asked, "A Dr. Montgomery has been questioning you?" Her breath stilled as she waited for his answer. She needed to confirm that the information she'd been given was correct, but she hated the idea of Jonah in Montgomery's clutches after what she'd read about the man. He was an expert interrogator, skilled in the use of intimidation, behavior modification techniques and drugs. And when those methods didn't achieve the desired effects, he'd been known to use torture.

"He's helping me deal with post-traumatic stress."

"Did he prescribe medication?"

He didn't answer for long moments. Finally, he said, "Yes."

"Stop taking it."

"What if I…need it?"

"You don't," she said, trying to make her voice authoritative. "Stop taking it. That will help you sort out your memories."

His voice turned hard and urgent. "How do you know?"

"I was told."

"By whom?"

"Let's get back to Montgomery. He's asking you questions, right?"

"Yeah."

"Don't tell him anything about Afghanistan," she said, hearing the plea in her own voice.

"Why not?"

"Because the moment he gets what he wants out of you, you're expendable."

He made a sound that could have been a harsh laugh. "That's just great."

"Don't forget that. He'll act like he's your friend, but you mustn't trust him."

He raised up, his face inches from hers. "Did you really come here just to talk?"

Before she could figure out how to answer, he rolled toward her again and wrapped his arms around her, pulling her tight against his body.

Apparently he'd thought of a more pleasurable activity than their disturbing conversation.

She knew she should push away from him, but she craved the contact as much as he did. When he tipped her chin up, she was helpless to do anything besides let him bring his mouth back to hers for another searing kiss.

There was only one man who had kissed her like that, and it was Jonah Baker. And then he had walked away.

Of course, he hadn't wanted to. She had comforted herself with that undeniable truth. He'd been scheduled to report to boot camp. Still, he could have made an effort to contact her after basic training.

She'd waited weeks to hear from him, and she'd been devastated that he hadn't called. Later, she'd thought maybe she should have reached out to him, but she'd been too proud and too hurt to ask why he'd walked away from what they'd found together. And too immature and unsure of herself to go after what she so desperately wanted.

None of that had stopped her from volunteering for this assignment—even when they'd laid out all the details so she would know the danger involved.

Maybe she secretly thought this was her second chance. She wasn't going to blow it this time.

She didn't want to think about her motives too deeply. Not now. Instead, she focused on the kiss, letting it consume her.

A few minutes ago, he'd been the aggressor. This time she gave as good as she got, feasting from his lips, then deepening the kiss, her tongue exploring his mouth the way he'd explored hers and sliding tantalizingly against his tongue.

She couldn't see him with the light off, but she reached out to touch his face, stroking her fingers over the familiar contours of his brows, his cheeks, his nose.

She felt him smile against her mouth, then turn his head so he could nibble at her earlobe, then her jaw and finally her throat. So he remembered how much she liked that!

She arched her neck, his lips on her there making her as hot as the mouth-to-mouth contact.

He nibbled with his teeth at her sensitive skin, then soothed her with his tongue. At the same time, she felt his fingers on the top button of her shirt. Once again, he slipped it open, then the next one, so that he could bury his face between her breasts. He turned his head to kiss first one inner curve and then the other.

At the same time, he shifted his position so that his erection was pressed to the cleft at the juncture of her legs.

And that felt so good.

She stifled a cry, loving what he was doing, loving the heat blazing up inside her. Yet she knew that if she gave herself over to the man and the pleasure, she could be steering them both to disaster.

She had to be the one in control. The one whose sound judgment would get them out of this trap.

With the last shred of her resolve, she slipped from his grasp and rolled away from him, then sprang off the bed, standing on legs that barely held her weight. When she backed up and stepped on something soft, she jumped, then realized it was her cap. Sweeping her hair into a quick twist, she shoved it under the protective covering. Still shaky, she buttoned her shirt, then moved back so that her shoulder was leaning against the wall.

"Sophia?" His voice sounded so raw that she almost came back to the bed.

But she stayed where she was. "We can't. You know it's too dangerous. Neither one of us can afford to stop thinking straight."

"But you wanted me?"

"Do you really have to ask?"

"I want to hear you say it."

"You know I did. Yes. I wanted you."

He huffed out a breath, then climbed off the bed. When he stepped toward her, she moved farther along the wall.

With a shaky finger, she pressed the button on her watch, lighting the dial so she could look at the time.

"It's three-eighteen. The guard could be coming back, and I have to get out of here before he does."

"Or what?"

"Let's just say it's a lot better for both of us if I don't get caught."

"So you admit you're here illegally."

"You could put it that way."

"How would *you* put it?"

"I've already said what I can. I have to leave, but I'll be back. Just don't talk about Afghanistan."

"Am I in prison?"

"No!"

"Then what?"

She felt her throat tighten. "Just play your cards close to your chest, okay?"

His voice turned gritty. "If I'm in so much trouble here, take me with you now."

Her throat constricted even more, so that she was barely able to speak. "I can't. Not yet."

He exploded with a string of curses that tore at her resolve.

"Jonah, please!"

She couldn't see his face, but she felt him glaring at her. "You come here like…like a thief, and you expect me to go for this crap? You have to give me more information if you want me to go along with you!"

Her insides clenched. "Jonah, I'm sorry."

"Just give me a straight answer. Why can't I leave now?"

She closed her eyes for a moment, then opened them again. "Your leg."

"What about it?"

"The route out of here isn't easy. You have to be in better shape."

He cursed again.

She pushed the light on her watch once more, not just to see the time. She wanted to make the point that she couldn't stand here arguing with him any longer.

"I have to go."

"Yeah, go on."

The bruised tone of his voice made her stomach knot so tightly that she almost doubled over in pain.

She lingered, pushing her luck because she wanted to take him in her arms and reassure him. And she had one more thing to do. Crossing the room, she opened the closet.

"What are you doing?"

"Making sure I'll recognize you." Quickly she stooped down, found his shoes and stuck a small monitor under the flap where the tongue was attached.

"Everybody wears the same thing."

She stood. "I see." It was a nonsense reply but it was the best she could do. "I'll be back."

"When?" he asked, as if he thought the answer was going to be a lie.

"I can't tell you exactly."

"Sure."

She pressed her hand against her stomach, trying to hold back the pain that twisted in her gut. She had known this would be difficult, but she'd had no idea how difficult emotionally.

She'd been so hopeful when she came in. But now she knew that she'd been feeling what she wanted to feel.

Seeing him again. Touching him. Kissing him. Lying to him. The combination was devastating.

Turning quickly, she opened the door.

She didn't look back, but she knew that every fiber of Jonah's attention was focused on her.

Thankfully, she saw that the hallway was empty, so she exited quickly, then sprinted down the corridor.

WHEN THE DOOR closed, Jonah clenched his hands at his sides. He wanted to charge down the corridor after Sophia, though he wasn't even sure why. Did he want to shake her and scream at her, or beg for her help? Probably he couldn't even catch her, because of his damn leg.

She was right about that. He couldn't move fast. So what was she saying about the route out? It wasn't the elevator that he remembered?

Was he remembering it wrong? Or maybe they couldn't use the elevator, and he was going to have to climb an endless stairway. Well, good luck with that!

He clenched his right hand into a fist and pounded against his left palm, frustration surging through him.

He didn't know whether to trust her or go find the guards and tell them somebody had broken into this place.

No. He canceled that thought. He didn't want her to get hurt.

For old times' sake? Or because of how their bodies had responded to each other?

She could have been faking arousal. But he didn't think so. Still, if he believed what she had told him, he was in deep kimchi.

Well, it seemed as though he'd already been thinking that. Apparently, he'd decided not to take his damn pills.

He sat down on the side of the bed, leaning over and cradling his head in his hands.

Sophia had accomplished two things during her brief stay. She had brought back buried memories, and she'd made him think about this place and the people. The latter impressions were still vague. He could barely remember anything besides this room. He must have been walking around like a zombie. A chemically induced zombie.

He felt a cold chill go through him. What was he taking, exactly? Was that why his memories were cloudy? Skipping one pill was making them better? Or had he skipped more?

He couldn't remember. But that still left the question of Sophia. Friend or foe?

He didn't have enough information to figure it out.

He lay down, stacking his hands behind his head and thinking about his life before this place. At least her visit had given him some glimpses into his past. They had talked about high school, and she hadn't mentioned where it was. But he knew now. Ellicott City, Maryland.

They'd gone to Centennial High on Centennial Lane. She'd lived in one of the big new houses that were going up in Howard County. He'd lived in a dinky apartment across from Chatham Mall.

The familiar names gave him something to grasp on to. And also made his stomach clench.

He remembered the kid he'd been back then. A lanky teenager, standing tall even with the enormous chip he was carrying around on his shoulder. So many of the kids who went to school with him had all the money they wanted, lived in McMansions, and drove late-model cars, while he and his mom were crammed into a tiny apartment that was one step up from a housing project. His transportation was a clunker that he worked on himself in the parking lot of the rental complex.

The only reason Mom could afford the place was because of Section Eight—rent assistance—and food stamps.

They'd been okay when Dad was alive. He'd had a dead-end job in a warehouse, but at least he'd brought home a steady paycheck.

But he'd died in a car wreck when Jonah was twelve, and Mom didn't have the education to get a good-paying job. She'd worked fast food or in the service department of a car dealership. Sometimes one in the day and the other in the evening.

More details of his life were coming back—and they were ones he'd rather forget.

When he'd been old enough to get a job at a fast-food restaurant, he'd kept the money for himself. The memory made him cringe, because he understood now that he should have contributed some of it to their living expenses. But with the logic of a juvenile jerk, he'd figured he deserved some of what the other kids had. The only way to get it was to pay for it out of his earnings. Or steal it.

Yeah. He'd done some shoplifting back then. Mostly at the upscale mall in Columbia.

He whistled through his teeth. No wonder he didn't want to remember his misguided youth.

But the present wasn't much better.

Let's see. What did he know?

He ticked off the facts on his hands.

He was stuck in a secure facility. He'd thought he was here to rehabilitate. Now, from what Sophia had said, it looked as though this was a carefully controlled environment designed to extract information.

From him.

And mind-altering drugs were part of the package.

He didn't really know how long he'd been here. Maybe it was three weeks. Maybe not. He couldn't trust his memory. And a woman from his past had showed up to warn him not to trust his doctor.

He shuddered. How was that for a paranoid scenario? He wanted to stride down the hall, find someone in charge and demand answers about what was really going on in this place—wherever it was. But he suspected it was dangerous to do something outside the pattern they were expecting.

Still, in the morning, he was going to start taking charge of his life again.

SOPHIA HURRIED along the corridor, keeping her head down, even though she wanted to glance up at the security cameras.

They were supposed to be off, but she wasn't going to take a chance on getting her face photographed in case the jamming device had malfunctioned.

Her senses were on alert. This was no place to lose your focus. She wasn't supposed to be here, and if someone caught her, she'd have to go into her song and dance about a surprise inspection—and pray that the story would hold up long enough for her to figure out a way to escape.

At all costs, she couldn't let them know that she had come here to talk to Jonah.

Her heart squeezed when she thought about their meeting. She wanted to think that it had gone really well with him, that they'd connected on a very basic level. In truth, however, because she hadn't been able to tell him much, she'd made him wary. As he should be, unfortunately.

Did he believe her enough to keep his mouth shut with Montgomery?

She prayed she'd gotten that through to him. And prayed that she could get out of here without being seen.

Starting to turn a corner, she saw a man in a blue uniform coming toward her and stopped dead in her tracks.

One of the guards.

Backing up, she turned and ran along the hallway, hoping she could make it to safety before the guy discovered there was an intruder in the facility.

Chapter Four

Sophia zipped around a corner.

As part of her training for the mission, she'd gone over and over the plans for this bunker. It was vast, and she knew there were places she could hide—if she could get to one.

The corridor walls were cinder-block. The first door she came to was locked. The second one, too. She wanted to look over her shoulder, but that would slow her down, and the guy behind her might see her face.

She reached a door marked Danger High Voltage. This time, when she tried the knob, it turned. She slipped into a darkened room, listening for the hum of electrical equipment. She heard nothing. Was this really part of the electrical plant? She couldn't remember. But she knew that if she bumped into a transformer, she was a cooked goose.

She could feel her heart pounding as she retrieved the small flashlight from her pocket. The narrow beam showed her only a small area at one time. Most of the room was still swathed in darkness.

Behind her, out in the corridor, she thought she heard footsteps.

There was no time to plan anything tricky. All she could do was slide along the wall and press herself into the shadows where the guy's line of sight would be blocked when the door opened. She killed the light and waited with her pulse pounding, clutching her flashlight handle. It had Mace in it—her only weapon. She'd drawn the line at killing anyone when she came in here.

The door opened and a powerful beam swept the room. But the man didn't step inside and look behind the door. After long seconds, the door closed again, and she breathed a sigh of relief.

She stayed put for several minutes, then pressed her ear to the barrier. When she detected nothing, she turned the knob and peered out.

Thankfully, she saw that the hallway was empty and she didn't hear any alarm bells. She reasoned that the guard hadn't really seen her; he was just following his rounds. Now, however, she was headed in the wrong direction; she could easily bump into another guard coming on shift.

Forcing herself not to run, she headed back the way she'd come. When she reached the cross corridor, she turned right, then took a flight of stairs down into the lower reaches of the facility, where she passed rooms with enormous tanks for water and fuel. The storeroom she wanted was about a hundred yards from the stairway.

Stepping inside, she played her light over shelves with boxes of canned fruit, pork and beans, tomato sauce, toilet paper, soap.

She was almost home free.

Unable to stop herself from running, she sprinted to the back and squeezed behind a line of shelves, where she pressed on a panel in the wall. It slid back, revealing a hidden doorway.

She stepped through, and ducked around a rock wall, then said a little prayer of thanksgiving that she'd made it out of the bunker in one piece.

She'd exited through the back door—a door she'd been told the men using the place didn't know existed.

Out here was a natural cave, with a couple of tunnels cut through the living rock.

"Well?"

The sound of a gruff voice in the darkness made her jump. She turned to find herself facing a man wearing night-vision goggles. He took them off and switched on a flashlight of his own. In the dim light she could see his wide face, close-cropped brown hair, and the SIG Sauer in his free hand.

"You're alone?"

"Yes."

His name was Phil Martin, and he had been her guide through the maze of underground caves that led to the back door of the bunker. He holstered the gun.

At first, she hadn't liked working with him. He could be brusque and bossy. Sometimes it seemed as though his mind was far away—in some place where it was impossible for her to follow—but she'd quickly found that he knew every aspect of his job, from weaponry to spelunking to psychological motivation. To be honest, she knew she never would have gotten this far without his help.

He'd wanted to come with her into the bunker. Because sending in two people increased the risk, she'd done it alone—and made it back.

Still, she knew she was in for an interrogation. As he led her along the corridor, she was glad of the chance to collect her thoughts. She was sure he'd want to look at her face when he asked her questions, so he escorted her down the tunnel to a place where she could see warm, artificial light shining. It was coming from inside a twelve-by-twelve-foot room that had been carved out of the rock. At the back was a side tunnel that led to a smaller room used for sanitary facilities.

As soon as they stepped inside their living space, Martin

turned toward her, the way she'd known he would, and she saw that his skin was flushed.

"Are you okay?" she asked.

He dismissed the question with a brusque jerk of his arm. "I'm fine. Did you make contact with Baker?"

"Yes."

"How is he?"

"Confused, like we expected."

"What happened?"

"We talked," she answered, making her voice as matter of fact as possible. They'd done a lot more than hold a conversation, but she wasn't going to get into anything she wouldn't have told her mother.

"Talked about what?"

"Old times. And his current situation."

"But you didn't give anything away."

"I didn't like lying to him. I told him not to spill his guts to Montgomery."

"We don't know how much we can trust him."

"I trust him!"

"They could already have messed with his mind enough to make him report that he talked with you."

"No!" she said automatically.

Ignoring her, Martin went on, "He could have a time bomb ticking inside his head. You don't know what kind of crap they've shoveled into his brain."

She couldn't deny that. When she sighed, Martin picked up on it immediately.

"What?"

"He thinks he's in Thailand. They told him he was part of a diplomatic mission that got caught in a bird-flu epidemic. They have him in the bunker for his own protection."

"Or that's a story he told you."

"I'm sure he believed it."

"Why?"

She kept her gaze steady and her voice even. "First, because that's a lot to make up on the spur of the moment. Second, I'm a trained psychologist. That's why you picked me for this job."

"And because you went to school with Baker."

"Look, you can't have it both ways. Either he's lying to me, or he's saying what they made him believe."

"Unfortunately, you don't know which."

"I volunteered to go on this mission because I want to save him. Don't make my job harder."

Something she couldn't quite read flashed in his eyes. "Believe me, I'm not trying to add to your problems. I'm trying to make sure you get out of this alive."

"Don't you want to come out of this alive?" she snapped.

"What do you think?" he answered.

She stared at him for another moment, then turned to one of the cots along the wall and sat down. She'd told him she could tell when someone was lying to her. She wished that applied to Phil Martin. He was hiding something. She knew that much, and she hoped it wasn't something that would sink the mission.

She stretched out her legs, rotating her ankles in their low-rise hiking boots. She would have lain down and slung her arm over her eyes, but she didn't, because she knew Phil was watching her carefully.

"When I said he was in danger, he asked to come with me. That was a logical response on his part."

"What did you tell him?" Martin asked immediately.

"That his leg isn't strong enough."

"What about his leg?"

"He was shot. He thinks that happened in Thailand."

"Good answer on your part." He waited a beat, then asked, "Can he make the trip out of here?"

"I think so."

"But you don't know."

"He won't be worse off than he is now."

"True," Martin conceded.

"I need to relax. Twice I was almost caught." She didn't explain how she'd hidden in Jonah's bed with him lying on top of her.

"Yeah. Try to get some sleep. I'm going to see if I can contact home base."

"Okay."

He turned down the light to a soft glow, then stepped out into the corridor. She heard him trying to use the special radio that he'd been given, but it was obvious that they were too far underground, and the tons of rock above them were preventing him from getting through.

So they were on their own.

He'd looked sick when he'd gone out. Sick or in pain. But moments later when he came back, he appeared to be in better shape.

Was he on drugs? His behavior was consistent with an addict. He'd seem sick and shaky, then he'd disappear and come back looking a lot better.

Did that mean he'd fooled everyone else involved in this assignment—and she was the only one who had picked up on the secretive behavior?

That certainly left her in a precarious situation.

He came back in and leaned against the wall for long moments, staring at her as though he had similar doubts about her.

Finally he turned down the lights farther, then lay down on the other cot. Mercifully, he didn't ask any more questions about her encounter with Jonah.

She was left alone with her own thoughts.

She wished that Martin would turn the light all the way off. She didn't want him to see how shaken she was. On the other hand, that would leave them in total darkness, and she didn't like that alternative either.

She wanted to fold her arms across her chest and hug herself. Instead, she pulled the covers up to her chin, which made sense in the chilly air of the cave. To give herself the illusion of privacy, she closed her eyes.

As she'd matured, she'd come to the conclusion that there was no point in lying to herself. Truth be told, she'd been in love with Jonah Baker all those years ago. A very stupid move, since he apparently wasn't planning to return any deep emotions.

But that one night with him had been the most wonderful experience of her life. Even at twenty-one, he was a fantastic lover. From her previous—and very scant—experiences, she'd thought that sex must be overrated. He'd proved that she didn't have a clue about how good it could be.

Behind her closed lids, she found herself reliving the memories of that night—reinforced by the very recent memories in his bedroom. Every touch. Every kiss. Every whispered word.

Those brief, intimate moments with him in his room proved that nothing had changed inside her head. Jonah Baker was still the man who did it for her.

Sliding her hands to the side of the cot, she gripped the aluminum frame, willing herself to calm down.

Maybe if she focused on the bad stuff, she could regain her cool.

Like what he was going to say when she told him she'd gotten married in an effort to forget him, then given up and gotten divorced two years later because she'd finally admitted she'd married the wrong man.

For an unwelcome moment, George's face floated into her

mind. She hadn't done him any favors by walking down the aisle with him. She hadn't known it at the time, but she'd been using him. Of course, she'd figured out that he'd been using her, too.

But maybe she wouldn't even have to tell Jonah about her mistake of a marriage. Maybe it wasn't going to be an issue at all because nothing would really change. He wouldn't tell her why he hadn't called, and she wouldn't tell him how devastated she had been. After this, they could go their separate ways again, and she'd return to searching for a man who could substitute for him—even when she knew the quest was doomed to failure.

She clenched her teeth, struggling not to make any noise and give anything away to the man lying in the next cot. She could hear him breathing. It wasn't a pleasant sound.

She didn't much like Phil Martin. But she was a realist. She was stuck working with him. If she wanted to help Jonah, she was going to have to rely on Phil's judgment.

When Phil had first come to her office at Howard County Mental Health with the information that Jonah Baker was in danger, she hadn't believed him. The documents he'd brought along served as proof she couldn't ignore, and once she understood what was at stake, she'd had no choice but to go along with the scenario Phil had outlined.

She wanted to save Jonah. She wanted an excuse to be with him again.

Of course, she'd come to realize that Phil had thought someone working in a low-paying government job couldn't pull her weight on the mission. She'd found out later that some of the others on the team had informed him she didn't need the income, and she'd picked the job because she saw it as an opportunity to help people who'd gotten shafted by "the system."

After that, he'd settled down and gotten to work. And the team had given her a lot of information about Jonah. She'd eagerly lapped it up because it filled in so many of the blank spaces that had kept her wondering over the years.

He'd had ranger training at Fort Benning. After that, he'd been on some hair-raising missions—every one of them successful. He was good at his job. He'd served with distinction and he'd earned a Distinguished Service Cross, no small achievement.

Then he'd gotten sent to a village in Afghanistan, on an assignment that had obviously had a hidden agenda. Only she didn't know what it was. And neither did Phil Martin.

When nobody on Jonah's team had reported back, he had been declared missing in action, presumed dead. Only it turned out that he was alive and at the mercy of a bastard named Carlton Montgomery.

And now he needed her help.

She shuddered.

Martin and his group had made her go through a week of intensive training. She'd thought she was prepared, but now she knew she was in over her head.

Because the training exercises had been just that—exercises carried out in an environment that she knew was safe. Or maybe she'd felt comfortable because she hadn't been able to cope with the enormity of what she had to do.

But everything had changed. Once she'd stepped inside the bunker, reality had slammed into her like a speeding train.

JONAH LAY AWAKE for what seemed like hours, staring into the darkness.

He still didn't remember enough about his personal life to fill a two-hour made-for-TV movie. But he was pretty sure he'd never been married. He had the feeling that his memories of Sophia had kept him from hooking up with anyone else.

He blinked in the darkness. If that were really true, why hadn't he tried to make something work out with Sophia?

Because he'd been too young and too stupid to realize what he was throwing away. Or maybe he'd been afraid that one night was enough for her. A novelty. She'd made love with him because it fulfilled one of her own fantasies—connecting with the big bad boy of Centennial High on a very intimate level.

Tonight, though, it had seemed as if she cared. They'd touched each other, and they'd been right back where they were ten years ago. Or that was the way it had seemed to him.

He sighed in the darkness. The longer he lay here, the more he second-guessed their encounter. And second-guessing her wasn't doing him any good. Gritting his teeth, he switched to another topic—his work.

He was more certain about that. At least Sophia had triggered his memories. Bits and pieces of his military career were coming back to him.

The enemy weapons ship he and a crack team had blown up in the Persian Gulf. The helicopter mission to raid a desert stronghold in Iran. The operation to rescue an army team captured by Shiite militia. Expeditions into the territory along the Pakistani border where you could get shot by troops from either Pakistan or Afghanistan.

As far as he knew, he'd been good at his job—until that village that shimmered in his dreams.

If he'd ever really been there. Clenching his fists, he struggled to relax when he wanted to get up and pace around the room.

He stayed where he was, because pacing wouldn't do the leg any good. Besides, he needed to get some sleep.

Finally he fell into a restless slumber. Soon after that, he was back in the heat and dust of Afghanistan.

The sun beat down on him as he pressed against the wall of a house that looked as though it had stood in that place for three hundred years. Again he heard the gunfire in the brown hills. This time the members of the team had split up and he was sneaking around, trying to get in back of Lieutenant Calley so he could shoot him.

He woke, covered with sweat. Swinging his legs over the side of the bed, he cradled his head in his hands, wondering if he'd ever fragged an American officer.

He was still sitting up when he heard a knock at his door.

His heart leaped. Sophia!

But when the door opened, he saw a man wearing the same blue uniform and cap that she had worn the night before.

Jonah squinted at the black name tag the guy was wearing. Sergeant Lopez. That was the only indication of the guy's rank.

Did Jonah's own shirts have a name and rank?

He hadn't even thought to look.

"You're up. Good. Breakfast at 0630. Get a move on."

He tipped his head to the side, looking at the man. "You come around and wake everyone up?"

SOPHIA AWOKE with a start. Jonah was up. And he was talking to someone. And more important, the bug she had planted under the slat at the side of the bed was working. She hadn't really had much faith in the small device, but apparently the men who had designed it knew what they were doing.

There was still a problem. Would someone find it?

She glanced to her right and saw that Martin's bed was empty. Glad of the privacy, she listened to the conversation.

Jonah had just asked the other speaker if he came around to wake everyone up. And the guy answered in the negative.

"Why me?" Jonah asked.

Several seconds passed before the man answered. "Your alarm clock was broken. I said I'd wake you."

"Thanks," Jonah said. Then asked, "This place doesn't have a public address system?"

"No. It was built in the fifties."

"Yeah. Okay," he answered, thinking that even his high school had had a public address system. It wasn't exactly advanced technology.

"I have your morning pill."

Sophia went rigid. This guy had come to give Jonah his medication. That was the real reason he was there.

"Uh, thanks."

There was a long pause, and Sophia waited with her heart pounding.

"Let me get you some water."

"Thanks," Jonah said again.

Seconds stretched, and she strained to hear what was going on. Had he taken the pill?

There was no more conversation on the other end of the line. Several seconds passed before the door closed again. The transmitter was so sensitive that Sophia heard Jonah let out a sigh. Then the bed creaked as he got up.

"Did you take the pill?" she demanded, knowing he couldn't hear her.

Of course he didn't answer.

She strained her ears and heard him make a small sound of pain, probably when he put weight on the injured leg. She'd used the injury as an excuse for not taking him out of the bunker right away. Now, though, she wondered how much of a problem it really would be.

Footsteps crossed the room, then another door shut, and she thought he must be in the bathroom.

So now what?

Either he'd taken the pill, or he'd convinced the guard that he'd taken it. Then he'd be going out into the general population of the bunker, and she was sure that meant everything she'd worked to make him believe would come into question.

JONAH WALKED to the bathroom and closed the door behind him. After using the toilet, he peered at his face in the mirror and rubbed his fingers over the stubble. He looked like a man who hadn't gotten much sleep. That might actually be his normal state, if nightmares kept waking him up any time he drifted off.

As he showered, he thought about the night before. Had Sophia really been there? Or had he summoned her from his imagination because he needed something positive in his life? Something that didn't involve this bunker.

Turning off the water, he reached for a towel, thinking that if he was desperate to wrap himself in fantasies of Sophia Rhodes, maybe he was cracking up.

Back in the bedroom, he pulled on a T-shirt and briefs and did a few stretching exercises, noting how his wounded arm and leg reacted. They were stiff, but better than the night before, he thought.

So was he getting physical therapy in this place?

He took down a uniform shirt and found that it did indeed have a name tag. Major Baker.

Not the usual kind of military insignia. But this wasn't the usual kind of military facility, either.

He noted that he didn't have a cap. Maybe only the enlisted men wore them.

After dressing, he inspected himself in the bathroom mirror. Then he crossed the room to the bed, intending to make it. Instead, he picked up the edge of the sheet and brought it to his nose.

He thought he detected the faint scent of Sophia's skin, and his body reacted instantly.

He made a strangled sound. All he had to do was think he smelled her to get hard.

Did the scent mean she'd really been here? Or perhaps he was just kidding himself, inventing the sensory input along with the encounter.

He went back to making the bed, trying to wipe away the evidence of his tossing and turning the night before—or of anything else that had taken place in the bed.

After exiting the room, he stood for a moment looking up and down the corridor. Did he know where to find the mess hall? If he'd been here for three weeks, he must have been there many times. So he turned right and let his feet carry him along, striving not to limp.

When he reached a cross corridor, he turned right. Then left down another hallway.

The sound of forks clacking against china and men talking drifted toward him. Apparently he was walking in the right direction.

He found the mess hall, where ten uniformed men were sitting at tables eating breakfast. They all looked tough and capable. More than tough, actually. Many had the hard edge of guys destined to get kicked out of the service.

Some glanced at him, while others kept their eyes trained on their plates. He felt like the center of attention. But maybe that was paranoia again.

A stainless-steel counter was fixed to one wall of the room. On it were several large, rectangular stainless serving dishes. Crossing to them, he found scrambled eggs, bacon, toast, butter, jam and oatmeal. A large urn held coffee.

As he served himself, a question popped into his mind.

Turning, he addressed the man closest to him, his face a study in guilelessness.

"So how do they get eggs when they've got a bird-flu epidemic?"

Chapter Five

Jonah heard somebody across the room cough.

Then a man whose name tag read Colonel Edwards, who looked to be in his fifties, with a lined face but a trim body, answered, "Freeze-dried."

"Oh. I hope we don't run out," Jonah answered.

One of the enlisted men laughed. "Yeah."

"We're well supplied," Colonel Edwards advised.

Jonah stood with his tray, looking around, feeling like a character who had stepped into a play without knowing his lines.

One of the men noticed him standing there and motioned him over. "There's a seat over here."

"Thanks."

He sat down across from two lieutenants, Faraday and Olson, and took a bite of eggs. They didn't taste freeze-dried, but he wasn't going to challenge the colonel.

"How you doin'?" Faraday asked, like they knew each other and had talked yesterday.

"Okay." He took a bite of bacon, wondering how much he would give away by asking questions. Finally he cleared his throat. "Is there any way to get news from outside?"

"I'm afraid we're restricted here," Olson said. "The communications equipment was old and broken."

Jonah considered that inconvenient turn of events. "Then how will we know when it's safe to come out?"

"I assume they'll come and get us," Faraday said.

"Yeah," Olson chimed in, then looked at his watch. "I've got to leave soon. I have an appointment with Montgomery."

Jonah shifted in his seat. "How come?"

"I've got some trouble coping with the stress of getting into this place."

"You mean you didn't like shooting those civilians who were trying to keep us from escaping?" Faraday asked.

"Not much."

Jonah nodded. He didn't like it, either. If it was true. Before he'd walked in, he'd been ready to believe Sophia's story—that nefarious forces were holding him captive in an underground bunker.

Now he wasn't as sure.

"Are you on medication?" he asked Olson.

The man looked startled. His gaze darted across the room. When nobody came to his aid, he cleared his throat. "I don't like to talk about that," he muttered.

"Yeah," Jonah agreed. He could understand that.

Apparently, he wasn't the only guy under stress because of the circumstances. Or was this all a setup?

Under the table, he clenched his fist, wishing he knew which way to jump.

DR. CARLTON MONTGOMERY muttered an oath under his breath. Calling on his self-discipline, he gave himself thirty seconds to deal with his anger, then rearranged his features and pressed one of the buttons on his phone. Moments later, Lieutenant Tobias knocked on the door.

"Come in."

The lieutenant stood across the desk, waiting for instructions.

"I was looking at the security tapes from last night," Montgomery began. "There's a gap of several hours."

"I'm sorry, sir."

"How did it happen?"

"It must have been a malfunction."

Montgomery kept his voice even. "Were there any reports of out-of-the-ordinary incidents? Any personnel who were some place they weren't supposed to be?"

"I'll check the log."

"Do that." He forced himself not to drum his fingers on the desk.

"I want to see Baker. As soon as he's finished breakfast, tell him he has an appointment with me."

Tobias shifted his weight from one foot to the other.

"Yes?" Montgomery asked, unable to keep an undercurrent of annoyance out of his voice.

"Um—we discussed having one of the men in the cafeteria say he had to leave early for an appointment with you. That way Baker wouldn't think he was the only one."

He remembered that now and struggled for calm. A lot was riding on this assignment, and he didn't intend to blow it because he was being pressured to produce.

"Send him to physical therapy after breakfast. Then have him come here." He looked at his watch. "In an hour and fifteen minutes."

"Yes, sir."

Tobias left, and Montgomery shuffled through the papers on his desk. He didn't like the camera failure. Then again, that was what you got when your bunker had been built more than forty years ago. Your equipment wasn't state-of-the-art.

He leaned back in his chair, thinking about the upcoming interview. And about security.

No one in this place had a cell phone, and all the desk instruments were internal only. The only outside communications were through the phone on his desk and the computers in this office.

He reached out his hand toward the phone, thinking he might ask for some instructions. Then he pulled his arm back. He'd been the one who wanted to try this experiment. He'd been so sure it would work. Unfortunately Baker's wounds had gotten infected, and he'd been on too much pain medication for any psychiatric sessions. When he'd finally recovered physically, his damn dreams had started, and Carlton was pretty sure the man didn't want to face the truth.

Carlton sighed. If he admitted that he was beginning to doubt the protocol, that would show weakness, and weakness was the last image he wanted to project. No matter what, he had to make it clear he was calm and in control.

JONAH WAS PUSHING around eggs and bacon on his plate when he noticed an officer striding toward him. He sat up straighter and looked inquiringly at the man, whose name tag read Lieutenant Tobias.

"I want to remind you that you have a physical therapy appointment scheduled in twenty minutes. Then you're scheduled to see Colonel Montgomery."

He struggled not to react to the mention of Montgomery—or to the realization that until the present moment he'd had no idea what he was supposed to be doing today.

From the corner of his eye, he could see several of the men in the mess hall watching him. When he made eye contact with one of them, the guy glanced quickly down at his plate.

Now that everyone was listening, Jonah wondered what he should say. Did he want everyone here to know he was having memory lapses? Or did they already know? After all, Olson had said he was going to see Montgomery. So apparently it was no secret.

He settled on a simple, "Thank you."

At least they were making an effort to rehab him.

As he stood, another question occurred to him. He assumed he would wear gym clothes to physical therapy. Were they in his room?

He guessed he'd find out. And maybe his feet would tell him where to find the gym.

He was halfway down the hall when another thought struck him. This was pretty poor planning. Physical therapy right after breakfast? Lucky he hadn't eaten a full meal, because that was a setup for stomach cramps.

He hurried back to his room and shuffled through the chest of drawers—where he did indeed find gym shorts and a T-shirt. And there were tennis shoes and socks in the bottom of the closet.

After he dressed, he lay down on the bed, trying to picture the route to the gym. Feeling a little shaky, he gripped the wooden slats at the sides of the bed and encountered something that shouldn't be there. A flat metal strip attached to the far side of the frame. When he pulled it out and held it up, he felt his stomach knot.

It was a bug. Somebody had put it there to listen to him.

But who?

The encounter of the night before came zinging back to him. He and Sophia had had plenty to say to each other. Stuff that could get him into trouble. So far, nobody had reacted to the conversation, or come to arrest him, for that matter.

Was Montgomery going to say something or somehow use the information?

He carefully put the thing back where he'd found it, wondering if he'd made a lot of static in somebody's ear by handling it.

A small detail from the night before came back to him. Sophia had banged her knuckles against the wall.

Had she been planting the listening device? Was she the one checking up on him? Better her than somebody else?

He glanced toward the side of the bed. "So, did you plant the bug I just found?" he asked, grinning as he pictured her startled expression when she heard the direct question. Too bad he wouldn't get an answer.

He thought about the pill Lopez had brought him this morning. He'd pretended to take it. Then, when the sergeant had left, he'd flushed it down the toilet.

He'd like to tell that to Sophia since she'd warned him not to swallow the medication. He couldn't take the chance, though, in case he was wrong about how the bug had gotten here. He hadn't given her away. If someone else was listening, they'd think he was addressing *them*. Wondering if he'd made a mistake by talking out loud, he moved restlessly on the bed.

Damn! He was starting to feel as jumpy as a tomcat staring down a Doberman.

Maybe he'd made another mistake not taking the medication. Maybe it would have calmed him down.

Or would it muzzy his brain again?

Instead of getting up, he folded his arms across his chest and lay with his eyes closed for a few minutes, ordering himself to chill.

When he thought he was going to be late if he waited any longer, he got out of bed and started down the hall again—in the direction of the mess hall. Only he kept going and did indeed come to a gym. So, even if he thought he couldn't remember squat about this place, his feet seemed to have some kind of knowledge of their own.

The facility was empty except for one guy wearing gym clothes. Again Jonah was grateful for the name tags.

"How are you doing?" Sergeant Henry asked.

"Better."

The sergeant got out a folder and consulted a chart. "You've regained eighty percent function in the arm and seventy-five in the leg," he said.

"Yeah."

"Why don't you warm up with ten minutes on the bike? Then we'll do your exercises."

He climbed on the recumbent bike, set it to level four and started pedaling. The rhythm was soothing, and he focused on the physical activity.

"So, are you still having those dreams about Afghanistan?" Henry said in a conversational tone.

"I told you about them?" he asked before he could evaluate whether the question was a good idea.

"Well, you were on edge, so I asked you what was wrong, and you talked about it some."

Jonah nodded.

"You want to talk some more?"

"No."

"Sure."

When his ten minutes were up, Jonah climbed off the bike and got down on a mat, where he worked with a big blue ball for a while then went on to stretches.

They finished in time for him to rush back to his room, take another quick shower, then dress in his blue uniform.

He should be planning what to say to Montgomery.

But had he ever planned his conversation before? Would he come across as canned if he tried?

The hole in his memory made him want to scream, but he kept his face impassive as he strode down the corridor again. He let himself walk to the mess hall, then turn in the other direction from the gym.

The corridor ended at a closed door, which was solid at the bottom with glass at the top.

Beyond it he could see a small, square room and the Lieutenant named Tobias sitting at a desk. The man looked up, saw him and motioned him inside.

"Just a moment," he said.

On a sudden impulse, Jonah looked around and asked, "Olson's finished?"

Tobias blinked as though he didn't know what Jonah was talking about. After several long seconds, he nodded. "Yes."

Jonah half turned. It sounded like Olson hadn't been here at all. Or was he only looking for clues to bolster Sophia's side of the case?

He could have taken one of the chairs along the wall. Instead, he stood while the man lifted a phone receiver and dialed a number.

After listening to someone on the other end of the line, he said, "You can go right in." When he gestured toward a door in back of him, Jonah strode to it and turned the knob.

He stepped into a room that was a lot more homey than the rest of the installation. Someone had covered the cinder-block walls with drywall painted a warm apricot. Berber carpeting covered the tile floor. In addition to the desk at one side of the room there were two comfortable easy chairs grouped on either side of a lamp table.

It was a scene out of a fifties movie, except for the berber. That was more recent.

The man behind the desk was tall and slender, with slightly stooped shoulders, thinning salt-and-pepper hair and watery gray eyes.

It was the image that had come to Jonah the night before after he'd awakened from the dream. The doctor would have looked at home in a tweed sports coat with leather patches at the elbows, but he was wearing the same blue uniform as everyone else. His, though, had no name tag.

The man was fussing with a briar pipe, lighting it with a match and drawing on the tobacco, which had an aromatic tang.

As soon as Jonah smelled the aroma, he remembered it and remembered that the doctor smoked, which was not allowed in any other part of the bunker. But he supposed rank had its privileges.

What rank was the doctor, anyway?

Jonah was probably supposed to know, so he couldn't ask.

The doctor gave him a warm smile. "How are you doing?"

"Better."

"Good." Montgomery gestured toward one of the easy chairs. "Sit down."

Jonah lowered himself into the chair. He knew this whole setup was designed to help him relax, but he could feel his heart wildly pounding inside his chest.

The doctor took his pipe from his mouth, came around the desk and sat down in the other easy chair. When he was settled, he took another puff.

"How's your memory?" he asked.

"It's still spotty."

"That's one of the symptoms. The medication you've been taking should help with that."

Would it? Or was the truth just the opposite?

"How are you spending your days?"

Jonah drew a blank. Basket weaving? Volleyball? He shrugged.

"The food here is pretty good, considering," the doctor said.

"Yes."

"You went to physical therapy this morning?"

"Yes."

"How was that?"

"Fine." Jonah wanted to scream at him to stop making nice and get on with the real purpose of this little chat, but he managed to sit with his hands resting easily on the chair arms.

"Any more of those dreams about Afghanistan?" Montgomery asked.

In the gym, Henry had asked him the same question. Why were they so important to everyone? What the hell should he answer? If he said no, the colonel could get the truth out of the physical therapist.

Somehow Jonah had the feeling he was damned if he said yes and damned if he said no.

SOPHIA SAT in front of the monitor.

"Where is he?" Martin asked. He'd been out in the cave, and now he was back, looking winded.

"In Montgomery's office."

"Where else has he been this morning?"

"The mess hall. Then he went back to his room and stayed there for over an hour."

She didn't tell Martin that Jonah had apparently found the bug and spoken to her. He'd jump on her for putting it where Jonah could discover it, and it would no doubt show him she had been indiscreet.

"Did he stay in his room?" Martin was saying. "He could have changed his shoes and you wouldn't know he was somewhere else."

"Why would he do that?"

Martin shrugged.

She looked up at him. "Where were you all morning?"

"I went out closer to the cave mouth to make a report and get some instruction. But I still couldn't get through."

"Too bad."

When he didn't volunteer any more information, she turned back to the screen.

She wanted to scream at Jonah that Montgomery's office was

the most dangerous place in the bunker for him. She wanted to tell him to make some excuse and get out of there. But that wouldn't do any good. He didn't have any way of hearing her, except through some kind of psychic bond, and she wasn't putting any faith in that.

Still, she couldn't keep from sending him a silent message. *Don't talk about Afghanistan. Just don't do it. Please. Please believe me that it's important.*

Chapter Six

Jonah wanted to shift in his seat, but he managed to stay still as a rock.

"I did dream about Afghanistan last night," he said, his tone measured as he watched the doctor's expression turn eager.

Leading the man on a little more, he said, "There were brown hills. I could hear gunfire in the distance."

He stopped, pretending to remember.

Now it was the doctor who shifted in his seat.

Jonah let the silence stretch, waiting him out. Finally Montgomery spoke. "And then what?"

"Then Lieutenant Calley came striding into the village."

The doctor blinked. "Who?"

"You know—that guy who was court-martialed for murdering civilians in Vietnam."

"Oh. Right."

Jonah floated a hypothesis. "So the dream couldn't be about anything that really happened?"

The doctor shook his head. "It could—if you're using him as a metaphor for reality."

Jonah stroked his chin, struggling to keep his face sober as he plotted his next move. "I don't remember what Calley looked like in real life. In the dream, he was in his mid-twenties, clean shaven, blue eyes. And his teeth were very white and even. He had on a non-standard uniform. Maybe what they wore back in the sixties. But I can't be sure."

"What he looked like isn't all that important," Montgomery snapped.

"You're sure? Okay."

"Go on."

Still making it up, Jonah continued. "Well, what happened in the dream was that Calley had a big bag slung over his shoulder."

The doctor sat forward. "And?"

So Montgomery was interested in the bag. Why?

"And he started pulling out stuff. At first it was toys and candy and things for the kids. Fun stuff. But then he got serious. He had food rations—powdered milk, big bags of rice and meat in neat plastic-wrapped packages like they came from the grocery store back home."

He stopped short when he noticed Montgomery eyeing him with mistrust.

"You're saying he came to help the people?"

"Yeah. And make their lives more comfortable."

"Okay. What else?"

Jonah had been enjoying himself, and he could have manufactured some more of the tall tale, but he wanted to make another point.

"That's it. I had the feeling something else was going to happen, but before it could, someone woke me up."

"Who?"

"A guard came down the hall, opened my door and shone his light inside. I couldn't see his name tag, so I don't know who it was. Do they do that on a regular basis? It disrupts a guy's sleep."

Montgomery scowled. "I don't know the guard protocols."

Yeah, sure, Jonah thought, but he kept the observation to himself.

"But I'll make sure they don't disturb you again."

That was something, anyway. Next time Sophia came to his room, he wouldn't have to worry about a guy with a flashlight barging in.

Montgomery gave his a piercing look. "What are you thinking about now?"

"Why?"

"You have a strange expression on your face."

"I was thinking about an old girlfriend."

"Why?"

Jonah scrambled for an answer and came up with a plausible memory. "Well, we were talking about my room. About the guard opening the door. And I was thinking about a time when I was at Hanna's house. In her bedroom. We were…" He stopped as though thinking about how to phrase his next words. "Her parents were supposed to be out for the evening, and we were half-naked in her bed. When we heard her dad coming up the stairs, I had to duck into the closet. Then, when the coast was clear, I climbed out the window. I loosened the drainpipe on the way down."

The story wasn't made up. It had really happened, but he'd just pulled the girl's name out of the air.

The doctor was still watching him closely. "I thought you were having memory problems."

"Yeah. But your question *triggered* a memory."

"Maybe we can dig up some more memories," Montgomery shot back.

"How?"

"Perhaps hypnosis would be more effective than a dream."

Jonah felt the hairs on the back of his neck prickle. "I don't want to do that."

"Why not?"

"It doesn't feel…comfortable."

The doctor's expression grew brittle. "By not cooperating, you're jeopardizing the safety of everybody in this installation."

Jonah's throat tightened, but he managed to ask, "How?"

"We need information from you."

Wondering if he would get an accurate answer, he said, "Probably you told me before, but I can't remember. What is my diagnosis?"

"You're suffering post-traumatic stress connected with your assignment in Afghanistan. You were in a military hospital for several months after villagers turned you over to American troops."

Jonah considered the implications. He could have asked exactly what was supposed to have happened to him. But he didn't want to hear the doctor's story. If it was a story.

Instead, he asked, "And my next assignment was Thailand?"

"Yes."

"So I was cleared for duty."

"It was supposed to be an easy assignment. The bird-flu epidemic changed everything. You went berserk and endangered the lives of everyone with the diplomatic mission."

Jonah gripped the arms of the chair to steady himself. He had almost gotten a bunch of people killed?

He didn't want to believe it. He didn't want to believe anything this man had told him.

But what if it was true?

Montgomery was looking at him with satisfaction. "Are you sure you don't want to try hypnosis?" he asked, his voice gentle yet persuasive.

Despite his sudden feeling of horror, Jonah answered, "No." If he knew anything, he knew he didn't want this man having that kind of access to his mind. He didn't need Sophia Rhodes to tell him that.

He stared into space, not seeing anything around him. Then,

as if he'd discovered a gateway to freedom, his eyes focused on the clock in the bookcase to his right.

"We're over time," he said, his voice low and gritty.

Montgomery glanced at his watch. "Yes, but I don't have anyone after you. We could keep talking if you want."

"No. This session was…traumatic."

"I understand," Montgomery said, his tone grudging. Getting up, he consulted an appointment book. "We can start again at the same time tomorrow."

"Yes," Jonah answered because he was sure that appearing to cooperate was his only option.

He climbed out of his chair and headed for the door without looking back at the man he knew was watching his every move. The way he walked. The way he held his shoulders.

He'd started off the session feeling like he was in control. By the end he'd felt like he was sliding down a greased slope toward some region of hell. He'd hit the bottom and bounced, and now he was so numb he could barely string two thoughts together in his mind.

Stepping into the waiting room, he closed the door behind him, trying to collect himself. He had to think. He sensed danger from the doctor. He focused on that, trying to build some kind of case for his own sanity when he knew he was hanging on by his fingernails.

At first, Montgomery had given him no hard facts. Then he'd come out with some horrific statements about Major Jonah Baker. But the man's attitude had never changed. It was obvious he wanted information, which seemed to confirm what Sophia had told him.

Sophia. She had come to him in the night and started his mind working again. Well, her and not taking the pills. Before that he had barely been functioning. Had he given that away to Montgomery? He hoped to hell he hadn't.

As though coming out of a fog, he noticed that the waiting

room was empty. The lieutenant who served as a receptionist was gone. Well, he thought, maybe that presented an opportunity….

Montgomery was still in his office with the door closed. Hoping he'd stay there, Jonah crossed to the desk and looked at the computer. A screen saver was showing, indicating that Tobias had been away for a few minutes.

When Jonah tapped one of the keys, he saw a list of men and their duty assignments.

He skimmed it and found only routine stuff—until he came to a notation about checking on Baker.

Apparently several men were assigned to look in on him during the night. Was that really going to change now?

When he found nothing else of interest, he switched to the other window and found himself looking at a pornographic Web site.

So that's what the receptionist had really been doing. But he'd put up the duty list in case anybody saw.

Nice.

As he switched back to the previous screen, another interesting observation zinged into his brain. Olson had told him that they were cut off from the outside world. So how was this computer connected to the Internet?

Jonah's hand twitched. Before he could stop himself he moved the cursor to the taskbar and clicked the Internet button. Several sites seemed to be open. He flicked to another one and found he was looking at a news parody site.

So the bunker wasn't sealed off from communication.

Quickly he restored the screen to its original.

Taking more of a chance, he began quietly opening drawers. In each, he saw only the usual office supplies, until he opened the bottom right-hand drawer and found a metal box. In it, was a stack of ten-, twenty- and fifty-dollar bills.

Struggling to repress a grin, Jonah helped himself to a quarter of the stack, then closed the drawer. Knowing he'd be pressing his luck to stay any longer, he stepped into the hall.

His heart was pounding now, and he forced himself to walk casually—not to his room, the mess hall or the gym, or anywhere else he could remember.

Words and phrases from the conversation with the doctor were swirling in his head again.

Went berserk.

Endangered the mission.

Post-traumatic stress.

He fought to keep his hands at his sides and not press them over his eyes.

Was he really all screwed up? He didn't want to believe it. He couldn't believe it and retain his self-image.

Yet he'd just stolen some money. As a teenager he might have done it, but he didn't think it was the kind of thing the adult Jonah Baker did.

Still, these were extraordinary circumstances. If he got out of here, he was going to need the money. American money. He suspected he would have no problem spending it in Thailand.

He kept walking, knowing he needed something constructive to do instead of thinking about what Montgomery had told him. Since he had no idea what this facility looked like, he decided to do some exploring. Would somebody stop him or follow him? He'd soon find out.

SOPHIA'S GAZE was glued to the screen. "He's left Montgomery's office."

"Let's hope he's walking under his own power."

She glanced at Phil. "What do you mean?"

"They could have drugged him. They could be carrying him somewhere."

"No!"

Phil came over and looked at the screen. "Then what's he doing?"

"I don't know."

"Montgomery may be getting desperate."

She dragged in a breath and let it out. "Let's see where Jonah is going."

"Okay," he agreed.

She felt him standing behind her, watching the action like a guy glued to a televised sports event. She wished she had gotten to work with some of the other men who had been in on the briefing sessions, but Phil had volunteered for the assignment, and she was stuck with him.

"Have you been on a rescue mission like this before?" she asked, partly because she couldn't stand the silence.

"No."

Not the answer she wanted to hear. But she felt as if her choices had been taken away when she'd signed up.

"If he gets into a good position, I can pull him out now."

"Not you. Me."

Her head jerked up. "What do you mean? I'm his contact."

"But you could get caught."

"So could you. And he may not trust you."

"He may not trust you, either. You don't know what Montgomery said to him. Or what he said to the doctor. He could have spilled the beans about you."

Containing a spurt of annoyance, she said, "Let's see where he ends up." Instead of looking at Phil, she kept her eyes on the screen.

He shrugged and went to the back of the room, and she saw him taking a drink of water. Was he swallowing a pill? she wondered. She thought she'd seen his hand slide out of his pocket a second before.

This could be further evidence of drug addiction, she thought. Or he could simply be taking stimulants to stay awake.

When he turned a corner, she knew he was heading for the portable toilet. Because there was no door on the facility, they tried to give each other privacy.

She was glad he'd gone there now. At least she'd have a few minutes when he wasn't hanging over her shoulder.

She turned back to the screen, seeing a moving blip that represented Jonah.

In her mind she spoke to him. *Jonah, come on. Come closer to the exit and we can get you out of there.*

CARLTON MONTGOMERY repressed the impulse to smack his fist against the apricot-covered wall.

Instead, he took several deep breaths, then sat down at his desk and opened his laptop computer. In his file on Baker, he wrote down a summary of their session. At first he'd thought he was going to get something from the man this time. Instead, the information was useless.

Was Baker reporting his dream accurately? Or was he working some kind of con?

He wouldn't have considered that possible a few days ago, but the man had seemed different today. More alert and more sure of himself—at least until Carlton had started feeding him the story about his going berserk. That had shaken him up. But he'd still declined the offer of hypnosis.

Montgomery pondered that logic. Baker was being given powerful medication every morning and evening. Had he skipped a dose? Had the sergeants failed to give it to him? Or was he only pretending to take the stuff? Was he in a rebellious phase? What?

After consulting his patient notes, he scribbled a note on the pad next to the computer.

"Question the sergeants about Baker's meds. Have them make damn sure he's taking the pills."

He put down the pen and leaned back in his chair. He'd been giving the man a drug that would induce confusion and interfere with his short- and long-term memory. But was that enough? Maybe it was time for something heavy-duty.

Unfortunately, the strategy could blow up in his face. The drug he was thinking about could fry the man's brain. He'd have to be careful. But if that was his only alternative, he'd have to use it.

JONAH WALKED DOWN the hall in the direction of his room and went past it. Resisting the urge to look behind him or to walk more quickly than normal, he kept going as though he knew what he was doing. He stopped at a random door and opened it to what looked like a dormitory with at least thirty bunk beds arranged in rows. All of them had mattresses but no sheets, which must mean nobody was sleeping there.

He wondered if most of the men here slept in dorms and if he was one of the few with a private room. Perhaps just the officers had that privilege.

He shut the door and kept going down the corridor for several dozen yards, then turned down a side hallway to another door with a sign that said Stairway.

He opened the door and stepped into a stairwell where he descended one level.

As he stood looking around, he flexed his leg. It was sore, but not as bad as it had been the night before.

The corridor wasn't much different from the one on the floor above, except that the lighting wasn't quite as bright.

The first door he came to led to a room with three upright tanks about twenty feet tall and twelve feet across. They were labeled Fresh Water. That made sense in a closed facility. But he didn't see a spigot on the side of the tanks.

He stared at the sign. It was in English, with no translation into anything that looked like Thai.

Well, he'd been told this facility had been constructed by the U.S. government.

He exited and continued down the hall to the next door, which opened into a storeroom lined with shelves of cans of food and boxes of medical supplies, toilet paper and linens. As he walked among the rows of shelves, he noted once again that all the labels were in English, with additional information in Spanish on some of the cans.

It was difficult to believe that they hadn't stocked any indigenous products. It certainly would have been cheaper to buy from the locals than to import everything from the States.

SOPHIA GLANCED over her shoulder. Martin was still in the bathroom, and she wasn't going to go back there for a consultation.

Snatching up the portable GPS locator, she rushed down the corridor toward the hidden door that she'd used to enter the bunker. Jonah was in the storeroom. She knew it. And if she could just get to him in time, she could bring him through. That would solve her biggest problem—how to get him out of there.

"Jonah, stay right where you are," she called out. She knew he couldn't hear her with rock walls between them, but it helped to feel that she was communicating with him.

And he was so close. So close.

Before she could open the door, a hand came down on her shoulder, and she screamed.

JONAH HEARD a muffled scream. Either it was far away—or on the other side of a thick wall. It sounded like a woman, and the only woman he'd seen here was Sophia.

Now it seemed as if she was in trouble, and his heart leaped into his throat, blocking his windpipe.

He wanted to call out to her, but he knew that was the wrong thing to do. Where was she? Had he really heard her?

He moved toward the shelves at the far end of the room, from where he thought the scream had emanated.

As he crossed the room, the door in back of him opened, and a hard voice called, "Hold it right there."

Chapter Seven

"Don't move," a low voice ordered.

Sophia went stock-still. She knew that the man holding her was Phil Martin. And she knew that he was doing his job—as he saw it.

"What the hell are you up to?" he asked, his voice so low she wouldn't have heard him unless he'd been speaking directly into her ear.

"Jonah's out there."

"And so are a lot of other guys."

She turned toward him. "How do you know?"

"Because I was looking at the seismic indicator. It's very sensitive. And it told me there are eight people about to enter the room on the other side of that door."

She felt her whole body go cold. She ached to open the door and prove Phil wrong, but she knew that was a dumb move. He was the expert at covert operations and she was the rank amateur. So she followed him back the way they'd come.

When she reached their staging area, she looked down at the GPS she'd brought and saw that Jonah was now on the stairs, on his way back to the living area of the bunker.

"They came and got him," Phil said, his voice hard.

"They could hurt him."

"They won't. Not unless they already got what they wanted from him."

It was all she could do to keep from bashing her fists into something. "But we don't know what they've gotten! Why did they come after him just now?"

"Let's be optimistic. Probably they didn't want him messing around down there."

She nodded. That made sense. There was dangerous electrical and mechanical equipment on this floor. Still, she had to ask, "What are we going to do?"

"I'll make a decision and let you know."

FOUR MEN walked in front of Jonah and four in back. Quite a large group to retrieve one lone guy. When the door to the storeroom had opened, he'd been prepared to fight whoever came through the door, but he couldn't handle eight armed men.

The guy in charge of the "rescue squad" had said he could get hurt down in the service area of the bunker. Yeah, sure. Hurt by them. He'd gone along quietly, half expecting them to take him back to Dr. Montgomery for an evaluation of his mental state. Instead they brought him to the mess hall, where lunch was being served.

Why had they come charging after him? Perhaps they were afraid that he'd somehow escape, or at least hide from them. But why did they think he'd do that? Either because he was crazy or because he'd come to his senses.

The speculation brought him back to Sophia. Had he been unconsciously looking for her? And how close had he gotten? She'd sneaked into the bunker *somehow*. It made sense that she'd come through a back exit, not the front door, wherever that was. But why had she screamed? Unless he'd only imagined her startled, frightened cry....

He got a lot of curious and resentful looks when he entered the mess hall. It was obvious these guys considered him a badass. If he'd really put all of their lives in danger, that would certainly generate resentment.

He grabbed a tray, then a plate and helped himself from the buffet on the steam table. He wasn't hungry, but he filled his plate with food and carried it to a table against the wall.

This time, nobody came over to be friendly. Well, what did he expect? He'd just caused them a lot of trouble.

As he took a bite of chicken, he thought again about what was supposed to be going on here. First eggs and now chicken. In the middle of a bird-flu epidemic?

Surely this poultry hadn't come from the countryside, nor did this taste like canned chicken. So was there a henhouse somewhere down in the bunker?

He ate a little bit, then set his tray in the clean-up area and walked down the hall, wondering if he could get back downstairs. But this time, he was thinking more clearly and looked for security cameras. He found them immediately.

He wanted to slap his forehead. That was how they'd known where he was when he'd gone exploring. Which also told him that someone was actively monitoring the security system, so if he strayed from his routine, they'd be right there. His head down so nobody could see his tense expression, he went into a room that served as a recreation area. Some guys were watching an action adventure movie on DVD. Ignoring them, he went to the shelf filled with paperback novels and looked through the collection. All of the books looked well-used. He took a mystery and an adventure novel, which he brought back to his room.

But instead of reading, he pictured the diplomatic mission. The bird-flu scare. The mad rush to safety. And his own failure to keep a cool head.

He made a disgusted sound and picked up the book, forcing himself to scan the pages, even when he wasn't taking in much of the story. Anything was better than thinking about himself.

The exercise got him through to dinner time.

Then he sat in the back of the recreation room for a while, watching another shoot-'em-up movie. Again, he wasn't much interested in the action, but it kept him occupied until ten hundred hours. When he left, he picked up a uniform cap someone had left lying on a table. He jammed it under his arm as he headed for his room like a good boy. But he wasn't planning to stay there long. As soon as the place settled down for the night, he was going to see if he could find Sophia. The hell with the cameras. If he kept his head down, maybe they'd think he was supposed to be in the hallway, patrolling. Of course, he'd heard the scream hours ago. If she was hurt or in danger, maybe he was too late. He hoped to hell not.

But he'd forgotten something important. As he was getting ready to leave the room, a knock on the door startled him. Then Lopez came in.

"Time for your evening medication," he said.

"Yeah. Right." The guy gave him a narrow-eyed look, and Jonah wondered why. Had the sergeant gotten in trouble for not doing his job?

"I watched you take it last time," he muttered.

Jonah nodded.

Lopez brought the pill and a glass of water from the bathroom and handed them to Jonah.

"I DON'T LIKE IT," Phil muttered.

"You've got a better suggestion?" Sophia countered as she tucked her hair under a cap.

"No."

"I go to his room and I get him out of here tonight." She

wanted to shout that they should have done it last night, but there was no use getting mad at Phil. He'd been following the procedure outlined. He'd been instructed to get a report on Jonah's sanity before getting up close and personal.

"I can't keep the cameras off as long as last night."

"It will work out fine." She made herself sound confident although her insides were tied in knots.

This time she was armed—with a gun and the portable GPS. It told her Jonah was in his room.

When she got there, would he trust her enough to leave with her?

As she thought of a half dozen nasty possibilities, she couldn't stop a shiver from racing over her skin. But there was nothing she could do to change anything that had happened now.

Her lips set in a grim line, she turned the handle and opened the door, half expecting someone to spring at her from inside the storeroom. But as far as she could tell, it was empty.

So far, so good. All she had to do now was make contact with Jonah, tell him they were leaving, and hope to God he would come with her.

CONSCIOUS THAT Lopez was watching him like a store security guard tracking a suspected shoplifter, Jonah took the pill. Hoping he looked like a man with nothing to hide, he put the pill in his mouth and managed to get it into the space between his gum and his cheek before swallowing the water.

"Okay," he said, handing back the glass.

But Lopez stayed for more than a minute, watching him. And Jonah had to stand there feeling the pill start to fall apart.

When the guy finally left, Jonah rushed into the bathroom and dug out as much of the thing as he could. Then he rinsed out his mouth, praying that he hadn't swallowed any of the damn stuff by accident.

Heart pounding, he sat down on the edge of the bed, trying to figure out if his brain was getting that muzzy feeling again.

SOPHIA FELT as if razor wire was twisting in her guts. Last night it had seemed that Jonah believed her. But she didn't know what false information Montgomery had fed him during the day. All she knew was that Jonah had figured out she'd bugged him.

She glanced at the screen and saw that he was still in his room. Good!

But just as she'd breathed out a sigh, everything changed.

He stepped into the corridor. He was on the move. Headed for God knew where.

Because she'd thought she was going to meet him in his quarters, she'd plotted a course through the maze of tunnels that made up the bunker. All at once, she was in unknown territory.

She studied the GPS, trying to determine the safest way. She knew the guard schedule along the route she'd intended to take, but she didn't know who might be in the other corridors.

After reading the schematic, she slipped the device into her pocket and hurried along the hallway.

When she came to a cross corridor, she stopped and slid her face just an inch around the corner. Good thing, because a guard was coming toward her.

She hurried back the way she'd come, opened a door, and closed herself into an empty room. With her pulse pounding in her throat, she waited for the footsteps to pass.

It seemed to take forever, but finally she opened the door a crack and found the hallway empty again.

Though she didn't want to waste time, she knew that Jonah could have changed directions while she'd been hiding, so she glanced at the GPS screen again. She was right. This time he was heading toward her. Finally, she'd lucked out.

She kept moving on a collision course with him, so intent on the screen, that she didn't see another guard until he was almost on top of her.

"Hold it right there," he said in a hard voice.

She froze.

Now what? If she ran, she could get shot. And if she stayed where she was, she could end up in Dr. Montgomery's clutches.

"Who the hell are you?"

She didn't answer, only waited for the guard to approach her. When he was close enough to touch, she lashed out a leg, trying to disable him with a kick in the crotch.

He must have been ready for her to try something because he dodged to the side and grabbed her.

As his arm brushed her cap, it fell off, and he made a low exclamation when he saw her blond hair.

"A chick! How the hell did you get in here?"

"Special assignment."

"We'd better ask Dr. Montgomery about that."

"Of course."

She pretended that she had every right to be there. But when he got out a pair of handcuffs, she panicked and flailed out with her arm.

In response, he landed a flat-handed blow on her face that stunned her.

Staggering back, she saw him go for the microphone on his collar. As he reached the button that opened the communications line, a blur of movement made him whip his head to the side. But it was too late. Someone crashed into him, knocking him to the ground and taking Sophia along with him.

Jonah!

When the guard went for his gun, she twisted to the side and bit down on his wrist. He screamed, and slashed toward her face with his spread fingers.

While the man was attacking her, Jonah unsnapped the catch at the top of the man's holster, pulled out his gun and brought the butt down on the guy's head.

He made a gurgling sound and went limp.

"Thanks," Sophia gasped.

"No problem."

Before they could exchange any information, a loud siren blared.

Jonah looked up, his eyes narrowed. "How do we get out of here?"

"Through the storeroom where you were this morning." He helped her up, and she swayed on her feet. Looking wildly around, she expected to see armed men coming at them from both ends of the corridor. But so far it was clear.

"Did I hear you scream?"

She looked at him. "Yes."

"What happened?"

"I couldn't come get you."

"But—"

"We'll talk about it later."

"How did you know I was in there?"

She pulled out the GPS and showed him the blip that indicated where he was. Then she pressed her hand against her forehead, trying to orient herself. "I don't remember how to get there from here," she admitted. "Do you?"

"I hope so."

He didn't have to urge her to hurry. They sprinted down the corridor, then into a cross passage and down a flight of stairs.

Jonah was limping badly by the time they were in sight of the storeroom. Worse, the corridor was suddenly full of uniformed men rushing toward them from both directions.

She opened the storeroom door and flung herself inside. As soon as Jonah was through the door, she turned and locked it, thinking that it wouldn't hold the guards off for long.

"This way."

Behind them, fists pounded on the door. When it didn't open, she heard bullets tearing into the metal.

Jonah swore. "They'll get in. We're trapped."

"Keep going. In back of the shelves."

She led him toward the rear of the room, then behind the shelving where the exit was located.

Behind them, the storeroom door burst open, and guards poured in. "Halt."

Sophia kept running. But one of the pursuers saw Jonah as he followed her behind the shelves.

"Over there."

Guards rushed after him.

"Hurry," Sophia shouted.

Ignoring her, Jonah turned and pushed at the shelves. At first they didn't move. Then they rocked on their base and tumbled forward, hitting several men on the way down and blocking the others.

Jonah turned and dashed after Sophia, through the opening and into the stone tunnel.

WHEN JONAH saw a tough-looking man in a blue uniform waiting on the other side of the door, he reared back. "Who the hell are you?"

"Philip Martin. Better known as the cavalry."

He reached around Jonah, slammed the door, and pulled down an iron bar, sealing off the opening. Then he gestured down a tunnel hewn out of solid rock.

In the dim light, Jonah stared at the man who'd obviously been waiting for Sophia. Who was this guy, really? Could he trust him? Could he trust Sophia, for that matter? Last night she had come to his bedroom with a story about his being held captive. Was she truly trying to rescue him or was Montgomery the one trying to help him? He had no way of knowing what was fiction and what was reality.

"I want some answers," he said in a gritty voice.

"Later," the man named Philip Martin answered.

He grabbed the guy's shoulder. "Don't tell me later! I want answers now. What's your motivation for getting me out of there?"

Phil gave him a hard look. "Special assignment for the DOD."

"What's that supposed to mean?"

"We don't have time for a discussion now."

When Jonah failed to get an answer, he turned to Sophia. "And how did you get involved?"

Before she could speak, loud pounding sounded against the door.

"I think you're going to have to wait for an in-depth discussion," Phil said. "Come on." He turned and hurried down the tunnel.

Sophia cupped her hand over Jonah's shoulder. "We'll talk later."

Not knowing for sure whether they were the good guys, he listened to his gut, then turned and followed Phil.

As they hurried toward a light glowing in the darkness, an enormous blast sounded behind them, the pressure wave throwing them backward down the tunnel.

Jonah grabbed Sophia and curved his body over hers as the floor shook and stones rattled down from the ceiling.

His mind flashed on some of the mine disasters he'd read about in the newspapers. Lord, was the whole tunnel going to come down around them?

He held his breath, praying that the structure was solid. After a few moments, the shaking stopped, leaving them coughing as dust settled around them.

Phil stood and brushed himself off, glancing back the way they'd come.

"It looks like they're through the door."

Jonah still didn't know what was going on. But he knew that armed men would be in the tunnel before the dust cleared.

He gripped Sophia's hand. "Which way?"

Phil pointed toward the light. "There's a room to the left. Stop there and arm yourself. Then keep going. There's a maze of natural caves down there."

Turning, Jonah followed Sophia down the tunnel, toward the lighted area. Beyond his vision was what appeared to be a vast area of blackness.

They stepped into what looked like a campsite. How long had Sophia and Phil been there? he wondered.

He found the gun rack and took two SIG Sauers plus extra clips. While he armed himself, Sophia pulled a pack from under one of the cots and slipped her arms through the straps.

"My emergency supplies," she explained as Phil lifted an Uzi from the rack. She looked at the GPS. "This is broken. I might as well leave it."

They had only taken a few steps toward the blackness beyond the camp when Jonah looked back and realized that Phil wasn't following them.

"What are you doing?"

He gave Jonah a hard look as he pulled out more heavy weaponry. "Getting a surprise ready for them. Go on."

"You—"

"Go on," the other man said again. "I'm going to handle this. You need a head start with that bad leg."

"Okay," he said, conceding the point and assuming Phil would join them quickly.

He and Sophia had covered a hundred yards when someone behind them started shooting. Someone else returning fire.

Phil and the guards.

The exchange went on for several moments, sporadic at first, then with more fury, and he pictured the guards advancing on the lone gunman.

"Come on," he muttered to Sophia. "What are you waiting for?"

The words were barely out of his mouth when the firing suddenly stopped.

Chapter Eight

Wide-eyed, Sophia looked at him and made a strangled sound in her throat. "Phil…"

He shook his head. "Either they captured him, or they shot him. And I'm not betting he's still alive."

"Lord, no!"

He heard the horror in her voice as the reality slammed into her. It reflected his own feelings. The man was dead—because of him. He would have turned around and charged back, guns blazing, but Sophia grabbed his arm, grounding him.

"You can't go back there."

He might want to even the score—for Phil, a guy he hadn't known very long, and for himself, too—but he'd end up getting himself killed. That wasn't an option because the men who had shot Phil would shoot Sophia, too. After they tortured her to find out who she was and why she was here.

The hell of it was that he didn't even know the answer to that question.

He didn't share any of that thinking with Sophia. Instead he said, "I assume you know the way out of here?"

"Yes."

She breathed out a sigh as he hurried along beside her. In a few minutes, they reached a place where the tunnel opened out into blackness.

"Now what?"

"Give me a minute."

Sophia pulled the pack off her back and fumbled inside. Bringing out two pairs of night-vision goggles, she handed him one.

With no natural light in the cave, it was still almost impossible to see. Then she brought out flashlights that emitted an infrared beam—which illuminated several markings on the wall.

"Bread crumbs," Sophia whispered.

Behind them, he could hear voices. "We've got to hide," he said in a barely audible voice.

"Not to worry. This place is hide-and-seek heaven."

She grabbed his free hand and led him to the left, behind an outcropping of stalagmites, then around another bend so that they were further sheltered from the tunnel. They both switched off their infrared lights.

Almost as soon as they'd ducked into hiding, three guards appeared. All of them were holding flashlights, which they swung in an arc. With the night-vision goggles, the light hurt Jonah's eyes, and he took off the goggles.

"Baker and the woman went down here."

One of them swore. "But this is a big mother of a cave. They could be anywhere."

"We go in there, we could get lost," the third one said. "We'd better go back and get some more lights."

The others agreed.

The lights swivelled in the other direction, but Jonah waited until they had disappeared back into the tunnel. "We have to hustle," he said.

"Right." She stood unmoving beside him, and he wondered

what she was doing, until she reached for him and wrapped her arms around him.

For a moment he was startled. Then he circled her shoulders and pulled her against him. He could feel her trembling.

"Cold?"

"Scared."

"You did fine."

"I didn't know it was going to be this rough." She swallowed hard. "I didn't know Phil was going to get killed."

"Yeah. Let's make sure it wasn't for nothing." He waited a beat, then said, "Maybe this is when you tell me who sent you here."

She hitched in a breath. "An outfit called the Light Street Detective Agency."

"Who are they?"

"They're in Baltimore. They do some government contract work, and they were contracted by a Department of Defense office that wanted to know what Montgomery was up to."

"So the point of the exercise wasn't rescuing me."

He felt her tense. "No. But it was the point for me."

"Okay."

"You don't believe me?"

"I don't know what the hell to believe anymore."

He wanted to ask if she would have backed out if she'd known the guards were out for blood, but he kept that question locked behind his lips.

Last night, she had kissed him passionately. Today she kept her head tipped down. So was she trying to change the terms of the relationship?

If he kissed her again, he might find out. But he couldn't do it now. Not when the guards were coming back.

She held him for long seconds before easing away.

"We'd better go."

They both put on their night-vision goggles and switched on their beams again. She moved hers in a circle and found one of the marks on the floor. Once she had her bearings, she began leading him across the cavern, where they had to keep detouring around stalagmites and ducking under stalactites.

Figuring he had nothing to lose, he began asking questions in a low voice. "How long was I in the bunker?"

"Three weeks."

He muttered a curse under his breath. "And I don't remember any of it—until last night, when you woke me up. Well, I do have a few memories. I could find my way to the mess hall, the gym and Montgomery's office."

"At first your wound was infected. You were on heavy pain meds, so there was no chance of getting information out of you. They had to get you well first."

"How do you know all that?"

"The Light Street people had a lot of information on you."

"Like what?"

"Your service record."

"Some of that information is classified."

"I know. You did some really heroic things. You got the Distinguished Service Cross."

"I did my job," he answered.

"Right. And how many guys get the DSC?"

She changed the subject abruptly. "I need to know—did you take any medication today?"

In the darkness, he could hear her draw in a breath and hold it.

"No. A guy named Lopez came to give it to me, and I only pretended to take it."

"I heard that—over the microphone."

"So you *were* the person who planted it."

"Yes."

"Lopez was more persistent when he came back this evening. I'm thinking he got chewed out."

"Good."

"Yeah." He laughed. "I didn't take it the night before, either. I found the pill under the pillow."

"I guess you had come to the right conclusions. But your logic was still a little fuzzy."

"It's a lot better now."

"I can tell."

Another thought struck him.

"You said the GPS was broken, but show me where you put the transponder."

"Your right shoe." She knelt down and reached under the laces. When she pulled out a small metal disk, he took it away from her and crushed it in his fingers.

As they resumed walking, he kept hitting her with questions so she wouldn't have a chance to prepare her answers.

"How exactly did you get hooked up with the Light Street people? I mean, why did they come to you?"

"I'm a clinical psychologist."

"Convenient. So you're in a great position to evaluate the escapee's mental state."

"That's not why."

"But Phil wouldn't agree to have you bring me out until you gave him a report."

Her breath caught. "How do you know that?"

"It made sense. And you came looking for me tonight. So the leg was just an excuse. It's about the same as the last time you saw me."

After a pause she said, "You asked how I got involved. It's because Kathryn Kelley, another psychologist, is a friend of mine. She's got an office at 43 Light Street and her husband,

Hunter Kelley, works for Randolph Security, which is associated with them. She came to me after they found out you knew me."

He still didn't get all the implications, so he let her continue.

"She told me you were in danger. When she explained what was going on, I couldn't leave you there."

Her voice sounded sincere. He wished he could see her face, but that was impossible in the dark.

Although he kept pushing ahead, the injured thigh was starting to show the strain. Finally he knew that he had to stop for a few minutes.

He cleared his throat. "I hate to slow us down, but I need to rest the leg."

She turned toward him immediately. "I'm so sorry. I should have thought of that."

"Not your problem."

"Of course it is." She made a low sound. "I mean, we're in this together."

Turning, she ran her light over the trail ahead. "Actually, we stopped a little way farther along on the way in. There's a place we can sit."

"So we're about halfway?"

"Yes."

She led him to a flat rock that could serve as a bench.

He eyed the height. "It's better if I sit on the floor and stretch out my leg."

"Sure."

Gingerly, he lowered himself to the ground, and she sat beside him.

Stretching his leg straight out, he massaged the sore muscles. Then, because he wanted to torture himself some more with all the reasons why he and Sophia had nothing in common, he said, "So you went to college after I left."

"Yes. I went to Radcliffe. Then Hopkins for my Master's and Ph.D."

He pictured what her life must have been like. Probably her parents had paid for her to live in an apartment while she was in school. She would have had a car, joined a sorority, gone to parties and football games.

All the while, he'd been crawling through muddy obstacle courses and learning how to kill people. Then relaxing in the evenings with the guys at a local bar or picking up willing women in town.

"What are you thinking?" she asked.

"You know I never furthered my education after high school. And I was lucky to graduate from there."

"Because you didn't apply yourself. After that, you got a lot of life experience in the army."

"That doesn't give us much in common."

"Are you worried about that?" she asked in a soft voice.

He wasn't sure how to answer. A yes implied he was thinking about the future. A no would make him sound arrogant.

"It puts us on an unequal footing," he finally said. Because the night-vision goggles were starting to get uncomfortable, he took them off. Beside him, Sophia did the same.

"I don't see that as a major problem."

Either she was trying to say that they wouldn't be together for very long or that she didn't see their wildly different educations as a barrier between them.

When he remained silent, she asked, "Are you trying to push me away?"

He honestly didn't know. And why would he? Because he didn't trust her, or because he thought she didn't want him, and he was trying to strike first?

While he was mulling that over, a sound seeped into his consciousness. At first he thought the guards might have caught up with them. Then he realized he was hearing a deep rumbling.

He swore sharply.

"What?" she asked, her voice turning anxious.

Without the goggles, he couldn't see into the darkness, but he was pretty sure what was happening.

"Get down!" As the rumbling grew closer, he pushed her to the ground beside him and flung his body over hers.

It was difficult to hear anything besides a roaring noise now, but he pressed his mouth to her ear and said, "Landslide. The explosion must have triggered it."

To their right, where they would have been walking, he felt debris tumbling down a steep slope.

As he had earlier, he shielded her, draping his body over hers. He was aware of her breasts pressing against his chest, her hips sandwiched between his and the ground, one of her legs thrust between his.

He tried to ignore the intimate position as rocks pounded to their right. A few small ones hit him, but he stayed where he was.

She clung to him, her face pressed to his shoulder as the rubble tumbled downward. After long moments, the earth finally stopped shaking.

Once again, dust wafted around them, and he kept her face shielded until the worst of it settled to earth.

Then he raised his head. Unable to see her in the darkness, he asked urgently, "Are you okay?"

"Yes. Are you?"

"Some small stuff hit me."

"You'll have bruises," she said, reaching up to stroke her hands gently across his back.

"I'm not worried about that."

"If you hadn't stopped to rest, we would have been under a pile of rubble now."

"Yeah," he answered in a gritty voice.

"Thank God for that."

The emotion in her voice mirrored what he felt. When she pulled him back down and angled her head so that her lips met his, he was as eager for the contact as she.

He made a rough sound as the reality of their narrow escape hit him. A little while ago, he had been wondering about her motives. Now he felt her clasping him against her breasts.

His lips settled on hers, sealing their mouths together, and he knew by her response that was what she wanted.

His emotions leaped up to meet hers. He had made love to many women since the night they had spent in bed together. A lot of those times had been good. But none as good as it had been with Sophia Rhodes.

He'd known all along that he was comparing other women to her. Nobody else had ever measured up.

Now, though, she was back in his arms and he was lying on top of her.

Holding her to him, he rolled over, reversing their positions so that he was the one lying on the hard ground.

As his hands stroked up and down her back and over her hips, molding her body to his, he felt a wave of need so strong that he could not deny it.

Their mouths broke apart so that they could both gasp for breath. Then, tenderly, he drew her lower lip into his mouth, sucking, nibbling, listening to the small sounds of arousal that she made.

She moaned into his mouth, moving her hips against his. He pulled her uniform shirt from her waistband so that he could slip his hands underneath and splay his fingers against her warm skin before fumbling with the catch of her bra.

Frantic for skin-to-skin contact, he eased her a little to the side so that he could push her bra out of the way and cup his hand around one of her breasts, entranced by her softness, the warmth of her skin, and the way her hardened nipple stabbed into his palm, telling him that she was as aroused as he.

She moaned as his other hand cupped her bottom through the uniform pants, pressing her against his erection.

The way she moved her hips in response turned his blood to molten fire.

He heard himself say, "I want you."

And heard her answer, "Yes."

She brought her lips back to his, devouring his mouth.

The world had vanished. Only the two of them existed as he rocked her in his arms, loving the friction that inflamed them both.

"You're wearing too much," he murmured.

She laughed softly. "We can do something about that pretty easily."

He was totally absorbed in her. They might have been the only two people in the universe, until the sound of voices penetrated the haze around them.

Men, coming closer.

On top of him, Sophia stiffened, and Jonah knew then that he'd made a big mistake. While he'd let himself get all wrapped up with her, he'd trapped them between the rubble and the gun-toting guards coming down the trail.

Chapter Nine

Sophia clamped onto Jonah's hand, feeling her fingers dig into his flesh. What was she thinking? She was supposed to be getting him out of here. Phil had already died in the effort, and now she'd gotten the two of them into a hell of a fix.

Just a little while ago, Jonah had seemed so distant. Then, after the landslide, when he'd wrapped her in his arms, she'd been helpless to stop herself from kissing him. When he'd responded, she'd let her craving to connect with him overcome good sense.

Now they were in deep trouble, and she had to get them to safety. Too bad she had only a superficial knowledge of the cavern's interior, because she'd expected that once they got in here, it would be a straight shot to the other end.

With the voices coming toward them, the logical move would be to go in the other direction. But that way was blocked. Her only option was to take a chance on going back a little way and praying that they found another route.

She grabbed her pack, and they each scrambled for their goggles. Staying low to the ground, she slithered a few yards back, so she could wiggle around the ledge they'd been leaning against when the landslide had struck.

Trusting her judgment, Jonah followed, moving as quietly as a snake.

They made it into a narrow vertical shaft just as she saw lights coming toward them.

She had always hated closed-in places, but she kept going down because her life depended on it.

Jonah came in after her, wedging himself between her and one of the rock walls.

There was only a narrow ledge for them to stand on, and she hated to think how far the drop would be if they lost their footing.

It sounded as if the men who had come down the path were now where she and Jonah had been sitting earlier. There were two of them, and she guessed they were only part of the search party, other men no doubt having taken different routes through the cave, looking for the fugitives.

"That's a hell of a landslide," one of the guards said.

"If they're under that, they're dead."

"Maybe they made it to the other side first."

"I'm going to see how stable it is."

"Okay. But they could still be over here. I'll look around."

His friend made a sound of agreement, and Sophia heard rock crunching.

She felt Jonah moving beside her, doing something at his waist, then raising his arm. Though she wanted to tell him to stay still, there was no way they could talk now.

Above her, she could see a light swing around the area, then move closer.

She wanted to duck her head, but she kept looking up, hoping that the man would miss the tunnel.

Then suddenly a blinding light hit her in the face.

She gasped as the man above them exclaimed, "Got ya."

A boom reverberated in the tunnel. Then another and another.

Even as her ears kept ringing, she knew what had happened. Jonah had fired one of the guns he'd taken from the weapons rack.

The light flicked away from the opening of the shaft, and Jonah pushed past her, scrambling up and disappearing over the rim.

She followed him up, where she saw him leaning over a man lying on the ground.

"Buck?" a voice called.

When she heard rocks sliding around, she knew the other guy was coming. Jonah pulled her down behind the ledge where they'd been sitting.

The sound of tumbling rocks grew louder, and then she heard a scream that faded away as though someone was falling through space.

"Sounds like he went over the edge," Jonah said. "And this one's dead. Still, the shooting and the scream might bring more guys. We've got to get out of here."

"Where?" she asked, hearing her voice tremble.

"Across the rock slide."

"But that guy just slipped and fell on the loose rubble."

"He was in a hurry. We'll be careful."

He sounded confident. Then she remembered why they'd stopped here in the first place. "Your leg."

"It will be okay. We've got to get going."

He had barely finished speaking when they heard more voices behind them—farther away than last time, but coming closer.

"You were right," she whispered. "We drew their attention."

"Unfortunately."

As they put the night-vision goggles back on, he led her quickly toward the rubble. Stepping onto the gravelly surface, he tested his footing, then reached for her hand.

"Don't put your full weight down until you're sure of the surface," he said.

"Okay." Together they started across, leaning over so they could grasp the rocks with their hands and moving cautiously. The voices were getting closer, and she wanted to hurry, but she knew that would be a fatal mistake, given what had happened to the last man who had walked out onto this unstable surface.

They were almost to the other side, when the blinding beam from a flashlight hit them.

"Over there," one of the guards called.

"Keep going," Jonah ordered.

"What about you?"

"I'll be along in a minute," he assured her.

One of the guards spoke up again. "Who the hell is that with him?"

"It looks like the woman who got into the bunker."

"Where the hell did she come from?"

"Who knows. But don't shoot him if you can help it," one of the guards ordered. "Montgomery wants him for questioning."

"Get behind me," Jonah whispered. "Press against the wall on your left."

She did as he asked, knowing she was using him for a shield.

She could see the men trying to line up a shot, but it looked like they couldn't do it with Jonah in the way.

One of the guards started after them across the rubble field, moving too quickly, and the rocks shifted again.

He cursed and slowed down.

Looking back, she saw that Jonah had put a boulder between himself and the men and was digging furiously with his hands.

"What are you doing?" she whispered.

"Loosening this thing. It's big, and not much is holding it in place."

She came around and started helping him.

"Get back."

Ignoring him, she kept digging.

They worked frantically, as one of the guards inched toward them.

Finally, the boulder shifted. "Get back. Now! It's going to go."

This time she followed orders, making it to the other side of the unstable area just as the boulder tumbled down the slope, loosening the whole pile of rocks again.

For a horrible moment, the ground shifted under Jonah's feet, and she thought he was going over the edge. Sophia screamed and grabbed for his hand. Their fingers brushed, but he couldn't hold on. She lunged closer, her hand closing over his, pulling him off the unstable surface. He teetered on solid ground, and she pulled him the rest of the way.

He swore. "You could have gotten killed."

"I couldn't leave you there."

The exchange was interrupted by a scream as the man who had come after them lost his footing and was carried over the edge by the rock fall.

She watched him, feeling sick.

But Jonah didn't give her time to worry about the carnage.

"The whole mess is shifting again. Run!" he shouted.

She ran as rocks rumbled after them. This time the slide sounded bigger than before.

They kept moving down the tunnel at a fast pace, and she knew Jonah's leg must be aching with the strain.

"You need to stop."

"We need to get out of here before they figure out some way to get across."

He was right, but she heard the pain in his voice as he answered her.

Finally she could see light ahead of them and knew they were almost home free.

"Thank God."

But her thanks were short-lived. When she had come this way a few days ago, she and Phil had forded an underground stream. Today it was much deeper and moving faster.

"You have a boat stashed somewhere?" Jonah asked.

"Last time we waded across."

He looked at the fast-flowing stream. About ten feet wide, it was too far to jump across. "We can't wade now."

"But we have to get to the other side."

"Yeah. Let's see what's in your pack."

When she took it off, he rummaged inside and found some supplies. First he pulled out a waterproof bag. It was small, so he sealed the gun and the magazines inside and tucked them into his waistband before pulling a length of rope out of the pack.

After scanning the other side, he cursed under his breath. "There's nothing I can anchor it to." Instead he tied one end around his waist and the other around hers, then looked down the passage where the water disappeared into the gaping darkness.

She followed his gaze and shivered.

"You know where the river comes out?" he asked.

"No."

"In that case, we don't want to get swept away." He reached for her hand. "We should stay close together."

She had no intention of being anywhere else. Locking her fingers with his, she waded into the water with him, testing the current.

The water was cold and it covered their feet, then their knees, then rose to their waists. But the depth was only one problem. The current was another. She struggled to keep her footing as the water came up to her breasts, numbing her from that point downward.

When she wavered, he steadied her. "Okay to keep going?"

"Yes."

Jonah was almost to the other bank when she slipped and went down. She lost her grip on his hand, and her head dipped below the surface. If she hadn't been tied to Jonah, she would have been swept downstream.

He pulled on the rope, reeling her in, then dragged her up and helped her toward the opposite shore.

She gasped, clinging to him, trying not to drag them both to destruction.

"Steady."

"I'm trying," she sputtered.

Somehow they made it to the other side. But now they were downstream where the rock walls made it difficult to climb out. So they had to wade upstream again, against the current, aiming for the cave opening.

It was tough going. When she slipped, she grabbed for Jonah, only her hand went to the pack, pulling it off his shoulder. It bobbed in the water, then disappeared into the darkness.

This time she was the one who cursed.

"It's okay. All we have to do is get to the opening."

She gritted her teeth and concentrated on pushing upstream, knowing the struggle would have been impossible if she were alone. Jonah stayed beside her, and when he finally threw himself onto the shore he pulled her after him.

Flopping onto dry ground, she lay panting beside him.

The cave opening was small and almost hidden by vines trailing down a rock wall. When Jonah pushed the vines aside, the light hurt her eyes. He used a hand for a sunshade and peered into the early-morning sunlight. They were about fifty feet up, on a rock outcropping. Below them, sunlight dappled the new green leaves of tall oak and locust trees.

Jonah turned back to her. "This is the middle of nowhere. But it doesn't look much like Thailand. I'd say spring in the eastern United States."

"Good guess." She wrapped her arms around her wet shoulders. "It's West Virginia."

He gave her an accusing look. "It would have been easy enough for you to tell me that two days ago."

"Like I said, it was safer for you not to know. It might have changed the equation with Montgomery."

He scowled. "Yeah. Maybe I was already being too assertive with him yesterday."

"Like how?"

"I told him a long story about Lieutenant Calley."

She laughed. "I'll bet he loved that."

He glanced back the way they'd come. "I don't suppose you know how that bunker got there?"

"Actually, I do know. It was a fallout shelter left over from the Cold War. For some important government officials."

"How were they supposed to get to West Virginia in case of a nuclear attack?"

"God knows. There's a train line that runs down from D.C. It's not too far from here. Maybe they were supposed to take the Eisenhower Special."

He laughed, which she took as a good sign. She imagined he hadn't had much to laugh about in the past few weeks.

"There's a similar bunker under the Greenbrier Hotel. That one was for members of Congress."

"Another waste of taxpayers' money." He eased back so that his head and shoulders were propped against a rock. She heard him sigh.

"What?"

"I was trying to orient myself. I hate to ask, but what month is this?"

"May. Does that help you figure out a time frame for yourself?"

"Unfortunately, no," he answered in a gritty voice.

"We'll work on getting your real memories back."

"First things first. We've got to get out of here and get some dry clothing."

"Yes."

"How did you find out there was a back way into the bunker?"

"The Light Street guys scrounged up some old plans."

"And you're assuming Montgomery didn't have them," he asked.

She nodded and looked over her shoulder. "I hope not."

"Yeah. But they know you got in through a back door. So even if they don't know this specific exit, they're going to figure out where it is, so let's get going."

Conceding the point, she scrambled to her feet and ducked so that she stepped outside the mouth of the cave. When the wind hit her wet clothing, her teeth started chattering.

Jonah moved to her side, looking down from the rocky promontory. "We're exposed up here. You remember the way down?"

"I hope so." She pointed toward a rock ledge that they could use as an oversized step.

He kept the rope on them, and they climbed steadily downward. She was sure his leg was screaming when they reached the bottom, but he didn't complain.

When they were on level ground, he untied the rope and slung his arm around her shoulder. "Did that Light Street group tell you what to do when you got out of the cave?"

She sighed. "I had a cell phone in a waterproof case. But it was in the pack. I'm sorry. It's gone."

"Don't beat yourself up over it. The important thing is that we got across the river."

"Okay," she answered in a small voice.

"Let's head that way." He pointed to his right.

"Why?"

"It's downhill. Better for the leg."

"Right."

They started walking, and she didn't feel any warmer than when they'd been up on the rocks. It might be May, but the wet clothing felt like ice on her skin.

She tried to clamp her teeth together, but that was too much effort, and she finally gave up and let them click like props in a graveyard movie.

Jonah stayed right beside her as they staggered through the woods, occasionally detouring around patches of brambles or poison ivy or large rock outcroppings.

Too bad the cave entrance was on a rock wall in the middle of nowhere. But that was probably why no one had discovered it. Or maybe they had, but they'd decided it was too inconvenient to develop as a tourist attraction like the other caverns in this part of the country.

As their feet crunched across dry leaves, she started wondering how she was going to keep going. She wanted to sink to the forest floor and cover herself with leaves to get warm.

Jonah urged her along, and if he could keep walking on his mangled leg, she could damn well keep up.

"I'm not much help," she muttered.

His hand tightened on hers. "Oh yeah? If you hadn't risked your life to go into the bunker and get me out, we wouldn't be here now."

"True."

He turned toward her and wrapped her in his arms. She clung to him for long moments, glad of the warmth and the comfort.

"Just a little farther," he said, easing away.

"How do you know?"

"Because we're due for a break."

He knitted his fingers with hers, and they kept walking. She started off with more resolve, but soon her head drooped and her feet shuffled through the leaves and sometimes slid over the rocks. When she stepped into a foot-deep hole filled with water, she almost fell over. Thanks to Jonah she remained upright.

When he stopped short, she made a small sound and looked up.

"Over there." He pointed ahead of them and to the left.

She squinted, trying to follow his gaze. "What is it?"

"A cabin."

"Maybe somebody's home."

"And maybe not."

Chapter Ten

Sophia waited in a stand of trees, leaning against the trunk of a massive oak, while Jonah went to investigate. It was all she could do to stay on her feet now, and she watched him through dull eyes. Wet and cold for too long, she knew she was in trouble if she didn't get inside soon.

When Jonah came back she watched his face anxiously and picked up his look of relief.

"It's an empty hunting cabin." He gave her a concerned look. "Come on."

When she pushed away from the tree, she wavered on her feet.

"Too bad I can't carry you."

"We could carry each other," she mumbled.

He slung his arm around her waist, holding her up as they crossed the fifty yards to the cabin, which was set on blocks, raising it two feet above the forest floor.

She stared stupidly at the open door. "They left it open?"

"No, but they left a key under a rock out front," he said as he helped her up four steps. He closed the door behind them and dropped a length of wood that acted as a bolt into a slot, sealing them inside.

She looked around, registering a simple and homey interior,

with a fireplace of local rocks against one wall and a double bed with a metal frame opposite. The warm quilt drew her eyes.

"Take off your clothes and get under the covers," Jonah told her. "I'm going to make a fire."

She staggered to the bed and plopped down, but that was as far as she got. Too tired to undress, she kicked off her shoes, lay down and closed her eyes, listening to Jonah moving around.

She dozed until he shook her gently. "Can you get undressed?"

"I don't think so."

Sitting her up, he peeled off her wet shirt and pants, then her bra. She might have been embarrassed that she was almost naked in front of him, her nipples drawn into tight points by the cold, but she was too tired to make the effort.

He left her damp panties on, then moved her aside to pull down the blankets and help her under.

As she snuggled into the warmth of the bed, she could see a fire crackling and realized he must have made it while she was dozing.

"Come to bed," she whispered.

"I will, but I've got a couple of things to do."

She watched him through slitted eyes, seeing he had exchanged his wet shirt and pants for others he must have found in the cabin. They looked too big.

She was sure his leg must be beyond painful, but he kept moving around. He laid their wet clothing on the back and seat of a rocker by the fireplace where it would dry. Then he went outside. Her heart pounding, she waited for him to return. A few minutes later he came back with more wood and an ax.

She dozed again, then woke when she heard him doing something in the corner of the room. She tried to sit up and see what was going on, but all she could manage was a question.

"What?"

"Just go to sleep."

"Um."

She watched him take the SIG out of the waterproof pouch and replace the clip with a full one before setting it on the table by the bed. Then he stripped off his borrowed clothing and climbed under the covers.

It felt as if an ice cube had joined her.

"You're cold."

"Sorry."

He scooted away from her.

"I didn't mean to complain." She used the last of her energy to roll toward him, sling her arm over his chest and press her face to his shoulder.

"We're safe," she murmured.

"Let's hope so." He cleared his throat. "Those guys in uniform, they're not regular army, are they?"

"No. They're from a private military group. Like Blackwater."

"Montgomery hired them?"

"Not sure." She couldn't manage any more conversation. Her eyes were already closed, and she drifted off to sleep.

Some time later, she was sucked into a dream. It started off with a hazy warmth that heated her all the way to her bones. She and Jonah were finally together again after all the years of separation, and the feeling of relief was like a living thing.

They were both naked, lying together in a cozy bed. She clung to him, kissing him deeply, running her hands over his back and shoulders. She wanted to tell him how much she'd missed him, how her life had been incomplete without him. Before she could speak the words, an enormous wind came pounding at them, dragging them apart.

"Jonah?"

He was gone. Panic gripped her as she tried to find him. Then she was running through the woods—wet and cold and searching desperately for him. Only she was being pursued by men in blue uniforms who were determined to keep her from him.

"No," she moaned.

"Sophia!"

He called her name, but his voice came from a long way away.

One of the men caught up with her and grabbed her, and she tried to fight him off, but he captured her flailing arms and held her still.

She kept fighting with all her strength, because she knew she had to get back to Jonah.

His voice reached her again.

"Easy. Take it easy."

"No!"

"Sophia, wake up."

Her eyes blinked open, and she looked up into Jonah's face. He was pressing her against the mattress while he held her arms, and she knew that she must have been hitting him.

"Oh Lord, did I hurt you?" she gasped.

"It's okay."

"I'm sorry."

"You were dreaming."

They had been naked in the dream, and they were almost naked now. She felt his muscular leg against hers, his hip pressed to her thigh.

But it was obvious his mind wasn't in the same place as hers.

"We can't stay here too long. In case they figure out where we are."

She kept her gaze fixed on him. "Don't we have a little time?" She didn't say why she wanted more time. She simply wrapped her arms around him and pulled him to her. This was like the dream. They were warm and cozy and finally together again after so many years of separation.

Unlike in the dream, his body had stiffened.

"Sophia…" His voice held the sound of refusal.

"Don't deny us what we both want so much. Come here."

He made a strangled sound as he cradled her against himself. At the same time, his mouth came down on hers for a hot, thirsty kiss. The taste of him was familiar and heady.

Electricity arced between them as past and present merged. She remembered that night so long ago and all the emotions he had kindled in her—emotions that she hadn't dared to share with him because that made her too vulnerable.

She had thought nothing in her life could ever be that good again. But here he was, back in her arms, and it was everything she had dreamed of.

She opened for him, telling him with her mouth and body and hands that slid over his shoulders and down his back that she was his for the taking.

He lifted his mouth a fraction. He was breathing hard, yet his words tore at her.

"You should be afraid of me."

She kept her gaze locked with his. "Why?"

"My mind's a mess."

"I understand why you feel that way. You've been through a terrible experience."

"It's not over."

"It will be. You grew up tough. You know how to cope."

His face hardened. "I grew up tough and no good."

"Don't say that. You turned into a man who should be proud of the life he's made for himself."

"How do you know?"

"Like I said, I read about your career. You went on some amazing missions."

"That was then. This is now."

"Jonah, don't sell yourself short. Even when you don't remember specifics, it's obvious that you're drawing on the training you got in the Special Forces. If you need it, you reach for it, and it's there."

When he only stared at her, she went on.

"I may have had the trail markers, but you were the one who got us out of that cave, across the river and through the woods to this cabin. You have most of what you need, and we'll get the rest of it back."

"How?"

"We can start by getting in touch with more of your memories." She struggled to keep her voice steady. "Like memories of that night."

"Which night?"

"Don't pretend you don't remember."

She knew from his expression that he knew exactly what night she meant.

"I missed you so much," she whispered, then knew she had given a lot away. Maybe too much. If he didn't feel the same, something inside her would shrivel and die.

She waited with the breath frozen in her lungs.

"Oh yes."

He gathered her to him again, and she sighed out her relief.

He brought her mouth back to his, sending heat coursing through her. Sliding her hands down his body, she cupped his buttocks, pulling his erection against her thigh.

He made a low sound, and she thought for a moment that he would tear off her panties and his shorts and plunge into her.

Instead he rolled to his side, taking her with him so that they were facing each other on the bed.

Outside, sunlight filtered through the trees and seeped through the window. He looked into her eyes, sliding his hands through her hair, then kissing her gently as he stroked his fingers over her cheeks, down to her jaw and over her collarbones.

She touched his body with the same tenderness, awed to be playing her fingers over his broad chest, burrowing into the thick dark hair she found there, then grinning as she drew circles around his flat nipples and heard his quick, indrawn breath.

"You like that," she murmured.

"You know I do."

He pulled the covers down so that he could see her breasts. They weren't quite as firm as they had been ten years ago, and she had a moment of uncertainty.

But his tender look told her what she needed to know. He sighed as he cradled them in his hands, stroking his thumbs across the tightened nipples.

"I love the way you feel."

"That's so good. What you're doing is so good."

He bent his head, circling one tight peak with his tongue, then sucking it into his mouth while he plucked at the other with his thumb and finger.

She heard herself make a sobbing sound as the pleasure of it surged through her.

They were almost naked, but the two thin layers of clothing between them had become intolerable.

She reached down, finding the waistband of her panties so she could push them over her hips and down her legs, where she kicked them away.

Seeing what she was doing, he followed her example. When they were both naked, he grinned at her, then sobered as he reached down to touch her intimately, his fingers tangling in the triangle of blond hair at the top of her legs before slipping lower, into the wet heat between her legs.

The way he caressed her said volumes. She knew that he remembered what she liked. His finger dipped inside her, then moving all the way up to the site of her greatest sensation before traveling downward and starting all over again.

The pleasure was exquisite. She wanted to give him that same joy, but when she reached down the front of his body, he stopped her hand before she found her goal.

"Don't." He caught his breath. "I need you too much."

"No more than I need you."

When he stroked her again, heat and raw emotion surged through her, and she heard his ragged breathing mingling with hers.

"I want you inside me. Now."

She rolled to her back and held out her arms to him. Finally, he covered her body with his and plunged inside her.

Sexual need surged between them. At the same time, she felt that an old wound was finally healed.

He brought his mouth back to her, his kiss hot and greedy as he moved in a steady rhythm, plunging into her and withdrawing.

Even as her need for release spiraled out of control, she felt him holding back, waiting for her to reach the peak.

She climbed to the top of the mountain, then toppled over the edge. As she did, she felt him follow her.

The intensity of her climax brought a cry to her lips, and his voice joined hers as he shouted his pleasure, then he collapsed on top of her and lay breathing hard and fast.

Wanting to keep him close, she stroked his damp shoulders and kissed his cheek.

When he started to move, she tightened her hold on him.

"I'm going to crush you," he whispered.

"No. I like the feel of your weight on top of me."

He stayed a few moments longer, then kissed her once more before rolling to his side, clasping her to him.

She snuggled against him, still trying to absorb the reality of this reunion. He had made wonderful love to her, and she felt as though the years of separation had been wiped away. But she knew it was only an illusion.

She knew too that he wasn't going to be satisfied with himself until he remembered everything—not just making love with her.

His hand glided to the back of her thigh, and he touched the small mole just below her butt. "I remember that," he murmured.

"Yes. You thought it was cute."

He brought her back to the present with his next words. Practical words.

"We need to eat."

In response, her stomach growled.

"You're hungry."

"I hadn't even thought about food." She turned toward the window. "Is this lunch or dinner?"

"I'm not sure."

"Are you going to go out and shoot a wild turkey?"

He laughed. "With a SIG? I don't think so. But I checked the kitchen area. There's some food we can steal. Maybe we can leave some money."

"Where would we get it?"

His face twisted. "I liberated some money from Montgomery. His lieutenant had a stack of bills in his desk drawer."

"How did you find it?"

"It was after my last session. Montgomery was in his office, and his lieutenant was away from his desk, so I did some poking around."

"That was taking a chance."

"Yeah." He climbed casually out of bed, giving her a nice view of his magnificent body. Without bothering to find his pants, he walked across the room to a kitchen area with cabinets, a sink and what looked like a wood-burning stove.

He might be comfortable naked, but she walked to the chair and quickly pulled on her pants and shirt he'd dried in front of the fire.

Reaching up, he opened one of the cabinets and got some bottled water, then followed with some cellophane-wrapped packages.

When he turned back with the food in his hands, he saw that she'd pulled on her clothes and straightened the bedcovers before sitting with her back against the headboard.

"Are we getting formal?" he asked.

"Decent."

He put the food on the bed, then grabbed his pants from the chair and put them on. After plumping up his pillow, he sat back down.

She picked up one of the bottles of water, giving him a sideways look. They had just made love. Now they were sharing a meal, and that felt almost as intimate.

She wanted to talk about the two of them, but she didn't want to push him into a discussion he wasn't ready for. Not when they'd just found each other again. The connection was too new—and too fragile. She wasn't going to kid herself. He could pull away from her if she didn't handle this right. So she let him set the pace.

Pointing to the packages on the bed, he said, "We've got beef jerky, peanut butter crackers and apricot leather."

"What's that?"

"Ground-up fruit mixed with sugar and hardened. It's pretty good."

He opened one of the beef sticks and handed it to her. "Excellent protein. But you've got to have good teeth."

"I do."

She tried some of the meat, then took a swallow of water. He did the same and opened the peanut butter crackers.

They focused on the simple meal, but she sensed tension building inside him.

After a sip of water, he cleared his throat. "I guess the first thing we need to do is figure out what Dr. Montgomery thinks I know."

Chapter Eleven

Jonah waited with his breath frozen in his lungs. Dinner—or was it lunch?—had been a way of stalling.

When they had made love, he had trusted Sophia with his emotions. Now he had dared to confront her with the problem that held him in its iron grip.

She laid her hand lightly over his. "We don't have to do it all at once," she murmured.

"Yeah, but the longer I can't access my memories, the more threat I am to you."

"Why are you a threat?"

"Because Montgomery wants information from me. And if his guys catch up with me, we're a hell of a lot better off if I have the big picture."

She knitted her fingers with his. "We can start with easy stuff. Let's do some more of what we tried before."

"Which is?"

"I'll tell you about your life, and you'll see if what I say triggers more memories.

"Okay."

She closed her eyes, thinking for a moment.

"What are you trying to do—dredge up something good?"

"I'm trying to see what's most effective." She squeezed his hand. "Do you remember the fireworks incident?"

"Not in those words."

"Do you remember Arty Hillman?"

He blinked as a pudgy face leaped into his mind. "The fat kid with the crew cut?"

"Yes."

"What about him?"

"Try to put that together with fireworks."

He closed his eyes, and suddenly a memory was there. Arty Hillman at twilight, out in a field, setting off fireworks—and a bunch of kids including Sophia and Jonah watching.

"A Roman candle fell over as it started to go off, shooting balls of fire toward the crowd."

"Good job."

He shrugged. "Okay. I'm remembering stuff from school. Does that mean whatever Montgomery was drugging me with is out of my system?"

"I hope so. But I don't know what it was. What else do you remember about the fireworks?"

"A fireball hit Danny Vera," Jonah said.

"And…"

"And I ran over and threw him on the ground and smothered the fire."

"Right. You got your arm burned, as I remember."

"Yeah."

Her hand tightened on his. "Everybody else scattered, but you ran toward Danny. When you threw him down, two fireballs flew over your head."

"I heard them," he whispered.

"Nobody had cell phones back then. One of the guys ran to the pay phone at a gas station and called 911."

"Yes. They took him to the hospital in an ambulance. But I wouldn't go," he finished.

"Why not?"

"Because I was afraid they were going to charge me for treatment, and I knew my mom didn't have the money."

"So you went around with blisters on your arm."

He winced. "They hurt like hell."

"Do you remember anything else connected with the incident?"

"My mom got mad because my shirt was ruined."

"You were a hero, and that was her focus?"

He shrugged. "After my dad died, we didn't have a lot of money. Every penny counted. That's why I don't like remembering that I kept the money I earned at my job and spent it on myself."

"Most kids would have done that."

"I should have given some to Mom."

"Did you make it up to her later?"

"Yeah. I bought her a condo in Daytona Beach."

"You're allowed to feel good about that."

He nodded.

"What else do you remember about your family?"

"I had an older sister. She got married right out of high school and moved away. We didn't see much of her after that, but I gather she was in an abusive relationship." He shrugged. "No wonder I wanted to forget all of that."

"But you're doing good bringing it back."

He snorted. "I've tried to bury all that stuff."

"What do you remember about my family?" she asked in a low voice.

He turned his head toward her, then looked across the room, his eyes unfocused. "Your background was a lot different from mine. Your dad was the president of the local bank, and your mom spent a lot of her time playing tennis at Turf Valley Country Club. They wouldn't have liked to know you spent the night with me."

Sophia felt her stomach knot, hating to let his judgment stand. "They were decent people," she said, defending them. "My mom also raised money for the Humane Society. And she spent a lot of time doing her own gardening."

"And if she needed help with the heavy work, she could ask someone from the lawn service."

"Are you faulting her for that?"

"I'm just pointing out that she had more choices than my mom."

"We both know that."

"What happened to your parents?" he suddenly asked.

Her voice lowered. "You didn't hear about it?"

His gaze sharpened. "What did I miss?"

"My dad was flying my mom and my little sister back to college. He ran into bad fog and crashed into a house. They were all killed. Luckily nobody was in the house."

He winced and took her hand again. "Sophia, I'm so sorry. I never heard about it. How old were you?"

"I was twenty-two. My family was wiped out. Then it turned out there were some things wrong with their will, and I had to fight my aunt and uncle for control of the estate."

"I didn't know."

"You were long gone."

"Yeah."

"There's something I want to tell you."

The way she said it put him on alert. "Something bad?"

"Yes." She looked like a swimmer plunging off the high board when she said, "I was lonely and adrift after they died. I got into a relationship—with a guy who seemed like he could make me happy. When things started going bad, I wondered if he'd been in love with me or my money."

"Your boyfriend?"

She cleared her throat. "My husband."

He stared at her. It was none of his business. Still, he couldn't help feeling as though she'd stuck an ice pick between his ribs. But what had he expected—that after the night they'd spent together, she'd become a nun? He certainly hadn't given up sex after that. But he hadn't gotten into any serious relationships, either.

She was still speaking, and he strove to listen above the roaring in his ears.

"I knew within a year that I'd made a big mistake. But I stuck with it another year. I ended up giving him a cash settlement."

"I'm sorry."

"I learned my lesson." Her face changed. "But I didn't need to tell you all that."

"Apparently, you did."

"I guess I wanted it out in the open."

"You don't owe me any explanations."

"I felt like I did." She huffed out a breath, then said, "Let's get back on track. We got into your early life, but what about later? What about the army? What do you remember about that?"

He leaned back and closed his eyes, inviting memories. To his relief, they came—clear and crisp—telling him that his brain was no longer muzzy.

"I remember basic training. I remember Ranger training. I remember…a lot of assignments."

"What about them?"

"Most of them are classified. But you read about them anyway." A thought struck him. "How did the Light Street people get hold of my classified records?"

"I guess they have connections. But let's keep this focused on you. You remember details you didn't remember the other night?"

"Yes." He gave her a fierce look. "I can account for my time—until a few months ago."

"Do you remember leaving for Afghanistan?"

"No."

She looked down at their joined hands. "So a lot of stuff has come back to you, but not that."

"Yeah. Why not? Does it have something to do with the drugs?"

"Maybe. Or maybe it was so traumatic that you don't want to deal with it."

He nodded. "So I'm stuck."

"We could try hypnosis."

As she made the suggestion, he felt his face go hard.

"Montgomery wanted to try hypnosis."

"That doesn't make us alike."

He answered with a tight nod. But he still hadn't liked hearing the suggestion. "It makes me vulnerable," he managed to say.

She kept her gaze fixed on him. "Yes. So what about it?"

CARLTON MONTGOMERY stared at the computer screen, reading his latest e-mail. The message made the back of his neck prickle. According to his correspondent, it was his fault that the bunker was vulnerable to invasion. His fault that Baker had escaped. And he'd damn well better get the man back.

He'd done his best. But who in hell could have predicted that two people would have shown up to spring Major Baker?

The guards had killed a man in a rock-hewn tunnel outside the developed part of the bunker. But there was apparently another person involved. Graves had seen her and said it was a woman.

So why had she volunteered for what could have turned into a suicide mission?

Maybe she was doing it for money. Maybe she believed in the

cause. Or maybe she was personally involved. That was an interesting angle and probably worth pursuing.

A knock at the door made him sit up straighter and switch the screen to another window. "Come."

Lieutenant Olson walked into the room.

"Have you found him?" Montgomery demanded.

"Not yet. But it looks like we've lost four men."

Montgomery kept his face impassive. "They didn't report back?"

"Patterson got shot by the guy who covered Baker and the woman's exit. Scottinger and Marks were on the search team. We found Scottinger's body. No sign of Marks."

"He could be lost in the cave."

"He doesn't answer his comm unit. And some of the men saw Templeton go over the edge of a cliff in a landslide inside the cave."

"Do you have any good news?"

"The cave is huge, but we know how the woman and the other man found their way through it. They laid a trail, using infrared markers."

"And?"

"We're following the trail. When we get to the end, we'll know where they exited the cave. And when we know that, we'll know where to search."

The information gave him a glimmer of hope, but he kept his voice hard. "What makes you think they're still in the area?"

"Baker's leg was injured. He can't walk all that far. We'll get him."

JONAH STARED at Sophia for long moments, and she kept her gaze steady. He needed to know what had wiped out his memory of the past few months and he needed to know whatever facts were now hidden from him.

So what were his options? He could trust her. Or he could go it alone. Too bad he felt as if he was trying to play poker with a rigged deck.

He sighed. "All right."

"You're sure?"

"No."

"Thanks for being honest. But it won't work unless you trust me enough to let me put you under."

"Yeah."

He watched her climb off the bed and walk to the fireplace, where she grabbed the rocking chair and carried it over.

"What do you want me to do?" he asked.

"Make yourself comfortable. You can prop yourself up with both pillows. I'll sit over here and give you suggestions."

"Okay." He stacked the pillows, then lay down with his arms rigidly at his sides.

"Relax."

"Easier said than done."

"Hypnosis is a way to go back and visit a threatening experience. But you won't really be there."

"So what good does it do me?"

"You'll be observing. You can watch it happening on a big television screen. And you can change the date to this time and place any time you want to."

"How?"

"You just have to tell me 'I need to leave this place.'"

"Okay."

"And if I need to wake you, we'll have a trigger phrase. 'Jonah, wake up now.'"

He kept his gaze focused on her. "You're sure that will work?"

She kept her eyes steady as she looked back. "Yes. So, shall we go ahead?"

He dragged in a breath and let it out slowly. "Yes."

"Good. A convenient way to do it is to look up to the line where the ceiling meets the top of the wall. Why don't you do that now?"

He took the suggestion, wondering what good it would do.

"Relax…now. Relax…now," she said, her voice calm and soothing. "Across the room is a big television set. It's one of those expensive flat screens. Sixty-inch. It takes up a big part of the wall in this small cabin. You're going to watch a movie about the life of Jonah Baker. Do you see the screen?"

"Yes," he answered, because he did. It seemed very wide and solid.

"You can see yourself on the television. You won't be there, but you can watch what happened. You're not involved. You're only an observer. All right?"

"Yes."

"You're back in school. Eighth grade."

"Okay."

"You're in the cafeteria. With your friends Roger and Kevin."

"Yes."

"It's the day Jeff Bolton lost his retainer."

He laughed. "He took off his retainer at lunch and wrapped it in his napkin. I can see him throwing it in the trash by accident. Now he's digging through the garbage looking for it."

"Does he find it?"

"Yeah. And he had to take a shower before they'd let him back into class."

"Good. Let's move forward. To the year after you graduated from high school. It's six weeks into basic training. You're still watching on TV. You're not really there. Do you see yourself?"

"Yes."

"Where is basic training?"

"Fort Bragg."

"And now you're in the mess hall, getting breakfast."

"Yes."

"Who are your friends?"

"Costa and Stevenson."

"So you're eating with them."

"Yes."

"Any time you want to stop watching yourself and come back to this place and time, just say, 'I want to come back.' And you will."

"Okay."

"In basic training, what's your best skill?"

"I'm good on the firing range. And on the obstacle course. I have the record for the shortest time."

"Good. So you're trying to keep that record. Who's the next fastest guy?"

"Wolinsky."

"You're going up against Wolinsky. You're going to try your damnedest to beat him again."

"Yes." On the screen he was watching himself back there in the hot fields, crawling under barbed wire, then scrambling up and running through a nest of tires. Wolinsky was right behind him. They got to the rope-and-barrier climb and after Jonah almost lost his grip, he pulled himself up, then vaulted over the wooden barrier and let himself fall to the straw on the other side. He picked himself up and ran the last fifty yards to the finish line, with Wolinsky puffing along right behind him.

"I made it. Ahead of him."

"Do you feel good?"

"Yeah. I'm good at this. Good at army stuff. Not like back in school when I had to be…a rebel to make myself stand out."

"That's why you did it?"

"Yeah."

"You could have done better in school if you'd wanted?"

"Yes. And I learn fast in basic training. I think they're going to ask if I want to join the Rangers."

"Good."

"Let's move forward. Your first assignment."

"Germany."

"Do you like it there?"

"It's cold and rainy. But the beer is good, and the women like American soldiers. They think they can get us to marry them and take them home. I won't be here long. It's only temporary duty for me. I'm going to Iraq next. We're going to be training their military."

"Let's move forward again. You're going to Afghanistan."

He shifted on the bed. He'd felt safe and relaxed, watching himself on television, but now he felt unsettled.

"It's all right. You're not there. You're only watching on television. Can you see the scene on the television?"

"Yes."

"That's good. It's safe to watch it on television. You're learning about the assignment. Who's briefing you?"

"Colonel Luntz."

"What does he look like?"

"He's tall. He holds himself very straight. Dark hair with some gray. A scar cutting his left eyebrow. He's lucky he didn't lose his eye."

"What's he saying?"

Frustration made his voice sharp. "I should be able to hear him, but I can't."

"That's okay. Try to tune in on him."

"I can't."

"Who else is there?"

"The guys on the team. Hall. Shredder. Fromer." As he said that name, a wave of cold swept over him.

"Jonah, what?"

"He's getting out of his seat. He's coming toward me. He's got a gun. No—"

"Who?"

"Fromer." His heart was pounding now, and sweat beaded on his forehead. "Stay away from me, you bastard," he shouted as he looked for a way to defend himself. He lunged for the gun on the bedside table.

Chapter Twelve

Sophia gasped as Jonah surged off the bed, his expression fierce. Afraid he was going to grab her, she reared back in the chair, almost knocking it over, then went rigid as he snatched up the gun and whirled to face her, holding the weapon in a two-handed grip, pointing it at her chest where she still sat, trying to stop the chair from rocking.

When he spoke, his tone was hard and direct. "I've had enough. Stay away from me, you bastard."

When she saw the murder in his eyes and heard the coldness in his voice, terror threatened to swamp her.

She'd hypnotized other people before, and nothing like this had ever happened. It *shouldn't* have happened.

The process had been working fine. She'd taken him back to school, then to basic training and then through his first assignment. Then something had gone terribly wrong.

Stay calm, she ordered herself. Speaking slowly and directly, she gave him the trigger phrase that they had agreed on. "Jonah, wake up. Wake up now."

She had told him that the trigger would work. It always had worked when she had hypnotized a client in the past.

Now nothing was going according to plan. He didn't seem to

hear her, and to her horror, he took a step toward her, still holding the weapon pointed at her chest.

She stayed where she was, her gaze glued to him—and the gun in his hands. She wanted to run, but deep in her consciousness, she knew that trying to get away would be exactly the wrong move. Showing fear would be fatal.

It took every scrap of determination she possessed to keep her voice steady and even as she faced this man she thought she knew.

"Jonah, wake up. Wake up now."

Totally ignoring anything she said, he whispered, "You did it, damn you."

"No. It wasn't me. I'm not—" In her desperation, she had spoken automatically, but she stopped herself before she could say the man's name. That was exactly the wrong thing to do. Maybe hearing the name of his enemy would make him pull the trigger.

"Jonah, it's Sophia. Wake up. I'm Sophia Rhodes. We're in the cabin that we found after we escaped from the cave."

His gaze was still fixed, but she detected something different in his eyes.

"I'll kill you," he repeated, but this time he didn't sound quite so sure of his mission, and she wondered if she was making progress? Or was that just wishful thinking?

All she could do was keep speaking to him, hoping to make a connection. "I'm Sophia. You don't want to kill me. You'd be killing the wrong person. I'm Sophia." When he didn't respond, she went on. "I wasn't at the briefing. I'm Sophia Rhodes, and we're in the cabin that we found in the woods."

The gun came up a few inches, pointed at her head. Sweat drenched his forehead and his skin had turned a pasty shade of white. "I…."

She gripped the arms of the chair, bracing for the worst. He could pull the trigger and shoot her, and he wouldn't even know who he was killing—until she was slumped in the chair. And then what would happen to him?

He was already in trouble. Either the guards from the bunker would get him or the police. Then who would help him figure out what had happened?

Her mouth was so dry that she could hardly speak. But she managed to say, "Jonah, wake up now."

The trigger phrase still didn't seem to be working, so she tried a different approach.

"Jonah, this is Sophia. You're holding a gun on me. But you don't want to shoot me. We made love a little while ago. You care about me. Put the gun down. Wake up now and put the gun down."

He shook his head, looking confused, his eyes darting from her to the interior of the cabin, and she thought he might finally be taking in his surroundings.

"Jonah, wake up now."

He opened his mouth and closed it again. The gun wavered. Then he lowered his arms. But he was still holding the weapon in his right hand.

"Put the gun down," she said. "Jonah, wake up now. Wake up now."

He went very still, his gaze turned inward. Then he raised his head, looking around again. This time she thought he was seeing his surroundings. Eons passed before his gaze came back to her.

"Sophia?"

"Thank God. You're back with me. Jonah, put the gun down."

He looked at the gun in his hand as though he'd just realized he was holding on to a poisonous snake.

With a strangled sound, he carefully set the SIG down on the table where he'd found it.

"What happened?" he whispered, looking from her to the gun and back again.

She swallowed, wondering what she was going to say now that she finally had his attention.

When she didn't speak, he asked, "Was…was I going to shoot you?"

She managed to speak around the lump clogging her windpipe. "No."

His expression turned dark. "Then why was I holding the gun on you?"

She took a step toward him, and he stepped quickly back. "Stay away. It's obvious I'm dangerous."

She couldn't let him think that she was afraid of him. Not now. When his legs hit the edge of the bed, she hurried forward and wrapped him tightly in her embrace, pressing her face against his broad chest. He felt real and solid and she knew that they had just come through a nightmare together. His nightmare.

Still, he remained stiffly in her embrace. "How can you stand to get near me?"

She stroked her hands up and down his back. "Because…" *Because I love you.* She knew that was the truth, but she thought that would be too threatening for him to hear at the moment. Maybe it would always be too threatening.

Instead, as she continued to caress his shoulders, she said, "I care about you. Very much."

He wouldn't even accept that much from her. "Apparently that's a big mistake."

"Don't say that. You're upset."

When she tried to hold him, he broke away, his eyes blazing.

"You're damn right I'm upset. I could have killed you. You damn well know it. Tell me what the hell was going on a few minutes ago."

"Okay. Just take it easy. We'll figure out what happened…"

"Don't hand me a load of psychologist bull. Just tell me why I blinked awake and found out I could have shot you!"

"Do you remember that I hypnotized you?"

"Yes."

"You remember the scenes you watched?"

"School. Basic training. Germany," he answered.

"Then we were talking about the briefing before you shipped out for Afghanistan."

"I remember," he said in a low voice. His gaze locked with hers. "With Colonel Luntz."

"Good."

"He was the guy who gave us the information about the mission."

"Do you remember the mission?"

His gaze turned inward again and she could see he was straining to bring the scene into focus. After half a minute, his face contorted. "No!"

"Okay. Don't get upset."

His jaw hardened. "Don't tell me what to feel. Just tell me what happened next—because I sure as hell don't know. Luntz is the last thing I remember. He was standing in front of a screen with a light pen in his hand. I guess he was doing a Power Point presentation, but I don't remember what he said."

"You said someone named Fromer was there."

"Fromer. I remember him. He was a hothead. I knew he was trouble the minute I saw him."

"In the scene at the briefing, he apparently attacked you. Could that have really happened?"

He flapped his hand in frustration. "I don't know."

"You said, 'You did it.' What did that mean?"

He answered with a curse. "I don't know! All I know is that I went for the gun. Well, I don't *know* that. What I remember is waking up with the gun in my hand."

"I should have put it away."

"No. We had it there for protection. We need the gun. You weren't expecting anything like that, were you?"

"No."

He shifted his weight from one foot to the other. "Anybody else go berserk on you during hypnosis?"

"You didn't go berserk."

"Oh yeah, what would you call it?"

"I don't know. Something…unusual happened to you."

He snorted. "You're trying to put the best possible face on this. But the truth is I'm sick and dangerous, whether or not my mind is free of the damn medication. You should be running in the other direction as fast as you can."

She shook her head. "Don't put the worst possible interpretation on it. Or to put it another way—stop assigning blame."

"What do you want me to do?"

The light had grown dim in the cabin, and she wanted to see his face more clearly. She thought about getting up and lighting one of the oil lamps that sat on the shelf, but she stayed where she was because she didn't want to interrupt, not at such a critical point in their conversation. They were close to some vital information—if they could just figure out how to do it.

She reached out a hand toward him and watched him follow the movement with his eyes.

"Let's try to figure out what part Fromer played in what happened to you. Maybe the incident between you took place in Afghanistan and not where you were being briefed."

"We were in Maryland for the briefing."

"Ah. Another fact. Do you remember exactly where?"

"Somewhere out in the country. I…remember thinking that it looked like an abandoned location. But inside it had been… modernized."

"What does that mean?"

"I guess that they wanted it to look like a dump on the outside, so no one would think they were using the interior."

"Good. What else?"

He sighed. "I can picture the briefing room. A table at the front. Chairs. A computer. A screen." He waved his arm. "But I can't remember anything Luntz said."

"But you came up with the location."

"Like I said. Nothing else," he bit out. "And I assume you're not crazy enough to insist on trying hypnosis again to dig it out of me, right?"

Though her chest felt tight, she had to agree with him. "Right."

"So what's next?"

"I'm not sure," she admitted, wondering if some other technique would trigger the same response. Although she hated to admit it, she was going to have to tread carefully now. But she didn't want to explain that to him.

He gave her an assessing look, and she wondered if he was reading her mind. As he waited for her response, he ran a hand through his hair and finally turned away from her.

She kept her gaze on him, and when he went rigid, she was immediately on guard.

Then she realized he was looking at something outside the window.

"What is it?"

He spoke in a harsh whisper. "I saw a shadow flicker through the trees."

"A deer?"

"No. Someone on two legs. There's a person out there." As he spoke, he moved to the wall.

"Who?" she asked, unconsciously lowering her voice.

"If we're lucky, it could be the guy who owns the cabin." He slipped along the wall, then along to the window, where he peered out.

"Shit."

"What?"

"I see one of the guards from the bunker, dressed in a hunting outfit. If he's here, there are more of them."

Suddenly, she couldn't draw in a full breath. "What are we going to do?"

"Get out of here."

She looked wildly around. As far as she could see, there was only one door to the cabin.

"We can't go out the front door."

"No." He gave her a quick inspection. "Take off that uniform and put these on."

He crossed to the closet and pulled out jeans and a work shirt. She pulled them on and then rolled up the pants legs. He put on a shirt; then he walked to the corner of the room and pulled up two floorboards. She remembered he'd been doing something in the corner while she was lying in bed cold and exhausted. She hadn't known what. Now she saw that he'd chopped a hole in the floor.

As soon as he'd removed the boards, he returned to the closet and pulled out a brown jacket. "Put this on, too. It will blend with the leaves on the ground."

When she complied, he came back to the wall, looking out the window again without showing more than a sliver of his face.

"How close is he?"

"He's holding his position. We've got a little time." He handed her the gun and she wrapped her fingers around the butt.

"Go down through the floor. There's a crawl space under the cabin. Stay flat to the ground. I'll be there as fast as I can."

Her heart was pounding as she lowered herself into the hole

and lay flat on the damp soil, clutching the gun and smelling the musty odor of earth that hadn't dried out in a long time.

Earlier, when the guards had been after them, they must have had orders to kill her and capture Jonah. What were their orders now?

Above her, she could hear him walking rapidly around, obviously making some kind of preparations he'd had in mind all along, in case the guards found them.

She turned her head toward the hole, watching and waiting for him to join her. The seconds ticked by, and she imagined the man outside and the others closing in on the cabin.

Above her, she heard the sound of breaking glass. She wanted to call out to Jonah, but she knew she had to stay quiet. Instead, she only took her lower lip between her teeth and bit down to focus herself. Finally, his feet dangled through the hole, and she let out the breath she'd been holding.

"Stay down!" he ordered in a harsh whisper as he crawled toward her and covered her body with his.

"What?"

Before he could answer the question, she saw flames flickering in the opening above them.

Chapter Thirteen

"Sorry about the cabin," Jonah muttered. "Maybe the DOD will pay for it."

"What did you do?"

He answered in a harsh whisper that was barely audible above the roaring sound rising above them. "Sprinkled kerosene around the cabin. Then I lit an oil lamp and smashed it into the corner."

"Why?"

He kept his voice low. "To create a diversion. They don't know we could get out through the floor. All they'll see is the burning cabin and they'll think we're inside."

She looked back toward the opening and saw flames licking at the floorboards.

Outside, Jonah's maneuver was having the desired effect.

"Fire," one of the men shouted. "The damn place is on fire."

"They're in there," said another voice. "I didn't see them come out."

She could hear someone pounding on the door.

"Open up. Open the damn door," the same guy shouted, his voice rising with his fear.

"They're busy trying to get inside. Come on," Jonah whispered.

Slithering along the ground, he reached the edge of the cabin, and looked out. Above them, flames were creeping up the wall. And now she could hardly hear anything else above the roaring of the fire. It felt as if the whole structure was going to explode. And if it did, fire would come raining down on them.

At the front of the building, she could hear the men still trying to get in.

Someone cried out, and she wondered if they were in trouble, but she had to worry about herself now. The floor above her was hot to the touch, and she heard pops and cracks in the wood.

The whole thing could come crashing down on them at any minute.

Jonah slithered out, keeping to the ground for several yards, then standing up and bending over as he made for the woods.

She exited after him, imitating his stance and following the same route, running for the thick underbrush a hundred yards from the cabin.

Jonah was way ahead of her, and as she hurried to catch up, she hit a patch of rocky ground and went sprawling. She lay there for a minute, catching her breath. When she started to rise, she saw a pair of feet and legs in front of her.

"Hold it right there."

A sick feeling rose in her throat, but with no other option, she flopped back to the ground. When she found a large stone under her hand, she closed her fingers around it.

The man's expression was menacing. "You're the chick who got into the bunker. Who are you?"

She shrugged. "Nobody."

"We'll find that out later. What the hell happened back there? Where's Baker?"

"I don't know. Maybe he's still in the cabin," she answered. "All I wanted to do was get out."

"Uh-huh."

"May I sit up?"

"Yeah."

She sat up cautiously, her hand still on the ground and still curled around the rock.

Now that she had a better look at the guy who stood over her, she saw that he was dressed like a hiker, wearing boots, rough pants and a plaid shirt. His hair, however, was cropped military-short and his face had the hard look of the guards she'd seen in the bunker.

Apparently, he was the only one of the security men in back of the cabin. The others were all closer to the building and in front where they hadn't seen anyone exit. It appeared that this guy hadn't seen Jonah.

Did he have a radio? Would he call for backup, or did he figure he could handle one lone woman on his own?

"How did you get out?" he demanded.

Seeing no point in lying, she said, "Through a hole in the floor."

"You mean there was an escape hatch."

"Yes."

She caught a flicker of movement and risked a quick glance behind the man. It was Jonah. She tried to keep her eyes off him, struggling not to give him away.

His gun was drawn. But if he fired it, the other guards would come running.

As Jonah crept closer, she moved the rock under her hand, getting ready to hit the guard in the leg.

Trying to buy Jonah a little time, she wavered where she sat, putting her other hand to her head. "I feel sick."

"Yeah, sure. Get up. We're going back to the front of the cabin."

"I can't."

He was about to give another order when something inside the cabin exploded. When his hand and head jerked up in surprise, she slammed the rock into his leg. He cried out, just as Jonah sprinted the last few yards to him and brought his gun down on the back of the man's head.

The guard slumped to the ground, but in the process, he squeezed the trigger of his gun, firing off a shot.

"Run for the tangle of brambles in back of me," Jonah ordered.

Without stopping to look back, she scrambled up and ran for the thicket. He was right in back of her. When they reached the tangle of underbrush, she spared a glance behind her to see another one of the guards running toward his fallen comrade.

Behind him the cabin was engulfed in flames that were shooting toward the trees, and she hoped they hadn't started a forest fire.

Jonah cursed under his breath and looked wildly around. The underbrush in this part of the forest wasn't thick enough to allow them to fade into the landscape.

"I hoped we could get away clean. Now we've got to put distance between us and them. Come on."

She didn't spare the breath to reply. Instead she took off after him, amazed that he could run so fast with his injured leg. Even though he'd been in the bunker for three weeks, he was in better shape than she was.

She was soon breathing hard and she had a stitch in her side, but she kept going.

After what seemed like miles, he stopped, and she saw he was trying to breathe quietly.

"What are you doing?" she puffed.

"Listening."

She did the same, but she heard no one behind them.

He allowed them a few minutes of rest, then said, "Come on."

They had started off again, when she picked up a noise somewhere above them.

"Down," Jonah ordered.

She got down, flattening herself under a tangle of brambles, the way he was doing.

"What's that?" she whispered.

"Helicopter."

"I guess it's not some random tourist flyby."

"No."

"Will they see us?"

"Don't know."

The noise grew louder, and she caught a glint of metal above the tops of the trees.

"Keep your face down." Jonah scooted away and she saw him gathering up handfuls of leaves. He threw them over her, then lay down beside her again and tossed more leaves over himself.

She could hear the helicopter getting closer and closer until it sounded like the spy in the sky was hovering above them. From the corner of her eye, she could see Jonah's hand gripping the SIG. She held her breath until the noise finally receded.

"We've got to get going while we can," Jonah told her.

"I know."

They both scrambled up, heading away from the burning cabin.

Once more, they heard the chopper coming back and once more they got down, digging into the leaves and waiting as the motor noise grew louder.

"If they didn't see me at the cabin, they may think I'm dead," Jonah muttered. "Unfortunately, when they start poking through the ashes, they won't find a body."

"I don't think the guy who caught me saw you."

"But he knows he was hit from behind."

When the noise receded, Jonah stood up and started jogging downhill.

They detoured around a large rock. "Lucky you looked out the window when you did," she said.

"I'm due for some luck."

Neither one of them was capable of moving quite as quickly now. "Did the fire trigger any memories?"

"You mean like when Mr. Luskin caught me and Teddy smoking out behind the garage?"

She laughed. "Teddy Luskin. I haven't thought about him in years."

"He came up with all kinds of ways to get into trouble. He was the guy who broke the gym windows."

"Did the fire trigger any memories from Afghanistan?"

His lips firmed. "Maybe."

"But you're not sure."

He balled his hands into fists at his sides. "I can see a house burning. But I don't know if it's anything real or if I'm making it up."

She knew she wasn't doing his nerves any good, and since right now their main job was to get away, she stopped trying to pry information out of him.

They kept moving at as fast a pace as she could manage. She wasn't sure how much territory they covered. She knew that Jonah's leg must be aching, but he didn't complain.

Ahead of her, she saw blue sky. Cautiously they peered through the screen of trees, and she spotted the black ribbon of a road.

"Could the guards come driving along here?"

"They could. I don't know where this road comes from or where it goes."

When a car passed, they ducked back into the trees.

"We've got to get out of here. Maybe we have to take a chance," Jonah muttered.

They could hear another vehicle approaching, something larger than a car.

"See if you can get us a ride," Jonah said.

"How?"

"Get out there and look charming."

She wasn't sure how to look charming, but she stepped to the side of the road and frantically waved her hand as a truck came around the curve.

At first she thought the driver wasn't going to stop, and she was getting ready to jump back into the woods when the truck slowed.

The driver rolled down the window and leaned toward her. "You need help, honey?"

He was a middle-aged man with thinning hair, broken veins all over his cheeks and nose, and what she'd call an honest face.

She started thinking fast. Yes, she was in trouble, but she wasn't going to tell him that she and Jonah had escaped from private security guards.

"Some crazy guys went after me and my boyfriend," she said, deliberately making her sentence ungrammatical. "We got to get away from them."

Jonah stepped out of the woods. "We'd surely appreciate a ride."

The driver eyed him, and she held her breath waiting to see if the offer of help extended to both of them.

"Sure. Hop in."

She exhaled, amazed that he didn't question their story. They both climbed into the cab, and the truck started off again.

"Name's Hank Keller," the driver said.

"Jim Baker," Jonah said without missing a beat.

"Like the preacher?"

Jonah laughed. "Yeah. They used to get me mixed up with him all the time." He gestured toward Sophia. "And this is Sara, my main squeeze."

She struggled to keep a straight face.

"So what happened to y'all?" the driver asked.

"We was camping," Jonah said, continuing the speech pattern

she had started. "And these guys came into our camp and started helping themselves to our stuff."

The driver jerked his head away from the road and Sophia had to clench her teeth to keep from telling him to watch where he was driving.

"You get hurt?"

"We was out fishin' at the time. We lit out and figured we'd come back for any gear that was left when it was safe."

The driver reached for the cell phone on the dashboard. "You want me to call the cops?"

Jonah pulled a long face. "Naw. Truth is, I had a beef with one of the guys. He reckons I owe him some money—and he reckons that gives him the right to rob us and kick us out of our own campsite."

"That's a plumb shame."

Jonah launched into an amusing tale about how he and Tommy had been best buddies until they'd had a misunderstanding.

Sophia kept her mouth shut, amazed at the way Jonah was spinning the tale out of whole cloth and at the way the truck driver was taking it all in.

"Where you headed?" he asked.

"Away from here."

"Y'all in trouble with the law?"

"Naw," Jonah allowed. "I got into some scrapes when I was a kid, but Sara keeps me honest now." He patted her on the knee.

The driver laughed. "Yeah. My old lady and me have the same arrangement."

Sophia kept silent while the men talked about beer and baseball and cars.

About fifty miles from where he'd picked them up, Hank brought the conversation back to their problem. "So they got all your money?"

"I have some hidden in my boot."

Sophia blinked, then remembered that Jonah had raided Montgomery's cash drawer.

A few miles farther on, Hank pulled into a gas station.

"This is close enough for us to walk home," Jonah said.

Hank got out, and she and Jonah did the same.

"Much obliged," he said, and the two men shook hands.

While the driver was inside paying for the gas, they turned down a side street and kept going.

"I can't believe the way you bonded with that guy," Sophia murmured. "Where did you pick up the gift of the gab?"

"Maybe I always had it."

"True. I do remember you could always tell a good story when it came time to collect homework."

They both laughed. She sobered as she looked around at the darkened road, suddenly conscious that they were in a rural area with no means of transportation. "What are we going to do for a car?"

Jonah kept his voice matter of fact. "I believe we're going to have to steal one."

"I was afraid you were going to say that."

"You have a better suggestion?"

"We can call the Light Street Detective Agency from a pay phone."

He stopped short. "I don't know anything about them, except what you've told me."

"They got me into the bunker. When we were in the cave, you asked what we were supposed to do when we got out. Doesn't that mean you were willing to ask for their help?"

"Maybe I was, but I'm thinking more clearly now. As far as I know, they have their own agenda."

"One of them got killed getting you out of there."

He had the grace to wince.

"Are you saying you have a different agenda?"

"Right. Now that I've got a name, I'm going to contact Colonel Luntz and find out what he knows about that briefing."

"Is that a good idea?"

"I guess I'll find out." He sat down on a fallen log and took off his boot. Reaching inside, he fished out the money he'd taken from Montgomery's office. After shuffling through the bills, he held them out to her.

"Maybe you'd better take this. You can call your friends and get them to pick you up."

"I'm not leaving you."

He tipped his head to the side. "And what if I say it's time to split up?"

Chapter Fourteen

In the moonlight, Sophia turned to face him. She knew pride had something to do with the decisions he was making. He'd been held in hostile captivity, then rescued by her and Phil. Now he needed to prove that he was in charge of his own destiny. Yet she wasn't going to let him shove her out of the picture.

"You are not going to walk away from me. Not after…" She had been about to say, "not after making love with me and getting my hopes up." Instead she switched the comment. "Not after what we've been through together."

She saw his jaw tighten.

"What are you thinking?" she demanded. "That I'm a spy? That Montgomery sent me along with you to make sure I get the information?"

"No," he allowed.

"Well, that's something."

"I know you risked a lot to get me out of there. I know a man got killed in the process. But I don't know what's going to happen when I find Colonel Luntz."

"Which is a good reason for me to stay with you."

"It could be dangerous."

"No more dangerous than what happened in the cave. Or

almost getting burned up in that cabin. Or my getting caught by that guard."

When he answered with a tight nod, she swallowed hard and managed to ask, "If you had your choice, would you want me with you or not?"

Her chest was so tight that she could hardly breathe as she waited for the answer.

"With me," he finally said.

"Good," she managed to say. It was a mild representation of what she was feeling.

She wanted to reach for him and pull him close. She needed that contact, needed to feel him respond to her. But she forced herself to stay where she was.

"Let's find some transportation," she suggested.

"I doubt that you're going to charm anyone out of a car."

"Right."

He kept his gaze fixed on her face. "I'm planning to fall back on the skills I learned in high school. You still have the opportunity to opt out of this expedition, you know."

"No." She stood. "Let's get it over with."

She fell back a pace, watching Jonah walk. The leg had to be paining him, but he wasn't complaining. That was the kind of man he was—and the kind of boy he'd been. His life had been a lot tougher than she'd imagined. Too bad she hadn't known back then that he'd put up such a tough-guy front. But what would she have done about it? She'd just been rich little Sophia Rhodes—not Dr. Sophia Rhodes with the professional training to give her insights into Jonah Baker's character.

The moon provided some light as they walked down the road, passing rural mailboxes. Jonah chose a darkened lane and started up it. The house at the top of a hill wasn't a very impressive residence. From what she could see, it looked like a small box with a gabled room and a front stoop that was listing to one side.

Below the house, several cars were parked. Jonah studied the collection, then walked to one that looked as though it had been in a couple of minor accidents. The back bumper was caved in and the right front wheel barely cleared one of the fenders.

"Nobody's gonna miss this thing," he muttered. "If it will start." He looked at her. "Keep watch."

He handed her the gun.

"You don't want me to shoot anyone, do you?" she asked, hearing the quaver in her voice.

"Use your judgment."

He tried the front door of the vehicle and found it open. A good sign, she supposed. Nobody cared enough to lock it up.

Slipping inside, he wedged himself onto the floor below the steering wheel and began fiddling with wires.

She watched nervously, expecting someone to discover what they were doing and come charging out of the house with a shotgun. She was thankful when nobody appeared.

When the car started, Jonah eased up from his position on the floor. But as she hurried around to the passenger door, a light came on in the house.

Trouble!

"Hold it right there," a voice boomed out.

She almost jumped out of her skin, then jumped again as a blast from the shotgun she'd pictured earlier split the air.

Lucky for her, the guy was too far away to do any serious damage.

"Get in," Jonah shouted.

She jumped into the car and slammed the door as he headed down the hill.

The engine sputtered, and he cursed. Behind them, another blast sounded.

She cringed down in the seat. "I guess he'd rather get us than save his car."

"Better fire a couple of shots across his bow."

"Are you crazy?"

As Jonah kept driving, he reached over and took the gun from her, then leaned out the window and got off several shots.

"Stop."

"I'm not trying to hit him, just scare him."

"Great."

She had been looking behind her. When she swiveled to the front again, she gasped. "Jonah, watch out."

He brought his attention to the road again, then yanked the wheel hard, barely missing a fence post.

She breathed out a sigh, then looked behind them again. "The good news is that he's stopped."

"The bad news is that he may call the cops. And we don't want to get nailed for armed robbery."

She winced.

Jonah kept going, picking up speed as he barreled onto the road and turned right.

"You know where we're going?"

"I wish I did."

He drove for another few miles, then pulled into another darkened lane.

"Now what?"

"We have to change the license plates."

"How do we do that?"

"Borrow some. Stay here."

He got out and cut the engine, then opened the trunk and

rummaged inside. He must have found what he was looking for because he went to work on the plates.

When they were off the front and rear of the car, he trotted up the hill and disappeared.

She sat rigidly in her seat, waiting to hear gunfire again.

Finally, Jonah came limping back down the hill and held up a set of plates for her to see. Then he replaced the ones that had been on the car.

When he climbed back inside, he sat for a minute with his head thrown back against the headrest.

She reached over and laid her palm atop his right hand where it rested on the steering wheel.

"Your leg is hurting." She didn't wait for affirmation. "Let me drive."

His head turned toward her. "You're sure you want to drive a stolen car?"

"What's the difference between driving and being a passenger?"

"Not much, I guess."

He twisted the wires together to start the engine again, then pulled up the emergency brake while they switched places.

She accelerated slowly, getting the feel of the vehicle as she headed down the highway.

When she came to a sign that pointed to Blackwater Falls and Morgantown, she started to ask Jonah which way to go. But he had fallen asleep.

She decided to head northeast, toward a more populated area.

When she found herself getting sleepy, she started looking for a place to spend the night. She pulled into a one-story, inexpensive motor court and laid her hand on Jonah's shoulder.

He came awake with a jerk, pointing the gun toward her.

"Jonah!"

He focused on her and lowered the weapon. "Sorry. I told you I was dangerous."

"No, you're not. I just startled you."

"Stop denying the obvious."

"That was your army combat instincts kicking in."

"Is that your professional opinion?"

"Yes. And I'm too tired to argue. I just want to get us a room."

"How far are we from where Hank let us off?"

"Seventy-five miles."

"I hope that's good enough."

"You think they're going to check every little motel between here and D.C.?"

"If they're desperate enough. Is that where we're headed?"

"In that general direction. I figured we'd be better off in an urban area."

His expression sharpened. "You're not taking me to your friends in Baltimore, are you?"

She sighed. "Not unless you want to go there."

"I don't!"

She wanted to tell him he was being stubborn, but she knew that wouldn't help the situation. Instead, she asked for some of the cash so she could pay for the night.

"Tell them you want a room in back where it's quiet."

He gave her all of the money, and she paid cash, then climbed in again and drove to the other side of the building. The room wasn't palatial but it was clean.

She wanted to talk to Jonah, but he was making it clear that he wasn't much interested in communication. Instead she used the facilities and took a quick shower, then turned the bathroom over to him.

Wishing she had a change of clothes, she climbed into bed in her underwear, then listened to the shower running. He stayed under the water for a long time, and when he opened the bathroom door, she could see him in the light coming in around the edges of the curtains.

Wearing only his briefs, he slipped into the other side of the bed, and she lay for a minute, listening to the sound of his breathing.

When she couldn't stand it any longer, she closed the distance between them and turned on her side, reaching for him and snuggling close.

She could feel his instant tension.

"Don't put barriers between us," she said.

"I have to."

It was hard to speak around the constriction in her throat. "Is that a moral imperative or a personal decision about us?"

"Both."

She cradled her head against his shoulder. "Maybe you can explain your thinking."

He dragged in a breath and let it out. "I have a big fat hole in my memory. I don't know what's true and what isn't. I don't know what happened in Afghanistan, but I'm pretty sure it's something bad. And if that's not enough, when you tried to dig into it, I attacked you."

"We'll fix all that," she murmured.

"How can you be sure?"

"Because of your determination," she answered. "You *want* to fix it, badly, so you *will*."

"Are you telling me every nut case who *wants* to get well does?"

"You're not a nut case. Montgomery screwed with your mind."

"What's the difference?"

"A lot." She sighed. "Look, right now, you need to relax."

"Easier said than done," he muttered.

"Turn over. Let me massage your back and shoulder muscles."

He hesitated for a moment, then rolled to his stomach.

"There's some hand cream in the bathroom." She went to get it, then pulled down the covers.

He was lying with his eyes closed, his arms folded under his head. She poured some of the slippery white liquid into her hands, then straddled his body at his waist. She leaned over him and started massaging the tense muscles of his neck and shoulders and back.

After a moment, he gave a deep sigh of pleasure, and she kept working on him with slick hands, trying not to notice that straddling him and touching him was turning her on. Her breasts started to feel full and achy, and she couldn't stop herself from pressing her sex downward to increase her own pleasure.

Partly to distract herself, she began talking to him in a low voice.

"Where was the briefing with Luntz?"

"Beltsville, Maryland."

"Ah, so you came up with the location."

He sounded surprised. "Yeah. I didn't remember it before. But I guess it popped back into my head."

"That's good. Why there?" she asked, trying to focus on business and not the heat rushing through her body.

"They used some abandoned buildings on the campus at the Agricultural Research Center."

She sat up straighter. "Was Montgomery there?"

"I don't think so."

"Just Luntz and the group going on the mission?"

"Yes."

"How long were you in Afghanistan?"

"Eighteen hours," he answered. "Then it all blew up in our faces."

She wanted to ask how, but she didn't push in that direction.

"Was Luntz with you in Afghanistan?" she asked instead.

"No."

"Do you know the real mission?"

"No."

She had felt his tension coming back as she asked the last few questions.

"Sorry," she murmured.

"You got some stuff out of me," he said in a gritty voice.

"I should stop being so aggressive."

"Or maybe you shouldn't." He laughed. "I know what you're doing. And I don't mean your questions. I can feel the heat coming off you."

He slowly rolled under her, giving her time to adjust to the changed position. When he came to rest on his back, she realized that she wasn't the only one who had been turned on by her slippery hands moving over him.

She made a strangled sound as she felt him pressing against her. When he reached up to pull her down to his chest, she came willingly.

She had thought he was trying to stay away from her. Apparently it hadn't worked.

Reaching around her, he unhooked her bra, and she pulled it out of the way and tossed it to the other side of the bed. Then he pulled her down, kneading her back the way she had done his.

Her breasts swayed against his chest, making her crave more. She raised up only enough to pull her panties off one leg, leaving them clinging to the other. Then she did the same with him, pulling down his briefs far enough so that she had full access to him.

She was already swollen and slick, and she rubbed herself against him, loving his wonderful hardness and heat.

He made a strangled exclamation as she drove them both wild with need. Then she brought him inside her.

Her eyes locked with his, and she stayed where she was

without moving for half a minute, teasing them both almost beyond endurance.

He was the one who forced the issue, raising his hips and pressing farther into her.

She cried out and began to move, because that was her only option.

"I want to see you play with your breasts," he said, his voice thick.

She did as he asked, boldly lifting her breasts toward him, then plucking and twisting at the tips because it gave them both pleasure.

It was wonderful to move in this dance of sexual fulfillment with him. Wonderful to see his face and so much of his body as she moved above him.

She pulled back as far as she could and still remain joined to him, then she looked down at the place where their bodies merged, marveling at the way that intimate connection looked.

She watched him follow her gaze, his face molten with heat.

With an exclamation of pure joy, she plunged down again, driving them both to the brink.

Her movements became wilder. Less controlled. She pushed them both to a high peak of pleasure, then tumbled over the edge, taking him with her in a rush of deep fulfillment.

Breathing hard, she collapsed on top of him, wrapping her arms around him and holding him tight.

"I love you," she whispered.

She heard his sharp indrawn breath.

"No."

"I think a while ago you advised me not to tell you what you feel. Give me the same courtesy."

"You don't want to get mixed up with me."

"Like I said, let me be the judge of that."

Sitting up was too much work, so she bent forward, clasping

his sweat- and lotion-slick body as she stretched out on top of him, keeping him inside her.

She longed to hear him say the same thing she had said. But she knew he wasn't going to do it. Not until he had dealt with the memory problem.

Or maybe never, if he let his stubborn pride rule his emotions. In the vulnerable recesses of her heart, she understood that she had to be prepared for that, too.

Chapter Fifteen

Jonah found a house where the people were obviously on an extended trip and traded in the old clunker for a newer model. The trade involved breaking into the house and taking a spare set of keys. He wasn't enjoying all the illegal activity, but he made himself feel better about it by keeping a list of people he had to reimburse.

As they headed toward Washington, D.C., he pulled into a fast-food restaurant and got in line for the take-out window.

They were using the money from Montgomery's office as sparingly as possible, but they were going to need an infusion of cash if they didn't change their fugitive status soon.

He and Sophia each ordered burgers, french fries and sodas. As they sat in the car eating, he slid her a sidewise glance. Since the first car heist, she hadn't complained about his problem-solving solutions, even though he was sure she didn't like being on the wrong side of the law.

She dipped a french fry in ketchup. "I have a suggestion for how to approach Luntz."

"Why do I think I'm not going to like it?"

"Because you don't trust my judgment."

He felt a pang of regret. "That's not true."

"Then at least listen to my plan."

He took a bite of his burger and leaned back against the seat. "Okay."

When she began to talk, he knew his suspicions had been right. He didn't like what he was hearing. Unfortunately, her scheme made sense. But he told her they were going to look for every flaw they could find in her logic before they put it into action.

Since he couldn't dredge up any objections, they checked out Luntz's house. He lived in Potomac, Maryland, in what had once been prime horse country. In recent years, many of the horse farms had been turned into McMansion subdivisions. There were still some old estates where the owners had kept the property intact. Colonel Luntz's was one of them.

Jonah drove past the entrance several times. The approach to the house was up a curving driveway, screened by trees. He didn't know what was going on up there. And he needed to find out.

Next they stopped at a mall and bought some equipment, including two prepaid cell phones, and a directional mike so he could pick up conversations at a distance.

"That's about it for our money," he said as they headed toward the colonel's house.

Sophia nodded.

"Maybe I could play guitar outside the mall and collect tips."

"Do you know how to play?"

"Yeah," he answered. "I learned at Fort Benning. I used to amuse my friends with raunchy ballads."

She laughed. "I'd like to hear them."

"But then I'd have to steal a guitar—which would defeat the purpose of the exercise."

She laughed again as they turned down the road where Luntz lived.

Jonah drove past and turned off into a patch of woods. Then

he got out and started back to the estate on foot while Sophia waited in the car.

Once he'd slipped under a split rail fence from the neighboring property, he waited and listened for signs that the place was being guarded.

He heard only the rustling of small animals in the underbrush.

Staying low and slipping through the woods, he came out into a well-kept garden, surrounding a redbrick Georgian two-story house.

As he approached the structure, he could see lights on inside. A gray-haired man in casual clothes was sitting in a den watching news on television. He looked to be in his fifties, and Jonah felt a spark of recognition. As he stared at the man's face, he tried to come up with more details of the briefing.

He could picture Luntz standing at the front of a room full of troops. But that was all. None of what the guy had been saying was coming through.

Jonah clenched his fists, then ordered himself to stop trying to force memories. It didn't do any good. They came back when they were good and ready—or not at all.

What he had to do was focus on the present assignment—determining that it was safe enough for Sophia to come calling on the man inside the house.

He strained his ears. As far as he could tell, there was no sound coming from the interior except the television.

As he circled the property, he noted the exterior features and looked in other windows, but he saw no one else. When he checked the detached garage, he found two cars.

It was almost too perfect, with Luntz at home alone and watching television.

Was this a setup? Or was the man entirely comfortable in his own surroundings and sure that he wasn't in any kind of trouble?

Slipping back into the woods, Jonah called Sophia on the cell phone.

"Give me ten minutes. Then come on ahead."

"Okay."

He hung up, then hurried back to the house, where he secured his pack on his back, then climbed up a drainpipe to the top of the covered patio. From there he crossed to an upstairs window and carefully cut a circle in one of the panes with a glass cutter. Then he slipped inside and tiptoed toward the stairs.

He tried to stay calm, but his stomach was tied in knots.

Stationing himself in the shadows of the hall, he waited for the doorbell to ring.

It did—on schedule.

Moments later, he heard footsteps on the stone floor of the lower hall. Then Luntz turned on the exterior light and opened the door.

"May I help you?" he asked.

From the top of the stairs, Jonah could hear Sophia's voice drifting through the doorway. "I'm sorry to bother you so late in the evening."

"Yes?" Luntz said.

"I'm Sara Rollins," she said, giving the name they'd agreed upon. "I'm a clinical psychologist, and I've been working with a patient named Jonah Baker. He's mentioned you several times in our sessions, and I'm hoping you can give me some information about him."

"Come in."

She did, and he closed the door behind her.

"Where is Baker?"

"I'm not at liberty to say."

"Why not?"

"He's at a secure government facility."

"Because?"

"He apparently had some kind of breakdown on an assignment in Afghanistan. And I understand that you set up the mission."

"Where did you get that information?" Luntz asked sharply.

"I was able to hypnotize Baker."

"Interesting."

"I'm not making much progress with him, and I was hoping you could give me some useful information about him."

He gestured toward the back of the house. "Why didn't you call me?"

"I was afraid you wouldn't see me if I did. I was hoping that if I just came here, you wouldn't turn me away."

"Why don't we sit down?"

"Thank you."

She started down the hall, and Jonah had started to walk down the steps when two more men came out of another doorway and moved quickly up on either side of Sophia, grabbing her arms.

Sophia cried out as they hustled her toward the room where Luntz had been sitting like a goddamn decoy, pretending he was totally alone.

Jonah knew that now. He also knew something else. Luntz wasn't an innocent bystander. He was up to his eyeballs in this, and he'd been prepared for trouble.

Jonah didn't recognize either of the men who had grabbed Sophia, but they looked like they'd been cut from the same mold as the security guards in the bunker.

Were there other guards in the house?

And how was he going to get Sophia out of here?

Cursing his own stupidity for letting her put herself in danger, Jonah tiptoed back up the main staircase. He'd thought it was safe for Sophia to come in here. Now he knew how wrong he was.

With his heart pounding, he looked back over his shoulder.

He'd seen another set of stairs which led to the back of the house. Maybe that was his best bet.

Scrambling for a plan, he pulled out his SIG and hurried to the alternate stairway, then quickly descended. At the bottom he paused to make sure he was alone. No other men had materialized, but that didn't mean they weren't here.

He flattened himself against the wall and moved down the hall toward the family room. Through the doorway he saw that they had pushed Sophia into a chair and were grouped around her.

"He sent you," Luntz growled.

"No."

One of the men answered. "She was at the bunker. And she sure as hell wasn't part of the team there."

"Shut up," Luntz growled. "We're asking questions, not giving out information."

The man clamped his mouth shut.

"Where is he?" Luntz demanded.

She raised her chin. "I don't know."

"I don't believe you." For emphasis, he pulled back his hand, then slapped her across the face.

She made a startled sound.

"You're going to tell us."

When he saw Luntz strike her, Jonah's anger flared. Yet he knew that if he let emotions rule him, they were both going to end up dead.

"Where is he?" Luntz asked again, his voice menacing. "It will be easier on you if you tell me."

Jonah pulled the phone from his pocket and called Luntz's number.

As it rang, all of the men focused on the sound.

Jonah dashed forward and hit one of them on the back of the head with the gun. He went down, but when Jonah struck at the other guy, he had already moved.

From the corner of his eye, he saw Sophia lash out at Luntz, her foot catching him square in the crotch. He doubled over, groaning.

But Jonah had his own problems. The other guard was trying to pull his gun out of the holster on his belt so he could get off a shot.

Jonah chopped at the guard's gun hand, and the man cried out. But that didn't stop him from springing forward.

Sophia backed up a step and swung her purse by the strap, hitting him on the back of the neck. It was enough of a distraction for Jonah to come up with a fist to the man's chin.

He went down, joining his partner on the floor.

It had all happened in a matter of seconds. The uniformed men both lay unconscious at his feet. Luntz was still doubled over.

Jonah ripped the cord off a lamp, pushed Luntz into the chair and handed Sophia the gun.

"Cover him," he said as he tied the man's hands behind his back.

When he'd secured the colonel, he gave him a narrow-eyed look. "What the hell is going on?"

"You won't get that information from me."

"We'll see about that."

"If I were you, I'd get out of here. Reinforcements are on the way."

"Why am I the key to your Afghanistan plot?"

The colonel lifted his chin. "Who says there's a plot, and who says you're the key? You're giving yourself too much credit."

"Oh, come on. You had me locked up in an underground bunker to get information out of me."

"Not me. Montgomery."

"So you know him."

Realizing he'd made a mistake, the man paled. But his voice remained firm. "I repeat, you'd better get out while the getting is good."

One of the guards groaned and started to roll over. Jonah gave him a kick in the head with his boot, and the guy went quiet again.

Sophia winced. "We should leave."

"She's right," Luntz confirmed.

Sophia put a hand on Jonah's arm. "I think we'd better split. He's not going to tell us anything."

"I wouldn't bet on it."

As Luntz had done to Sophia, Jonah swung back his arm, then delivered a flat-hand blow to the man's mouth.

He gasped, and when he opened his mouth again, it was bloody. He glared at Jonah. "How dare you."

Jonah felt his blood surge. He had been angry and frustrated for a long time, and finally he had an outlet for that anger. "There's a lot more where that came from. Who's running the show? You or Montgomery?"

The colonel pressed his lips together.

"I can find out who was authorized to use that bunker," he said, wondering if that was really true.

He was pleased to get a reaction out of the man.

"I'll bet you didn't know there was a back way in."

Luntz's face showed that the guess had been right.

"Too bad you couldn't control access," he taunted. He wanted to strip off the guy's clothing, tie him down on a bed and make him think he was going to end up with his balls handed to him on a platter. But not with Sophia watching. Maybe it was good that she was here, because that would keep him from stepping over a line that he could never come back across.

Outside, Jonah heard a car door slam.

Luntz gave him a triumphant look.

Jonah turned to Sophia. "Come on."

He hurried out of the room, and she followed. In the doorway he reached into his pack, then tossed two tear gas canisters inside.

As the room filled with gas, Luntz began to cough, and Jonah guided Sophia out the back door and around the side of the house.

Inside he could hear shouts, coughing and cursing.

"You're driving. Get in the car."

Sophia got into the driver's seat while Jonah turned and shot out all four tires of the SUV that had pulled up in the driveway. Someone came running out the front door, shooting.

Jonah ducked into the passenger seat and slammed the door as Sophia took off down the driveway. Careening through the decorative brick posts, she headed for the route that they'd agreed on earlier in case they had to make a quick getaway.

THEY DROVE for several miles.

"Now what?" Sophia asked.

"I don't know."

She cleared her throat. "Would you consider calling the Light Street Detective Agency?"

"I don't want to."

"I know. But we're out of options and out of money."

He sighed, finally conceding the point. "Yeah."

She pulled the phone out of her purse, put it on speaker phone and pressed in a number. Someone answered on the first ring.

"This is Sophia Rhodes."

"Thank God," a woman answered. "This is Kathryn Kelley."

Jonah remembered she was the woman who had recruited Sophia for this assignment.

"Where are you?" Kelley asked.

"In Potomac, Maryland."

"You, Phil and Baker?"

She sucked in a breath. "Phil didn't make it. But I have Jonah Baker with me."

"You want us to pick you up?"

She glanced at Jonah.

"Yes," he answered.

"Okay. Give me a moment." They waited without speaking for Kelley to return. When she came back on the line, she said, "Take Route 108 across Montgomery and Howard counties. Do you know how to get there?"

"Yes."

"Turn off on New Hampshire Avenue, then right onto Brighton Dam Road and head for Brighton Dam Park. We'll meet you in the parking lot across the highway from the park. Do you know where that is?"

Jonah had no idea, but Sophia answered, "Yes."

When she hung up, Jonah slumped in his seat, and Sophia reached out to touch his knee.

His leg twitched. "That didn't work out so well."

"Sorry. I guess it wasn't such a great idea."

"I shouldn't have let you risk it. I'm obviously not functioning at top efficiency."

"Stop blaming yourself."

"He hurt you."

"It was only one slap."

"That was enough."

"I'm tougher than I look."

"I know."

"Thanks for that, at least."

"What's that supposed to mean?"

She huffed out a breath. "You're trying to distance yourself from me."

"For your own good."

She turned her head toward him. "You have to let me be the judge of that."

"I'm not used to answering to anyone besides myself. Well, at least when I'm not following orders."

"That's obvious."

He wasn't sure how to respond, so he pressed his lips together, waiting for her to demand some answer that he wasn't ready to give.

Maybe he never would be.

To his relief, it seemed that Sophia had decided not to keep pressing him.

They traveled in silence until she said, "Here's the turnoff."

They rode past woods, then came to a parking area on their right. In the moonlight, he could see the ground sloping along the side of a dam into what looked like a black chasm.

"What's down there?"

"Picnic tables. Playground equipment. A stream where the water spills off from the dam."

"It's relatively open?"

"Yes."

"What about the other side?" he asked, looking to his left where he saw a wooded area with water sparkling in the moonlight. "Is that a lake?"

"That's a reservoir, with a naturalized park along the shore. It's full of huge azaleas planted all through the woods. Right now, they're blooming. In the daylight, it's like a fairyland with big splashes of color."

He stared into the woods. Some of the flowers must be white because they stood out in the moonlight.

"There are trails with blooming bushes towering over your head on either side. I tell people that if they live around here and don't visit in the spring, they're crazy." She laughed. "And here we are. Perfect timing! Too bad we can't see much in the dark."

"Yeah."

In his life, he hadn't given himself much time to stop and smell the flowers. He didn't even know if azaleas had much scent.

Climbing out of the car, he was glad to stretch his cramped muscles. He'd been doing too much walking on the damn leg. He was just leaning down to massage it when a noise made him stop short.

Sophia came around to his side, her look questioning. "What?"

He swore, listening for another moment to be sure. Unfortunately, the noise was all too familiar. "Another helicopter coming this way."

"You think?"

He took a quick look at their surroundings, wondering if the moonlight was a help or not. It gave him some additional night vision, but that was also true for the enemy.

The open area below the dam was deep in shadow now. But a searchlight would illuminate anyone down there like roaches running for cover when you turned on the kitchen light in the middle of the night.

He swung the other way, seeing the trees and flower-covered bushes along the lake.

That was their better bet.

"Into the woods. Hurry."

Chapter Sixteen

Headlights knifed down the road, setting Jonah's heart pounding. Were more guards on the way?

He held his breath until the car sped past. Grabbing Sophia's hand he led her across the four-lane highway. She took the lead, running down a wide path lined with huge bushes that towered over them.

After twenty yards, she veered off onto a narrow track leading uphill between eight-foot tall azaleas. When she found a small opening, she plunged under the foliage on the left, wedging herself in and making room for Jonah.

"How did they figure out we came here?" she whispered as they curled around each other.

He made an angry sound. "Unfortunately, it looks like they put a transponder on the car."

"Like I used to track you around the bunker?"

"Yes."

He looked out, wishing he'd driven the car over the side of the parking area before they'd crossed the road. It would have plunged down into the stream valley below the dam, and the bad guys might have thought that he and Sophia had gone over the edge with it. But it was too late for that now. The helicopter was almost above them.

In fact he could hear two choppers. One right here and the other a little farther away.

Across the road, he could see lights moving back and forth, confirming his assumption about the transponder. The bad guys were starting with the car. When they realized it was empty, they'd widen their search.

As he expected, the helicopter began to circle, the light striking the bushes, making sudden splashes of color leap out of the blackness as the wind from the rotors whipped the branches, sending blossoms swirling into the air.

He brought his mouth to Sophia's ear. "Don't move."

Reaching for his SIG, he worked his hand into firing position as he wrapped his free arm around her and pressed his lips to her cheek.

The spotlight wove through the wooded area, still illuminating the blooming bushes, still tearing the blossoms off their stems. On its first pass, it missed them. Then it swung back, and he tensed, waiting for the light to strike their hiding place.

When it did, he stopped breathing.

The machine hovered, and he was pretty sure the spotters had found them.

He brought his mouth to Sophia's ear. "Stay under the bushes, but see how far you can get from this spot. If you can make it to the reservoir without being seen, maybe you can swim across and get away."

She turned her head. "What about you?"

"They can't land in the trees. They have to use the open space in the parking lot. I'm going to take out as many of them as I can."

Before she could object, he left her, wiggling through the bushes and slithering out. Climbing to his feet, he started running back up the trail toward the road.

He reached the fence that marked the edge of the wooded area as the helicopter zoomed toward the parking lot. It was still a hundred feet in the air when the rotors choked and sputtered, and the machine came crashing down to the blacktop—where it burst into flames.

Jonah leaped back, his gun at the ready.

In the light from the burning machine, a shape materialized out of the darkness, something rushing at him so fast that he couldn't see anything but a blur of motion. Then hands with super-human strength grabbed him, lifting the gun from his grasp before he could fire.

"Sophia?" another voice called. "Are you there? Are you all right? Come out. It's Hunter Kelley, from Light Street."

"Here. I'm here." Sophia came running up the path, her eyes wide.

The man who was holding Jonah let go, and he stepped quickly back.

Sophia ran to Jonah. "Are you all right?" she asked.

"Yes." Before he could say anything further, more figures materialized out of the darkness, and he stared at the group gathering around him. They were all tough-looking men, but different in some fundamental way from the guards at the bunker.

"What did you do to the chopper?" he asked.

The one named Hunter Kelley answered. "We thought they might try something like this, so we brought a device that jammed the rotor."

He stared at the guy, taking in the words but not crediting them. "That would be very convenient for terrorists. But as far as I know, it's not possible."

"Our technology is beyond current state of the art. The jamming device isn't something we've made public or that we use very often. But this is one of those times. When the authorities investigate, it will look like a mechanical failure."

Stunned, Jonah stared at him. "And when the cops find a

chopper full of tough guys here, what are they going to think was going on?"

"Hell if I know," the man who had grabbed Jonah's gun answered. "But we'd better split. By the way, my name is Nicholas Vickers."

"Nice to meet you," he said, wondering how the guy had moved so fast.

"Likewise."

He led them down the stretch of highway to the other side of the dam, where another chopper had landed.

In the distance, they could hear the sound of fire engines.

"Better hurry," Vickers said.

They all climbed into the helicopter and strapped in. As soon as they were secured in place, the machine took off. From the air, Jonah got a quick look at the burning machine before they flew away.

Sophia sat next to Jonah, holding his hand tightly.

He squeezed her fingers, glad that it was almost impossible to talk above the noise.

Though he expected to see the lights of Baltimore ahead of them, they were heading toward a sparsely populated area. About an hour later, they landed in a clearing beside a long, low building in the middle of a pine forest.

When they had exited and were far enough away from the rotor to talk, he asked, "Where are we?"

"The Randolph Security research facility in western Maryland," Hunter Kelley answered.

They walked into a spacious front hall.

"We were in kind of a rush to get away, so I didn't get to introduce myself," the man who had been piloting the helicopter said. "I'm Jed Prentiss."

The others also offered names.

"Max Dakota."

"Cameron Randolph."

"And Thorn Devereaux."

Two women came down the hall, one of them a redhead and one a blond.

"I'm Kathryn Kelley, Hunter's wife," the redhead said, moving to her husband's side.

"And I'm Jo O'Malley, head of the Light Street Detective Agency. Cam's wife and partner."

"Glad to meet you all," Jonah said, trying to relax. Though he didn't know these people and had been afraid to trust them, so far, things were going surprisingly well.

"I'm afraid I'm the one who got Sophia into this," Kathryn Kelley said.

"I'm glad you did," Sophia answered.

Jonah gave her a long look. "You almost got killed a time or two."

She swallowed. "What's important is that we got you out of the bunker."

"But not your friend Phil," Jonah reminded him.

Cameron Randolph gave him a grave look. "We're all mourning him. He wasn't with our organization long, but we knew he was a good man. However, there's something he didn't want us to tell Sophia before they left for the cavern. He had inoperable cancer."

"What?" Sophia gasped.

"That's why he volunteered for the mission. He didn't have long to live and he was prepared to go out with his boots on—if that's what it took to get you out of there."

Jonah tried to cope with the shock of this new knowledge. "So that was why he was so insistent on holding off the guards while we went down the tunnel."

"That sounds right."

Kathryn turned to Sophia. "I'm sorry we kept you in the dark about his condition. He wouldn't let us tell you. He was afraid you wouldn't go with him if you thought he was unreliable."

She opened her mouth then closed it again, obviously reevaluating everything she'd known about the man.

"I was starting to think he was a drug addict," she whispered.

Randolph nodded, then said, "After what you've been through, you need some R and R. Let's start with food. Then sleep."

The thought of food and sleep made Jonah realize how hungry and tired he was.

"We've got a spread set out down the hall."

They kept walking and came to a comfortable lounge with sofas, chairs and tables. Plates and dishes of food were spread out on a long sideboard at the back of the room.

Jonah wandered over and looked at the selections, which included steak, baked potatoes with all the trimmings, roast turkey with gravy, stuffing and cranberry sauce and candied sweet potatoes.

"How did you get all this together on short notice?"

"We've been waiting for you to arrive," Jo O'Malley said. "And we wanted to make it a festive meal."

"Well, thanks."

Everybody helped themselves to food. Jonah opted for the turkey and trimmings, thinking how much it was like the Thanksgiving meals he'd seen on television—and better than anything his mom had been able to scrape together.

He brought his food to a sofa and leaned back with the plate on his lap.

Sophia sat beside him.

"You okay?" she asked.

"Yeah," he answered automatically as he ate and watched how the other men and women interacted. They had obviously been together for a long time, and they were all perfectly comfortable with each other.

All of them were eating, except the guy named Nick Vickers. He'd gotten a bottle of something red out of the refrigerator under the sideboard and was sipping slowly. From here, it looked like blood. What was he? One of those Goths who thought they were vampires?"

He felt a chill travel over his skin as he remembered the scene at the dam, when Vickers had moved through the night with super-human speed.

From across the room, Vickers smiled at him, and he got the feeling that the guy knew exactly what he was thinking.

He dragged his gaze away from Vickers and looked at the others again, enjoying the meal and talking in quiet voices.

He could dimly remember a time like that—when he'd been close to the guys in his unit. But that seemed like a dream that he only half remembered.

Cameron Randolph was looking at him. "So, why were they holding you in the bunker?" he asked.

"That's a pretty direct question," Jonah countered.

"We want to find out how much you understand about the situation."

Well, here it was. He was going to explain what a mess he was. He took a sip of the soda he'd gotten from the sideboard, then he told them about the memories of Thailand and about Afghanistan and about the nightmares.

As he spoke, he could feel sweat trickling down the back of his neck.

"I think you held up better than most people would have," Randolph said.

"Why do you think so?" Jonah challenged.

"Because you made it here."

"With Sophia's help. I couldn't have done it without her—and Phil."

"Yes. They played a very important role."

"Jonah and I made a good team," she murmured.

Randolph turned back to Jonah. "And don't minimize your achievements. You gave us a very coherent account of the past few weeks."

He hadn't thought of it that way.

Sophia covered his hand with hers and squeezed. "See? That's what I've been telling you," she murmured.

He wasn't sure what he would have said if he'd been alone with her, but Thorn Devereaux broke in to the exchange.

Clearing his throat, he said, "I sense that you're impatient to get to work."

"If you mean getting my memories back, then you're right."

"We have something that may help you, something we've tried with other people who had chunks of their past missing."

Jonah sat up straighter, all his attention focused on the man.

"You know that electroshock therapy often makes people lose their memories?"

He nodded.

"I've invented a machine that reverses the process. We've used it with success on a woman who came here from the future on a secret mission."

Jonah blinked. "A woman who came from the future? You're kidding, right?"

"No," Max Dakota answered. "She's my wife, Annie. She was sent here to prevent an event that set the world on a course with disaster. Only, when she got here, she didn't remember her mission."

Jonah glanced at Sophia and saw that she looked as thunder-struck as he.

"It sounds fantastic, but it's the truth. She's not here now because she's pregnant with our first child."

"Congratulations," Sophia said.

"Did it work?" Jonah asked. "I mean—the treatment."

"Yeah. But there's some risk involved," Devereaux answered.

"What risks?" Jonah demanded.

"If we bring back your memories from Afghanistan, you could forget everything you've learned since."

He nodded, considering that possibility.

"And there's some risk of brain injury."

"Then we won't do it!" Sophia said, her voice high and strained.

"Yeah, we will," Jonah answered, because he knew that he had to recover his past. No matter what.

"We should discuss this," Sophia said.

"No. I'm tired of being at the mercy of men like Luntz and Montgomery."

"For what it's worth, we think Montgomery is working for Luntz," Jed Prentiss said.

"Why didn't you tell me that?" Sophia snapped.

"We didn't know until after you left. We tried to communicate the information to Phil, but we couldn't get through to the cave."

"Yes, I remember his trying to contact you," she murmured.

Jonah stood. "Let's go zap my brain."

Sophia gave him a dark look, but she also stood.

"It would be better if you got some sleep first," Thorn said, and Sophia agreed.

Jonah looked at her, seeing the anxious expression on her face. Obviously she was hoping for the chance to talk him out of it.

"Maybe," he answered both her and Thorn. "But I'm not going to be able to sleep until we get this done. So let's get the show on the road."

Thorn stood and led the way down the hall to a wing of the building that looked like an outpatient clinic. They passed various rooms with medical equipment and ended up in what might have been a doctor's consultation room. Thorn sat down behind the desk, and Jonah and Sophia took the guest chairs. He wanted to tell her to leave now and let him handle this, but he was pretty sure she would ignore the request. And maybe she did have the right to stay, because he wouldn't be here if it weren't for her.

Not wanting any personal contact at the moment, he folded his arms in his lap and listened to Thorn explain the procedure.

When he slid Sophia a sidewise glance he saw that her face was as rigid as a sheet of glass, and just as transparent. She didn't like this.

"We'll start with a thorough physical," Thorn said. "Dr. Miguel Valero has just arrived from Baltimore so he'll be able to do that now."

"Okay," Jonah agreed. He glanced at Sophia. "I guess you have to wait outside now."

After she left, Valero came in and introduced himself. Then Jonah stepped into a dressing room, stripped and put on one of those white gowns that open down the back.

IN THE LOUNGE, Sophia tried to sit still with her hands wrapped around a mug of tea. Unsuccessful, she finally had to get up and pace the room.

Kathryn Kelley came over to her. "I know this is hard for you."

She nodded.

"Do you want to talk about it?"

Sophia glanced around. There were other people in the room, and she didn't want to bare her soul in front of them.

"Let's go down to the sunroom," Kathryn suggested.

She scuffed her foot against the floor. Although she wanted to talk about her and Jonah, she didn't want to get into anything too revealing. But who was she kidding? She'd already revealed a lot. Maybe Kathryn could give her some insights.

"Okay."

They walked down the hall to a room with huge windows and skylights. It had a warm, earthy scent, coming from the pots of plants that filled the room. Color came from orchids, bright tuberous begonias and cyclamens. But there were also large ficus and dracaena trees, many sparkling with tiny lights in the darkness. They gave the setting an ambiance that Sophia would have appreciated if she hadn't been so strung out.

She sat down in a wicker chair, staring out onto the grounds where spotlights illuminated the well-tended gardens.

"I guess they put a lot of money into keeping this place up," she remarked.

Kathryn sat in another chair. "Some of the researchers have to stay here for weeks, and Cameron Randolph wants to create a comfortable environment for them."

"I see."

The conversation died away, and they sat in the darkness for several minutes until Kathryn gently suggested, "Why don't you tell me what's been going on."

"You already heard Jonah's account of our adventures."

"Right. Your adventures. The guy version. Very fact-filled. But I didn't hear anything about your emotions. Or his."

Sophia grimaced. "He's pretty uptight."

"And you're being pretty guarded." Kathryn spread her hands. "We don't have a lot of time for extended therapy here. If you tell me what's going on with you, I'll give you my considered opinion."

Sophia lowered her eyes. "I guess the bottom line is that I told him I was in love with him, and he didn't bother to respond."

"I guess that was hard for him to deal with—under the stress of running for your lives."

She nodded. Then, because she had nothing to lose, she said, "I had a crush on him in high school. I know he liked me, too, but he always acted like he thought he wasn't good enough for me. In the past few days, we've talked about his life back then. I didn't realize how hard it was."

"How does that make you feel?"

"Like I was too self-centered to notice."

"Or he hid it from you. Probably not just from you—from a lot of people."

She huffed out a breath. "I think you're right. But it doesn't make me feel good about myself back then."

"But you did reach out to him?"

"Yes. Just before he left for Fort Benning, I brought him to my house when my parents were in Europe. I mean, it wasn't a kid sneaking around," she added quickly. "I was nineteen. And he was a couple of years older. I never forgot that night, and I think he didn't, either. Later, when I got married, it didn't work out partly because I kept comparing my husband to Jonah. And partly because George married me for my money, I think."

"That's a lot to walk around with."

"Yes. But Jonah and I are both a lot more mature now. I think we could build something together. But he won't let me close." She heaved a sigh. "Well, he let me get physically close, but he's guarding his emotions."

"You might have gathered from his behavior that he feels like he's damaged by what happened to him in the bunker and in Afghanistan," Kathryn said.

"Yes," Sophia answered in a small voice, still unwilling to meet the other woman's eyes.

"So perhaps he's putting your relationship on hold until he feels he has more to offer you."

She gave Kathryn a fierce look. "He doesn't have to do that!"

"But he's a proud man, and he obviously feels he has to."

Sophia had thought of his pride, too. Now she felt as though a giant hand was squeezing her lungs. Nervously, she looked toward the door. "That physical is taking an awful lot of time." As she thought about the implications, she stood.

"Show me where to find the lab."

"That may not be a good idea," Kathryn murmured.

"Show me!"

"All right."

She followed Kathryn down the hall, silently urging her to move faster.

They stepped into the medical wing of the building again.

Kathryn pointed. "Down the hall."

Sophia hurried toward an area where white light shone through an interior window. As she got closer, she could hear voices. When she drew abreast of the window, she looked through and gasped.

She'd thought Jonah was only going to have a physical. At least, that's what he'd let her believe. Now he was lying on a table with his eyes closed, apparently unconscious.

She took in the scene in the blink of an eye. He was dressed in a white gown, his arms and legs strapped to the table. That was bad enough, but then she saw that electrodes had been attached all over his head.

"No!" she cried out.

Through the window Thorn looked toward her. And when she ran to the door, Kathryn was right behind her, grasping her shoulder to hold her back.

Chapter Seventeen

"No. I've got to…"

She didn't know what she intended, but she had to do something.

She'd known it. Known it on some unconscious level she hadn't been able to deal with.

Jonah made his own plans. He was going ahead with this with no regard for her.

When Kathryn's hand tightened on her shoulder, she whirled to face the other woman.

"Were you in on this? I mean keeping me talking in the sunroom so he could…could take a chance on frying his brain?"

"No, I wasn't." Kathryn stared into the room. "This is as big a surprise to me as it is to you."

Sophia clenched her hands at her sides. She wanted to hit someone, Jonah, actually.

Through the window she saw Thorn and another man watching her.

"Who's that?"

"Dr. Valero."

"So he okayed this?"

"I assume so," Kathryn answered.

"I want to talk to him, or Thorn."

Kathryn cleared her throat. "I'm sorry, but I think it might be dangerous to interrupt now."

Sophia glared at the other woman, but she silently acknowledged that the assessment was probably right. If she'd gotten here a few minutes earlier, she might have been able to make Jonah stop and think about the risk he was taking.

Now it was too late.

She stayed where she was with her hands clenched at her sides as Thorn fiddled with the damn equipment, then walked to a computer console and started typing on the keyboard.

Sophia tensed, then gasped as Jonah's body jerked. Kathryn leaned toward her. "I know it looks scary, but Thorn knows what he's doing. This isn't the first time he's used this procedure."

"Easy for you to say," Sophia snapped. "They're not experimenting on the man you love."

"They did," she answered.

Sophia whirled around, her eyes questioning. "They did this to Hunter?"

"Worse."

Outrage bubbled inside her. "How could it be worse!"

Kathryn continued quietly, "Hunter was a clone—raised for a suicide mission. He didn't even have a name. I met him because I was hired to…socialize him, but I had no idea what I was getting into."

Sophia gasped. "You're kidding."

"No." Kathryn held her gaze steady. "A lot of the people who work for Randolph and Light Street have been through some pretty harrowing experiences. We're a very resilient group."

Sophia swallowed. "I guess," she murmured.

"As you can imagine, Hunter and I had a lot to deal with after we escaped from the secure facility where they were training him to be an assassin. So I'm pretty in tune with what you're going through."

Sophia nodded, hearing the strong emotion in Kathryn's voice. Kathryn and Hunter had gotten through the worst, but that was in her past. Jonah was strapped down to a table right now. And the sight was pretty frightening. What if this "treatment" damaged his brain?

Beside Sophia, Kathryn whispered, "I think it's working."

"How do you know?"

"See his eyes moving under his lids. He's dreaming."

"About what?"

"I hope we'll find out."

JONAH TRAMPED forward through a kind of twilight country where the landscape was a series of indistinct blobs. Where was he? Afghanistan… West Virginia… Thailand?

No, Thailand wasn't real. It had never been real. Those were memories Dr. Montgomery had fed him. He knew that much.

The thought of the doctor made him wary, and he glanced over his shoulder. There was nothing behind him but more indistinct shapes. When he faced forward again, he saw light ahead of him.

The closer he got, the more he was certain it was Afghanistan, and the more his chest tightened with determination. He had to go back there to find out what was so bad that he had no memory of the events.

He was almost there. Except that he seemed to be standing behind a translucent curtain. Beyond it he could see the brown hill he remembered.

He stepped toward it, and then a shadow crossed his path. It resolved itself into a man—Dr. Montgomery.

"Stay out," the doctor ordered.

Confusion swirled in his mind. "You want me to go back there. That's what the bunker was all about."

"You can't go until I say you can. Not until I'm beside you, recording your experiences."

Anger surged, and Jonah answered with a curse. "The hell with you."

He felt Montgomery grabbing the back of his shirt, trying to keep him in the twilight.

He yanked himself free, and suddenly he was through the curtain, walking toward the village. He wasn't alone. Shredder was beside him and Hall and the other men who were part of the rescue operation.

Rescue operation! Yeah, that's what it was. He remembered that now.

They'd come in by helicopter, landing twenty miles from their intended destination to keep the mission secret. They were wearing native garb, not their usual combat outfits.

This was an important covert operation, and Colonel Luntz didn't want anyone getting wind of their presence in the area.

The Colonel had sent them here to pick up Jamal Al Feisal, an al-Qaeda defector with valuable information.

Sweat trickled down the back of Jonah's neck and down his face. He wiped his brow on his sleeve and looked to his left.

"You think somebody's following us?" he asked.

"Naw. It's your nerves jumping," Hall answered. He always had been overconfident.

"Yeah, but I can't shake the feeling that there's someone out there."

He reached in his pocket and pulled out the map they'd been given. There was supposed to be a village just ahead. But he didn't see the damn place.

The map was a piece of crap. Maybe the whole mission was a piece of crap. They'd already made a couple of detours around huge rock formations that weren't supposed to be there.

Shredder looked at him. He could tell his buddy was thinking the same thing. But they couldn't go back. Al Feisal was too big. If they left him here, he'd be killed by his own people who thought he was a traitor. He was counting on Colonel Luntz to hold up his end of the bargain.

Too bad the unit was on radio silence so they couldn't ask for directions.

"What do you think?" Jonah asked.

"Let's see what's over the next ridge," Shredder said.

They plowed ahead, and when they climbed the rise, they could see houses in the rocky landscape. So was this the place where they were supposed to pick up Al Feisal?

If so, there was supposed to be a contact in the village, a young guy who had helped the Americans before—assuming the map was correct and it was the right place.

They started down the slope toward the houses, moving cautiously.

From the village, he heard the sound of music. A foreign melody that could have been a dance tune played on flutes and percussion instruments.

He stopped short.

"Something wrong?" Hall asked.

"I don't know," Jonah answered. But he was lying. The music told him that the bad part was coming. The part he didn't want to remember. He felt his head whipping from side to side as he tried to get away. Still, the images pummeled him.

The gunfire. Men lying on the ground, some of them already dead, some of them screaming in agony.

Through the memories he heard a voice. "Easy."

Jonah gasped, his body jerking as blinding pain shot through his head.

His eyes flew open, and he felt himself shaking as he looked around in disorientation. A moment ago, the Afghan landscape had been spread out in front of him in vivid detail. Now it had vanished.

Not just the landscape. The ambush.

He struggled to grasp on to that memory, but it flitted out of his mind, and he cursed.

When he tried to sit up, he found he was strapped down to some kind of table. He screamed, then screamed again as he looked wildly around, trying to figure out where he was. All he could think was that Montgomery had him. Montgomery was doing something horrible to him.

He heard a door bang open, heard a woman's voice call his name, her panic leaping toward him.

Turning his head, he saw her rush forward, her face contorted with fear.

"Jonah. Oh God, Jonah."

He stared at her. Who was she? Why did she care about him? Was she one of the villagers?

No. He could tell she was an American from her clothing and from her golden hair.

For a terrible moment, he was lost as he scrambled for context. And then memories came flooding back. "Sophia?"

"Yes!"

"What are you doing in Afghanistan?" he asked, even when he knew that the question had no meaning. He wasn't in Afghanistan. He was…

The location wouldn't come to him.

Her voice captured his attention again. And her beautiful eyes—so full of fear. "You know me?" she asked with such urgency that he could tell the answer was important to her.

"Yes. But I don't understand where we are," he managed to say.

"We're at the Randolph Security research facility—in western Maryland."

He tried to take that in, but it wasn't making any sense. He stared at her helplessly.

She leaned over him, loosening the straps that held his hands and feet. He was aware of activity behind him. Turning his head, he saw a man removing some kind of wires from his head.

He stiffened. "What's going on?"

"Jonah, everything's okay. You're okay," she said, but he could tell from her voice that she wasn't sure it was true.

When he tried to leap off the table, someone pressed a firm hand to his shoulder.

"The music," he gasped out, panic almost closing off his windpipe. "The music."

"What music?"

"The woman was playing it. No wait—this time the woman wasn't there." He blinked in confusion, trying to sort through what was real and what wasn't.

Sophia leaned over him, then brushed her mouth gently—so gently—against his. "Let's start with the good part. Do you remember making love with me?" she asked softly.

A sizzle skittered over Jonah's nerve endings.

"Making love with you," he murmured against her lips. "Yes, I remember that." His gaze burned into hers. And he did remember. Making love all those years ago, and a few days ago. It had been wonderful back then, and just as wonderful when he'd found her again.

He stared at her in amazement. "I remember," he said, just to make sure it was true—and that she understood how much it meant to him.

"Good."

He dragged in a breath and let it out. "I mean, not just us. I remember the assignment in Afghanistan." He felt as though a terrible weight had been lifted off his chest as relief flooded through him. "I remember. I can tell you about it."

Chapter Eighteen

Sophia's look of relief almost took his breath away.

"Why is that so important to you?" he murmured.

"Because it's important to *you.*"

When she reached for his hand and linked her fingers with his, he held on tight.

But there were still questions whirling around in his mind. "Why couldn't I remember the mission? What the hell was wrong with me?"

"Did you feel betrayed by Luntz?"

"Yes!"

"That's the key, I think. You had to drive Afghanistan from your mind because the whole thing was such an enormous betrayal of everything you believed in—everything you'd devoted your life to. He was in your chain of command, but he sent you to do something bad."

"We didn't know it was bad."

"Of course not."

His gaze turned inward. "Is that why Montgomery cooked up that false story about Thailand? Because he knew I couldn't let myself go back to Afghanistan?"

"I think so. He knew that was safer for you than reality. He gave you memories that were more acceptable."

When he grimaced, she continued. "Probably he started with the diplomatic mission. And when you wouldn't cooperate, he added the part about you going berserk and endangering everyone—to give you more reason to cooperate with him."

"How did he do all that?" he asked, the question making his mouth so dry that he could hardly speak.

"With mind-altering drugs."

"Just drugs?"

"And techniques to induce the behavior he wanted. Then he started digging back into the Afghanistan mission. Maybe he planted the idea that it was just a dream."

He thought about that. "Yeah, that makes sense," he answered, although deep in his consciousness he felt a small scrap of doubt. He banished it.

"I kept dreaming about it. But not what really happened. I guess I couldn't face it—even in a dream."

"So you twisted it into something else."

"You'd think I'd make it into something good."

She gave a hollow laugh. "Apparently, you couldn't go that far. But when you put Lieutenant Calley into the middle of it, you had someone to blame."

"Yeah." He heaved in a breath and let it out. "So—am I really suffering from post-traumatic stress?"

"Well, not in the classic sense if you list all the symptoms."

"Is that good or bad?"

She shook her head. "We don't need to fool with labels now. Let's just deal with what we have."

He considered that, then said, "Okay. I guess the most important thing is telling you the real story."

"Yes. I want to hear it. But maybe you'd be more comfortable if you put some clothes on first."

He looked down, seeing he was wearing one of those hospital

gowns that left your ass flapping in the breeze when you walked around. "Right. Let me get dressed."

A man came forward. Dr. Valero. And Jonah realized that he and Sophia had been engaged in this private conversation in front of an audience.

"How do you feel?" the doctor asked.

"Fine," he said automatically.

"I want to check you over. Then you can meet with the rest of the team."

Jonah might have objected, but he was pretty sure the doctor was going to insist. So he went back to the exam room, where he got a medical okay.

Half an hour later, dressed in jeans and a Ravens T-shirt, he sat in a comfortable lounge area. Sophia was beside him, holding tightly to his hand, while other men and women were grouped on chairs and couches around him. Apparently they all knew him. Only when Sophia introduced him to each of them, did they became familiar to him.

As he spoke to them, flashes of memory came back to him like waves lapping at a beach when the tide comes in.

These people worked for the Light Street Detective Agency and Randolph Security. They were more than coworkers. They were good friends who were always there for each other.

They'd sent Sophia and a man named Phil Martin into the back door of the bunker to get him out. And now he was going to tell them why he was being held at the bunker.

Some of the pieces were still missing, but he was pretty sure the rest would come back to him when he started talking.

Clearing his throat, he said, "The whole thing was Colonel Luntz's show. He had us detailed to a covert operations unit. Then he created a false mission—something he could put down on the record. He sent us to pick up a guy named Jamal Al Feisal, who was supposed to be an al-Qaeda defector. He said that the guy had information valuable to the War on Terror. But all of that was a lie. He was really an Afghan warlord who was funneling millions of dollars in illegal drug money to Luntz. Well, not just that. Antiquities. Gems and gold that were illegal to export."

Hunter looked as if he was taking that under advisement. "How do you know the cover story was a lie?" he asked. "I mean, how did you get the real story?"

"Because I heard the attackers talking when they thought they'd killed us."

"Back up," Cameron Randolph said. "Who thought they'd killed you?"

"A rival faction. They had a couple of American guys with them. Nixon and Fromer. I guess they were mercenaries who were hired to protect the opium. They were speaking to each other in English, which is why I could understand them."

Sophia made a small sound.

"What?"

"When I hypnotized you, you thought a man named Fromer was at the briefing with you. He attacked you."

"Yeah, he attacked me. But not at the briefing. In Afghanistan. I guess I still had that jumbled up."

She nodded.

"They were working for a rival warlord who was getting ready to kill Al Feisal. He'd found out he was in danger and wanted out. That's why he contacted Luntz—who sent us in to rescue a guy we thought was a defector. They shot us all, including Al Feisal."

Jonah had to stop and swallow as the gruesome scene came flashing back to him. The blood, the heat, the flies. The shock and horror had penetrated his soul. He hadn't been able to deal with the enormity of it, so he'd turned it into something else.

But he remembered everything now.

He kept his voice even when he said, "The rest of the unit was dead, and the bad guys thought I was, too. I was shot and bleeding, and I had blood on me from the other men. Then, when it got dark, somehow I got out of there and into a cart that was leaving the area. I ended up in a friendly village and was eventually turned over to the Americans. The villagers thought they were doing the right thing, but Luntz swept in and got custody of me. As far as anybody knows, I'm still missing in action."

"And Luntz is afraid you're going to tell what happened to the rest of the team," Sophia said.

Jonah laughed, and it wasn't a pleasant sound. "He could have killed me right away if that was all he wanted. He was going to do that to shut me up, but before he could, I got out of there with the money and the treasure. He wants to know where I hid it."

A babble of voices broke out in the room. When it calmed down, Sophia asked, "You know where the loot is?"

"Yeah, I do," he said with satisfaction. Then he realized the victory wouldn't do him much good. "He's going to hunt me down and kill me. And kill you," he said in a strangled voice.

"No," she answered.

"He's desperate, and he's got a private army working for him. Guys who were in the military. Badass guys. I'll bet a lot of them were dishonorably discharged, but he offered them a job because he valued their skills."

"Why didn't he send his own men to pick up Al Feisal?" Hunter asked.

"Because he couldn't get them certified. Remember, they were already known troublemakers. So Luntz had to work through official channels."

"Couldn't they use false names?" Sophia asked.

"Not with their fingerprints on records."

"He thinks he's got the upper hand, but we've got the resources to stop him," Cam said in a hard voice. "So let's start planning our operation. Starting with a visit to his house."

Jonah looked around at the men and women in the room, seeing the determination on their faces. He remembered that he hadn't trusted them. Now he understood that they were his friends—and the key to whether or not he could rescue Sophia from the nightmare he'd dragged her into.

SOPHIA WAITED with Jonah and some of the others for a report from Max Dakota, who had taken a team to the Luntz house. While she waited, she made her own plans.

The bad news came when Max and the team returned by helicopter. "He's gone. Cleared out."

As she and Jonah exchanged glances, Max continued talking. "The place is empty. We got inside, and there's no indication of where he went."

"Great," Jonah muttered.

"My guess is that you shook him up with that invasion into his turf. He's obviously worried that you'll come after him again, and the next time, you won't bother with talking."

"Funny thing," Jonah answered. "It sounds like a Mexican standoff. I can't find him as long as he's hiding, and as long as I hole up here, he can't find me." He glanced at Sophia, who was sitting beside him on the sofa. "Or you, either."

She nodded tightly, waiting for Max to finish his report. When he was done, she cleared her throat.

"What?" Jonah asked.

"I have an idea."

"You mean like when you thought of strolling into his house and telling him you were a psychologist working with me?"

She kept her gaze steady. "No. This time you're the one who has the major role."

"Let's hear it," Hunter said.

She continued to stare at Jonah. "What if you can convince him you're no threat to him?"

"Like how?" he demanded.

"Like you're in such bad mental shape that you can barely function. You escaped, and now you don't know what the hell to do. You're paranoid. You think everybody's after you. You just want this nightmare to be over." She gulped. "I've left you high and dry because you're so whacked up that…that you attacked me. All you want is to get back into the bunker so Montgomery can make the pain and confusion in your head go away. But you don't know how to find the front entrance to the place. So you're out in the West Virginia woods, looking for the back way in, through the cave. But you can't find that, either."

She dragged in a breath as everyone in the room stared at her.

"It might work," Jed Prentiss said.

"But it's dangerous," Sophia admitted. "You'd have to…" She stopped and started again. "Jonah, you'd have to make yourself a target."

"Whatever it takes, it's worth it," he growled. "Pretending to be a mess isn't going to be so difficult."

She took her lower lip between her teeth. She wanted some private time with him. She knew he wanted her, physically, just as she ached to kiss him. Just a kiss—if that was all he was willing to give her.

But he built a wall between them again. She understood why. He still thought he was dangerous. He didn't know what the future held for him, and he was afraid to let himself reach for happiness. There was nothing she could do about any of that—not until Luntz and Montgomery were rounded up.

While all that churned in her head, Cameron began speaking. "Okay, let's get the sting operation set up."

"We should start with a phone call," Jed added.

"To his house, even when we know he's split?" Jonah asked.

"Yeah, because *you* don't know that. And there's no evidence that we were there."

"Did he have security cameras?"

Max laughed. "His security system had a malfunction."

Jonah grinned, and Sophia could see that he liked these people and trusted them.

"Before you make any calls, we have to decide what you're going to say," Sophia told him.

She'd thought that might give her some time alone with him while they did some planning. But he thwarted her plans by quickly saying, "You and Kathryn can coach me."

JONAH WAS dead tired.

He, Sophia and Kathryn had found a smaller room where they could work on his monologue. Now, two hours later, he figured he was as ready as he'd ever be. And Randolph Security was also ready with a special hookup to a prepaid cell phone.

With Sophia beside him, he walked back to the lounge. Jed, Cam and Kathryn gathered around him as he dialed the number.

As he expected, he didn't get Luntz himself, only voice mail. When it beeped, he went into the monologue he'd rehearsed.

After a string of fiery expletives, he finally got around to saying something semicoherent.

"You're not there! Where the hell are you? I need to talk to you." He stopped and swallowed. "Oh yeah, right. Forgot to say. This is…this is Jonah Baker," he said, his voice making it clear that just saying his name required a tremendous effort. "I…I'm in trouble. And I need your help. Please, call me back. The number is…."

He gave the number of the cell phone, then gulped. "I feel like my brain is on fire. Do you know what that's like?" he shouted, then added another string of curses for good measure. When he was finished with the blast, he apologized with a shaky, "Sorry."

He paused for effect, then went on. "Listen, I can't hold a thought for more than a few seconds. Please, I need some more of that medication I was taking. That made me feel better. I want to hook up with Dr. Montgomery, but I don't know how to reach him, and I don't know how to get back to the bunker. I went down to West Virginia and started searching, but I'm so turned around that I can't find my ass with a flashlight."

He glanced at Sophia.

"Good," she mouthed.

He gave her an apologetic look. "That chick who got me out of the bunker—she left me high and dry. Just because I roughed her up a little. She said I was crazy as a bedbug, and she couldn't take it anymore. She told me I needed medical treatment. I didn't want to believe her, but now I think she's right. Only the bitch took off while I was sleeping and she didn't even leave me with any meds," he whined, going back to the previous topic. "I can't handle this. I need help. If Dr. Montgomery is willing to take me back, I'll do anything he wants. He said hypnosis could help me. I didn't want to do it before, but I'll try anything. Please, call me back." He gave the number again, then hung up.

"Now we wait to see what he says," Cam said.

"And if he doesn't respond?"

"Then we go to plan B."

"Which is?"

"We'll figure that out if and when we need to."

Jonah leaned back and closed his eyes. He was completely wiped out.

"You should get some sleep," Sophia murmured.

He didn't have the strength to object.

"When Luntz calls, you can talk to him and we'll monitor the conversation," Cam said.

Jonah nodded, then looked around. "I don't even know where I'm bunking."

"I'll show you," Jed said.

He followed Jed down the hall to a room with a double bed. He half expected Sophia to barge in after him, but when she didn't appear, he figured she was giving him some space.

He fell onto the bed with his clothes on and was instantly asleep. This time, there were no dreams.

SOPHIA PACED back and forth in the hall. She knew Jonah had to sleep. But she also knew that he could have asked her to share the room with him.

She walked past his door and stopped, thinking that she could go in and lie down next to him. That way, he'd have to speak to her when he woke up. Or maybe not. Maybe Luntz would wake him up, and then he'd have to be on his toes.

Other people at the complex passed her in the hall. She tried to return their greetings, but it was difficult to focus on anything else besides Jonah.

He had been through a horrible ordeal, and it wasn't over yet. In fact, she'd suggested that he put himself in danger. But she knew it was necessary and not just for the reason she'd given everyone. Montgomery and Luntz had damaged Jonah's self-esteem. They'd used him in the worst possible way, first by sending him on that mission and then by screwing with his mind. They'd intended to get what they wanted out of him—then kill him.

Well, he'd escaped from the damn bunker. Now he needed to show them that he was the winner in this situation.

Once he proved to himself that he was back in charge of his life, they could deal with their relationship.

What if Jonah walked away from her again when this was all over? That would be like a kind of death.

She clenched her fists. It was all she could do to stop herself from charging into his room, waking him and demanding that he tell her what he intended when he had his life back.

But she knew he wouldn't give her the answer. Not yet.

Was he smart enough to realize that the two of them belonged together and had always belonged together? Or would he throw their future away because he thought he wasn't good enough for her?

All she could do was pray that he came to the right conclusions.

Chapter Nineteen

Jonah sat up with a start.

Something was jangling in his head.

Music?

His stomach clenched.

No. Not music. It was the cell phone ringing.

It must be Luntz. Nobody else besides Sophia had the number.

Glancing at the clock, he saw that the colonel had waited six hours before responding.

He rubbed his eyes and cleared his throat. Then, feeling better than he had in days, he picked up the phone. "Colonel Luntz?"

The man on the other end of the line drew in a quick breath. Jonah could imagine him rearing back. "How do you know who this is?"

"I didn't know." He lowered his voice. "I was praying you'd call me back."

"Where are you?"

He gave a hollow laugh. "I'm not *that* stupid. I'm where you can't find me—unless I want you to."

"I wouldn't count on that."

Jonah glanced up as Cam came into the room and sat down in the easy chair. Sophia stood in the doorway. They'd both been waiting for the call, too. The phone volume was turned up so both of them could hear the other end of the conversation.

Jonah swore. "If you can trace this call, maybe I should hang up."

"No! Wait. We can help you," Luntz said.

He shoveled despair into his voice. "Sometimes I think nobody can help me."

"The problem is, that girl screwed with your mind."

"You said it!"

"I can take care of her for you."

"Like how?"

"She left her fingerprints in the bunker. We know her name. She's Sophia Rhodes. She's supposed to be working for the Howard County Mental Health Department." He made a deprecating sound. "But she took a leave of absence to go and get herself into trouble. Who's she really working for?"

Jonah's skin went cold. He glanced at Sophia, knowing his expression looked sick. "She didn't tell me."

"And now she's disappeared," Luntz said. "We know you grew up in the same town. Ellicott City, Maryland. Is she your lover? Is that why she got you out of that bunker? And how did she do it?"

He glanced across the room at Sophia. This was a development he hadn't expected. "She said she vacationed in the area. She knew about the cave entrance."

"Ah. But how did she know you were there?"

"She didn't tell me. I think someone paid her to do it."

"How do I know you're being straight with me?"

"What do I have to do to convince you?"

"Meet me at the location of my choice. Come alone."

Jonah heaved in a breath and let it rush out. "How do I know I can trust you to help me?"

"You don't."

His curses ranged over the phone line. "I don't know if this is such a good idea. Maybe you're after me, too."

"And maybe I'm the only one who can save you," Luntz said.

"Screw you," Jonah answered and pressed the "off" button.

He looked at Cam and Sophia. "He'll call back. He wants me bad."

"Yeah," Cam agreed.

Jonah pressed his hands against the mattress to keep them steady. He was shaken, and he knew Sophia could see his reaction. The conversation had taken more out of him than he'd expected.

Sophia took a step into the room, and he stiffened.

"Are you okay?" she asked.

"Yeah," he answered, praying it was true. He had to do this. It was the only way they could get Luntz.

Was he up to playing his part? He had to be. Yet a tiny splinter of doubt had lodged in his brain. He had remembered Afghanistan. Everything should be okay. Yet he was afraid to trust that the rest of it was going to work out.

"Maybe you want to take a shower and shave," Sophia murmured.

"Do I look that bad?"

"You look like you'd feel better if you cleaned up."

"Yeah. But I'd better not shave. I've got to look like a wreck when I meet Luntz."

"Right. I wasn't thinking about that. Take a shower and change your clothes. Then we can eat."

"If I can swallow anything."

Sophia laughed. "They made you some chicken soup. That should be easy enough."

She was right. He did feel better after showering, brushing his teeth and eating. The soup was good. But he had to wait three long hours for that bastard Luntz to call back. And he couldn't stop himself from pacing back and forth across the lounge as he waited.

When the cell phone finally rang, he snatched it up. "Hello?"

"I have a counteroffer," Luntz said.

"It better be good," Jonah growled.

THE NEGOTIATIONS went on for the next two days, with Jonah coming across as a man at the end of his rope, a man who was willing to do anything to stop the pain in his head. But still a man who was afraid to show himself.

He was pretty sure Luntz didn't trust him, but he was the key to a great deal of money and treasure that the colonel thought he deserved. Too, Jonah had information that could hang Luntz, which meant the colonel had to deal.

Jonah said he was afraid to travel far, making it sound as though he was deteriorating. If the colonel didn't get to him soon, he would be too whacked out to do anyone any good.

They finally settled on a meeting place in the Prince William National Forest.

The Light Street team scoped out the area, then dug themselves in where they couldn't be detected. By the time Luntz sent his men to reconnoiter, it looked safe.

Or that's what Jonah was hoping by two in the afternoon— the appointed meeting time—as he waited on a gravel road by a sign that said, "For law enforcement purposes, the right side of the road is West Virginia and the left side is Virginia."

Jonah turned in a full circle, his eyes probing the forest, wondering if one of Luntz's men was already watching him.

He looked like a man who'd been sleeping rough. His beard was growing out and he had on grubby clothes. He also had a Glock in his hand—for all the good that was going to do him. Still, he knew that the nut he was portraying would never come unarmed.

There was no time for self-doubt now. They had planned every detail of this operation.

Of course, Luntz was probably thinking the same thing.

Jonah heard tires crunching on gravel a long way off, and his hand began to shake.

Good, he told himself. That would add to the verisimilitude.

Two Land Rovers pulled up on the Virginia side of the road. The windows were all darkly tinted, so that he couldn't see inside. He stood with his heart pounding as the back door of one opened, and Luntz got out. He wondered how many other men were in the vehicles.

"Major Baker."

"Colonel Luntz."

"Good to see you again."

Jonah shifted his weight from one foot to the other.

"You asked for my help."

"Yes."

"Put the gun away."

"I feel more comfortable holding it."

"You understand why I don't."

Jonah shrugged.

"Let's go to a safe place where we can get you the help you need."

Jonah looked around at the forest. "This is a safe place."

The colonel followed his gaze. "Not for me. But if you insist, we can secure the area." He waved his hand, and more car doors opened. Six men in blue uniforms got out. Men he remembered seeing in the bunker. They stood with their backs to the cars, automatic weapons pointed in all directions.

"Ambush," Jonah shouted, taking a step toward the side of the road, cowering back, making it look as though he was terrified out of his mind.

"Take it easy," Luntz ordered.

"Afghanistan was an ambush."

"What the hell are you talking about?" the colonel demanded.

"You wanted Jamal Al Feisal to give you the money from the opium trade, but another warlord was way ahead of you."

Luntz goggled at him. "How do you know about that?"

"I remembered. That was the thing I didn't tell you." He giggled like a maniac about to crack in two. "That's what you really wanted, wasn't it? The money."

"You couldn't have remembered. That was part of the conditioning for the mission. Your memory was supposed to be wiped the moment you finished. That's why we had to dig it out of you."

Jonah stared at him, then swore. "You screwed with our minds before we left for Afghanistan?"

"Yes," Luntz hissed.

As he stood there—vulnerable and exposed—Jonah scrambled to assimilate this new information. Sophia had suggested a perfectly reasonable explanation for what had happened to him. She'd thought he couldn't deal with what had really happened. But there had been no way for her to know what Luntz had actually done to him and the other men.

"I didn't finish the mission," he croaked, giving a reason for why his memory had suddenly come back.

"Who else did you tell about this?"

Jonah stared at him. The man had already implicated himself in something illegal, but Jonah wanted enough on tape so that the Defense Department would have the information they'd hired Light Street to obtain.

He was planning what he was going to say next when a sound stopped him dead. From inside one of the Land Rovers he heard musical notes. An Afghan dance tune, such as they might play at a village celebration.

"No," he shouted, clapping his hands over his ears.

Dr. Montgomery stepped out the back door, holding a metal box. He closed the car door behind him and thrust the box toward Jonah. It must have had some kind of recording device inside, because when the doctor turned a dial, the music grew louder, faster.

"No," Jonah screamed, going down on his knees.

Luntz turned to the other man. "You said it would disable him, but it's hard to believe it works. How could music do that?"

"Part of the treatment." Montgomery laughed. "A nice little method for controlling him. I implanted the trigger when I gave him the false memories of the assignment in Thailand. Whenever he heard the music, he'd go incoherent."

"But he remembers Afghanistan."

Luntz came forward and took the gun from Jonah's hand, tucking it into his own belt. Jonah looked up at him with watery eyes. He tried to crawl away, tried to get away from the tune.

But Luntz stepped in front of him, blocking his escape. "Too bad I didn't have that music box when you came to my house. This charade would all be over by now. We'd have the money, the treasure, all of it. We could already have gotten rid of you."

Still down on his knees, Jonah fought for coherence. "You killed those men," he shouted. "The other men on the patrol with me. You killed them."

Luntz waved his hand. "Collateral damage. That wasn't how I planned it. You were supposed to come back, then forget about what had happened—and Dr. Montgomery would give you false memories. I had no way of knowing another warlord was going after Al Feisal." He came down beside Jonah. "I'd like to kill you now. But not until you tell me where you hid the damn loot."

Jonah struggled to make his mind work, despite the jangly tune threatening to blot out coherent thought.

"We'll get the information out of you, then we'll put you

out of your misery. Where is the money and the treasure?" Luntz demanded.

"Screw you."

Montgomery brought the music box closer to Jonah's head, and he screamed in pain.

The doctor's leering face loomed over his. "Are you trying to pull something on us?"

Fighting for control of his tongue, Jonah managed to get out one syllable, "No."

And then above them, the treetops exploded in a series of concussions that blotted out the sound of the music.

The men in blue uniforms were instantly on the alert, raising their guns, pointing toward the threat in the trees. But they didn't know that the concussions were no more than fireworks.

A diversion.

"What the hell…" Luntz shouted and jumped back, heading for the safety of the car. But Montgomery had closed the door when he got out. As they fought to open it, Jonah scrambled to his feet and leaped forward, grabbing for the box.

The tune almost robbed him of thought. He had only one goal—making it go away.

Montgomery flailed at him with one hand, grasping the box tightly with the other.

Jonah snatched at it, the music making his movements jerky. It felt as if hours were dragging by, though it was probably only seconds.

Finally he wrenched the box from the doctor's grasp, threw it to the ground and stamped on it with his boot, crushing the thin metal sides.

The music stopped, and the blessed relief was like the sound of angels' wings beating around him.

Then, from the woods, a curtain of choking smoke enveloped all of them.

The men around Jonah began to cough. Jonah himself was immune because of an injection Thorn had given him earlier.

He knew he had won. Still, he needed the personal satisfaction of socking Montgomery on the jaw, watching the man gasp in pain as he went down.

The colonel had gotten the car door open. Jonah yanked his hand away and whirled him around.

"Damn you," Luntz shouted between coughing fits. "Damn you. It was a perfect plan to bring the money and the treasure back to the U.S. And you spoiled it."

More men poured onto the road, the men from the Light Street Detective Agency and Randolph Security, but there were others with them. Operatives from the special Department of Defense unit that had asked them to find out what kind of illegal operation Luntz was running in Afghanistan.

They were the ones who hustled the colonel, Dr. Montgomery and their men into secure vehicles that pulled up behind the Land Rovers.

Sophia came running out of the woods, and he knew she must also be protected from the smoke. Still he gasped when he saw her.

"I told you to stay out of this," he choked out.

"I wasn't going to leave you here alone."

He looked from her to the receding vehicles.

"It's really over," she said, punching out the words. He swung back toward her, his face registering disbelief.

"It's over," she said again. "Believe it."

"Did you hear the part about their planting a trigger in our minds before we left?"

"Yes. I'm sorry. I didn't think of anything like that."

"Who would?" He considered that for a moment, then

laughed. "I guess they thought they were so clever—giving us a command to forget. Then the mission blew up in our faces, and they got me back. But they'd made it so I couldn't remember."

"So they had to set up the whole bunker scenario to pry the information out of you." She took his arm and led him away from the smoke to a shelter that the Light Street men had commandeered. Part of a Defense Department installation that had been built in the area years ago, it was underground, dug into the forest floor and invisible unless you bumped into one of the ventilator shafts.

Cam Randolph had studied the area, which was why he had suggested the meeting place, and Jonah had knocked down all of the colonel's proposals, insisting that he had to meet on this road.

Sophia switched on the light, then closed the door behind them before turning to face Jonah.

"Are you all right?" she asked.

"Yes."

"That music! Oh God, that music. You were talking about music when you woke up from Thorn's treatment. I should have paid attention to you."

His face turned grim. "You couldn't know Montgomery was using something like that. I didn't understand the implications. Nobody could," he said, softening his voice.

She kept her gaze on him. "In case you haven't figured it out, the bad stuff is over," she said, her tone very sure and authoritative.

He stared at her, trying to take it in. Was he really free from the nightmare of Afghanistan? The nightmare of the bunker? Of Montgomery's diabolical interrogation methods?

She kept her gaze fixed on him. "So you have no more excuses."

"Excuses for what?"

"For turning away from me," she said in a strangled voice. "To make it perfectly clear, I mean, either you admit you love me and we go on to make up for all the years we lost, or you walk away because you can't stand the idea of the two of us being happy together."

He swallowed hard, then said the words. "I love you."

"Thank God."

"But I'm no good for you," he said, in the spirit of full disclosure.

"Of course you are. You were ten years ago and you still are. We loved each other back then, but neither one of us could admit it. And since then, no relationship has ever worked for either one of us."

He silently nodded in agreement.

"We belong together. We always have."

"Yes, but you have a PhD. I'm—"

"A patriot. A man with his feet on the ground. A man with values I admire. A man with courage and strength."

"You make me sound like…a saint."

She laughed. "Hardly. Thank the Lord, you're a human being, with flaws. But I know your strengths are greater than your weaknesses. I knew that back in high school."

"You might be overestimating me."

"No. As you said, I'm a trained psychologist. I'm a very good judge of people. So stop looking for excuses to back away from me. "I love you, but I can be objective."

He stared at her. "But—"

To keep him from saying anything he might regret, she reached out, brought his head down to hers and pressed her mouth to his. When she did, all the emotions he'd been holding in check exploded through him.

It was as if someone had finally given him permission to be happy. Or maybe he'd given himself permission. Finally, after all the years of missing her.

She was in his arms and nothing was keeping them apart. Not anymore. He kissed her with all the passion that had been pent up inside him since they'd arrived at the Randolph research facility. She kissed him back with the same intensity, her mouth moving under his, opening so that she could taste him with greedy enthusiasm.

As her hands stroked over his back, down his body, pulling his hips against hers, his did the same, touching her everywhere he could reach.

The need for her burned through his blood, and he was about to raise his head and look for a place where he could make love with her when the door slammed open.

They both looked up in shock to see Max Dakota staring at them. He grinned.

"Sorry."

Jonah stayed where he was, his arm protectively around Sophia.

"Cam wanted to make sure you were okay."

"Yeah, I am."

"We've moving out. Unless you want to spend the night here, you've got five minutes." Max grinned again and stepped back outside.

Jonah dragged in a breath and let it out.

Sophia laughed. "I can walk in front of you, if you want."

"I'll be okay in a minute—as long as I know there's a bed waiting for us in the very near future."

She laced her fingers with his. "Oh, yeah."

He dragged in several more breaths and ran his free hand through his hair. "Okay. Let's go."

The rest of the Randolph–Light Street group was waiting in several vehicles that had been hidden in an underground garage.

"Ride with me," Cam Randolph said.

They both climbed into the back of his SUV, and he pulled away.

"We were a little worried back there," Cam said, "when Montgomery pulled his stunt with the music box."

"Luntz wasn't going to kill me until I told him where to find the money and the treasure."

"Luckily, because he sure looked like he wanted to."

Sophia winced.

Cam drove through the national forest, then headed north.

"You did a fantastic job of getting Luntz and Montgomery to talk. The military will be able to go back to the area where he sent you and get the loot. And the villagers can verify what happened. So it's over for you, except testifying at the trials."

"Yeah," Jonah murmured. "And I'd say my military career is over, too. It may be illogical, but I'll never trust the chain of command again."

"But you trust us," Cam said.

"I know that now," Jonah answered.

"Good. Because I was hoping you'd join our organization. We've got a lot of ex-military and ex-spies. You're just the kind of guy we need, and you obviously fit right in."

Jonah took a breath. "I…"

"You don't have to give me your answer right away. But I did talk to the Defense Department, and they're willing to expedite your army discharge—if that's what you want."

Jonah felt his chest expand. "I don't have to think about it. I know the answer. I felt at home the moment I sat down and started talking to all of you."

"Good."

Sophia gripped his hand tightly. When he looked at her, she smiled.

He pulled her close, and she leaned her head against his shoulder.

"It's over," she murmured. "I can hardly believe it."

"No, it's just beginning," he said, feeling happier than he had since the night he'd first made love with her. There was so much he wanted to say to her, but not in front of anyone else—even his friends.

Still, he knew by the warm look in her eyes that she was on his wave length. As soon as they were alone, he was going to start making up for all the lonely years. She grinned at him and he grinned back, sure that the rest of his life would be so much different from anything that had gone before—except for that one glorious night that had kept him going for all these years.

"Happy?" she whispered.

"Yes."

"Well, I predict you ain't seen nothin' yet."

SEDUCING THE MERCENARY

BY

LORETH ANNE WHITE

Loreth Anne White was born and raised in southern Africa, but now lives in a ski resort in the moody British Columbian Coast Mountain range. It is a place of vast, wild and often dangerous mountains, larger-than-life characters, epic adventure and romance – the perfect place to escape reality. It's no wonder it was here she was inspired to abandon a sixteen-year career as a journalist to escape into a world of romantic fiction filled with dangerous men and adventurous women.

When she's not writing, you will find her long-distance running, biking or skiing on the trails, and generally trying to avoid the bears – albeit not very successfully. She calls this work, because it's when the best ideas come. For a peek into her world visit her website at www.lorethannewhite.com.

"Nearly all men can stand adversity, but if you want to test a man's character, give him power."
– Abraham Lincoln, 16th American president
(1809–65)

Prologue

15:00 Zulu. Friday, November 8.
Ubasi Palace. West Coast of Africa

"The American embassy is being evacuated—all U.S. citizens are being advised to leave the country at once." The general paused. Silence permeated the room and hung heavy in the equatorial heat.

Jean-Charles Laroque nodded at his aide and walked slowly over the vast stone floor of his war room, toward the long arched windows cut into the walls of the palace he'd called home since he'd taken Ubasi by force just over a year ago. His leather boots squeaked softly, and his black dog, Shaka, moved like a shadow at his heels.

He clasped his hands behind his back and surveyed the dense jungle canopy that undulated for miles beyond the walls of his fortress, toward distant mountains shrouded in afternoon haze.

Four Americans had been killed in Ubasi, allegedly geologists with a Nigerian oil concern.

The killings had occurred simultaneously in different parts of Ubasi. The bodies had been gutted and strung from trees, left in the steaming sun for predators, *exactly* the same way his father used to exhibit his kills as warning to his foes.

Laroque's mouth turned bone-dry.

This had clearly been a coordinated operation, and it had clearly been intended to frame *him.*

As hard as he'd tried to shed the stigma of being the son of infamous South African-born mercenary Peter Laroque, the notoriety of his late father proved impossible to shake. And it followed him now with this gruesome display of bodies.

He pursed his lips in concentration.

On the heels of these murders had come even more disturbing news. His rebel allies who controlled the northern reaches of the Ubasi jungles had crossed into neighboring Nigeria, where they had raided the barracks of a U.S. oil corporation security outfit and captured five employees. Laroque's rebels maintained *these* captives were the killers of the Americans. They also maintained that the four dead geologists were in fact CIA agents who had been poking around Laroque's oil concessions in the north.

Laroque had been given nothing to prove this, just the word of his rebel leader with whom he had now lost contact as the cadre had entered the dense jungle at the foothills of the Purple Mountains. When the rebels reached base camp in a few days, word would be sent to Laroque and he could go and interrogate the captives himself. But until then, he had nothing.

He cursed softly in his native African-French.

Ubasi had just been welcoming back tourists. The U.S. embassy had recently reopened with two officers offering basic emergency service. Foreign currency was trickling in again. Telecommunications were gradually being restored. Even the electrical supply was becoming slightly more reliable. The war-torn economy was actually picking up for the first time in fifty years.

Now those same tourists were being told to evacuate.

And if those dead Americans were indeed CIA operatives, and if Washington thought Laroque was personally responsible for their deaths, that he had killed them as some kind of warning to the superpower to stay out of "his" country, and away from "his" oil, then some major form of retaliation was certain.

Ubasi was set to blow.

Adrenaline hummed through Laroque's blood as he turned to face the general, his dark mahogany skin gleaming in the equatorial heat. He touched Shaka's fur as he spoke.

"Contact every single foreigner who obtained a visa from the immigration office within the past six months," he commanded his general. "Order them all out. Shut the borders. I want as few innocent lives lost as possible."

Innocent lives like his sister's. Like her small children.

Bitterness filled his throat. It was always the innocent who suffered in this business of war. His business.

"There is also that science team sponsored by Geographic International—"

The image of the woman he'd seen in the street earlier that day once again took haunting shape in Laroque's mind. She'd stood out like a siren among the crowds that had gathered to greet him. Something about her had unsettled Laroque deeply. It was the way her violet eyes had looked at him, right *into* him. Cool fingers of warning raked through him, indistinct like mist over a jungle swamp. He blew them off sharply.

Perhaps she was part of the science team, perhaps not. It didn't matter. Either way she and every other foreigner would be out of his country by nightfall.

Laroque checked his watch. "The team should have landed in Ubasi nine hours ago. Turn them round, tell them they no longer have my sanction for their study."

"If they refuse?"

"Anyone who has not left for the airport by curfew hour tonight is to be brought here to the castle. Tell them it's for their own safety—Ubasi could turn into a war zone at any moment."

Laroque watched the heavy doors swing shut behind his general, and he clenched his jaw.

Someone was trying to manipulate him into a violent confrontation with the United States. He needed to know who and why, and he needed to know ASAP. If anyone defied his orders to leave Ubasi, he wanted them in his palace and under his watch, because it might just give him a lead, some small clue as to what the hell was going down.

And God help anyone trying to undermine him. Laroque would sacrifice *nothing* for his dream of freedom now. Because he had nothing left to lose.

And that made him the most dangerous kind of man.

Chapter 1

Nine hours earlier. 06:02 Zulu. Friday, November 8. Ubasi airport. West Coast of Africa

Perspiration dampened Dr. Emily Carlin's blouse as she neared one of two customs checkpoints.

There was no electricity in the cramped Ubasi arrivals room this morning. Fans hung motionless from the ceiling, the only light in the terminal coming from doors flung open to white-hot sunlight. Even at this early hour everyone was already dulled into slow motion by the rising temperatures and humidity.

The line of passengers shuffled slowly forward and Emily moved with it, people jostling her on all sides. She'd been informed Ubasi possessed no

X-ray equipment and the additional lack of power made it even less likely they'd find the knife strapped to her ankle under her jeans.

It was small protection, but she didn't expect much trouble. Her mission was simply to get into the beleaguered war-torn country wedged between Nigeria and Cameroon and assess the sociological situation. Most importantly, she was to compile a psychological profile of notorious mercenary Jean-Charles Laroque, known on this continent as Le Diable, a fierce and deadly guerrilla war expert, master military strategist, and now, a dictator.

She had exactly one week to do her job. Laroque's life depended on her assessment.

Just over twelve months ago the Parisian-born Laroque had sailed into Ubasi on a Spanish boat with a scruffy black Alsatian at his side, a rough band of mercenaries under his command, and a cache of black market weapons in his hold. After putting up a weak fight, the beleaguered Ubasi army had surrendered to Laroque.

Xavier Souleyman—the despot who had overthrown Ubasi's King Douala eight years previously and ruled the country with a bloody hand ever since—had escaped Laroque's capture and fled the country with the aid of a small band of loyalists.

Laroque had wasted no time moving into the royal palace, installing himself as de facto leader, and after negotiating with the rebels who had seized control of the northern jungles of Ubasi during

Souleyman's reign, Laroque had assumed *personal* ownership of massive tracts of land where his geologists had proceeded to strike oil—enough to potentially rival production in *both* Nigeria and Equatorial Guinea combined.

That fact alone had catapulted the once-forgotten country and renegade warlord instantly onto the world stage.

In less than a year Laroque had managed to broker unheard-of treaties with disparate rebel factions over the border in Nigeria and Equatorial Guinea—radical militants who opposed their own corrupt governments' financial ties with Western corporate interests in the Gulf of Guinea.

This placed Laroque in an exceedingly powerful anti-status-quo position. He now had the power to spark a major civil war in the region that could cut off oil supply to the rest of the world for decades to come—oil that had recently become critical to U.S. foreign policy, given the current tensions in the Gulf of Arabia.

On top of this, four deep cover CIA agents in Ubasi had just been slaughtered, their bodies displayed using the same gruesome signature technique once employed by Laroque's mercenary father as he'd cut an increasingly bloody swath across the continent before meeting his own violent end two years ago.

Laroque seemed to be sending a message to the U.S.: *Get out. Stay out. Or else.*

And here Emily was going in.

She mopped her brow with a damp and tattered

tissue as the queue inched forward again and heat pressed down.

Emily was a Manhattan-based expert in tyrannical pathology with a military background of her own. The minds of dictators, organized crime bosses, renegade warlords and murderous despots were both her passion and her professional specialty. Alpha Dogs, she called them.

She'd been contracted by the Force du Sable, a private military company based off the West Coast of Angola, to profile this particular Alpha Dog. The FDS in turn had been retained by a CIA-Pentagon task force in a clandestine bid to control the Laroque "situation." His threat in the region was becoming too great for corporate and political comfort.

The U.S., however, could in no way be overtly involved in a bid to oust the new Ubasi tyrant. Nor could the CIA trust its own at the moment—the source of the intelligence leak that had resulted in the deaths of the four CIA agents represented a grave internal security breach, which was why the FDS had been brought in.

Emily's assessment of *Le Diable* would be used by the FDS to formulate strategy. She needed to identify where the tyrant's psychological weaknesses lay—and in her experience, they *always* lay somewhere—and she had to pinpoint what fired him. While much was known about Laroque's military exploits in Africa, virtually nothing was known about the man himself.

No one knew what made him tick.

Emily's job was to figure out what did.

She also needed to ascertain whether taking him captive would exacerbate an already volatile situation in the Gulf. To do this, she'd have to determine how his subjects viewed him—as evil despot, or charismatic leader. Tyrants wore both stripes, and the last thing the U.S. wanted was to make the man a martyr.

If taking Laroque prisoner was not an option in Emily's opinion, the result would be death by assassination before midnight on Thursday, November 14.

Meanwhile, a team of FDS operatives was infiltrating Ubasi from the north. They would gauge the power of the exiled Souleyman faction, and start negotiations to back Souleyman in another coup to overthrow Ubasi. The FDS team on the ground would also get Emily out of Ubasi if she ran into trouble.

Emily didn't like the idea of swapping one murderous tyrant for another, but the U.S. did. Souleyman was easy to control. Laroque wasn't.

The oil business made strange bedfellows, she thought as she removed her water bottle from her bag, but politics was not her concern. Her sole interest was the Alpha Dog.

But while Alpha Dogs like Laroque were her intellectual thrill, they were also highly unstable—and dangerous. And she hadn't been on a mission for a while.

A combination of anticipation and anxiety shimmered through her stomach as the queue inched closer to the customs checkpoint. She uncapped her water bottle and took a swig of the warm contents.

She could not afford to screw this one up.

She couldn't afford to screw *anything* up. She'd left enough of a personal mess in Manhattan as it was. She *needed* this job. And she needed to do it right—for both professional and personal reasons.

Her nerves tightened as she glanced at the line of passengers on her left, the one with the rest of the Geographic International science crew—her cover. It was moving much faster.

She'd been separated from them by a soldier who called himself the "document man" and roughly shunted to the line on the right. Emily wondered if she'd have been assigned to the faster queue if she'd given the "document man" cash. But she was saving her two hundred dollars in bribe money for the big important-looking guy manning the customs booth ahead. She had another two hundred dollars U.S. stashed in her Australian-style bush boots as backup.

Perhaps she should have brought more.

She was uncharacteristically hot and edgy this morning, and it was not a sensation she enjoyed. Emily liked to stay cool and in control—always. She tried to shrug off her uneasiness, putting it down to the pathetic mess she'd left in New York. She was tired, emotionally drained, still reeling from her recent relationship fiasco.

The angry heat of humiliation once again flushed her cheeks. She'd been lured over the boundary between professional and personal, made to look like a fool. It had been a damn stupid mistake, and it would never, ever happen again.

She irritably swiped the sweat off her lip with the base of her thumb. This FDS contract could not have come at a better time. She wanted to put as much physical distance between herself and her ex—if she could even call him that—as humanly possible.

She needed to focus on someone *else's* pathology, not her own.

Emily was almost at the customs booth now, and her pulse quickened. She shot a look at the other line, saw the last of the science team leaving the terminal, and cursed silently.

While FDS leader, Jacques Sauvage, had hastily cobbled together a deal with their sponsors that allowed her to tag on to the Geographic International team, the scientists themselves had no idea why Emily was actually here, and they were under no obligation to coddle her. In fact, they'd been instructed by their sponsor to ask no questions at all. She cursed herself again. She should have forked over the damn bribe.

The customs official motioned for her to approach.

"Passeport?" he commanded in heavy African bass.

She handed it over along with her currency declaration form.

He flipped open her passport, glanced at her photo, looked up and met her eyes.

Her mouth went dry.

He smiled, teeth bright against gleaming ebony

skin. "And what have you got for me today, Dr. Sanford?" he asked in deeply accented English, using her alias.

She slid a hundred dollar bill across the counter, watching his face. He stared at the money, his smile fading.

She pushed another note slowly across the counter. "It's all I have," she said in English.

"Vous êtes Américaine?"

Her heart beat faster. It was patently obvious from her passport what her nationality was, and now he was refusing to speak English. *"Oui, je suis Américaine."*

"Raison de visite?"

A ball of insecurity swelled suddenly in her throat. "I'm here with the Geographic International science team," she said firmly, in English, wishing to hell the crew hadn't left without her. She unfolded and handed him another piece of paper that had the Ubasi palace stamp on it. "See?" She pointed to the signature. "We have permission from the Laroque government."

The official didn't even pretend to look at the piece of paper. His eyes continued to hold hers. "Currency declaration form?"

"I gave it to you, with the passport."

"Non—"

"I did! Look, it's right there," Emily said, pointing.

The man shook his head, raised his hand high above his head and clicked his fingers sharply. Two armed guards left their station at the exit doors and started making their way toward his booth. Emily's heart pounded wildly against her rib cage. "What's going on?" she demanded.

"There is a problem with your currency declaration," the customs official said in French, before turning to the next person in line. *"Passeport, s'il vous plaît?"*

"No, there isn't. Wait! You haven't even looked at my form. You—"

The guards took her arms roughly. *"Venez avec nous."*

Emily jerked back. "Why? Why must I go with you? Where to?"

But the guards hauled her briskly away.

"What about my luggage?" she snapped, dangerously close to losing her temper. "I haven't collected my bags yet."

But they remained mute as they forced her through a crushing crowd of people, all of whom studiously averted their eyes. The reaction of the crowd wasn't lost on Emily. She saw it as a blatant sign of fear of government authority. These people were terrified of Laroque's goons, she thought as the guards forced her into an interrogation room. She whirled round as they shut the door and locked it.

Stay calm. Breathe.

But no matter how Emily tried, she couldn't. The room was airless. The temperature had to be more than 100 degrees, humidity making it worse. Her jeans clung to her legs, her hair stuck to her back, and rivulets of sweat trickled between her breasts. Emily shoved the damp strands of hair back off her face. She *refused* to let this man or his country get the better of her!

She refused to let *any* autocratic male make a fool of her.

The heat of humiliation burned into her cheeks again. Damn, she was displacing her anger and she knew it. She needed to focus on this tyrant, not her ex. That's why she was here. She was a profiler for God's sake. She could do this.

She clenched her jaw, forcing herself to take stock. She still had her knife, her traveler's checks, her satellite phone, camera and, most important—her computer.

Anything she typed or downloaded into her laptop would be relayed via satellite to a monitor on the FDS base on São Diogo Island. It was state-of-the-art military communications technology, and it was how she would file her daily briefs, along with her final report on Laroque.

Just as she was thinking she'd be okay, the door banged open against the wall. Emily jerked in fright, heart pounding right back up into her throat.

The customs official loomed into the room. "I will see your checks and francs." He held out his hand, palm up.

"I…beg your pardon?"

He didn't budge.

Emily reluctantly opened the pouch strapped to her waist and forked over the wad of traveler's checks and francs she'd had to declare on the form.

The man thumbed through the wad slowly, mouthing the amounts as he did. He looked up sharply. "There is a discrepancy. The amount here is not the same as you declared on the form."

"It is. I—"

"This is illegal. You are smuggling currency. You will pay a fine of fifty thousand francs."

"What! That's ridiculous. That's…almost ten thousand dollars. I don't have that kind of money on me!"

"But you can get it, yes? You will have your *passeport* confiscated until you return to the *aéroport* with the francs for me personally, *ça va?*"

Emily looked at him, stunned. Without her passport she was a prisoner in Ubasi. And illegal. She wouldn't be able to obtain the visa all tourists had to buy in Basaroutou within twenty-four hours of landing. This was pure corruption. She cursed viciously under her breath. These men had targeted her because she was American, female, separated from her crew, and because she possessed expensive equipment. She was, in their eyes, a perfect candidate for extortion. And who the hell could she complain to? Their dictator, Jean-Charles Laroque?

She cursed again as the customs official abruptly departed, leaving the door swinging open. A guard waited outside with her bags, which no doubt had been searched.

Emily grabbed them from him as the guard took her arm, marshaled her toward the exit doors, and dumped her and her belongings unceremoniously onto the dusty streets of Basaroutou.

A riot of colors and sounds slammed into her, and for a second she just stood blinking at the chaos. People jostled her on all sides, dressed in everything from swaths of brightly colored fabric to tattered western dress and stark white tunics. Women carrying baskets on their heads hawked the contents, and on crumbling sidewalks vendors peddled everything from exotic fruits and strangely shaped vegetables to mysterious oils in brown bottles and weird-looking shriveled animals.

Poverty was clearly evident, as was a mélange of cultures. But the faces Emily saw were not ones of milling discontent. Her first impression was an air of industry and purpose.

She hadn't expected this, but then virtually nothing was known about Ubasi under Laroque's rule.

She shaded her eyes, sun burning down hot on her dark hair. Most of the buildings were dun-colored and flanked by impossibly tall, dull-green palms that rustled in the hot wind. Cerise bougainvillea clambered up walls pockmarked by years of war and roads were dusty and cratered with disrepair.

Emily squinted into the light as she searched for something that vaguely resembled a roadworthy cab.

Thankfully she still had what was left of her bribe cash in her boots. Passport or not, she had a job to do. She'd contact the FDS from the hotel and see what she could do about getting her papers back.

But as soon as she tried to elbow her way through the people thronging the sidewalks, she sensed a shift in energy that made fine hairs at the base of her scalp stand on end. She stilled, suddenly acutely cognizant.

There was a strange tension in the air. The mass of humanity around her was growing tighter, quieter. A dark anticipation began to throb tangibly through the crowd.

Emily's pulse quickened.

Soldiers were beginning to clear the street and line the road, holding people back with automatic weapons.

The air literally began to crackle with a mounting expectancy. Then the crowds grew suddenly hushed, and now she could hear only the rattle of palm fronds in the wind. Something was coming.

Emily's heart beat faster.

She began to look for exit routes. She knew from experience situations like this had a way of rapidly flaring into extreme violence. But anything vaguely resembling a cab was a good hundred yards off, and the crowds were closing her in even as her brain raced to comprehend what was going on. She was trapped, being wedged and jostled down toward the curb that edged the main street. She gripped her bags tight against her body and peered down the road, trying to see what was happening.

A burst of automatic gunfire suddenly peppered the air, and she jerked back as a convoy of military Jeeps rounded the corner at the bottom of the road. Soldiers triumphantly brandished AK-47s high above their heads, firing with abandon, the sound ricocheting between buildings as the convoy roared up the street.

Emily ducked as the vehicles neared her vantage point, but to her surprise, instead of fleeing in terror, the crowds around her surged forward, singing, ululating, chanting in such a strangely harmonious and resonant chorus it chased shivers over her skin.

Emily slowly stood, awestruck by the elemental effect of the primal sounds on her body.

The first set of Jeeps raced past in a cloud of fine dust. Then the haunting hush returned, silent anticipation thrumming in the humid air. Emily's heart began to pound like a drum as she leaned forward, trying to see all the way down the road.

A large open-topped military vehicle flanked by smaller Jeeps rounded the corner and crept slowly up the street. The crowd was so deathly silent that the only sound above the growl of engines was of the government flags snapping on the hood. As the big Jeep drew closer, Emily saw what they'd been waiting for.

Their leader.

Adrenaline dumped into her blood. She was seeing Le Diable in the flesh for the first time.

Jean-Charles Laroque sat high in the back of the vehicle, regal, utterly confident. Everything about him telegraphed power.

The sleeves of his camouflage shirt had been rolled back to reveal gleaming biceps. His shoulder-length black hair was drawn back into a ponytail of dread-locks that accentuated the aggressive angle of his exotic cheekbones. He wore pitch-black shades under an army beret cocked at a rakish angle over his brow.

At his side sat his faithful Alsatian, Shaka. The dog's fur glistened in the sunlight, its teeth starkly white against a pink tongue as it panted in the heat.

A hot thrill slid sharp and fast through Emily's stomach.

The Jeep drew close, coming right up alongside her, and a strange primal awareness prickled over her skin. Emily could not have looked away if she tried.

Laroque turned his head, slowly scanning the crowd, then his gaze collided with hers. His body tensed visibly. He raised his dark glasses slowly, looked right at her, *into* her, isolating her from the crowd, cutting her from the herd like prey. He was close enough for Emily to see that his eyes were ice-green against burnished mahogany skin, and just as cold, devoid of any humor or glimmer of kindness.

She could barely breathe. Her own eyes watered as she met his gaze, unable to blink. Not wanting to. The crowds around her faded into a distant blur, the silence becoming a deafening buzz as her world narrowed to focus solely on him.

Laroque shifted around in his seat, watching her as his convoy crawled up the road…then he was gone.

Emily stood rooted to the spot, dust settling around her as the crowd erupted in a riot of sound. She tried to catch her breath.

What in hell had just happened here?

This man clearly had the adulation of his people. She hadn't expected that. Nor had she expected the effect he would have on *her*.

She swallowed, suddenly gravely uneasy with what she was about to do, with the very real impact her profile would have on this country, these people and that powerful man.

Because Emily wielded a power of her own.

Her professional judgment could kill him.

In less than one week.

Chapter 2

"They're gone, Jacques. The entire science team had left by the time I arrived at the hotel about two hours ago." Emily spoke in low tones on her encrypted satellite phone from her hotel room, hot wind whipping through the ragged banana leaves outside her window. "Le Diable's militia has ordered all foreigners out of the country before curfew." She glanced at her watch. "Which is *now.*"

It was already getting dark out, night descending like clockwork so close to the equator. There was also a thunderstorm brewing. "He seems to have shut down the borders in retaliation to the U.S. State Department advisory issued earlier."

"The State Department is worried about hostility against U.S. citizens," said the FDS boss. "No one has any idea those murdered Americans were operatives. They were deep cover."

"You think he's preparing for some kind of military strike?"

"Could be. I'll keep you posted. Our men can extricate you within two hours from when you sound the alarm."

"Apparently there were also five hostages taken from Nigeria by his rebels early this morning. That's the word here at the hotel," Emily said softly.

"We're on to that," Jacques said. "Looks like three of those hostages are U.S. nationals, and two Nigerian. They were taken from the security barracks of an oil outfit. Apparently Le Diable's rebels are transporting them into the Purple Mountains and heading toward the Ubasi border. No ransom demands. Not yet."

"Unrelated incident?"

"I never assume anything on this continent, but it could be. It's a common enough occurrence. In the meantime, it's fortuitous your papers were confiscated—it gives you a legitimate excuse to stay in Ubasi and defy the evacuation orders. See how long you can play it, and keep us updated."

"Gotcha."

"And, Carlin…stay safe."

Emily signed off, and bolted the louvered shutters

against the hot storm wind, anxiety tangling with emotional fatigue in her body. Perhaps she wasn't ready for this after all.

01:27 Zulu. Saturday, November 9.
Hotel Basaroutou, Ubasi

The night was intensely humid and close. Tattered leaves slapped at her shutters while Emily tossed and turned in fitful sleep. She'd swapped her T-shirt for a skimpy camisole, and still she was soaked with sweat.

Her dreams that night were of Le Diable—dark, sultry images full of smoke and heat and pulsing drums, his green eyes piercing the blackness, his hands touching her in ways she shouldn't even begin to imagine. Her body was hot with desire—and panic. She was breathless. Running. Trying to escape. Someone was yelling at her, screaming that she *must* flee, that she was in danger. She awoke abruptly, confused, drenched.

She opened her eyes, trying to gather her senses, and realized with shock that the screaming was *real*. Emily jolted upright in bed, heart slamming against her breastbone.

Someone was banging on her door!

Before she could even think of grabbing her sarong and getting up, the door splintered open and crashed back against the wall.

She shrank back against the headboard as soldiers armed with Kalashnikovs burst into her room.

"What…what do you want?" she demanded.

They said nothing. One tore back her mosquito netting, motioned with the barrel of his weapon for her to get out of bed. Another scooped up her phone, computer and camera—*all* her communication equipment. Without it she was totally cut off.

"Allez!" The big soldier pointed his weapon to the door. "Go!"

Emily was suddenly horribly conscious of the fact she was wearing only provocative lace panties and a sheer camisole that stuck to her breasts with perspiration. She held up her hands. "Just…just one second, okay? Please? One second. *Comprends? S'il vous plaît?*" She reached cautiously for her sarong, watching their eyes as she spoke. She covered herself as she slid awkwardly down from the high bed. She tied the sarong tightly over her hips with shaking fingers as she mentally scrambled for where she'd left her sandals and knife.

"Allez!"

"Okay, okay. My…my shoes—"

They grabbed her arms and shoved her barefoot toward the door, through the hotel and out to a waiting battery of Jeeps. That's when she knew she was in trouble—serious trouble.

02:03 Zulu. Saturday, November 9.
Ubasi Palace

Laroque paced slowly round the massive eboya-wood table that sat squarely in the center of his cavernous war room. There was still no electricity—the room was lit by flickering torches that sent shadows to shiver and crouch in corners.

Thunder boomed in the distance, making his dog growl and edge nervously up against his leg. Laroque reached down and patted Shaka's head, studying the wood pieces he'd laid out on the table in the style of old generals to mark the positions of his allied rebel troops, and pockets of resistance fighters—pockets that were growing mysteriously.

He frowned. His spies had informed him that Souleyman had set up camp in the jungle beyond Ubasi's eastern border. He was once again amassing power, but where his weapons and financing were coming from was an enigma.

At first Laroque had suspected the CIA. He knew Washington—along with the rest of the world—would be eyeing the massive oil reserves he'd recently discovered. And because of his rebel alliance, they would be seeing him as a serious threat in the region.

But if it was the U.S., and *if* those dead men were in fact CIA agents—their murders made no sense. Something else was at play here.

Anger bubbled through Laroque's blood. Again he cursed himself for not killing Souleyman when he'd had the chance.

His father would have.

His father would have seen Laroque's mercy as a mistake. And it was.

Souleyman had overthrown Ubasi's King Desmond Douala in a violent coup eight years ago. The king and his family had fled to France, the former colonial power, and Souleyman had declared himself leader-for-life, running the country by a process of extortion, bribes, torture and corruption, instantly silencing any political opposition with his notorious death squad.

It was how he had silenced Laroque's sister, and her children.

Laroque clenched his jaw. The mere *notion* that someone might be helping that bastard back into power filled Laroque's mouth with bitter repulsion.

He swore violently, strode to the huge arched windows, and glared out over the black jungle. Thunder rumbled again, and a gust of hot wind lifted the drapes.

It was for the love of the women in his life, the women he'd lost, that Laroque was doing this. He owed it to them. To his sister. This was her dream. And now that he'd started down this road, there could be no turning back.

But as he stared into the stormy blackness, it was the image of another woman that crept into his mind—the one he'd seen in Basaroutou. A strange hot frisson ran through him.

His general had told him that a U.S. national who had entered Ubasi with the science team had defied his orders to leave the country by curfew. Laroque had an odd feeling that the woman he'd seen in the street might be that person.

The hot wind gusted again, and anticipation rustled

through him as he caught the scent of the coming rainstorm. He checked his watch. It was just after 2:00 a.m. He'd find out soon enough who she was.

They were bringing her to him this very moment.

02:17 Zulu. Saturday, November 9. Ubasi Palace

The soldiers threw open a set of heavy studded doors and thrust Emily into a dimly lit, cavernous room. The doors thudded shut behind her, and she heard an iron bolt being dropped into place.

She blinked, trying to adjust her eyesight to the coppery torchlight. She could sense another presence in the room, but couldn't see anyone.

Then he stepped from the shadows, his famous black dog moving at his side.

Emily's heart stalled.

Laroque.

He said nothing, just raked his eyes over her from head to foot and back again, making her feel even more naked than she already was.

Her palms turned clammy, and her throat tightened.

He appeared even taller than the six foot three indicated in the FDS dossier she'd memorized. He was wearing the military fatigues she'd seen him in earlier, except now his hair hung loose to his shoulders. His ice-green eyes glinted in the light.

Emily choked down a rush of fear and awe as she forced herself into professional observational mode. She was being handed a rare opportunity here—face time with Le Diable, a tyrant in the making, right inside his lair. This man was her subject. She was here to study him.

But he was clearly appraising *her*.

She tried to tamp down the hot flare of déjà vu, the uncanny sense that she'd woken up in her own erotic nightmare.

Focus, Emily. You know the dominance psychology here. You can do this. You're still in control.

She cleared her throat. "I'd like to know why you brought me here like this?" she demanded in French. "And I'd like my clothes."

Laroque angled his head ever so slightly and the light played over his mouth. Was that a twitch of a smile—or anger—on his lips?

Emily straightened her spine, her movement instantly drawing his eyes to her breasts. She felt her cheeks grow warm.

He took a step toward her. "And *I* would like to know why you are in Ubasi." He spoke in perfect but beautifully accented English, his voice rolling out from somewhere low in his chest.

"I'm with the Geographic International—"

"No." He cut her short. "Why are you *still* here? Why did you not leave when ordered?"

She felt herself bristle. "I couldn't leave. Your customs official confiscated my documents and cash."

His eyes narrowed sharply, the chemistry in the room suddenly becoming darker, edgier.

"Why?" He said the word very quietly.

She swallowed. "He…maintained there was an irregularity with my currency declaration form."

"Was there?"

"Of course not. The man didn't even look at my form. It was extortion, pure and simple. He cut me from the crowd because I was female and had become separated from my group. He said if I want my documents back I must pay a fifty-thousand-franc fine. I don't have that kind of money on me. That is why I'm still here."

Muscles corded visibly along his neck, yet his voice remained measured, calm. "What was the official's name?"

Emily's stomach tightened. She didn't yet know where this man's trigger points lay, and she didn't like the way his cold eyes and level voice clashed with the invisible anger that seemed to be rolling off him in disquieting waves. This man was barely leashed violence. He was dangerous.

"His name," he insisted, even more quietly.

"I…I didn't get his name."

Laroque spun on his heels, reached for the communications device on his desk and punched a button. He issued orders in rapid Ubasian, his tone completely unemotional. Emily didn't understand a word, but there was something about his concealed tension that said it all—the customs guy was done for.

He released the button, turned to face her, the muscles in his neck still bunched tight. Silence descended on the room. It was then that Emily realized she was shaking.

"I'm sorry," he said, taking a step toward her, his voice suddenly as smooth and rounded as cream liquor over ice. "I do not condone extortion in any form, especially concerning a woman. I'll have your passport returned by dawn."

She lifted her shoulder in part shrug, part nervous reaction, his sexist comment not escaping her. "It's the way of this continent—"

"*Not* in Ubasi." He took another step toward her. "We will not manage to attain a democracy unless we root this sort of thing out now. I need my people to trust authority. Not fear it."

She felt her eyes widen.

He smiled, a quick and piratical slash against his dark skin, so fleeting she almost missed it. "You did not expect an apology?"

"Honestly? No…no, I didn't."

He pursed his lips, the light of flames shimmering in his eyes. It was an unexpectedly intimate look, a trick of the firelight. It reminded Emily of her state of undress, and the fact that he still had not offered to make her comfortable in any way. He still wanted something from her.

And he wanted her on edge to get it.

"What…what'll you do to the customs official?" she asked, wanting to probe his character, to use her limited time with him as best she could. But at the same time she was wary of pushing him.

"He'll be punished."

"How?"

He arched a brow. "You're interested?"

"Well…I…" *Tread carefully here, Emily.* "I've heard about the Laroque legacy on this continent, and I—"

"I am *not* my father. I will never be like him." Although spoken quietly his words were terse.

Emily noted his reaction. His father was a sensitive point. "I'm sorry," she said gently. "I didn't mean to offend you."

He regarded her intently. "You don't believe the customs official should be punished?"

Watch yourself, Emily. He's assessing you, just as you are him.

"It appears," she said, selecting her words with care, "that this man broke the law. Certainly justice should be done. But perhaps you could define the Ubasi version of 'punishment' before I can offer a considered opinion."

"Ah, a diplomat?" He smiled quickly, turned, strode away, then spun suddenly back to face her. "As well as a scientist."

He was closing in, yet giving her the illusion of physical space by walking away. This man was good. He understood people, psychology. And he knew how to use it. Most tyrants did.

"Your name is Emma Sanford—Dr. Emma Sanford. You're from New Jersey. You're both a sociologist and a psychologist."

Emily nodded. "That's correct." He'd gotten those details from the papers she'd had to file with the palace before joining the G.I. expedition. He was probably having her background checked this very minute.

She knew the identity Jacques had given her would hold. They always did, whether she went in as a nun, aid worker or reporter. Yet she felt as though Laroque could see right through her.

She folded her arms over her stomach as she spoke, and his eyes followed the movement of her hands. *Damn.* He was reading her defensive body language. The movement had come so instinctively in response to his question that she'd covered herself before she'd even realized it.

She didn't make mistakes like this. Laroque had managed to throw her way off center, just as he'd intended by bringing her here half-dressed in the dark of night.

And there was something in his penetrating gaze that made her intimately aware of her own femininity. He was all male. All in control. A very real and personal panic suddenly sliced into Emily. It caught her off guard and she fought to regulate her breathing.

She needed to stay focused. Professional.

"So what is a sociologist-psychologist doing with a team studying a volcano?"

She swallowed. She'd known this was coming next. Jacques's idea had been for her to play as close to her identity as was comfortable so that she could legitimately ask questions about Laroque's mental state without drawing suspicion.

"It's not just the volcano," she said. "We also wanted to look into the sociology of the villagers who live on the flanks of an active volcano. My specific role is to examine the psychology associated with dwelling on the shoulders of a geological monster that could erupt at any moment." She hesitated, watching for some kind of reaction in his eyes, but he gave away nothing. "I'm professionally intrigued by what rationalizations a society uses for remaining in that kind of danger. I also want to examine the mythology and religion that has evolved around living on a live volcano."

A genuine interest crept into his eyes. It was the first real sign of emotion in him, and it emboldened her a little. "That's basically my goal here in Ubasi— to do that research and to compile a series of articles for our sponsor's magazine." She allowed her eyes to flicker briefly to the side, feigning a touch of coyness. "I was also hoping to examine life in Ubasi under the new leader. I'm told things are improving in the country," she said, forcing a soft smile.

He said nothing.

She tilted her head, met his eyes and deepened her smile, fully aware of what she could do to a man, if she wanted. "You're an enigma," she ventured. "A French soldier of fortune who came out of the blue to take an African country for himself. It's a bold and fascinating story." She stepped closer to him. "That's more than an article, Your Excellency," she said, using his official title. "That's a book."

His eyes flared briefly. "I gave no sanction for a book."

"I know. A book is my *personal* interest, an adjunct to my work with the Geographic team. I'd been hoping to request an interview while I was here."

This is where feminine flattery should work on an autocratic personality. This is where the Alpha Dog should be seduced into talking about himself. But Emily had just succeeded in unsettling *herself*— because not only was she physically ruffled by this man's proximity, the idea of a book on the warlord-turned-tyrant was something she actually wanted beyond this FDS mission. She was hewing too close to her own desires.

He studied her quietly, shadow and light playing over his features. For a moment she thought she glimpsed a softening in his eyes, a shimmer of sadness, even, a small window opening to the real man inside.

"I see." A ghost of a smile tipped the corners of his lips. "For a moment there I thought you were going to compare living on an active volcano to life in Ubasi under my rule."

Emily wasn't sure whether she was expected to laugh, or if he was playing her, just as she was playing him.

Confusion coiled inside her. Thunder crashed, right above the castle this time, unleashing the full brunt of the storm. Rain lashed against the walls, and wind howled, billowing curtains and ferrying a mist of fine droplets into the room.

He held out his hand in a sudden gesture of magnanimity. "It's late. Allow me to offer you accommodation, Emma—may I call you Emma?"

"I…yes, of course."

"Stay in my palace, be my guest for the night while we sort out your passport issue."

Hope fluttered in her chest.

"You will then leave Ubasi before noon tomorrow."

Her heart sank right back down. "So…there's no chance of an interview, then?" she asked, trying to push her luck.

He held her eyes for several long beats, as if deciding whether to even answer.

"What good would a book do me, Emma?" he said.

She decided to play her wild card. It was dangerous, and she knew it, but she'd glimpsed the little chink in his walls, and being bold enough to go for those barely perceptible vulnerabilities was what had made Emily the uncanny success she was at psychological analyses—so successful, in fact, her peers often joked about her being psychic. Plus, she was running out of face time with Laroque. If she didn't move now, she'd lose her window completely. She'd fail her mission.

"A book could show people that you are not like your father, Your Excellency."

His mouth flattened and his eyes narrowed to slits. He took a step closer to her, and she felt herself tense.

"It's not the truth the world wants to read,

Emma," he said darkly. "What is true is less important than what is widely believed. People prefer to believe in monsters."

"Monsters like Le Diable?" She watched his eyes. "Or monsters like Peter Laroque?"

He came close to her, very close, and he lowered his voice to a soft murmur near her ear. "What if I *am* like him, Emma?"

Heat began to burn low in her belly. But she didn't shy away from the penetrating intensity in his eyes, or from his closeness. "That's your fear, isn't it?" Her voice came out a whisper. "You're afraid that deep down somewhere you *are* like him. But I don't believe it." And she didn't. She was going on a raw gut feel here, taking one hell of a gamble. "Let me stay, Your Excellency," she said gently. "Give me the interview time. Please."

A muscle pulsed under his eye.

He leaned down farther, his mouth coming very close to hers. "What do you *really* want from me, Emma Sanford?"

She shivered at the sensation of his breath, warm against her skin, and for a nanosecond she wasn't sure *what* she wanted. Her heart began to race so fast she could barely breathe. She tried to moisten her lips. "Just…the interview time."

He studied her in silence that vibrated like electricity between their bodies, his eyes probing hers, searching for something. Emily felt herself begin to burn from the inside out.

"I need to know something first, Emma," he said softly, his eyes lancing hers. "Do you understand just how dangerous things are in Ubasi right now?"

Oh, boy, did she ever. In more ways than one. She was in trouble. Every warning bell in her system was clanging for her to step away from him. Right now. Run. Flee! This was a man who could convince a woman to cross the line into sin with one little crook of his finger. This was exactly the kind of man she *must* avoid, the kind of man who got her into personal trouble.

Except this time she couldn't flee. This time the man she feared on a very personal level *was* her professional mission. And this time, her life might be on the line.

Whether he was like his father or not, Emily had little doubt Le Diable would kill her if he learned she had come to destroy *him*.

"I do," she whispered, eyes burning from the effort of sustaining his gaze without blinking. "I know exactly how dangerous."

Chapter 3

A dark whisper of warning breathed through Laroque as her violet eyes held his steadily. "I saw you," he said, watching her carefully. "In the street this morning."

A nebulous look swam through her eyes. "I know."

Something rich and dark slid through his stomach. She'd felt the same connection, he could read it in her eyes, hear it in her voice. Every last strand of primal DNA in his body fought to override rational thought at this moment.

He loved the way her hair fell in a dark tangle almost to her waist, the way freckles ever so faintly dusted the pale skin over her nose. And he was particularly attracted to the sharp intelligence that sparked in her unusual eyes. This woman presented challenge.

And *nothing* fired Laroque like a challenge.

It fueled a voracious appetite in him—for victory, dominance. It made him want to play the game.

There was no doubt in his mind that he'd take her physically, should she dare offer.

But he didn't trust her.

He'd be damned if he didn't *want* to, though. The notion of sharing his personal story with her was strangely compelling.

He'd never told anyone his life story before. He'd borne his scars solo since the age of thirteen, pretending the opinions of others never bothered him.

But they did.

Deep down, if he really was truthful, Laroque wanted people to understand that while he'd learned the art of guerrilla warfare and the techniques of torture and death from his father, while he'd been forced to follow, and depend on, and fight with Peter Laroque for his very survival, he was not at all like him.

Yes, he'd become a mercenary, because it was what he knew, and he'd become very good at it. But he had his boundaries. His game was always an ethical one. And what he wanted for Ubasi—for the entire region—was good. Bold, yes. Overambitious, perhaps. But it was for the benefit of the majority who lived in increasingly abysmal conditions in contrast to the rapidly growing oil wealth of a few corrupt leaders.

The romantic part of Laroque actually *wanted* to believe that this woman had been dropped into his life like an angel.

But he wasn't a fool, and he did not believe in co-incidences. He also had trouble believing her science crew would just abandon her like this.

He needed to check her out. Thoroughly.

In the meanwhile, he needed to be sure she was safe. His castle was the best place for her tonight.

"You'll agree to the interview, then?" Her voice was midnight velvet, soft and powerful at the same time. It was the kind of voice that made a man aware of his sex. And that made her potentially dangerous.

"You're welcome to stay the night," he said bluntly.

Surprise showed in her eyes. "Is that all?"

"That's all. I'll have my men show you to the guest quarters. They'll escort you to the airport before noon."

He stepped back and summoned his guards.

Langley, Virginia. CIA headquarters

CIA director Blake Weston pored over the reports on his desk. The death of his men in Ubasi ate at him like acid.

He rubbed his face, inhaling deeply.

He had what appeared to be an extremely serious intelligence breach on his hands. His agents in West Africa had been deep, deep cover. The exposure of their identities indicated an information leak, and it could only have come from the *inside*. At least this is how it would be viewed in Washington. He pinched the bridge of his nose.

Blake was new to this top job, and the White

House was watching carefully to see how he handled his first major crisis. His agency had to be seen to be acting swiftly, decisively and ruthlessly to root out any possible mole. Blake was also aware that his career depended not only on his actions at this critical juncture, but on the political *perception* of his actions.

Which is why the Laroque-Ubasi situation had been instantly outsourced to the FDS, an objective organization, while the CIA could be seen to be dealing with its own internal security issues. Blake had no doubt the FDS would effectively eliminate Jean-Charles Laroque and pave the way to stability in the Gulf of Guinea.

But that didn't solve the disclosure of his men's identities. *That* was the problem that burned him. That was what would come back to haunt him.

He shoved his chair back, stood, unscrewed his bottle of pills, popped two into his mouth. This clandestine cooperation with the Pentagon only confounded things. He'd been put hands-on in charge of the new joint task force, and any failure would reflect directly on him. He chewed his medication slowly, thinking. This business was full of mirrors and shadows and smoke—one never really knew who or what one was dealing with. Or what the agenda was. He could use this to his advantage.

But getting off this particular tiger was going to be tricky. Maybe impossible. It could even cost him his life. If Blake was to have any chance of actually riding this one out, Laroque *had* to take the fall for the agents' deaths.

If Laroque died with Washington believing the tyrant had somehow discovered the CIA agents' identities on his own, the mystery—all the niggling questions—would die with him. Then Blake's problem would simply disappear.

There was just one little hitch—the profiler. The FDS had insisted on this approach. Blake had been dead set against it. He didn't need some academic from New York declaring the tyrant fit for capture, he needed him *dead.*

He glanced at the calendar on his desk.

The FDS profiler had less than one week to make her move. It had damned well better be the right one.

03:17 Zulu. Saturday, November 9.
Ubasi Palace

Emily lay on the king-size bed staring at the impossibly high ceiling. The door had been bolted from the outside. When she'd protested, the guards had said it was for her own safety. The balcony was too high to climb down. She'd checked.

She was imprisoned like a damn princess in a castle tower.

Her bags had been delivered to the room, but her computer, phone, camera and knife were all still missing. Emily had little doubt Laroque was going through her things with a fine-tooth comb, checking out her story—her identity.

She told herself she shouldn't worry. It was state-

of-the-art military issue, and everything was encrypted. The FDS techs were among the best in the
world. They'd have been careful not to leave digital
clues. Laroque wouldn't find a thing.

So why didn't she feel more secure?

She figured the only reason she was still here in
his castle boudoir was so that he could thoroughly
check her cover story. Perhaps he hadn't believed a
single word she'd said. She wondered if she'd even
see him again.

Emily tossed irritably on the Egyptian cotton
sheets as the wind moaned up in the parapets and
rattled at the French doors on her little stone balcony.

The more she thought about it, the more she really
liked the idea of a book. Laroque exhibited classic
Alpha Dog pathology, yet he'd only recently become
a dictator, which meant she had an opportunity to
witness a monster-in-the-making. Scoring a one-on-
one interview with Le Diable would not only secure
her FDS mission, it could earn her academic prestige
down the road.

It would give her something to take back to New
York.

Emily desperately needed some sort of professional—and personal—validation after being so thoroughly humiliated by her ex and her peers. Anger
surged through her at the memory. She sat up
abruptly in the bed, forced out pent-up breath with a
puff of her cheeks.

She did *not* want to go back to New York a failure.

The fiasco she'd left at home had forced her to question everything about herself, every choice she'd ever made in life—from her career to the men she dated. And she really didn't want to face those questions. Not now. Not yet. Maybe never, if she could help it.

She wanted excitement, adrenaline, something big to focus on right now, other than herself.

This wasn't running, she told herself. Sometimes you just needed distance.

She slid off the bed, snagged the water jug on the dresser and poured herself a glass. She took a swig but the liquid balled in her throat.

Her eyes began to burn and hurt tightened her chest.

She'd trusted her ex.

Hell, she'd even thought she loved him. But it had just been a game—a bet he'd taken with his colleagues that he could not only bed the brainy ice queen, but make her fall for him.

She plunked the glass down, shoved her hair back from her face and cursed viciously.

She *had* fallen for him. His name was Dr. Anthony Dresden. He was much older, an esteemed university professor who did consulting at *her* clinic. Not only had he made a mockery of her, but he'd lured her across a line she should never have dared cross—that line between personal and professional. A vital line in a field like hers.

What made it worse was the fact she'd once confided to Anthony that she was concerned about her consistent attraction to dominant and physically powerful males—men like her dad. She'd told Anthony she was beginning to think she subconsciously found ways to sabotage her relationships with men like this as soon as they showed signs of getting serious. That's why her relationships never lasted more than eighteen months. She invariably grew afraid that if she committed wholly to the alpha guy in her life she'd be trapped. That he'd undermine her independence and ultimately quash her. Like her dad had quashed her mother.

To death.

Emily was deeply afraid of not being in control, always. Because in her heart, Emily was terrified that she was really just like her mom. Weak.

Dr. Anthony Dresden, a man she'd once respected on so many levels, had used her secret fears against her.

He'd taken a substantial monetary bet one very drunken night over dinner with a group of his—*and her*—male colleagues. He'd wagered he could seduce the brainy ice queen—that's what they called her— and make her fall for him. He'd bet he could date her longer than any of her previous relationships. He'd told his friends that it was more than sex for Emily, you had to get her at her own game, a mind game.

It was pure betrayal.

When their relationship had gone over that eighteen-month hurdle, Emily's heart had begun to feel light, as if a huge weight had been lifted from her. She thought she might be truly in love, that Anthony was *the one*.

Tears slid hotly and angrily down Emily's face.

He hadn't collected on the bet.

When she'd found out about it via the grapevine, she'd been devastated. Anthony told her he'd called the bet off because he'd come to care deeply for her. He said it had been a lark, something he should never have allowed to happen. He'd pleaded with her for the relationship to continue. That's what made it worse—the fact that he said he really did love her.

All he'd done was reinforce her deep-rooted pathological fears. Because in a powerfully intellectual and physically subtle way, Anthony was an alpha himself. She'd fallen for his calculated seduction, and he'd used her own mind against her. And everyone who mattered in her career knew about it.

Emily threw herself back onto the pillow and closed her eyes tight. No, she could not go home.

Not yet.

Not until she'd proved something to herself.

05:45 Zulu. Saturday, November 9.
Ubasi Palace

A soft peach bled into the ink sky. Monkeys stirred in the branches below, and the sound of birds rose in a soft chatter. Laroque stood on his balcony, hands flat on the balustrade, surveying the dark jungle canopy.

The storm had blown through, and he was enjoying the rich scent of fecund earth. In a few hours the forest would be an oppressive place, steaming under the sun's fire. He liked these predawn hours best.

He hadn't slept, but he was used to not sleeping. He'd learned since a boy how to push, and keep pushing, to rest only when the battle had been won. He wouldn't be alive otherwise.

"Sir?"

He spun round to face Mathieu Ebongani, the technician who'd been busy with Emma's equipment.

"Mathieu, did you find anything?"

The tech stepped onto the balcony. "Her ID checks out."

"What about her equipment?"

"It's beyond my scope, I'm afraid. Her satellite phone and computer are fitted with highly sophisticated GPS and encryption technology," he said. "We're going to need Ndinga if you want to try to decode it."

"Is the technology consistent with a science mission of this nature?"

The tech's mouth twisted. "It looks more state-of-the-military to me." He paused. "It's her laptop that worries me. It appears to be communicating at a low-level-signal strength with another off-site station, even when turned off."

"GPS?"

"No, this is something different." He hesitated. "I haven't seen anything like this before. We'd learn more by opening the hard drive up in a forensic environment, but again, we'll need Ndinga and his team for that."

Laroque's pulse quickened. "What about her computer files?"

"Encrypted, but she does have a photo in there that I could access."

"Photo?"

"From the Parisian Press archives. The caption says it's you at age thirteen being taken from the hospital by your father."

A band of muscle tightened sharply across Laroque's chest.

His mind was yanked instantly back to a day he'd rather forget. His mother had been famous. She was always in the tabloids, and by default, so was he, the young boy hanging on to the skirts of the glamorous African model, or so it had looked to the world. It was logical Dr. Emma Sanford would have dug one or two of those out, especially if she wanted to work on a book. Yet it made him feel strange. Vulnerable. Especially *that* specific image.

Did she know it represented the turning point of his life?

"Anything in her e-mail?" he asked, his words unnecessarily clipped.

"Only correspondence with Geographic International headquarters."

"Thank you. Keep her equipment for Ndinga's return," Laroque said, dismissing his tech.

He turned to watch the peach sky deepen to burnt orange, then blood-red as the fiery ball of sun crashed over the Purple Mountains in a wild symphony of color. He breathed in deep. He loved the African sky. It was bold. Confrontational. Always changing.

It defined *him*.

He hadn't been born here, yet this place pulsed rich through his blood. His mother was an Ubasi native, his father a third-generation South African of Dutch heritage. Laroque himself had been born and schooled in Paris, but from the age of thirteen this continent had been his heart and soul.

People from other parts of the world didn't understand the differences, the laws of this vast and elemental land. They *couldn't*. The things that happened here just weren't in the lexicon of the West.

It made him mad…and, strangely, glad. He was as conflicted about this place as it was conflicted itself.

But he did know that if Ubasi and the rest of the Niger Delta was to survive, thrive even, he needed to bridge that vast gap between Western ideology and African. The rebel oil alliance was the starting point, the foundation of something big, a local OPEC and an army with some real negotiating power for the people of the Delta.

He wondered just what part in this unfolding melodrama Emma Sanford was to play, if any. There was a chance she was telling him the truth, but things weren't adding up well enough to make Laroque comfortable.

Her computer equipment had only raised more questions.

If she was broadcasting he wanted to know to whom—and why. He needed to hang on to her gear long enough for Mano Ndinga, his top IT genius, to return and look into it.

Laroque checked his watch.

Mano and his team were busy installing a network at the Nigerian base of one of Laroque's allied rebel militias. They'd be back in roughly four days. Laroque couldn't hold Dr. Emma Sanford prisoner until then. It would cause an international outcry.

He could just ship her out of the country. However, if she *was* some kind of informant, she might be a vital link to whatever was going on behind the scenes in Ubasi. He'd be a fool not to milk that angle—it was the only lead he had. And if worse came to worst, she might end up a valuable negotiating tool.

She'd have to stay on her own volition.

He'd have to make it *her* choice.

He drew the morning air deep into his lungs again, and breathed out slowly. If the lady was playing a game of deception, she was good. But he'd show her that he was better.

And keeping one's enemies close—very close— was never a bad idea.

8:07 Zulu. Saturday, November 9.
Ubasi Palace

A loud rapping on the door ripped Emily from sleep. She jolted upright, squinting as she tried to focus. Bright bars of sunlight streamed through shutters, throwing slatted patterns on the walls. Her head felt fuzzy, her mouth dry.

The banging continued, louder.

She stumbled out of bed and headed toward the door, belting the silk robe she'd found behind the bathroom door tightly around her waist as she went. She pulled on the brass handle, and it gave—the door had been unlocked from the outside. She drew it open cautiously, shoving her tangle of hair back from her face as she did.

Muscled pecs under a snug-fitting crisp T-shirt greeted her at eye level. She stared numbly, her brain trying to kick back into gear. She lifted her eyes slowly and met his clear, penetrating gaze. Her stomach somersaulted, and she grounded herself by reaching for the door handle, his eyes instantly tracking her movement. Did this guy not miss a damned thing?

"Good morning," Laroque said in his exotic African-French accent, a smile reaching right into his luminous green eyes, making them sparkle with un-speakable mischief.

The effect rocketed through Emily like dynamite. And damned if her cheeks didn't flush. She reached up to smooth down her hair.

"You slept well?"

"I…yes. Thank you." It sounded trite. She'd been abducted and locked in a turret, for goodness' sake. "I was tired. I *was* dragged here at 2:00 a.m.," she added defensively. "What…time is it, anyway?"

He held up her passport. "Time to leave Ubasi."

She stared at her passport in his hand, her ticket to freedom.

She reached up to take it from him, but as she tugged at the passport, he held tighter, his fingers connecting with hers, the sensation electric. Emily's breath caught and her eyes whipped to his face.

"I have a proposition," he said. "Take the passport, and leave Ubasi before noon. Or—" He paused, watching her way too intently for comfort. "*I* keep the passport, and you stay and interview me. Your choice. My terms."

Her heart was now racing so fast she could barely breathe. "Your...terms?" Her voice came out thick.

"Stay in my palace, under my constant guard. If we do venture beyond the fortress, you do not leave my side. Understand? Not for one instant. No exceptions. It's for your own protection, of course."

Emily appeared to be incapable of disconnecting from his touch, of letting go of her passport, her ticket to freedom. Her mind reeled. She should leave, for her own good. Perhaps she wasn't yet mentally ready to handle this man and the strange seductive power he had over her.

Then she recalled the mission, why she needed to succeed. She thought of New York, of her ex, of the utter humiliation and pain that awaited her.

She'd be Laroque's voluntary captive. She'd have exclusive access to Le Diable in his inner sanctum, an extremely rare opportunity to watch one of her Alpha Dog subjects at work. She'd have access to information that could help the FDS.

This was an opportunity that might never present itself again.

This was what she wanted—wasn't it?

A dark, sensual excitement tangled with rising adrenaline as conflict raged through Emily. He was making it *her* decision. He was making her a partner in her own captivity. It was a power play.

Laroque could destroy her if she stayed. He would kill her if he found out who she was working for.

This is life and death, Emily. This is the real thing. Wake up, here, think straight.

Logic screamed at her to leave, screamed that she was basing decisions on flawed reasoning, on personal issues, not professional ones. Logic told her that at some level she was dangerously attracted to this subject, and it reminded her of all the trouble she'd ever gotten herself into when she'd tangled emotionally with A-types. And those men in her past didn't even begin to hold a candle to the kind of power and sexual charisma Laroque possessed.

Neither were they killers.

But she *couldn't* leave.

"Keep the passport," she said quietly, dropping her hand to her side.

His smile was sharp and fleeting as he whipped the passport away and handed it to a sullen guard who materialized from the shadows at his side. Emily had a sinking sense that she'd just made a mistake. A grave one.

And now there was no turning back.

Chapter 4

Emily cinched the belt of her robe tighter around her waist, pulling herself together. She had less than six days left to file her report on Laroque, to decide whether he would live or die.

If she failed to submit by the deadline, Jacques's men would move in, and he'd die, anyway.

She moistened her lips. "My equipment is missing. I'll need it if I am to record our interview."

"We're looking into it," he said.

Yes, I'm sure you are, she thought.

"In the meantime, I'll make sure you have a replacement laptop."

"I need my phone. I *must* report in or my team will

be worried. They'll contact the U.S. State Department, alert the embassy in Cameroon, and—"

He held out a stubby satellite phone as if he'd been anticipating every word. Maybe he had. Maybe he didn't believe her at all. Perhaps he'd found something in her computer, but not enough to condemn her outright. Her eyes shot to his, and nerves once again skittered like butterflies around her heart.

"One call," he said.

"Why only one?"

"Things are unstable in Ubasi. I'm limiting communications."

"But why—"

"We agreed, Emma, my rules."

The nerves tightened in her chest.

"If you wish to change your mind—"

"No," she said, reaching for the phone, careful not to connect with his skin again. "I'm fine with that."

He waited.

"You…want me to call here, right now?"

"Is that a problem?"

"No, it's not," Emily said, racking her brain for the mobile number of Max Rutger, the science team leader. She punched it in slowly, praying it was correct. She put the phone to her ear. It rang once. Twice. Three times. Her mouth turned dry. She flicked a glance to Laroque.

He was watching her intently.

"Hello?"

Relief slammed through her at the familiar sound

of Max's voice. "Max! It's Emma." She couldn't give him a chance to speak, to blow her cover. "The Laroque government has come through on my passport issue. I—"

"Thank God," he interrupted. "We heard you had problems and felt terrible about the note we left when—"

Perspiration prickled under her scalp. "Max, I'm fine, really. Jean-Charles Laroque has apologized to me personally. And you know that project I was working on?" She didn't dare give him a chance to get a word in edgewise. "Well, he's granted me one-on-one interview time for the book. Isn't that great? I'll be staying at his palace as his guest, but communications are limited at the moment, so will you please let *the office* know that I'm still working on…my personal project while you guys wait things out in Cameroon? Let them know at once, please, Max. And tell them I'll be in touch as soon as I can. Thanks, Max." She quickly cut the call, heart pounding, palms damp, praying that Max would get the hint to call their sponsor who'd notify Jacques. She handed the phone back to Laroque.

His eyes were flat as he took it from her. "That was…brief."

She said nothing. She could hear the rush of her own blood in her ears.

"We'll discuss the parameters of the interview over breakfast," he said abruptly, his eyes flicking over her body. "As soon as you're dressed." He turned and started down the corridor. "My men will escort you down to the terrace," he called over his shoulder.

And he was gone, his black Alsatian moving like a ghost in his wake, leaving only the hollow tap of boots echoing down the castle corridor, and the click of his dog's claws on stone.

Emily slowly released the breath she'd been holding.

"I want to know when Mano will be back ASAP." Laroque delivered his words with staccato precision into the phone. "Tell him I have an important job waiting." He hung up, reached for his coffee cup and stretched his legs out under the garden table. He sipped from the white china as he watched a blue crane walk along the edge of the castle's rock swimming pool.

Shaka's ears twitched at the sight of the bird. Laroque reached down absently to stroke his pet, acknowledging his dog's restraint. His suspicions about Emma were even stronger now. But the telling evidence might come once his IT expert returned. Meanwhile, he wanted to find out as much about her as possible, as soon as possible, because he had a sense that the longer she stayed, the more damage she could do.

Emily paused at the entrance to the garden.

The man and his dog waited for her on the lowest terrace overlooking a vast swimming pool. Laroque's back was to her. He sat on a white wrought-iron chair in the shade of a broad tree with thick olive-green leaves, his long legs stretched almost lazily out in front of him, combat boots crossed at the ankles.

Shaka lay on the grass under his chair. In one hand Laroque held a white cup, the saucer resting on the glass-topped table. With his other, he ruffled his dog's fur.

It was an arresting vignette, an image for a magazine cover—the devastatingly handsome and powerful warlord at ease in his garden. A garden he'd *stolen,* she reminded herself, just as he'd stolen the whole damn country.

A king and his family had once lived here, a royal family that had mysteriously vanished from their Parisian home in exile just over a year ago.

It had been whispered that Le Diable and his French connections might even be responsible for the disappearance of King Desmond Douala and his wife and son, perhaps even their murder in Paris, before he'd come to take the country for himself.

She breathed in deeply, and began to walk over the lawn toward him, the grass springy under her feet. The morning sun was hot, the sound of birds riotous in the trees above. Shaka looked up as she approached, then glanced at his master for direction. The dog adored him, she noted. And he clearly loved his pet. It showed a human side to him, a capacity for care, for empathy.

From what Emily had learned about Laroque and his violent, transient lifestyle, Shaka might well be his *only* true friend in life. She wondered what he'd done for companionship before Shaka. As far as she knew the dog had only appeared on the scene with Laroque's arrival on that Spanish boat.

As she reached the table, she realized the sound that emanated from the tree above came not from birds, but from a troop of curious little monkeys that cavorted in the branches like naughty tufted gremlins.

Laroque stood the instant he saw her, his movement as fluid as a jaguar's. Emily guessed he was never truly at rest. He'd not have survived otherwise.

He held out his hand. "Take a seat," he said, motioning to the vacant chair. His eyes were lighter, somehow even less human in the stark sunlight. The juxtaposition against his smooth coffee-toned skin was truly startling.

He caught her staring. "I'm used to it," he said. "They're my father's eyes." A faint bitterness underscored his words. "That's why they call me Le Diable. Did you know that?"

Surprise rippled through her. "No. I...I thought—"

"You thought the moniker was a result of some terrible action of mine, didn't you?" He didn't give her a chance to answer. "Most assume the worst. Rumors grow legs of their own."

People want to believe in monsters.

She sat, momentarily self-conscious and trying to avoid the piercing green of his eyes. She could see that calling him Le Diable would have been a natural leap for the people of this continent. This was a place of animism and spirits and a powerful belief in dark magic, and while this man walked this territory with African blood and natural ease, he did so to his own drum. He was different in both looks and spirit, and that kind of independence always made people uneasy. It made them afraid.

But while Laroque had inherited his father's eyes and massive build, those strong Dutch genes were offset by his Ubasian mother's striking beauty and innate grace. He was an exotic blend of primal African charm, Germanic strength and a uniquely European finesse. He was a global man.

And the effect was totally captivating.

But Emily was more interested in what lay beneath the surface. She wanted to know how much more of his father was in him. She needed to know if this man would talk if captured and tortured.

He lifted a tall silver pot. "Coffee?"

The gesture, the question, was so simple, so normal. Yet it wasn't. She glanced up at his face, and was suddenly sideswiped by the fact she might be responsible for this man's death. "Thank you," she said, feeling guilty. "It smells divine."

"Ubasi grown and roasted," he said as he poured.

She watched the rich liquid stream from the spout, wondering how much of her discomfort stemmed from the fact that she was physically, and yes, even mentally, intrigued by him.

"What are you thinking?" he asked as he set the pot down.

Her eyes cut to his and she laughed lightly. "Men don't ask questions like that."

He smiled. "I'm not your average man."

He was right on that count. "I was thinking," she said reaching for the cream, "how badly I need a cup of coffee. You say it's local?"

"Grown in the foothills of the Purple Mountains." He settled back into his chair, hooking one boot over the other. "My dream is to see Ubasian coffee and cocoa exported around the world someday as a very exclusive fair-trade brand."

Another surprise. "Fair trade?"

He angled his head, studied her. "You did not expect this?"

"No, I mean, I have no reason not to. I just thought—"

"That I was a warmonger, after nothing but destruction and personal spoils?"

She snorted softly, unexpectedly amused, and sipped the coffee. Damned if it wasn't some of the finest she'd ever tasted. "It's good," she said. "Really good." There was something about this guy she was starting to really like.

The jolt of caffeine helped lift her spirits, too. "Shall we talk about interview parameters, or do you want to tell me your plans for the Ubasi economy first?"

His eyes narrowed. "I want to empower the people of my country, Emma," he said, watching her steadily. "If you've done your research, as I suspect you have, you'll know I was schooled by an assortment of Catholic nuns and priests at various missions across the continent, and that I obtained a masters in economics at the Sorbonne. I studied between my mercenary missions. I used the proceeds from my commissions to fund my studies, and to make investments, which have paid off very well."

Oh, she'd done her research, all right. Jean-Charles Laroque was not only a warrior, but a shrewd investor with a phenomenally solid portfolio of offshore holdings. He'd made war pay. Personally. By investing his spoils wisely. Yet here he was saying he'd overthrown Ubasi for the good of the people. It shouldn't surprise her.

A true tyrant often claimed to be acting in the name of "his" people, but Laroque would be the first to turn around and sacrifice those very same people to keep, or increase, his hold on power. And he'd crush any opposition with force.

Just as he would crush her if he found out who she really was. She had to remember that.

"You're an astute businessman, Your Excellency, as well as a guerrilla war expert and master strategist," she said, aiming to flatter as well as probe. "You clearly don't need the cash, but you still choose to fight. You must like it."

"I fight only for Ubasi," he said. "Once I have properly secured the country, that's it. I'm done."

"No more mercenary work?"

"No more."

Emily set her cup carefully into its saucer. "You're

telling me that Ubasi is somehow the pot at the end of your rainbow? That you've accrued enough oil wealth from this latest acquisition to set you up for life?"

"Those oil fields are mine in name only, Emma," he said quietly. "The wealth will go to the people."

"I don't understand."

"There's a lot you don't understand."

She feigned a smile. "Then we have much ground to cover, don't we?"

He gave a curt nod, reached for a platter of sliced fruit and handed it to her. "But first, you must eat."

The fruit was exotic and sinfully sweet. Emily wiped the juice from her chin with a napkin as a server materialized at their side with a basket of freshly baked French pastries. She studied the exchange between Laroque and his servant as the pastries were set on the table, detecting a genuine friendliness between the two.

Laroque's staff liked him, and from what she'd seen in the street yesterday, his subjects idolized him. Even more telling was the respect *he* showed his staff. This man was not at all what she'd expected. She filed this revelation with her other surprises.

"Tell me, Your Excellency," she said when the server departed, "why are doing this in Ubasi? You make it sound as though this place is some kind of endgame for you."

"It is," he said. "And you may call me Jean."

She nodded, a little nervous at the sharp flint in his eyes in spite of the step toward familiarity. She'd hit on something. She needed to keep probing, but the aggressive lines in his features warned her not to. She moistened her lips. "You're…making me think this is something you're prepared to die for, Jean."

He said nothing. His eyes narrowed to slits and a small muscle pulsed at the base of his jaw. Silence swelled with the rising temperatures. Even the monkeys had grown quiet.

"I am," he said suddenly.

Emily stopped chewing.

He leaned forward, his eyes sparking with cold green fire, a predatory danger crackling from his body. "Understand this, I will *not* go down without a fight…*Emma.*"

The pastry in her mouth suddenly felt dry.

"And…that fight will be to the death?"

"I don't like losing. I plan to win. But I *will* die fighting if that's what it takes."

She didn't doubt him, not for a moment. His intent was as crystal clear as the green in his eyes.

So it was unlikely Jean-Charles Laroque would make a good prisoner. He'd probably give nothing under torture. And capture could make this man a martyr. She'd witnessed firsthand the elemental passion of his people—he was like some kind of god to them. Such was the manipulative power of a shrewd despot.

Taking Le Diable alive could potentially spark a civil war.

Assassination—death—might be the only answer.

The idea left her strangely deflated.

"It's for my sister," he said suddenly.

"I…beg your pardon?"

"My sister, Tamasha. She was a key political activist here in Ubasi. She opposed the Souleyman regime during his bloody eight-year reign. Tamasha's voice of dissent was growing strong, along with her support. She had a gift for mobilizing an oppressed people. So Souleyman silenced her. Just over a year ago." His eyes flicked away briefly, but not fast enough to hide a flare of raw anguish that made Emily's heart squeeze.

"He killed her children first, slit their throats like goats. He made her watch. Then he cut her throat, in front of her home. He made the people of her village watch that."

Emily was speechless.

"You didn't know I had a sister, did you?"

"No… No, I didn't."

"Neither did I. Not until two years ago. That's when…" The words died on his lips, a small twitch tugging at a corner of his control. He looked away again, longer this time. When he turned back, she could see the savage emotion in his eyes. Not helpless pain, but the kind of bitter and raw hurt that fuelled revenge.

For the first time Emily felt like she was actually *seeing* this man and not some mask. He'd just made himself vulnerable to her and the gesture filled her chest with inexplicable emotion.

He reached for his pocket, withdrew his wallet, flipped it open and slid a battered black-and-white photo over the table. Emily picked it up. "This is her?"

He dipped his head silently.

"God, she's beautiful, Jean. She looks so much like your mother, like *you*."

A wry smile ghosted his lips. "She's pure Ubasian. Not a mongrel like me."

Her eyes shot to his. Is that how he saw himself? The impure son of a murderer and rapist, not a true African?

Something close to compassion unfurled inside her.

He pocketed the photo quickly, as if he'd made a mistake even showing her. "Can you imagine that?" he said, his mouth curling into a harsh smile. "The infamous Diable actually had family—a real sister, nieces, nephews." He leaned forward sharply. "Do know what that was like, Emma? To *discover* that? His eyes narrowed and his voice turned husky. "Souleyman took that from me. He took my family. He murdered them before I could ever meet them." His voice grew dangerously quiet. "It was a mistake not to kill him when I could, because now he's coming back for more. He's growing strong again. But this time I *will* end his life."

She had an impulse to touch him, to ease his spirit. She lifted her hand almost reflexively, caught herself and ran it through her hair instead.

He noticed the gesture, her indecision. His eyes connected with hers, and the air felt suddenly charged. It wasn't only the chemistry that had shifted between them, they'd connected on some deeper level. Emily felt as if she was at a critical turning point, unsure which way to go.

To her relief, she saw one of his guards hastening down the lawn, but relief segued into mild alarm when Laroque stiffened sharply at the sight of his soldier.

He launched to his feet, long strides taking him swiftly over the lawn to meet his man out of her earshot. Their exchange was urgent, conducted in low tones she couldn't pick up.

When he returned to the table his features were once again impenetrable. He held his hand out to her. "Come, I have something to show you."

"What?"

"My sister's village."

Nerves skittered through her chest. "Why?" She glanced toward the retreating militia guy. "Is…is there some kind of trouble?"

"There's been a skirmish near the palace," he said. "Some of Souleyman's insurgents have infiltrated deeper into Ubasi. They're getting closer to the capital. My men have subdued them, but there may be more. I cannot leave you here alone, and I must speak to the headman of Tamasha's village. I owe him a visit, and I need his help. He needs to prepare his people for battle, protect the women and children, and he must send out alerts to other rural settlements. I'm taking reinforcements to him."

He waited, hand held out, rock steady.

Emily stared at his hand, confusion tightening

inside her. She needed to talk to Jacques, tell him things were not what they seemed in Ubasi.

Maybe if she stayed behind at the castle, she could find a way to communicate while Laroque was gone. "I think I'd rather remain here while—"

His brows lowered sharply. "It's for *your* safety."

"I…I'm prepared to take the risk, thanks, Jean. I'm tired after—"

"We have a deal, Emma," he said very quietly. "Don't we?"

She studied the hard planes of his face, marveling at how different he'd looked in those few moments he dropped his guard. He could be manipulating her, working up her empathy, sucking her in with charismatic charm. Or he could be telling the truth.

Either way, she was trapped. The only way out was to see this mission through, knowing that any misstep might cost her.

"Yes," she said softly, placing her hand in his. "We have a deal."

His fingers closed firmly around hers as he lifted her to her feet. He didn't release her right away, and she didn't pull back, either.

Laroque looked deep into Emma's eyes, searching for some hint of truth. What he felt was desire. Unbidden and sharp. He felt himself swell with need as he held her hand, her skin so soft in his rough palm. His breathing quickened. Her scent was intoxicating. Everything about her was arousing. He could see she felt it, too. He could read it in her eyes. And

in this moment, as he held her close, Jean knew he'd
do whatever it took to sleep with her.

Enemy or not.

And if she *was* a spy? Well, then, she was equipped for the game. She knew what she was in for. She
knew his reputation, and thus her chances.

But was *he* equipped to deal with her if she turned
out to be a traitor? Something in her eyes warned him
he wasn't.

Chapter 5

Jacques Sauvage hung up the telephone, deep in thought. According to the Geographic International team leader, Max Rutger, Emily Carlin was inside Le Diable's fortress voluntarily. GPS confirmed her laptop and phone were there. So why wasn't she using them?

He leaned back in his chair. Carlin hadn't been active in the field for some time, but he was confident in the training he gave *all* his contractors. If they wished to remain on FDS books, they were compelled to do a refresher boot camp annually, regardless of whether there was work available. Emily was no exception. He had to trust her. If she was in trouble, she'd have sent a coded message.

Still, if for some reason she failed to make contact

by midnight Thursday, Jacques's men would move on the palace regardless, extract Emily, and eliminate Le Diable. This was the backup plan. CIA director Blake Weston had insisted on it.

Ideally, Souleyman's insurgents would be the ones to carry out the actual assassination. The FDS would simply arm and position them.

Jacques's operatives had already made contact with Souleyman's camp east of the Ubasi border, and they'd found Souleyman to have a surprisingly healthy opposition force and network of spies already active inside Ubasi. He was planning a coup of his own. This made the FDS job incredibly simple.

Still, little things troubled Jacques. The source of Souleyman's weaponry and funding was, as yet, a mystery. He clearly had a rich source of income. The men he was hiring to retake Ubasi were not local.

And then there were the five hostages, taken by Laroque's rebels from Nigeria. There was still no official claim of responsibility for their capture, nor any ransom demand.

This was unusual, especially given the fact three of the hostages were American citizens. Things were just too damn quiet on that score. Not even Weston seemed overly concerned.

If Jacques were in Weston's shoes, he'd want answers on that front ASAP. But his job was not to second-guess the policy or strategy of his employer, in this case the United States of America.

Nevertheless, Jacques was having the backgrounds of those five hostages checked for himself. He liked to have *all* his bases covered. He liked his questions answered, and right now things were not quite adding up.

12:00 Zulu. Saturday, November 9.
Northwest of Basaroutou

They traveled in convoy, armed men standing in the backs of Jeeps scanning walls of dense foliage that encroached on either side of their vehicles with a keenness that unnerved Emily.

The sun was at its zenith, white-hot and small in a hazy sky. As the temperature peaked, the humidity began to press down on them, leaching color and clarity from the landscape. They'd been traveling for more than two hours. Emily's throat felt dry, and her body was drenched in perspiration.

Shaka sat between her and Laroque on the backseat of one of the Jeeps, panting hard, his black fur glistening in the sun. The dog was growing accustomed to her, and Emily was grateful for the buffer against Laroque's body. Her physical reaction to his touch in the garden had alarmed her. It was that potent.

She pet Shaka's head. "He's thirsty."

Laroque's eyes remained locked on to the dark green tangle of jungle, his muscles tense. "It'll have to wait. Can't stop now."

"You're worried about an ambush, aren't you?"

He grunted, which didn't ease her nerves.

"Do you have some kind of intelligence alerting you to the possibility?"

His eyes shot suddenly to hers, held her gaze. Christ, she'd have to watch herself. He was highly suspicious, as if waiting for her to make a mistake. She had no idea how much of her story he believed.

"He's a great dog," she said, trying to shift focus. "You're really fond of him, aren't you?"

"You can trust dogs," Laroque said tonelessly, turning once again to face the jungle.

"Where'd you get him?" she asked, trying to hold back the hair flapping around her face.

"Senegal. He was a stray on the docks where we stopped to collect a weapons cache."

"So you just took him in out of the goodness of your heart, while out shopping for black-market weapons?"

He snorted without looking at her. "No. He was the right color."

"Oh well, *that* explains it."

The convoy slowed to an easier pace more in keeping with the abysmal road conditions. The danger, whatever it was, must have passed. Laroque's body relaxed somewhat, too. He turned to her, but he didn't smile.

"This is a complex land, Emma, steeped in voodoo tradition and magic. People follow a different set of beliefs. When Souleyman took power, the Ubasi high priestess issued a prophecy. She decreed that Souleyman would remain leader until a man with demon eyes and a black spirit-dog came to destroy him." He paused, watching her carefully. "And do you know what Souleyman did? He ordered every black dog in Ubasi shot on sight. That was eight years ago."

"So you purposefully taunted him with the prophecy by bringing a black dog with you?"

"No. I simply made it come true. Like I told you, Emma, what is fact is far less important than what is believed, especially in this part of the world. Souleyman believed the high priestess. So did his men. So did the people of Ubasi. I brought Shaka with me as a tool to crush him psychologically."

"And your eyes—"

"They sealed the deal."

"That prophecy could be interpreted a hundred ways, Jean."

"Yes, but when Souleyman got word that a man with 'devil eyes' had sailed into port with a black dog at his side, and that he'd come with men and guns, he was instantly psychologically defeated. He panicked. His men fled in terror. His army was in disarray as it was—most of his soldiers hadn't seen stipends in more than six months. They had no intention of dying for a man who'd already given up."

"So *that's* how you managed to overthrow an entire kingdom in a few hours without killing a single person."

"Strategy can be more powerful than the sword. You have to get a man at his own game." He tapped his temple. "A game of the mind."

She swallowed. "So…Souleyman just gave up and surrendered?"

"Like a pathetic bastard."

"Smart," she said, and looked away. That's exactly how her ex had gotten her—a game of the mind.

Was that what Laroque was doing now, playing her at her own game? She wasn't sure what to trust anymore.

"No, not so smart," he said suddenly. "I should have slit his throat, done it right there as he surrendered. My mistake has allowed him to regroup and come back for me, for Ubasi."

Emily shot a look at him, and saw a moment of pure hatred in his face.

"Why didn't you kill him?"

"I have no taste for cold-blooded execution. I fight a man on equal terms, not one who lies whimpering at my feet." His jaw tightened. "But I've learned my lesson."

"It's strange, Jean, don't you think, how a stray black dog just sort of happened to be waiting for you at those docks in Senegal?"

"Don't read too much into these things, Emma. If you think too much about them you give them power, they become real."

She laughed, but inside she felt murky, strange, off center. "You don't believe in that voodoo stuff yourself, do you?"

"My people do. That alone makes it something I

have to work with. One cannot ignore the influence of voodoo and magic in local politics."

She studied the arrogant lines of his face. Laroque was clearly a master at propaganda. He'd managed to portray himself as Ubasi's rightful leader by linking himself to the high priestess's prophecy and thus aligning himself with the country's most popular religion, almost shaping himself into its cult figurehead. His dog was a tool, part of the image. It was classic tyrannical behavior.

"But you *do* love your dog?"

He cocked a brow in surprise. "Shaka?" he said, touching the animal's head. "He's my one friend."

She believed him.

The stray may have initially been a strategic tool, but Shaka had become much more to Laroque. The man did have a soul, of that Emily was becoming certain, but even tyrants had soft spots in their hearts. Weak spots.

She watched his hand resting protectively on Shaka's head, and for a brief moment wondered how it might feel to have his protective touch on her. Her cheeks went hot and she glanced away quickly, shocked with herself.

It was just an atavistic female reaction, she told herself. But she was lying. It was even more simple. *She'd* been specifically wired to go for men like him. Just as her mother had been.

And look what had happened to her.

Their Jeep swerved suddenly to avoid a small

yellow monkey that scampered into the road with a baby clutched to her back.

Emily gasped, grabbing the side as their vehicle jolted into a ditch and kicked up a cloud of sand as it accelerated and fishtailed back onto the road. Her heart skittered wildly.

She tried to catch her breath, not sure what had rattled her more—the near accident, or the realization she was becoming dangerously attracted to Laroque.

As they drove by the small primate sat up and bared her teeth, screeching at them in a high-pitched staccato, her small eyes wild.

Emily's heart thudded as their convoy began a descent into a lower plateau knotted with tropical growth. The air trapped in the hollow of land was intensely close. Trees grew taller, forest giants punching high up out of the canopy. Moisture dripped.

Two vultures circled up high on hot currents of air. Emily watched the birds, unable to get the sound of the monkey's screech out of her mind. She felt as though Laroque was taking her deep into an untamed place where strange magic seemed all too possible.

The village was nestled into a red valley alongside a twisting chocolate-brown river. As they negotiated the dirt track down into the lowlands, Emily could make out thatched wattle-and-daub huts painted with bright colors clustered in groups around a central well. Crop gardens had been cut back into the jungle, and the scent of cooking and wood fires tinged the humid air.

She felt she was journeying back in time.

Their convoy rumbled into the encampment with a town crier heralding their arrival on an ancient loud-hailer. People began to emerge from the gardens and huts—men with the physiques of hunters carrying ceremonial spears and shields, women wrapped in brightly colored swaths of fabric, some with babies strapped to their backs, and elders with bent bodies, hair white as hoarfrost against dark skin.

Barefoot children with bony little bodies in ragged clothes scampered ahead of the adults to greet the visitors, smiles wide and bright. A few emaciated curs joined the excitement with yelps of encouragement. Emily's heart did a tight little tumble.

"Your sister lived *here?*" she whispered as she watched the timeless scene unfolding in front of her, not knowing why she kept her voice low. Perhaps it was because speaking out loud might pop the fragile spell the village had woven around her. Perhaps she instinctively felt that some sort of deference was required.

He pointed to a thatched hut on the outskirts of the encampment. It was painted with green-and-orange patterns, small windows hewn into mud walls. "That was her home."

Where she'd been killed.

Emily swallowed.

She hadn't expected *this* when he'd said Tamasha had been a political activist. She wasn't sure what exactly she'd expected.

Their convoy slowed to a halt in the town center and the townsfolk converged on them.

Laroque's soldiers shook hands and joked with the men as cigarettes were passed around. The children crowded around the Jeeps trying to touch everything— children like Tamasha's, thought Emily. Innocent smiling faces just like these had been slaughtered by Souleyman's men while she'd been forced to watch. While this whole village had been forced to watch. Emily's throat grew tight and her eyes burned unexpectedly.

She tried to shake the disturbing image, and became aware that Laroque was watching her.

"You all right?"

"I...did Tamasha have a man in her life?" She *needed* to know if their father was among the faces that greeted them.

"He was killed by Souleyman's men a few weeks after their youngest child was born," Laroque said, his voice strangely tender in a way she hadn't heard before. "It's what made Tamasha so angry. She channeled her grief into fighting for a democratic Ubasi, free of Souleyman. She began to travel from village to village on that small motorbike over there—" he pointed to a rusty old scooter resting against the wall of Tamasha's hut "—to spread her ideas."

He clasped her hand, helping her out of the Jeep. "There's no other form of communication between the villages apart from travelers and word-of-mouth."

She looked up into Laroque's face. "She was like you, Jean."

His brow lifted in question.

"She was a fighter. A person who physically needed to fix what was broken." *You also fuel your actions with grief. You won't allow yourself to heal, to let her death go. You want to "fix" it instead, with bare hands and guns.*

"You want revenge," she added.

"Justice," he answered.

"It's the same thing, really."

His eyes held hers for a beat, then he moved sharply away. "Come, I'll introduce you to everyone, then I must talk to the men and tell them how to prepare."

Emily watched the children scampering alongside Laroque as he crossed the village square ahead of her. He touched the head of each child in acknowledgement, then he stooped suddenly to pick up a little girl. He raised her high up onto his shoulders, and she shrieked with laughter as he swooped back down to catch the hand of another very small barefooted boy.

Laroque laughed with them as he walked, a warm and elemental sound that caught Emily right in the gut. She noted with mild shock that the notorious Diable was totally free here, in this village. It was home to him. It was his symbolic heart of Ubasi—it defined the country's people, the traditional lifestyles, the purity of his continent.

That's why he'd come personally to talk to the

headman, and that's why he was bringing militia to
protect them. He wanted to protect his home.
Emotion rose like a warm tide through her chest, and
with it came a very real sense of affection for this
enigmatic man.

She tried to remind herself that Jean-Charles
Laroque was a tyrant. His rule here wasn't legal. It
wasn't ethical. But somehow, being here, seeing it all
with her own eyes—and beginning to understand
why he'd done it—it just didn't seem wrong. And in
that moment, Emily's trusted moral compass no
longer read true.

She suddenly wanted no part of a coup that would
attack this lifestyle—these people. Their ideals. Their
dreams. Her throat tasted bitter, dry.

She was more trapped than she'd realized.

Chapter 6

Laroque exited the hut with the men, Shaka at his heels, and stilled as he caught sight of her.

Emma was at the well, surrounded by a group of women and children all giggling hysterically as she tried to walk without dislodging the bucket of water she had balanced on her head. A bolt of bright turquoise fabric with yellow squares had been wrapped over her T-shirt and khaki pants, restraining her movements, and tears of laugher poured down her cheeks.

She saw him looking, and froze.

The bucket fell to the ground with a dull thud and rolled over the packed red earth, spilling water that darkened the ochre soil to the color of blood. Everyone fell quiet for a moment. Just the raucous call of birds and a handful of small monkeys chattering in branches above filled the afternoon.

Silently he approached her and placed his hand proprietarily at her waist. "That color brings out your eyes," he said in a whisper. "But it's supposed to be worn without the regular clothes underneath."

Her cheeks flushed, and she quickly began to unravel the wrap.

A frisson of heat chased up his spine at her reaction. Laughter made her beautiful, blushing even more so. It showed a softness she tried to hide. It made her look incredibly feminine, and even more desirable to him.

Seeing her wrapped in traditional Ubasi dress, right here in Tamasha's village, laughing with *his* people, was dangerously provocative to him. For the first time in his life Laroque wondered what it might be like to take a wife and build a home, in this country. The thought shocked him to his foundations.

His heart began to beat boldly as he watched Emma hastily rolling up her bolt of fabric, as if trying to bundle up her embarrassment. She tucked it firmly under her arm, straightened her back, and looked him coolly in the eye. "It's a gift," she said, jutting her chin toward the fabric. "They were showing me how to wear it."

"And the bucket?" He was toying with her now; he couldn't help it any more than a cat could restrain itself from chasing a mouse.

Uncertainty washed back into her eyes. He

smiled, again unable to help it. He liked her this way. Natural. No games.

He knew he had to be careful with her. Her sophisticated equipment was suspicious, as was the timing of her presence in the country. But right now all he wanted was for her to be who she claimed she was. All he wanted was to touch her.

And he did.

He placed his hand at the base of her spine, and she inhaled softly as he did. He guided her with subtle pressure from hut to hut as he greeted each family individually, introducing her by name, Shaka obediently following at their heels.

She felt good under his hands. He enjoyed the sense of ownership as he escorted her through the small town. And he liked the way she was coyly avoiding his eyes. She wanted him. He could tell. And it made him feel good.

They came to the humble abode his sister had called home. Laroque dropped his hand and motioned for the others to leave them alone for a moment.

They didn't enter Tamasha's dwelling. He couldn't.

"It's remained empty all this time?" she asked, meeting his eyes with a new openness.

He nodded, replacing his black shades, distancing himself from the genuine empathy he saw in her face. Sympathy made him edgy.

"Tell me about her, Jean," she said gently. "How did you finally learn of her existence? Why did it take so long?"

He inhaled deeply, wondering how much of himself he should expose to her. The silence between them grew thick, but not uncomfortable. The jungle wrapped its sultry-afternoon cloak around them and palm fronds rattled as birds moved through leaves, pecking at fruit. He reached down to touch Shaka and ruffled the dog's fur, drawing strength from the connection.

"Tamasha's birth was my mother's darkest secret, Emma, and she died keeping it." Laroque stared at the small, brightly painted hut. "My mother had an affair with a cousin of the king's family while visiting her Ubasi homeland, and she returned to give birth to her in this village, in secret, while my father was on an extended contract. My father had begun to change, you see, and my mother had grown very afraid of him. Too afraid to leave him. She believed that if Peter Laroque had discovered her affair, he'd have killed both her and Tamasha." He paused, his chest feeling oddly tight. "She made Tamasha promise she would *never* make contact with the family—including me, her brother—while my father was still alive."

"Was Tamasha older or younger than you?"

His mouth twisted in a grim smile. "She was my kid sister, two years younger."

"So she'd have been eleven when your mother died?"

His eyes whipped to hers, tension returning to his body as he recalled the photo she had in her computer. This woman knew too much about him.

"I did my research on you, Jean," she said softly. "I've seen the famous photo of you being dragged at age thirteen from the hospital bed of your dying mother."

It was as if she was reading his mind. He didn't like it. The silence grew charged.

"It must have been tough," she said.

"I never saw my mother alive again after that photo was taken," he said. "My father took me straight into the battlefields of Africa, where he taught me how to be a soldier."

"Who raised Tamasha?"

"Guardians. They instilled in her the importance of keeping the promise after my mother died, and when Tamasha grew older, she came to hear herself about the exploits of Peter Laroque. At that stage he was already rumored to have turned murderous. Criminal. Tamasha knew our mother was right, that he was an incredibly brutal man, and that there was a good chance he would hurt her. And later, of course, she wanted to protect her own children."

He paused, turned to look into her eyes. There was a directness in her gaze, and a compassion that made him uncomfortable. He looked away. "Because of my father's predisposition for violence, I remained estranged from my sister. And because I was in his custody and forced to fight under him from the age of thirteen, people assume I am like him. But I'm not. No one understood my relationship to him. No one knew me at all."

Even now.

"He was all you had, Jean," she offered. "You depended on him."

Laroque was quiet for a moment. "I *hated* him."

"You must have witnessed the most abysmal atrocities as a kid."

"I wasn't much different from many children on this continent. I didn't have a choice."

"When did you leave him?"

"When…" He hesitated. No. He wasn't going to tell her about that night. "The last time I saw him I was twenty."

"So when your dad was killed in that Congo raid almost two years ago, that was when Tamasha finally contacted you?"

"She got a letter to me in Paris."

Laroque wasn't going to tell Emma, either, that his politically active sister had made contact with him via King Douala, who'd been living in innocuous exile in Paris for the past eight years. The king's role in this Ubasi mission had to remain secret, for the royal family's protection.

Laroque's men had taken King Desmond Douala and his wife and son into hiding in rural Spain before mounting the coup. No one could know where the royal family was sequestered until Ubasi had been stabilized enough for their return. After living in France for eight long, unhappy years, Douala was aging, unwell. He'd wanted one last chance to reclaim his country from the hands of Souleyman. He wanted democracy, and he wanted his young son at the helm of the process. He'd paid Laroque handsomely in oil concessions to overthrow Souleyman and take back Ubasi. Laroque's brief from the king was now to establish a police force and strong military presence, so that it would be safe to bring back his son.

Laroque had initially refused the contract. There was no way he was going to masquerade as some tyrant until the king's rightful return. But then Douala had shown him the letter from Tamasha, a sister he never knew he had, the sister who'd followed *his* life, biding her time.

Tamasha had believed her brother ideal for the role of reclaiming the throne. She'd convinced the king of it. And she'd believed Laroque would do it because he had Ubasi blood.

Seeing that letter had changed the entire direction of Laroque's life in that one instant. He actually had family, a place he might belong, even call *home.*

He took the commission and began to prepare for war.

Then news came of her death. At Souleyman's hand.

The instant that news had reached him, the Ubasi mission became an all-consuming personal obsession for Laroque. He would succeed—or die trying.

And now, just as things were finally looking promising for the king's return, the CIA agents had turned up dead. The hostages had been taken from Nigeria. Souleyman had mysteriously grown in power.

And Emma had appeared on his doorstep.

Her voice broke through the silence. "But you never got to meet her?"

"No."

Emma reached out and placed her hand on the bare skin of his arm. Her eyes, so damn wide and luminous, met his. Eyes that were the exact same color as dawn breaking over the Purple Mountains.

Laroque sat in stony silence as their convoy negotiated the rutted track on their return. The sky was turning a dusky twilight that made visibility a challenge as his eyes adjusted to the gray zone between day and night. The air was thick and heavy with a sense of foreboding.

He stole another look at Emma Sanford. Not only had this woman managed to get into his castle, she was getting right inside his head, poking into his secrets. She was also aiming at some vague area around his heart. She was forcing him to *feel*. Worse, she was making him talk.

He'd overstepped the mark. He needed to be more vigilant until he knew exactly what he was up against.

An explosion suddenly split the air, and their Jeep lurched violently sideways. A hot whoosh rushed past Laroque's face. It happened so fast he barely saw the next one coming.

Another explosion ripped through the jungle as a second vehicle hit a land mine. He saw the Jeep up ahead buck into the air, hood flying up, pieces of the vehicle separating in a spinning blur of red soil and twisted metal. The Jeep flipped, landing on its back, wheels helplessly spinning. Black smoke billowed, the scent of fire was acrid.

The convoy screeched to a halt, soldiers yelling and diving for cover as machine gun fire peppered the air.

Bullets thudded into metal and barked into the dirt road in puffs of dust.

Laroque's first instinct was to protect Emma. He threw himself over her as he reached for his holstered weapon. Shielding her, he aimed up into the tree that hung low over the road, the source of the gunfire. And he returned fire with staccato precision.

Whoever was in that tree immediately turned fire directly on him. He felt Emma's body jerk and shudder sharply under his as she gasped. Laroque felt hot blood on his arm. His stomach tightened and his vision turned scarlet with rage. *She'd been hit!*

In a rage, he reared up, oblivious to his own safety, and fired into the tree, again and again and again.

He hit his mark, and the sniper tumbled out from the low branches. His body glanced off the side of a Jeep, thudding into the dirt with a bounce. Laroque's men scrambled up out of the ditches and converged on him.

Laroque grabbed Emma's shoulders, pulled her up and turned her to face him.

Her eyes were wide, her face pale against the blood that soaked her shirt.

Chapter 7

"Shaka's been hit! Quick, Jean, help me!" Emily pulled herself free from Jean's grip. "I need something to stop the bleeding!" She pressed her hands over a wound on the dog's neck as blood welled dark through her pale fingers.

Alarm flared in Laroque's eyes, then darkened to rage. He shot a quick look at his men, calculating casualties, assessing the status of the situation. Then he yelled something at her as he reached under the backseat of the Jeep, but Emily couldn't hear him. She was deaf, her ears still zinging from the explosions.

He yanked out a first-aid kit, flipped it open and pulled out a wad of bandages, urgency fueling his actions. He moved his mouth again. She shook her head. "I can't hear you!" she yelled.

He took her bloodied hand, pressed a roll of bandage against her palm, and closed her fingers over it. His eyes said it all: *Look after Shaka.*

The responsibility suddenly felt enormous. "Go!" she screamed. "Look after your men!"

He touched her shoulder briefly, then he was gone.

Emily quickly fingered through Shaka's bloody fur, her FDS first aid training skills kicking in. She could ascertain two wounds—a shot in the shoulder and one in the neck. He was losing blood fast. His eyes were rolling back and his mouth lolled open. His pulse was thready. Emily pressed the bandages firmly against the wounds, and glanced up. The dog was going to need proper medical attention, fast.

The scene she saw was apocalyptic. Acrid black smoke hung low over the burning and twisted vehicles. The battered bodies of two soldiers were strewn near the first Jeep that had hit the mine. Some of Laroque's men were scrambling to help injured comrades, others converged on the captive he'd shot from the tree, beating him as he writhed in pain.

Laroque pulled back his guards and jerked the captive up to his knees by the collar of his shirt. The sniper had been shot badly in the shoulder, and his shirt was bloody. Even from here Emily could see the stark whites of his terrified eyes against his dark skin.

Laroque demanded something, but the captive spat into his face.

Laroque stiffened with predatory anger, questioned the sniper again.

The man just stared up at him, breathing hard.

Laroque repeated his question.

The man winced as blood seeped from his shoulder, but still he didn't respond.

Laroque barked an order to his men and spun away as they dragged the captive into the jungle.

Emily heard a single gunshot, and bile rose in her throat.

Without missing a beat, Laroque strode toward her. Her heart kicked into overdrive and her stomach heaved as she tried to swallow the bitter taste in her mouth.

Not once did his eyes break contact with hers as his long legs ate the distance to the Jeep. And what she saw in those eyes frightened her.

She saw his father.

Emily forced herself to tear away from his lethal stare and quickly focused her attention on Shaka.

Laroque swung into the vehicle. *"Allez!"* he yelled to his driver as he pushed Emily's hands away from his dog and took Shaka gently into his lap.

He felt for the wounds himself, moving with experienced and fluid efficiency to staunch the bleeding.

The Jeep barked sideways out of the dust, and swerved around the carnage.

"You had him killed!" she yelled over the engine.

He looked up with eyes as flat and cold as a shark. "That sniper was one of my men," he said tonelessly.

"A soldier turned traitor. Working for Souleyman. Against my people."

In that moment Emily knew he would crush her if he ever discovered she was threatening what he held dear. This man operated on a take-no-prisoners basis, at least since he'd allowed Souleyman to escape. He clearly was not going to make that "mistake" again.

She wiped the perspiration from her forehead with the back of her wrist, before realizing all she was doing was transferring a gritty paste of blood and dust from one side of her face to the other, and suddenly she felt exhausted.

She stared at the dull green of jungle blurring by as they hit the ruts in the road at ridiculous speed, her teeth jarring with the impact.

Over the years events had taken an innocent young boy and shaped him into a brutal cold-blooded man with a dream he would now kill for.

And die for.

Just how far, she wondered, would Le Diable go if no one stopped him?

Would he really rest if he achieved his goal? Or would he take it to the next level, aiming higher, growing harder, hungrier, colder, bolstered by each success, fueled by each betrayal—a true tyrant on the rise?

Was it her job to stop him?

Or save him?

Was it even possible to alter the life course of a man like this once he was set in his tracks?

She closed her eyes, no longer even bothering to try to brace against the bone-jarring movement of the vehicle. She wasn't sure what her role in life was anymore. Yes, she was a profiler, but she was also a healer of broken minds.

In her previous FDS jobs she'd always maintained her objectivity. She'd always stayed removed from her subject. She'd always felt *right*.

Now she felt everything but.

21:48 Zulu. Saturday, November 9.
Ubasi Palace dining hall

The guards held back the doors, and Laroque swept into the dining hall, adrenaline pounding through his blood, making him rough, edgy. Frustrated.

Shaka's life was out of his hands. Whether or not his dog lived or died tonight was not in his command.

He stood still, steadying his breath as the double doors swung solidly shut behind him.

The long dining table had been set with white linen, candles, sparkling crystal and shimmering silverware. Emma stood next to the buffet at the far end of the room, her back to him. She wore a simple sleeveless black sheath that fell to her calves and molded to her figure in a way that made him think of sex. Her dark hair had been scooped back into a high ponytail. Functional. Undecorated. Elegant. And totally arresting.

She whirled round as he entered, and he saw what she was holding in her hands—his special photograph.

He walked slowly over to the buffet, his eyes holding hers as he drew closer, his stomach tightening with each step, his restless adrenaline spiking. He carefully took the framed photograph out of her hands and set it firmly back on the buffet.

He wanted it away from her.

He wanted distance between this seductive woman and that very deeply personal part of himself, that part of himself he kept on trying to find, and was losing tonight, perhaps in his dog.

"Is…is Shaka okay, Jean?" she asked softly.

There was that empathy in her violet eyes again—a genuine caring, a sense of something so incredibly personal.

He didn't want that.

He wanted to be back in charge.

"I had an army doctor check him. The bullets have been removed." His voice didn't feel right. "Shaka is stable, and sedated. If he survives the night, he'll stand a fair chance. The doctor is with him now." He hesitated. "There's…nothing more I can do."

She touched his arm. "I'm so sorry, Jean."

He glared at her hand, emotion tugging sharply at his mouth. He withdrew from her touch. "I know it's late," he said. "But I hope you will dine with me."

He should've eaten alone. But as much as he needed to feel in charge, he also couldn't be alone right now. He needed something he couldn't define—company, a connection. He wasn't the hell sure what he needed.

"Of course," she said, but she didn't move toward

the table. She was watching him with that all-knowing analytic gaze, and he knew she had to be thinking about what he had done today, about the traitor who had been killed.

"Look," he said. "I'm really sorry you had to see what you did."

"Was it necessary, Jean?"

He felt his energy darken. "I'm not in the mood for psychological games, Emma. He was one of *my* soldiers. He betrayed not just me, but my people, *my country.* He's been living under *my* roof while feeding information to my enemy's camp. I got wind of this from the captives apprehended during the skirmish this morning. That's why we took extra pre-caution on the way to Tamasha's village. Clearly it wasn't enough."

"He didn't have to die like that."

Irritation darted down his chest. "I don't need your approval." He held his arm out, sorry now that he'd asked her to join him. "Let's eat."

Her eyes flicked to the grandfather clock, as if she didn't have the luxury of time. "That old black-and-white photograph," she said, indicating the silver frame he'd just replaced. "That's your father, isn't it? With you and your mom. You look about five years old in that picture."

He lowered his arm slowly, feeling the pressure building inside him. He said nothing.

She gave him a measured look. "I didn't expect you to have a photo of Peter Laroque on display."

His heart pumped harder, but he remained silent.

"You kept it because it was taken when you were still a genuine family, didn't you? It represents a time when there was still hope and promise in your life, before things went wrong."

He snapped. "*Enough,* Emma!"

Her eyes narrowed sharply. Then she nodded. "I'm sorry, Jean. I don't mean to push. I…it's…it's just that I'm not sure how much time I'm going to have with you…for the book, given all that's happening in Ubasi." She took his arm, drawing him closer. "Come, why don't we eat?"

Conflict churned dangerously low and hot in his gut, and the cool touch of her skin against his unfurled ribbons of something dark and hungry inside him.

Tonight he needed someone.

Damn, he needed *her.* All of her.

He pulled out her chair for her, steeling himself against her scent as she seated herself.

He took his place at the head of the table, flipped open his napkin, laid it on his lap and lifted the silver domes off the dishes. He poured wine and they ate in awkward silence. When the chink of cutlery grew too annoying, he slammed his knife and fork down and looked up. "He killed her," he said. Then cursed himself for having said anything at all.

Emma's eyes flickered, a quick sweep of long dark lashes over buttermilk skin. "What did you say?"

"My father killed my mother."

"I...I thought your mother died of a recreational drug overdose, after several years of abuse." She faltered a little, clearly worrying that she was over-stepping her mark. "I...it was in the tabloid archives I studied before coming here, Jean." He heard the hint of apology in her voice.

He reached for his glass, took a deep sip of wine. "Peter Laroque introduced my mother to the drugs that killed her. My mother may have been beautiful and famous, but she was also emotionally fragile, and very dependent on her man."

Emma's mouth tightened and a strange look crept into her eyes. She set down her knife and fork as if she'd suddenly lost her appetite.

"The drugs he gave her were highly addictive," he said. "He had to have known they would destroy her."

"Why did he do it?" She almost whispered the words, a look of growing recognition in her eyes that piqued Laroque's curiosity.

"He was an insanely jealous man, Emma. He loved my mother's beauty and he loved the fame and money that came with it, yet he resented the atten-tion it got her, especially from other men."

She reached for her wineglass, took a swig, and when she set her glass down he noticed her hands were shaking. Laroque frowned inwardly.

"Peter Laroque needed a woman who wouldn't stop him from going away to fight," he said. "Yet while he was away he'd torture himself imagining his wife having affairs. He'd grow increasingly wild with jealousy until he'd come home to claim her physically, roughly. He wanted both his freedom and total domination of his woman. He couldn't seem to reconcile these two overriding desires." He paused, thinking. "It was as if he needed to sabotage her. My father grew increasingly paranoid, more destructive, and each time he came home…he'd take her more violently."

"You *witnessed* this?"

"Yes."

Intensity darkened her eyes. "Why didn't she leave him?"

"She *couldn't*. She was afraid of him, and at the same time strangely dependent on him. He could be a very compelling man."

Emma's breathing grew slightly ragged. Her eyes flicked toward the open French doors, as if she were seeking some sort of mental escape of her own.

Intrigued, Laroque held up the bottle of cabernet. "More wine?"

She nodded, too quickly, and he poured.

He filled his own glass. "It got to a point where my father would leave her a supply of drugs each time he went on another commission, as if he wanted her to blot herself out until he returned, as though he couldn't bear her actually having a life without him."

"It was his way of locking her up while he was gone," she said, her voice hoarse.

Laroque nodded, watching her eyes. "And he always

came back with more drugs. He was a sick man, Emma, and his demons grew more violent with time."

She paled visibly. "Why did he take *you* away? Why didn't he just leave you be?"

He snorted. "My mother was dying. He had another contract to fulfill, and he knew that if she died while he was away, the authorities might step in, and he'd risk losing me. In his own very sick way, he loved his son, he loved the fact that he even had one. It appealed to the male in him." Laroque leaned forward. "And you know what, Emma? As much as I *hated* him, as much as I blamed him for my mother's death, and for taking me away before I could say goodbye to her, I came to *need* him. Especially in those early years."

"That's perfectly understandable," she said, almost too quickly, her voice too light. "You were a child, totally alone in a foreign world, of *course* you needed him."

He shrugged. "I needed his approval, and that makes me sick to my stomach now. I endured the blood, the violence, and I fought alongside my father, because he *was* my father, because I wanted his praise, and…he was all I had." Emotion heated his eyes. "And because I was angry. I fought because I was angry. I hurt people, because of *him*."

She swore bitterly, turning her face away.

"Emma?"

She took a moment. When she turned back to face him, he could read distress in her eyes.

He placed his hand over hers. "Have I…I'm sorry if I have upset you."

She shook her head. "No…no, I'm fine. I was…" She inhaled sharply. "I was just thinking about family."

He studied her face. It bothered him that he knew nothing about her. Not once had she mentioned anything about her own past or her own family. His suspicions simmered back to the surface.

"What about you, Emma? What does your father do? Where is *your* mother?"

Her eyes shuttered. She wiped her mouth with her napkin. "I have a boring academic life, Jean," she said. "Besides, this interview is about you."

He picked up his knife and fork and cut into his meat, but from the corner of his eye he saw her take another deep swig of wine. She was trying to take the edge off something, and it deepened his curiosity.

"Tell me about the oil in Ubasi, Jean," she said, setting her glass down too carefully.

Laroque lifted his eyes, studying her as he chewed slowly. "You should eat something."

She smiled, nervously this time. "I will. You mentioned this morning that the oil was yours in name only. What did you mean by that?"

He set down his cutlery and dabbed his mouth with the linen napkin. "You won't talk about yourself, yet I must give."

"Jean, it's an interview. We had a deal."

"I don't see my oil plans as part of the interview, Emma."

"*Everything* in Ubasi is part of you. I don't think you can extract one from the other without missing the picture. Besides, you did mention the oil this morning." She leaned forward in an obvious way that drew attention to her cleavage.

He forced himself to look back up at her face. He was beginning to feel manipulated. Yet this woman was clearly uncomfortable doing whatever she thought she was doing.

"I mentioned it only in relation to your allegation that I had taken the fields for personal gain," he said. "And I'm sorry I did."

"You've discovered enough oil to make you one of the wealthiest men on this planet, Jean."

The leash on his control grew taut. He was too damn edgy to be having this conversation now. He should get up and leave. Yet a part of him couldn't bear the accusation in her voice. Part of him needed her to know he was good, hell alone knew why.

"It'll make Ubasi wealthy, not me," he said coolly. "It's too damn bad it takes something like a massive oil find to bring my country to world attention, *non?*" He leaned forward. "Ubasi was not sexy enough. It was small, poor, war-ravaged. But now?" He watched her steadily. "Now *I* have the country, and now I have something they *all* want." He paused. "Cheap black gold. Now Ubasi is suddenly sexy because we have it. Is that why *you're* interested in me, too, Emma? Because now *I'm* sexy enough for your book sales? Will this interview make you rich, bring you fame?"

Anger sparked in her eyes and her mouth went flat. "Call it sexy if you want, Jean. But we're talking about a lot more than a few barrels here. I'm told there's enough in those oil fields to rival production in Nigeria and Equatorial Guinea combined. And it's all *yours*. At least, since you stole it."

His body began to thrum.

The night suddenly felt unbearably hot. The call of an owl reached them from the sultry jungle outside, and in spite of his anger at her comments, he was turned on by her fire, her challenge. Desire burned through him.

If Laroque stayed with this woman one second longer, he was going to do something he regretted.

He got to his feet, placed his napkin on the table. "This interview is over," he said. He turned to go, but she grabbed his wrist.

He froze, turned slowly back to face her, lust and aggression swirling dangerously like the chemicals of a Molotov cocktail in his gut, just waiting for the spark.

"You're not telling me the whole story, Jean. *Why?*"

"Why should I tell you anything, Emma?"

"Because you don't want to be known as a despot. You don't want to be like your father, that's why."

Her fingers were hot on his skin, feeding the dark sexual energy in him. He stared at her hand as he spoke. "I take only one thing from the oil, Emma." His eyes lifted, lanced hers. "Power. When you have something others want, you are made strong in direct proportion to their need. I have used my new power to form an alliance with the rebels that govern the northern jungles of Ubasi, as well as with the underground militias of our neighbors. You see, Emma, all those rebels want the same thing as I want for Ubasi—a fair shake."

She removed her hand from his arm. "I don't understand."

"They see the massive transnationals drawing oil from *our* delta. They see incredible profits going to foreign countries. Meanwhile their own families starve, their land is raped, their rivers are polluted with oily rainbows that kill their fish and their game."

"You and the rebels want the West out?"

"No. We just no longer choose to be victims. In uniting, we have strength. By arming ourselves, we have negotiating power. We are now forming a petroleum cartel that will, among other things, coordinate oil policy in the Gulf of Guinea, manage supply, set pricing and stringent environmental rules. *We*—the people—will control the Gulf, Emma. Anyone who doesn't like it will have to convince the international community that they have a claim to go to war over what is ours. And we *will* fight them."

Incredulity filled her eyes. The pulse in her smooth pale neck pulsed rapidly. "You're *serious*."

"Do I look like a joker?"

"Jean, you do realize that any one of the superpowers or transnationals *will* fight you for this. They will go to war to keep the status quo."

He leaned down, close to the gorgeous mouth he just wanted to ravish. "Exactly, Emma. Which is precisely why we are preparing for war." He was so close to kissing her now.

He touched her neck and ran his hand very slowly down to her shoulder, feeling her pulse increase under his fingers. "And you know something else?" he whispered over her lips. "Any one of those superpowers or transnationals you just mentioned are also capable of sending spies into Ubasi to undermine me."

She swallowed nervously.

"But you've seen what happens to those who betray me," he said, his eyes tunneling into hers.

Hot spots appeared on her cheeks. "Do...do the deaths of those four American geologists have anything to do with this plan of yours, Jean?"

"Why should they?"

Her eyes flicked away from his.

"Look at me, Emma."

She lifted her eyes slowly and met his. Her lips were so close he could taste the wine on her breath, he could taste *her.* "You think *I* killed those men because those bodies were displayed in that fashion? After everything I have told you about myself?"

"I...I only—"

He angled her chin, forcing her not to break eye contact. "Do you know something that I don't about those men, Emma?"

Her eyes flickered.

His heart turned cold. He swore viciously, lurched to his full height and stalked out into the hot jungle night.

Laroque knew a liar when he saw one.

Chapter 8

23:03 Zulu. Saturday, November 9.
Ubasi Palace

He didn't trust her.

That much was clear. He was testing her, probably because he didn't yet have any proof she wasn't who she claimed to be. She needed to be more careful. She was walking a very fine line with him.

And she needed to move faster.

Emily's eyes shot to the grandfather clock. In less than an hour she'd have only five days left. If she didn't contact Jacques in that time, they *would* kill him.

Conflict churned inside her. Laroque was a revolutionary, his plan bold, brash. But it *was* conceivable. If he pulled this off it would represent a major power shift in Africa. The corporate interest behind the status quo in Washington wasn't going to allow that—they had way too much vested in African oil right now. Cutting off the supply could send the American economy into an instant downward spiral.

A cold feeling filled her chest. Just how much did Washington actually know?

Were she and the FDS being used as pawns to stop Laroque in this oil game?

It was certainly feasible.

They'd rather see someone like Souleyman in power, someone who could be bought, controlled. Because there was no way in hell anyone could hope to control Jean-Charles Laroque.

A sick feeling leached from her chest to her stomach. This also, however, gave Laroque motive to eliminate the CIA agents, especially if those operatives were informing Washington about his cartel. Emily knew he was capable after seeing what he did today. Yet she honestly did not believe he'd have used his father's signature display of the bodies. It didn't make sense.

Unless she was being manipulated on that front, too.

She was caught in the middle, way over her head. Jacques was probably not aware of the scope of this, either. He would not have accepted this commission otherwise. The FDS walked a fine line in Africa. When in doubt, they erred in the favor of the indigenous populations. Surely Laroque's cartel would be seen as a positive for the people?

She swore softly.

Maybe Jacques did know.

The only thing Emily knew for certain was that absolutely nothing was as it seemed in Ubasi. There were shadows behind shadows, puppeteers behind manipulators.

She wiped her damp palms on her napkin, then pushed back her chair and stood, nerves biting at her stomach. She had to try to learn more from Laroque, because while she'd been sent here to take him down, she might now also be the only person in the world who could save him.

If Jacques did know about this cartel, and she ended up going against him, her career with the FDS would be over. And possibly her life, too.

But without communication she was on her own. She had only Laroque to work with, and she was going to have to go all the way to push him to his limits, to get the information she needed. Because at some point in the next five days she was going to have to pick a side.

It was even hotter out on the wide stone veranda that overlooked the forest. A full moon hung low over the forest canopy, thick and dark with secrets.

The sounds of the night rose from the blackness and drifted on damp and verdant air tinged with the scent of flowers that bloomed only in the dark.

Laroque stood silhouetted against the moonlight, staring out over the jungle—a powerful and lonely specter.

She came up behind him. "Jean?"

He didn't respond.

She reached up and touched his shoulder. He whipped round, moonlight catching his eyes, his pulsing intensity startling her.

Emily took a quick step back.

"I…I'm sorry, Jean. I know you've said you don't condone what your father was, or what he did, but it's impossible to ignore the parallel."

"Don't you see, Emma?" he snarled. "That's exactly what was intended. Someone *wants* the parallel drawn. They want to frame me for those murders."

The hostility in his voice sent shivers over her hot skin.

"Why?" she asked softly.

His eyes narrowed, glinting in the pale light. "I thought I told you this interview was over."

"This is off the record. You need to talk to me, Jean."

"And why would I need to talk to you?"

Because I might be the only one who can save you.

She edged a little closer, and touched his arm tentatively. "Because you have no one else."

His eyes held hers, his energy turning darker, more palpable.

"I have my generals to confide in, Emma. My military advisers, the headmen of the villages, the council I am putting together. Those are the people I look to."

She moved her hand up his arm slightly. Her only chance was to get close to him, to make him care enough so that if she needed to tell him why she was here, he might not hurt her. "I mean just to share, Jean. You can't stand so alone."

"I always have."

"But it hasn't been by choice, has it?"

He said nothing. The moonlight threw an eerie glow off the mica in the cliffs of the distant Purple Mountains.

"What about the hostages, Jean?" she said gently, worried about pushing too far, too fast. "Why did you take those men from Nigeria?"

He swore and cupped her face roughly, his voice lowering to a darkly seductive pitch. "Why won't you give it up, woman?"

She swallowed. She could feel the thrumming strength of his fingers and she could see a muscle pulsing at his jawline. An owl hooted, its shadow momentarily blocking the moon as it swooped over the forest. "Why do you keep answering my questions, then, Jean?" she whispered.

He moved his face closer to hers. "Maybe I need you to understand me." He slid his hand down from her jaw and curled his fingers around her nape, drawing her closer. It was warm and rough against her skin, an outdoorsman's hand. A warrior's hand. A hand capable of love.

And death?

Emily felt herself melt inside, drawn to his complexity, his strange need for her.

He lowered his head, bringing his mouth near hers. "Maybe I want to trust *you,* Emma," he murmured, feathering his lips softly over her mouth.

"Maybe—" he said darkly "—I want to know how *you* know so much about those hostages." He brushed his lips even more firmly over hers, drawing her closer at the same time. "Maybe I want to know how *you* know there are even Americans among them."

Panic unfurled low in her belly. Her breaths became short, making her light-headed. A shriek in the jungle made her jerk back, but he gripped her arm suddenly, rattling her completely.

"I…the science team, the staff at the hotel, they were all talking about it…" Her voice came out in a rough whisper. "About why everyone was being ordered out of the country."

"News travels fast."

She tried to step back again, couldn't. Panic rose in her gut.

He slid his hand down her arm, encircling her wrist. He was edgy, wild.

She didn't feel right, either.

His eyes drilled into hers. "I did *not* kill those men, Emma. And I did not sanction those hostages being taken from Nigeria."

She swallowed, and nodded. "I…I believe you."

"Do you?"

Her eyes began to water. "I do."

His grip relaxed slightly and she exhaled.

"What else do you believe, Emma? Tell me about yourself. Where do *you* come from?"

It was a test. She felt his net closing around her. The flame of panic licked harder at her stomach.

She was a trained operative and a psychologist—she could talk her way out of this. She could control her emotions. But something was wrong. The panic was burning too fast, growing way out of proportion to the situation. Flames flicked through her belly, faster, rising up into her chest, burning through her lungs and searing into her throat.

She couldn't breathe, couldn't speak. She was dizzy. Her pulse began to race.

He was watching her intently, a hunter waiting for his prey to dash so he could strike. A dark breeze suddenly rattled fat leaves. The clapping noise made her jump, unraveling the last little shred of control she held over her mind. Him—this place—it was all getting to her, drilling down into the roots of her psyche where her phobias lay locked away. They were being chiseled free, and were sifting to the surface of her brain, taking hold.

"I…" Her voice choked in her throat. She tried again. "I…think I'm tired. I…need to sleep." She pulled her hand out from his hold and turned to leave, but he caught her arm, spun her back and kissed her hard on the mouth.

She froze momentarily as his mouth pressed over hers, then she melted almost as quickly as heat devoured her from the inside. Her knees buckled, but he caught her, pulling her hard up against his body, his lips moving hungrily and aggressively over hers. Something wild and primal surged violently up from her core, and she met his hunger with a hot urgency of her own, opening her mouth under him, her tongue twisting with his, her teeth scoring his lips, a soft moan releasing from somewhere deep in her chest.

His hand moved up from her waist and cupped her breast roughly. A spasm of pleasure speared right into her belly, and she pressed her pelvis against his thigh, needing to feel him against her.

In the back of her mind she heard the jungle sounds, felt the velvet cloak of humidity over her shoulders, but there was no logic to her thoughts. She moved her hands over his chest, feeling resilient pads of muscle moving under her fingers. It made her hotter, hungrier, and she slid her hands down his belly.

He pulled back abruptly, his breathing ragged, his eyes wild in the silver moonlight. He took her by the shoulders, held her steady, his eyes searching hers for…something, for some answer to an unarticulated question.

Confusion washed through her, and a coolness shivered over the heat of her skin. She suddenly felt embarrassed.

"Emma?" His voice was rough. "Do you want this?"

Her heart was beating so hard she ached. She wanted him like she'd wanted no other man. She wanted to ride his rough energy, tap into his power, obliterate the fears that plagued her mind. One kiss had opened a hunger so raw in her she had no idea it had even existed.

She swallowed.

This was a mistake.

This was a man who could destroy her. This was

her *job*—and he was her subject. Panic separated itself from the heat of her desire and began to writhe inside her again as rational thought resurfaced.

Had she learned nothing in New York?

"I…I can't do this."

She swiftly crossed the veranda and entered the dining hall, the noose of fear tightening, choking her.

She heard him coming behind her.

Her breathing quickened, and she rushed through the palace, right past the guards. She just had to get to her room, get somewhere safe.

"Emma!"

He was coming after her. She could hear his boots. She began to walk faster, faster, her heart pounding as she broke into a run. She knew it made no sense at all, but she couldn't *not* try to escape from the thing she feared the most—the power of her own attraction. The thing she tried to hide from. The fear she pretended she didn't have.

"Emma! Stop!"

He caught up to her, grabbed her arm, spun her round. She was panting, her body drenched in sweat.

"What the hell is going on, Emma? What are you running from?"

You. Everything you represent.

But she said nothing. She looked away, afraid of connecting with his eyes, afraid of his charisma, his growing sensual hold over her.

She should never have touched him. She'd assumed she could handle him.

"Talk to me, Emma," he said softly, feathering her cheek with the backs of his fingers. "It was you who said we needed to talk, remember?"

She struggled to hold back tears. She wanted to lean into his solid chest, feel those hands on her, protective, the way she'd seen they could be. At the same time, it's exactly what she *didn't* want. Off limits professionally or not, this man was bad for her. He had a rotten family record. She had no idea how much of his father lurked inside him.

She'd seen firsthand what men like him could do to women like her. And her mother.

"Who has hurt you, Emma?"

He was astute, she had to hand him that. But she couldn't tell him, not without blowing her cover. She could not tell him about her own father, about her own sick need for powerful men like her dad, and about how that need fed into her fear of being dominated, controlled, like her mother had been.

She couldn't tell him how General Tom Carlin had shaped everything she had become in life—from joining the military to getting her doctorate in psychology, to specializing in the minds of dominant males. She could not tell him how she *still* sought approval from her dad. She couldn't tell Jean about her own mother's suicide.

Emily couldn't even voice it all properly to herself. The only time she'd come close to talking about it was with Anthony. And look where that had got her.

Yet somehow Laroque had unearthed something in her, a yearning to share, to articulate it all.

He'd understand.

He'd seen that same kind of dependency in his mother. It made her feel connected with him because of it, even as the power of her attraction to him frightened her.

She'd been suppressing this all for far too long now, and she craved catharsis.

But Laroque was a stranger. And she was a spy.

She couldn't share.

He took her into his arms, drew her close and gently brushed his lips over her forehead.

It did her in. Tears slid over her cheeks. He kissed them away, and his kisses moved gently, hesitantly closer to her lips, but she placed her hands flat against his chest. "No," she whispered hoarsely. "Not now. I…I'm sorry."

He tilted her chin up gently and brushed a tear from her face with the rough pad of his thumb. "Later, then?"

Emily looked into eyes, softened with compassion, and she knew she was going to sleep with him.

She wanted to.

But she walked away, trying to coordinate limbs that felt like melting jelly.

In the dark hours before dawn, Laroque finally received word that Shaka had pulled through. A savage happiness ripped through his body. He threw back his head, closed his eyes, and he heard the velvet memory of her voice. *You need to share, Jean.* It curled through him. *You can't stand alone.*

He breathed out hard. Emma had opened a door he could no longer shut. She'd let him taste a need.

Laroque left his dog sleeping peacefully in his basket, and he took the stairs up to her room.

He knocked gently, listened, but there was no answer. He hesitated. He shouldn't do this. Then he thought of the sultry promise he'd seen in her violet eyes when he'd said "later." It was a look of longing that went well beyond the invitation he'd tasted on her lips.

He reached for the handle, opened her door, slowly.

She lay in a silver puddle of moonshine, louvered doors wide open to the hot sultry night, her sheets in a wild tangle on the floor. She wore only a thin white camisole and panties.

His pulse fluttered.

Her arm was hooked behind her head, displaying breasts that were small and firm under the sheer white fabric. Her skin was the color of alabaster in the moonlight and it was sheened with heat, giving her an ethereal quality. Her hair fanned out darkly over the white pillow. She was breathing deeply, fast asleep. He ran his eyes down her body, his mouth going dry.

The knee of her right leg was crooked, the ankle hooked loosely under her other knee in a way that opened to hint at the dark delta between her thighs.

His stomach swooped sharply and his breath

lodged tight in his throat. He gripped the door handle. He should leave. Now. Quickly. He should never have come in like this.

But he couldn't. Not after seeing her like this.

His heart began to bang hard against his chest wall, the rhythm echoing in a hot, heavy pulse between his legs.

"Emma?" he whispered, his voice rough.

Her lashes fluttered and she moaned softly, lifting and repositioning her hips in such a way that spat fire to his groin.

"Emma?"

She moved again, opening her eyes, staring straight at him.

"Jean?" she murmured.

He stepped into her room and shut the door quietly behind him.

Chapter 9

Emily had fallen asleep angry.

She'd returned to her quarters furious at losing control. She'd allowed her personal issues to interfere with a job in a way that was absolutely inexcusable, and she'd totally embarrassed herself.

She was going to take a break after this job. She needed to totally reassess her life, her career. That business with Anthony had been a wake-up call. She should have faced it, dealt with it properly before taking on another FDS contract. But, damn, she hadn't wanted to, even though the therapist in her knew it would have been the right path.

Shrinks were notoriously inept at dealing with their own neuroses. It's why they went into the profession in the first place—they were all bloody nuts.

It was with these irritable thoughts that Emily fell into a hot and tangled sleep. And once again, Le Diable emerged from black shadows and entered her dream. Once again the night was hot and velvet, and he was touching her in ways she shouldn't imagine.

"Emma?" The voice in her dream sent a low shiver of cool along the damp heat of her skin.

"Emma." She heard it again, his rolling bass turning thick, tugging at something elemental in her gut. She moaned softly, lifting her hips, feeling the ache in her belly for him again. She was hot, so hot.

She sensed him materializing from the darkness, coming closer, and the ache began to throb sharp and low in her pelvis. She instinctively opened her thighs a little wider as she moaned again, trying to escape the heat, trapped somewhere deep and humid in her dream. She felt a slight breeze ripple over her skin—a sense of real presence.

He was standing there. At her door.

She stared straight at him, her mind confused, her body still hot, ready. "Jean?"

He came to the bed, sat down beside her, the moonlight glinting in his pale eyes. "You are so beautiful, Emma," he said, gently tracing the line of her jaw with his fingers. Her nipples contracted sharply under her skimpy camisole as he watched. "I need you, Emma. But…just say the word," he whispered, "and I'll leave."

She shook her head, and he continued tracing his fingers down along the contour of her breast, circling around her hard nipple. Her eyelids fluttered and molten heat settled low in her belly.

He leaned over her. "Are you sure?"

She moistened her lips. Not trusting herself to speak, she reached for the hem of her camisole and pulled it over her head, then drew him down to her. He covered her mouth firmly with his, lowering his weight onto her.

He was hot, his body solid muscle, his military fatigues rough against her bare breasts. He moved his lips gently over hers in hesitant question, making any decision to move further solely hers.

She tried to think, but she couldn't. Didn't even want to. She wanted Jean, and she was ready for him. And she didn't give a damn about anything else in this world right at this moment. She needed this fundamental human connection.

She needed to feel like a wanted woman.

She just needed *him*.

She kissed him back, hard. Hungry. Desperate. Opening his mouth wider with her lips, she tangled her tongue slickly with his as she yanked his shirt out of his pants and rapidly worked the buttons. She splayed open his shirt and moaned involuntarily against his mouth as her hands met the firm skin of his iron-solid abs.

He lifted her buttocks, removing her panties, positioning her in the center of the king-size bed as he kissed her. Then he sat back and removed his clothes, his eyes never leaving hers until he stood fully naked.

He studied her brazenly, raking his eyes down the length of her hot, damp body in such a way she could feel them moving on her skin, stopping to rest on the mound between her thighs. A dark smile of satisfaction curled over his mouth and he leaned forward, placed his hands on her knees, opened her wider. He bent down and she felt the slick, hot tip of his tongue at the apex of her thighs. Emily bit back the sound that swelled from her chest. She closed her eyes, threw her head back, unable to control the shiver of her muscles as he flicked his tongue between her legs, going a little deeper each time, swirling, teasing. But when his teeth grazed the exquisitely sensitive little nub at her centre, the sound escaped her control, and she began to shake.

He lifted her hips higher, drawing her to himself, entering her with his tongue, going deeper with a wild and increasing hunger of his own until she felt she was going to explode.

But just as she was convinced she could hold back her climax no longer, he stopped abruptly.

Emily lay there, shaking, trying to catch her breath, the air suddenly cool between her legs.

He moved up, his body covering hers, heavy. She felt his knees pushing hers apart even farther, giving better access, and with one sharp and powerful thrust he entered her fully. She gasped, opening herself wider, arching her back, wanting him even deeper. He filled her completely, hot, hard and thick.

And he moved inside her, fast, quick strokes that seared her nerves. Limbs intertwined in a breathless, elemental rhythm that cut through the intellectual tangle of games and lies straight to the raw, physical core where the bond was rudimentary, savage and simple.

He rolled her on top of him so that she straddled him, knees wide on either side of his body. She sat back, sinking deeper onto his erection. She braced her hands on his shoulders, hair falling wild over her face, and she rocked her hips, breasts bouncing as he bucked under her, forcing himself deeper into her, so deep that she suddenly exploded with a rough cry. She'd never needed a man so badly, been so ready for him, that she'd screamed with the raw pleasure of release.

She was panting as he spun her over and sank back into her. He held her tight as he drove repeatedly into her before finding his own release with a powerful shudder that took control of his body.

They lay like that, in the puddle of silver moonlight, hot and intertwined, still breathing hard, neither of them wishing to break contact with each other or shatter the moment with speech.

Emily felt Jean's pulse gradually begin to slow and his body relax against hers, and a deep sense of physical peace washed through her.

She watched the shadows on the whitewashed walls, feeling at a loss to describe the sensation of just lying here, holding this powerful man naked against her skin as he fell asleep in her bed. So she didn't try. She just savored his body with a rare sense of belonging just in the moment.

They'd both known that he'd come to her tonight, that this would happen. They also both knew that something had shifted.

For whatever reasons they'd been compelled to this point. Where they would go from now, Emily had no idea.

06:33 Zulu. Sunday, November 10.
Ubasi Palace

Laroque propped himself up onto his elbow and moved a strand of dark hair from Emma's face. This morning she was a different person. She was a woman strong in her own sexuality, one who could give as hard as she got. Yet he'd glimpsed her vulnerability inside. This dichotomy intrigued him. He understood it. He knew himself how to be potently powerful while balancing on the shaky foundations of a rough childhood.

He knew how to bottle fear behind a cool facade of control, because giving your enemy the scent of weakness gave him an edge. It could cost the battle, and your life.

He wondered—not for the first time—if he needed to protect himself from Emma.

He trailed his finger slowly down her belly, smiling as she shivered slightly and opened sleepy eyes. He could make love to her forever—but he still knew virtually nothing about her.

"Do you want to talk about what happened after dinner?"

She closed her eyes and shook her head.

He didn't press it. He didn't want to break the connection they had right now.

Perhaps he just didn't want to acknowledge that the reason she was unable to talk about herself was because she was hiding the truth about who she really was, and why she was in his palace.

He lay back, choosing instead to be content in the moment as a pale dawn leaked into the sky. But his beeper sounded, slicing reality back into the morning.

Laroque tensed. Groping around the floor, he found his pants, took his pager from his pocket and read the message. He dressed quickly as she watched him, a growing wariness in her eyes.

He kissed her softly. "I have to go. I'll be back before dark."

She sat up, eyes strangely purple in the dim light. "Where are you going?"

He paused. "There's been an incursion. A skirmish with Souleyman's men near one of the villages. Several of his militants are dead. I need to take a look. My people need to talk to me."

She opened her mouth to speak and he covered her lips with his fingers. "Don't worry. I'll be back before dinner."

And he was gone.

Emily flopped back onto the bed.

What had she just done to the mission, to herself?

She got up, hair falling in a damp tangle over her shoulders, and padded barefoot onto the small stone balcony. The dawn sun was warm on her naked body. And for a moment, she didn't want the tangle of complications of her life. She didn't want to think about the FDS backing Souleyman, or the cloak-and-dagger operations of this mission. She just wanted to feel like an Eve, in the soft morning sun blanketing this Eden.

She closed her eyes, relishing the sensation on her skin, and with mild shock she realized that for the first time in a long, long while, she actually felt physically whole.

It was a sensation she didn't want to lose. It was a state she hadn't even known she'd been searching for. And she'd finally found it—in the wrong place, with the wrong man. She was falling for the enemy.

But *was* he?

She opened her eyes and stared out over the forest canopy. The jungle looked even more beautiful today. That made it deceptive, and even more threatening, because this jungle was not an easy place to survive. It was one of the most competitive arenas on earth, a place where you either hunted or *were* hunted, killed or *were* killed.

And she wasn't sure whether she was pawn, or power.

Somewhere out there, the *real* enemy might lie.

All Emily knew for certain this morning was that regardless of what Jean was doing, it was not in her to condemn him to death.

But that's exactly what would happen if she didn't find a way to break her radio silence—he would die.

In less than five days.

Laroque's Jeep pulled into a village which lay at the religious heart of his country. The headman of this community was a key ally of his, and a friend. Descended from noble warrior tradition, he was not only an astute military strategist, he was a persuasive orator, too. He also had a keen grasp of what was of traditional importance to Ubasi. This was a man Laroque hoped would form part of a powerful Ubasi democracy in a few years. He wanted him in cabinet.

He swung out of the Jeep and strode through the circle of mud dwellings toward the headman's hut. Laroque visited here often, but this was the first time he'd walked without Shaka at his side. He'd checked on his dog before leaving the palace, and things were looking good. Shaka had turned a corner. He was definitely going to make it. But the shock of nearly losing something so close to him had shifted Laroque's world slightly.

Making love to Emma had further unsettled him. He was falling for her, and that was going to make things difficult, especially if he learned she was deceiving him.

This alone put a kind of fierceness into Laroque's stride—he *wanted* her to be who she claimed she was. He wanted it so badly he was worried it would skew his judgment.

He instinctively felt for his weapon before ducking into the hut. He'd been called to this village because of an emergency during the night. The headman's soldiers had engaged in a shoot-out with a group of what appeared to be Souleyman insurgents. As far as Laroque knew, the so-called insurgents had all been killed. It was their bodies he'd been called to see, and he was keen to check their uniforms, weapons and communications equipment. He welcomed any small clue that might help him ascertain what the hell he was up against.

But as Laroque moved the bead curtain aside with the back of his hand, he saw it was not the headman, but the village *feticheuse* sitting in the center of the hut. The old fortune-teller squatted in the dull yellow glow of a paraffin lamp, as if waiting for him.

Laroque froze, almost backed out, until he saw the headman sitting on a small wooden stool across the room. He raised his arm, motioned for Laroque to enter. "I'm having my shells read, come in."

The wizened old woman stared at Laroque with cloudy eyes as she drew a handful of cowrie shells and worn ivory pieces from a leather bag. She cast them across her mat with a rattle.

She began to sway in rhythm to a moaning chant that sent a shiver over Laroque's skin. He had a sense it was not the headman's fortune being read, but his own. "I'll wait outside," he said.

But as he moved, the woman stopped dead. Her eyes flared, pupils rolling back, leaving glassy whites. "Yah!" she whispered, and refocused on Laroque. His heart lurched. The woman's one word had punched him physically in the stomach. He backed out quickly and stepped into the hot sun. A sheen of perspiration had formed over his forehead. He swiped it off with the back of his arm. Damn, this stuff could get to one.

"What the hell was that about?" he asked the headman as he finally emerged from the hut.

He studied Laroque intently. "Come," he said. "I must show you the bodies."

The headman led Laroque along a narrow jungle path to where the slain militants had been left in dense undergrowth. The forest was very dark, little light filtering through the dense canopy.

Flies and insects buzzed over the victims, settling on wounds.

Laroque tried to ignore the smell as he crouched down to examine them. "They're not locals," he said, moving one man onto his back.

The headman nodded. "Looks like hired guns from the Sahara region. Word is that's where Souleyman is getting his muscle. Those guys don't come cheap."

Laroque pursed his lips as he checked pockets. The uniforms were devoid of any insignia. He found no ID at all. "What about weapons?" he asked as he stood up.

"Czech-made Rachot UK-68s. Right out the box."

Laroque whistled. These guys had been carrying highly portable general-purpose machine guns, not the sort of weapons commonly found floating around African war zones.

"Where are the guns?"

"Back at the village."

Laroque frowned. "You find any communications equipment on them?"

The headman nodded. "It's also back at the village."

Laroque narrowed his eyes. "Why'd you bring me out here, then?"

The headman glanced nervously over his shoulder, then stepped closer.

A foreboding rustled through Laroque, raising the hairs on the back of his neck. He automatically felt for his weapon, every sense suddenly on keen alert, even as he maintained an outward cool.

"It's not the bodies I wanted you to see," the headman said, his voice low, his eyes intense, his face dark in the jungle shadow. "It's what that man—" he pointed to one of the bloodied bodies with the business end of his Kalashnikov "—told us before we killed him."

A muscle tightened over Laroque's chest. "What did he say?"

"He said that Le Diable is bewitched, that a sorceress has come to destroy him, and she is stealing his power."

"What!"

"He said that this witch is living in Le Diable's

castle, that she has hair like a raven and eyes like the Purple Mountains." He paused, the intensity of his eyes darkening to a smoldering black. "Do you remember the prophecy, Jean?"

"*What* prophecy?" But even as Laroque asked the question, he registered the earlier origins of his unease with Emma, the whispers of warning he'd felt when looking into her violet eyes, that feeling he'd forgotten something.

"When you came and took power from Souley-man," the headman said, "the Ubasi high priestess ordained you would hold power until a woman arrived and changed everything. Do you recall that the priestess said this woman would have eyes like the Purple Mountains?"

Laroque swore and dragged his hand over his hair. "This is ridiculous! I didn't believe it then, and I don't now."

But something *had* stuck in his mind—some dark little seed that had given rise to the sense of warning that something about Emma was dangerous, some-thing that went beyond the obvious.

He cursed to himself. He'd been too damn busy overtaking the country and installing some kind of functional government to worry about the mum-blings of some ambitious high priestess. It had been a mistake. Voodoo magic was the spiritual backbone of this country. He'd used it himself to gain power.

He glanced around. The forest was impenetrable here. It felt ominous, as if it had eyes. He cursed again. It was *him,* his mind, already playing tricks on him. It was that damned fortune teller.

He was giving it all value, emotion, where none existed. But *this* was where a curse, a prophecy, played with your head. You had to get it out of your mind, because it could drive you mad, make you paranoid, like it had Souleyman.

"So what?" Laroque snapped. "So what if they say this? It means nothing!"

The headman looked hard at him, and Laroque realized he'd have to tread carefully. He'd been done a favor in this man's eyes. This was a tribal leader who dealt with superstition on a daily basis.

"It means nothing to *me,*" he added.

"It means something to your people, Jean," the man answered. "To your people this holds real power. Souleyman knows of the prophecy, and through his spies he has learned of the woman in your presence. He is using this—coincidence or not—to spread the word that you are growing weak, that it is time for change to once again come for Ubasi. Souleyman has made this prophecy something you need to reckon with."

So Souleyman was using the religion just as he had—as a military and propaganda tool. The headman was right—you ignored this stuff at your peril. You had to fight it at the same level. Denying it, laughing at the priestess, would mean mocking his people's religion—mocking *them.*

"The rumors that Souleyman spreads, they travel

fast, Jean. You must stop them, and this is why I brought you here, to talk to you away from the eyes and ears of people who are searching you for weakness. Before it is too late. The Ubasi people can not be allowed to think you are weakening, Jean."

"I'm not, dammit! You know that." Although suddenly he wasn't so sure. After his night with Emma, he *felt* different.

A bird shrieked up high in the canopy.

Laroque jerked at the sound, then angrily spun on his heels and marched out of the grove, leaving the bodies behind. The headman followed as Laroque moved swiftly along the narrow jungle path, hacking unnecessarily at undergrowth with his machete, beating back things that stood in his way. He would *not* let anything stop him. He refused to allow some woman to steal his dream.

He stepped out into harsh sunlight where a group of his soldiers waited, but the colors looked different. Laroque imagined he could see a new wariness in the eyes of his men.

He was getting paranoid. He couldn't have that.

"The woman—" the headman whispered over his shoulder "—she must go."

Jean nodded curtly, saluted his men and got back into his Jeep. Without his dog.

Did they notice that, too? That his "spirit dog" was missing?

For the first time since he'd sailed into Ubasi, Laroque felt slightly unsure of himself. The headman was right. Emma had to go. There was too much at stake right now, and perception was everything.

But first he needed to know where her laptop was broadcasting to. He could send her out of the country without her computer. However, if Mano Ndinga *did* find something highly incriminating on her machine, Laroque needed her to answer questions.

He might even need her for leverage.

For that he had to keep her, at least until Mano arrived.

Never mind the other more personal reasons he felt like keeping her around. He'd been a fool. He'd been seduced by a woman he suspected could be an operative. He'd thought he could handle it. He had not anticipated the reach of her power over him.

Irritated, he snapped open his phone as he ordered his driver to move. "Any sign of Mano?" he barked into his cell over the growl of the engine.

"Yes. Ndinga's come early—just arrived."

Laroque closed his eyes briefly. "Give him the computer!"

He snapped his phone closed. Within hours he'd have an answer, then he'd have to deal with Emma. In a way that satisfied his people.

Chapter 10

It was early evening when Laroque returned to the castle compound. They told him Emma was down at the pool. He instructed his men not to bother them for a while, to close off that section of the garden.

He marched over the lawn, adrenaline thumping through his veins. He should have gone straight to see Mano, but he wanted to see her first, before he was told she was some kind of spy, that she was here to destroy him. The evening was incredibly hot, the air fecund. Distant evening drums reverberated over the forest. The cry of a fish eagle split the air, and small fruit bats flitted almost imperceptibly over a sky deepening to violet and purple. Like her eyes.

Like the eyes in that damn prophecy.

She *was* a curse. She'd stolen his focus.

He'd allowed it to happen to himself.

Such was the power of this strange religion.

He should never have slept with her, allowed himself to feel anything. Because he *did*—something that went well beyond whatever little charade they were playing.

But he had to put an end to it now—

He stopped dead.

Swallowed.

She was coming out of water that shimmered in dark, inky ripples behind her. Her underwear was doubling as a bathing suit. Wet, it left nothing—absolutely nothing—to the imagination.

A black slip of lace nestled between her thighs, and two small triangles outlined her breasts. In contrast, her skin was white, luminous. She shook her hair and a spray of droplets fell like black pearls to the dark water.

His arousal was instantaneous. Explosive. Hot.

He didn't allow himself to think. He began to walk. Steadily. Right up to her.

She stilled as he neared, her eyes reflecting the colors in the sky, water glistening over her skin. He fixated on a smooth rivulet that slithered from the base of her breasts down to her belly button, where it pooled momentarily before reaching a tipping point and sliding farther to disappear into the dark fabric at the apex of her thighs.

He looked up and met her eyes. The connection

was visceral, electric. Her breathing quickened, and her lips parted slightly.

In the back of his mind he could hear the beat of the drums, the sounds of evening in the forest canopy. The thick scent of flowers in his garden was sweet and provocative.

He lifted her hair away from her breasts, and through the sheer fabric of her bra he could see her nipples were hard. His groin ached as another shaft of hot need cut through him.

He cupped her breast roughly. She caught her breath, but she didn't step back.

Instead she tilted her chin and locked eyes with him. He met the dare in her gaze as he grazed her nipple, catching the nub between his thumb and forefinger. She swallowed and squared her shoulders slightly, which only lifted her nipples a little higher and shifted them in his direction.

He began to pound with need, barely able to breathe.

He reached for the clasp between her breasts, undid her bra, slid the straps over her shoulders and dropped the wet fabric to the shallow water in which she still stood. A sultry heat darkened her eyes. She wanted him. Right here.

Well, he wanted her.

With one hand he yanked his shirt over his head, and with the other he pushed her back into the water, deeper and deeper, waves sloshing and slapping gently between her legs as she moved.

He followed her in, pushing her in front of him,

water soaking into his pants. He guided her back toward the small waterfall that tumbled into his rock pool, undoing his fly as he moved, his eyes never leaving hers. The splash of water around them drove him higher. He grabbed her thigh, lifted her leg around him, yanked the scrap of lace aside and entered her sharply, pushing in deep.

She gasped, lifted her leg higher, broadening access for him as her nails dug into his back. She arched into him, moving with him, meeting his hunger with a voracious need of her own.

He lifted her other leg, wrapped it firmly around himself and held her hips as he thrust. She threw her head back, digging her fingers into his hair, finding purchase, gripping tightly as he moved faster, urged on by the searing pain of his desire. The water was syrupy and warm as it slicked between them, and she came so fast and suddenly it shocked him. A cry escaped her throat, drowned by the sound of the water, as she threw her head far back, her breasts exposed, her muscles clamping down on him, until she went limp.

He was still hard as rock. He lowered her, spun her around, braced her palms up against the rock. And he reentered her from behind, taking her in a way as elemental as the jungle around them.

They sat in silence beside the pool as it grew dark. Words defied what was happening between them, and the cloak of night felt comfortable. Laroque had wrapped the towel she'd brought down to the pool around his waist and given her his T-shirt. She looked almost girlish with her wet hair slicked back—so clean and innocent and pure. Yet there was nothing innocent about the way he'd taken her in the pool, nor in her desire for him. She was a mystery to Laroque, mostly because he couldn't fathom the source of their undeniable bond, given the circumstances. In spite of it all, he was still falling for this woman. Did she feel the same about him? Or was this an act?

He couldn't put it off. Not a moment longer. He had to go and see Mano in the communications room. He needed to put an end to this insecurity. He needed to know who she was.

He touched the side of her face gently. A part of him wanted to hold on to her for just one moment longer before it all blew apart. He had no idea what he'd do with her if he found evidence she'd come to destroy him. She could have hurt him, killed him, several times over if that's what she'd been trained and sent to do. He took some solace in the fact that she hadn't. It gave him hope.

She seemed distracted. "Hey there, *mon petite,* where've you gone?"

Her eyes whipped to his, suddenly vulnerable, then her subtle mask was back. His heart sank just a little.

She smiled, but it never quite reached those mystical eyes. "I was just thinking about tomorrow."

"What about it?"

She shrugged, and looked sad.

His pager bleeped. Twice. Thank God the thing still worked, thought Laroque as he fished it from his wet pocket.

He checked the messages—there were two.

Mano needed him ASAP, and the hostages had finally arrived at the rebel base camp.

"I have something I must attend to," he said.

"I'll stay out here a bit."

He hesitated. "It's getting dark."

"I'll be fine—you have guards everywhere, Jean." She smiled wistfully, her eyes hauntingly luminous in the dusky light. "I...I just need a while. To think."

He frowned, nodded and strode up the garden toward his palace, a knot tightening in his gut.

Emily drew her knees up close to her chest and hugged them tight. Anxiety ate at her. She was sinking deeper, falling more and more for this enigmatic man, the line between professional and personal blurring, making it difficult to be objective. She wasn't sure whether she could believe everything he claimed to be doing, but she *wanted* to. She sensed something truly noble inside Jean. In his sister's village she'd witnessed firsthand where his priorities lay. His people not only loved him, they *respected* him. So did his staff. He was tough, but that's what it often took to be a leader, especially in an environment like this. And underneath it all, she could see that he was just human—a man who needed family and a place to belong. A man who needed to protect the things—and people—he cared for. A man who made *her* feel like a complete woman.

Whatever his bold plans for this entire region, whatever his unorthodox methods, Jean-Charles Laroque had more integrity than most of the powerful men Emily had met in Manhattan. And he could do things to her body that no man ever had.

She closed her eyes, stress warring with a sense of duty to her mission and the growing tenderness ballooning inside her chest. By dawn she had four days left.

She had to pick a side.

Her mission. Or this man.

She couldn't have both.

"There is no way in hell this is an ordinary civilian system, Jean."

Tension streamed through Laroque. "Mathieu suspected as much," he said. "It's why I wanted you to take a deeper look at it."

Mano touched his fingertips to her equipment. "This laptop has been equipped with a rocket homing device."

His heart slammed once, then it thumped, steady, fast, hard. His throat tightened and his mouth went bone dry. "*What* did you say?"

"I took it apart, found a missile homing device in the hard drive."

Laroque stared at her computer, thinking about what he and Emma had just done in the pool. Bitterness filled his throat at the thought she had purposefully set out to seduce him, that she felt nothing. "Speak, Mano, tell me more."

"This machine—" he tapped the computer lightly "—is telling someone *right now* exactly what room in your palace it's in. The homing device can either be activated manually from this system, which could then be strategically placed close to a desired target, or it can be activated remotely from the same place to which it is now sending a satellite signal. Someone out on a ship, for example, could launch a warhead and hit whomever is holding this computer within minutes."

Fury burned in Laroque. He walked slowly to the dog basket he'd had brought into the room. He crouched down and touched Shaka's shaved fur softly, watched as his dog's gentle eyes turned trustingly to him.

His eyes shot back to Mano, but his voice remained absolutely level. "Why could Mathieu not see this immediately?"

"He saw there was *something* going on, Jean, and he told you what he could. But until we could take this thing apart in a forensic lab environment free of dust and static, there was nothing definitive. Even so, you need to know how to look for something like this. Look—" He pulled up a screen on a separate monitor.

"I took photos of her hard drive, enlarged them. See here?" He pointed. "This is where the homing apparatus is located. The device is barely visible to the naked eye. It contains sophisticated nanotechnology, is extremely small and deadly effective." He looked up. "You can't get this stuff on the open market, Jean. This is cutting-edge military technology."

"So you put the system back together leaving the homing device intact? It can still be activated?"

Mano's mouth twisted into a wry angle. "That's why I needed to see you ASAP. I don't have the skill to disable something like this without sending an alert directly to whoever is monitoring this thing. And I don't want to risk destroying it totally. It could be booby-trapped to trigger a missile launch instantly. A target-seeking warhead could launch the second I destroy this device, following the pulse of the last recorded coordinates like an echo." He held Laroque's eyes. "The rocket would still hit its target."

"Can you tell where it was manufactured?"

"No. There are no markings, no serial numbers, nothing. I've read about this technology, but I haven't actually seen anything quite like it yet. It could be anything, from Russian-, Chinese-, British- to U.S.-manufactured."

Laroque stroked his dog gently, as red-hot rage boiled inside him.

There was no doubt now. Absolutely none.

He almost shook under the strain of maintaining outward muscular control as he wrapped his mind around the sense of betrayal. Still, he could not stop himself from asking, "Is there no way that perhaps a science crew might have something like this—"

Mano shot his boss a sharp, querulous look. "No, Jean. No way."

Laroque sucked air very deep into his lungs. He stood up from Shaka's basket slowly, battling to subdue the fire of his rage, his feral impulse to storm out and physically confront Emma Sanford. He didn't like the violent urge pumping through his veins.

Had his father felt like this before rage had blinded and erupted from him, before he'd started hurting women? How had Peter Laroque lost control the very first time? And how much more quickly had the violence flared the second and third times? Was it the sense of betrayal of love, even if imaginary, that had driven his dad there the first time?

Distress twisted into Laroque's rage. It hurt. He hadn't felt this deeply rejected since he was a young boy. It made him furious with her, and with himself for being led by his libido.

Even more serious was the fact his staff would now see this proof of her betrayal as concrete evidence of the prophecy. This woman was challenging him in ways he'd never experienced.

She'd stolen his control. And she was threatening his country.

But he would not succumb to brute force. To do so would be his ultimate defeat.

If he wanted to get to the people controlling her, he had to stay very cool and continue to play her game. And he needed a strategy.

"If we move the computer to an outside location," he said calmly, "could we destroy the device with minimal collateral damage?"

"We could. But they will see it being moved. How that might play out is anyone's guess."

"So the GPS is showing them wherever that thing goes?" Laroque said, thinking aloud as he paced the room.

"Correct."

He stilled, bit the inside of his lip. "And you can't tell me *exactly* where it's transmitting to?"

Mano pulled up another screen. "Somewhere here, in this region along the west coast of Africa." He pointed with his pen. "The monitoring station could be on land or sea, but I can't tell you anything more precise. Not yet."

"When?"

"Her system is configured to send a low-strength satellite signal while at rest, and this signal is being rerouted through several hubs to throw electronic tracks. At this level of emission, I can't trace it. However, if her laptop is fired up, and an encrypted code entered, it'll ramp up to full signal strength. Whatever she then types into the computer is trans-mitted directly to a monitor off-site."

"So you're telling me that this laptop is essentially her communications system? Whatever she enters is relayed live to a screen somewhere else?"

Mano nodded. "With the signal at full strength for a few seconds, I could triangulate and pinpoint the exact location."

"So with her computer in a resting phase like this, whoever is watching her has no way of knowing whether it's actually in her possession or not? All they know is that it's in my castle?"

"To the best of my knowledge."

"Presumably, then, they'd refrain from activating the missile device unless there was some kind of distress signal from her, because they'd hurt *her* in the attack?"

"That would be my assumption, but—it's a risky one, Jean. This puppy is as good as a live bomb."

Laroque rubbed his face with both hands. "Is it possible to set it up so that if she enters her code, ramps up the signal and begins to communicate on that thing we can pick up her transmission on a monitor down here in the communications room?"

Mano pursed his lips and hummed in a low tone as he toyed with the logistics. "It'll take some time to configure things in such a way that doesn't clue either her or the other party into the fact we're watching them, but I think I can do it."

"And then you'd be able to pinpoint the precise location of the off-site monitor."

"Yes."

"Do it!"

Laroque leaned over a desk and pressed an intercom button, summoning his general.

The man arrived promptly, clicked his heels and stood at attention.

When Laroque spoke, his voice was ruthlessly cool. "Evacuate the palace of civilian staff. Retain only key military personnel. Do it as quietly and calmly as possible."

"Anything else, sir?"

"No. Thank you."

His general hesitated. "What about the woman, sir?"

"She stays. She must know nothing." Laroque turned back to Mano and pointed to her computer. "I am the target of that thing," he said. "I'm banking on the fact her people don't want to hurt her, and unless she sends a distress signal, they won't activate that device. I'll be safe, as long as I keep her close. For my own protection, for Ubasi's protection, she must not for one minute think she is in any real danger."

"It's a gamble, Jean."

He tensed his jaw. Mano didn't know the half of it. "I know. But I must find out who this woman is working for. If we learn *who,* we will know why. From there we can take action. Set her up, Mano. Have me paged when you're ready to roll." He hesitated. "The *instant* you are ready, *comprends?*"

"Oui."

Laroque turned sharply to his other aide. "I need you to do something for me. I want you to take the doctor and Shaka and whatever equipment the doctor may need to my sister's village. Tell the doctor he will be handsomely compensated. Tell him…" Emotion banked sharply in his throat. "Tell him to take care of Shaka."

He whirled on his heels and stormed out, boots echoing loudly down the cold and empty stone corridors.

* * *

She glanced up as he entered the dining room.

Laroque stood stone still at what he saw, his mind shattering into a kaleidoscope of emotions.

She was wearing the turquoise fabric the women in Tamasha's village had given her, nothing else underneath. Her hair had been piled up on her head, exposing the long, pale column of her neck.

He couldn't breathe.

She was so beautiful. So lethal.

His enemy, wrapped in the traditional cloth of his village. His people. His country. And she was here to destroy them all.

Fury hummed through his body.

Laroque had looked his enemy right in the eyes before killing him more times than he could count. But his foe had never been a woman.

This time when he looked into the eyes of his bewitching adversary, a whisper of doubt unsettled the steel of his will.

Whoever had sent this woman had known just how to get under his guard, and into his fortress. Right into his damn bed.

"Jean?"

He inhaled sharply, bracing against the allure of her voice, her body in that cloth. She was going to be his hostage, and she wasn't even going to know it.

"I can't dine with you tonight, Emma," he said simply. "I have meetings. Be ready to leave at first light, we're going north. We'll be gone at least two, maybe three days."

A wariness crept into her eyes. "Why?"

"The hostages have arrived at base camp. I'm going to question them."

Her eyes narrowed, grew calculating. Why had he not noticed that look before?

"Why do you want to take *me*?"

"Because you won't be safe here alone."

And that was a fact. If his men believed she was a sorceress out to destroy him, they were loyal enough to Laroque to eliminate her on his behalf, if he didn't do it himself.

He knew the ways of the jungle well enough, and he needed her alive, as his prisoner.

But although he had to keep his enemy close, the longer she was with him, the more his men were going to question his power to rule. He would lose their faith if they believed the ridiculous notion that he was under her spell, and doing nothing to stop it. He was in a double bind.

"I think I'd prefer to stay in the castle, Jean," she said firmly. "I'd like to spend some time writing up my notes."

"I'm sure you would."

He was also damn sure she'd go looking for her laptop in his absence. She'd try to find a way to communicate. There was not a shred of doubt in Laroque's mind she was an operative, and any spy worth her lies would not underestimate a man of his reputation. She'd know he had to have her computer in his possession, and she'd go looking for it at the first possible chance.

He wasn't going to give her that chance.

And if he was her, he'd also be nervous that something incriminating may already have been discovered in the laptop.

This woman was playing a very dangerous game, but if he'd underestimated her, she'd seriously misjudged him.

"We had a deal," he said flatly. "You're coming with me."

Chapter 11

Jacques and his crew watched the bank of LCD screens.

April Ngomo, one of Jacques's FDS techs, had summoned them to the situation room, alerting them to a small hiccup in Emily Carlin's computer signal. It had made April uncomfortable.

"It's back on track now," she told them in her rich, melodious voice. "The homing device is still intact, but something definitely interfered with her GPS signal."

"You think someone opened up her system?"

"It's possible."

The tension in the room mounted as they watched the steadily pulsing dot of luminous green on the monitor. "We still have a fix on the GPS in her laptop, right?" Jacques said, nodding toward the dot. "She's in that castle."

"Her computer is," April corrected. "That's all we can say for certain. She should have filed a report by now, Jacques."

"She's not using the laptop because she's not with it." The blunt statement came from Dr. Hunter McBride, FDS surgeon. Jacques had asked him to step into the communications room. Before requalifying as a surgeon, Hunter had been Jacques's top Africa guerrilla warfare expert, and his advice in strategy sessions remained invaluable.

"Either that," said Jacques, "or she's being too closely watched. She did say she'd be out of communication for a while."

"Perhaps she said it under duress," said Hunter.

"No, she'd have sent a coded message. We'll give her the full seven days. That's her brief. She'll do her best to meet it." He glanced at the computerized clock. "If Carlin doesn't make contact by the deadline, we move. We get her out, we activate the homing device."

"I don't like it," said Hunter watching the dot. "If Le Diable finds out she's working for us, she's dead. It's that simple." He looked at Jacques. "She may be already."

"No one ever said this was a safe business. She knew that going in."

Hunter nodded, his eyes serious. He jammed his hands into his fatigue pockets and jerked his chin toward the monitors. "How's the rest of our team placed?"

"The guys are beginning to mobilize with Souleyman's militia here in the east," said April, pointing her pen at a cluster of small flicking red triangles on the map. "The others are in position in the south, over there. We have the choppers on standby in Cameroon."

"Good. Contact me if anything changes, April." Jacques motioned with his head that he needed to talk to Hunter outside. They walked into the night together.

"I ran the IDs on those hostages," he told Hunter.

"You didn't like what you found?"

"They're mercs."

Hunter whistled through his teeth. "Working for who?"

"I don't know. Nothing's adding up. Two of the hostages are Nigerian and three are U.S. citizens by birth. I haven't got much on the Nigerians yet, but neither of those three Americans has been back to the homeland for decades. One is ex-military, was court-martialed, and discharged in connection with prisoner abuse. He left the U.S. shortly afterward. The other two have rough reputations with foreign private security companies and have hired out to wildcat operations in both the Middle East and Africa. These guys give outfits like ours a bad rep."

"And there's been no ransom demand?"

"None."

"What does Weston say?"

"CIA brass doesn't seem to give a rat's ass about these hostages. Weston has his sights trained purely on Laroque."

"Do you figure these hostages are somehow connected to the CIA agents' deaths?"

Jacques stilled, stared out over the inky blackness of the ocean, white foam cresting waves luminous in the moonlight. "Those mercs were hired by someone, but who? And why? And why did Laroque's men take them? Plus there's Souleyman's backing. He's getting hard cash and weaponry from some outside source that we haven't managed to identify yet. I wish to hell Carlin would make contact, because it feels like something else is going down in Ubasi, and Blake Weston doesn't give a damn."

"He's got tunnel vision. He's worried about his job. The Pentagon and the White House are putting pressure on him."

"Yeah, but if I were him, I'd be worried about a lot more."

"It's not our job to worry, Jacques."

"No, it's not. Not unless we're being played. I've got my team to think about." He glanced at Hunter. "They come first."

17:58 Zulu. Monday, November 11.
Ubasi jungle

Emily wiped thick sweat from her forehead with her sleeve, the scent of bug repellent nauseating in the sticky heat.

She and Jean had been traveling alone since daybreak, in one Jeep with three days' worth of supplies and weapons. They were moving into increasingly dense jungle in the direction of the Purple Mountains, and were now negotiating a muddy track being reclaimed by tangled growth.

Something had changed in Jean. He was terse, sullen, and she imagined she could read hostility in his eyes. His mistrust of her had deepened, she could sense it, and the farther they journeyed into thick jungle, the more vulnerable Emily felt.

He could cut her throat and dump her out here and no one would ever find her body. She'd made sure she knew the exact position of his rifle, machete and knives. Just in case.

When she'd questioned the lack of accompanying militia—especially given the size of the convoy they'd traveled with to his sister's village—he'd informed her that on that last trip they'd had information about a legitimate threat. The traitors had been dealt with. There was no immediate threat now.

He'd added that traveling into the northern jungle alone was preferable. The more quietly they moved, the less attention they'd draw to themselves. The rebels in these parts preferred a solitary visit—it was how he'd gained their confidence in the first place. "Besides," he'd said, "the jungle has eyes. Their scouts will be watching. They'll know we're coming."

That certainly didn't make her sit any easier.

She studied his rugged profile through the growing darkness, seeking some clue to his changed demeanor, until she couldn't take it anymore.

"What happened, Jean. Is it Shaka? Is he okay?"

"Yes." He wouldn't look at her. He steered their Jeep down into a water-filled pothole, spinning the tires as he edged it out the other end. His concentration was firmly ahead, his muscles too tense.

"I didn't see him in his bed in the usual place."

"He's safe."

Her stomach tightened. She hadn't seen the usual staff at the palace, either. She ducked as a branch whipped back over her head. She didn't like this. Murky blackness was closing in around the dusky yellow shafts of their headlights. Emily could no longer glimpse sky, and the growth around them seemed to develop a malevolent presence in the dark, as if watching them intently.

Another branch flung back and a thorn sliced her cheek.

She sucked in the pain, and clamped her hand down hard to stop the blood.

They were compelled to share a tent that night.

The air was soupy and their small fire belched thick, bitter-scented smoke. Laroque had fed the flames with green twigs to chase the bugs. Still, fat insects thudded against the tent fabric, sensing warm bodies inside. As the circle of firelight dwindled, so did the scope of their little world in the tangled heart of the forest.

Emily lay on lumpy ground next to Jean. Sleep was impossible. The night had come alive with a simmering orchestra of insects—a sound so loud and pervasive it seemed to have one physical shape. But if she concentrated, Emily could detect a million other little sounds layered into the composition—small clicks, groups of chirrups, rubbings, flutters, warbles, rattles, peeps, and pop-pop noises punctuated by startling screeches that echoed high in the treetops and were followed by low, aggressive warning barks.

Closer to the tent she could make out snuffles and grunts, the soft cough of an animal and an occasional crackling of twigs. Then something rustled sharply right outside their tent flap. Emily inhaled and reflexively backed up into Laroque's body.

She was shocked to find him hard. He seemed so angry, so cold and distant, yet he was aroused.

She held her breath, lay still against him, not wanting him to know she'd felt it.

Tension thickened in the smoky heat. She could hear her own heart thud until she couldn't bear his silence any longer.

"Jean?" she whispered into the darkness.

For a long time he said nothing.

Then she felt his fingernails trace the line of her neck, as if with a knife. She shuddered slightly at the mix of sensations that shivered up her spine.

A wry smile tugged at Laroque's mouth.

Her instant physical response to his slightest touch only intensified his arousal.

Why did sex with his enemy have to be the best in his life?

Thinking about it made him even hotter, harder. *Angrier.* What was he going to do with her once he had the information he needed?

Conflict churned inside him.

He touched her hair gently. It was so soft, so full, fragrant with the scent of the shampoo he'd stocked in the bathroom of the guest quarters. A bittersweetness blossomed in his chest, filling it to hurting point. He closed his eyes and nuzzled his nose into her hair, drinking in her scent as he slid his hand around to feel her breasts. Without thinking he began to undo her shirt buttons, unclasp her bra, listening to her breathing grow lighter and faster as he moved. Her breast filled his hand perfectly, her nipple hardening against his palm.

His mouth went dry. He kept his eyes closed, listening to the jungle sounds, alert to changes in the environment even as he slid his hand down her flat belly and into the front of her pants.

She sucked in air the instant he touched her between her legs, and she trembled slightly. His smile deepened. With his eyes still closed he cupped the mound between her thighs. Her slick heat brought his desire to feverish pitch. He slid a finger up into her.

She gasped lightly, opening her legs wider. Logic deserted his brain as he slipped another finger up into her, and he felt her clench her muscles around him in response, moving against him. A savage hunger surged through Laroque. He moved his fingers inside her, faster, coaxing her with small rhythmic movements, then hungry hard ones as he buried deeper inside her, and soft recurring sounds escaped her throat.

His breathing grew labored and he began to quiver against his own restraint when she suddenly arched, went stiff, swallowed a cry and shuddered, her muscles clamping down hard and spasming around his fingers. He sank his teeth into her shoulder as she climaxed again and again, until he thought he'd explode at the exquisite sensation.

Her body softened as she waited for him to move. When he did nothing, she rolled over to face him. He caught the glint of her eyes in the dark and could feel the question in her posture. She watched his face, clearly as unsure as he was about what had just happened. "Jean?" she whispered again, and he heard the vulnerability in her voice.

But when Laroque didn't answer, still didn't move, she reached for his shirt, yanked it open and kissed his chest, her lips hot, her tongue slicking his skin, teasing her way slowly toward his groin. His blood pounded. His vision turned scarlet.

He thought of the missile-homing device, of why he'd had to bring her with him into the jungle in the first place, and fury speared sharply through his belly, spearing right into the exquisite pain of his lust. He tensed, dug his fingers sharply into her thick hair and arrested her movement. There was nothing vulnerable about this woman.

She hesitated, unsure, then she opened his zipper, anyway, slid her warm fingers into his pants, exposing him. And he felt her wet, warm lips take him into her mouth. He groaned involuntarily, and reflexively tightened his grip in her hair. She began to massage him with her mouth. He sucked in his breath sharply, holding her still by the hair. *"No!"* His voice was hoarse. "No, Emma."

He had to force himself not to move against her. He wanted to ravage her, but with a ferocity that frightened him.

He pushed her quickly away, rolled out from under her touch, grabbed his rifle, unzipped the tent and stepped into the syrupy night. He pulled up his fly and forced a low and shuddering breath from deep in his chest.

His eyes burned.

He could *not* allow himself to mix rage with pleasure. He didn't want to go down that road. Ever. He point-blank refused to explore that particular combination of sensations because he was afraid he'd enjoy it—terrified he'd become his own father.

Peter Laroque had done terrible things to women in his later life. The boundaries between pain and pleasure, aggression and sex, had blurred for him.

From what Laroque had heard through the mercenary grapevine, killing had become almost orgasmic to Peter.

Laroque had even come close to slitting his own father's throat to save a woman under him. He could have—*should have*—done it, but he hadn't been able to. Instead he'd forced his father to allow the woman to crawl away for help. Then he'd withdrawn the tip of the blade from Peter's throat and walked away himself. It was shameful. And it was the last time he'd seen his father.

Laroque had been twenty years old that day. The incident haunted him still.

He'd argued endlessly with himself, that had he known just how bad Peter would become, he'd have had the courage to end his father's life that day.

When Laroque had finally heard about his father's terrible death at the hands of Congo militia, something had relaxed in him. But the news of his father's demise had not killed the fact that Peter's DNA still lurked in his body, nor the fear that the same sickness and rage could one day manifest in him.

He wiped the sweat from his face, and cursed softly.

He could not sleep with Emma now that he knew for sure she was a traitor. And what was she waiting for?

Why hadn't she stabbed him in the heart already?

She could have done it several times over, especially out here.

The uncertainty frustrated Laroque. He itched to confront her right now, get it over with. But then he might never find out who was watching her computer, who had a missile trained on his palace—

Twigs cracked suddenly in the brush.

Laroque spun, moving his weapon up in one fluid

motion. He aimed at the sound, waiting for another to come out of the blackness.

She crawled through the gap in the tent. "What was that?" she whispered.

He motioned with his head for her to stay back.

The sound moved into the night, and he lowered the gun slowly. Heart thudding.

"Jean?"

He glanced at her. She looked incredible, even out here in the jungle night, the light from the dying embers painting her face soft copper and peach. The face of a traitor, with the eyes of a sorceress. He swore again to himself.

"Have I done something?"

"Go back to sleep." He tossed a few more chunks of wood on the fire and sat on a log. "I heard something in the brush. I think I'll stay out here, keep watch."

She crawled out of the tent and came to sit beside him. He braced. Her scent was intoxicating and his pent-up desire hurt like hell. He wished she'd get back into that tent before he did something he regretted.

But they sat in heavy and uncomfortable silence as the night wore on—an hour, then another, then another.

"You asked me about my parents," she said softly.

Curiosity snaked into him. He turned his head slightly, resentfully, and listened.

Emily bit her lip.

The little details didn't matter, she told herself, the essence of what she wanted to communicate was true.

"My father was in a position of authority." She hesitated. "He was a firefighter, a fire chief," she lied.

"Was?"

She glanced at him. "He's retired." The fervor in his eyes unnerved her. "He's a charismatic and an extremely domineering man." She laughed lightly. "He's like you in a way."

He said nothing.

Emily moistened her lips. "My mother loved him with all her heart. So did—do—I. But I don't like him. My mom's entire life revolved around pleasing him, because when my dad was happy he was the most mesmerizing man around, and we adored him. He made me feel like a princess, and I suspect that's how he made my mother feel, too."

Jean leaned forward, his eyes riveted on her. But Emily no longer had the courage to meet his gaze. She barely had the grit to tell him this. She'd told no one—not flatly like this. Maybe she could do it now because she was still hiding behind an alias, because the names and professions she was using were not real. She was *still* bending the truth.

"But my dad has a very violent temper, low flashpoints, and I suspect, a pathological need to dominate the women in his life. The more my mother tried to please him over the years, the more worthless he made her feel, almost deriving pleasure from her desperation in the end." Emily inhaled deeply. "He couldn't help it. The more pathetic she got, the more it egged him on." She stared at the fire, her heart thumping. "Until one day she just…committed suicide. Killed herself. She couldn't take the rejection anymore."

Laroque remained deathly silent.

Slowly, she turned her face to him.

He was staring at her in some frightful way, conflicted emotions twisting his features.

"I was thirteen," she said. Emily tried to smile. "I lost my mom at the same age you lost yours."

He jabbed a stick at the fire, sending another cloud of orange sparks into the air. Then he sat, silently watching the flames.

"You're afraid you're like your mother?" he said without warning.

"What?"

"You're afraid you're weak, like her. You're worried that you actively seek dominant men like your father, and you're scared they'll end up controlling you. Am I right?"

She felt the blood drain from her head. "How… how do you…what makes you say that?"

"It's why you ran from me like that, after dinner, wasn't it? After I pressed you about your past. It's your dad that hurt you. He hurt you *and* your mother."

Emotion blurred her vision. Damn this man. He *could* see right through her. She turned sharply away, feeling raw, exposed.

She could feel him watching. Waiting. But she couldn't talk anymore.

"What did you do about it, Emma?"

The question surprised her. She turned slowly back to face him. "What do you mean?"

"How did you fight back? Did you talk to him?"

She swallowed. She hadn't ever had the courage to tell her dad that she thought her mum's death was his fault. And here *she* was the shrink. Guilt deepened in her.

"I studied psychology," she said, leaving out the army bit. "That was my way of fighting back. I needed the tools to understand men like him, and society's relationship to them."

"Do you?"

"Yes," she said, staring at the fire. "Yes, I do. I've become something of an expert in the field."

"But it doesn't change, does it? How you feel *inside?*"

Her eyes flicked to him in surprise. "No," she said. "It doesn't."

He swore bitterly.

She frowned at him. "What was that for?"

His eyes narrowed. "You and me, we're one of a kind."

"What do you mean?"

"You understand *me,* don't you?" Anger shimmered over his features, tightened his neck.

"I think I understand *some* of your conflict, Jean, about who you are. Your fear. I understand your need to belong. Your need for family."

Angrily, he lurched to his feet and cast another log into the fire, sending a scattering of small orange sparks into the blackness. He glared at her, then stalked around to the far end of their encampment.

They might be one of a kind, but right now they were on opposite sides of the battle fence.

He spun back to face her suddenly, the shadows hiding his features. "Why are you telling me this *now*, Emma?"

"Because…I needed to, Jean."

She needed him to know she cared enough to share this deeply personal part of herself, even though she couldn't tell him who she was.

She'd felt him retreating further and further from her the deeper into the jungle they'd traveled. He hadn't even been able to commit to making love to her properly in the tent, and it had left a hollowness in her stomach.

And in her heart.

She wanted him to like *her*—Emily. She wanted to try and connect with him on some deeper level, yet she was compelled not to blow her cover, or the FDS mission.

It was more than just her life at stake.

There were the lives of Jacques's men to think of.

21:19 Zulu. Tuesday, November 12.
Rebel camp. Northern Ubasi jungle

Laroque and the rebels conversed in turbulent tones around a large campfire. Ebony faces glistened with sweat, the whites of eyes flashed, muscles in cutoff shirts flexed—the men were agitated, aggressive.

Emily couldn't make out a single word of the dialect they used. The mood, however, was clear. These men spoke with a provocative anger.

Every now and then one would launch to his feet and yell something, his finger pointing at Laroque, muscles cording in powerful arms. She watched quietly from the darkness, captivated, as Laroque raised his hand in quiet authority, his response measured, unquestionably firm, brooking no argument.

He was undeniably the leader of this wild bunch, a respected power figure in a group of rough warriors. Le Diable's strength was elegant, his sharp eyes cool with shrewd intelligence. Yet his physical resonance matched the raw strength of each of these men.

Emily edged back into the shadows. She waited for a few moments, but no one seemed to have noticed her move. She backed farther out of their line of sight. Still no one looked her way.

She quickly surveyed her surroundings.

The compound was not big, and she'd seen where Laroque had been taken to interrogate the captives. She'd also counted every one of the militants as she'd moved around the compound earlier. They were all accounted for around the fire.

Her pulse raced. This was her chance.

She made her way across the compound quietly, halting every few steps to see if she was being followed, listening for a change in timbre or tempo of the voices around the fire. From Laroque's Jeep she quickly retrieved a flashlight and a knife, which she slid into the top of her boot underneath her pants.

She made her way along a narrow path, well screened from the fire by brush. She wondered why they'd left the small lean-to that housed the prisoners unguarded as she peered through the uneven slats of wood. The stench was awful, and she could see nothing but darkness.

"Hello?" she whispered. "Anyone in there?"

Dead silence greeted her.

She hesitated, glanced over her shoulder. She was taking one hell of a chance, but these hostages were somehow key to what was happening in Ubasi. She needed to try to talk to them, find out who they were, and why Laroque's men had captured them. She'd come up with an excuse if caught.

The lock on the door hung open. She figured she knew why—the men were either dead or close to it.

She also knew they had been alive *before* Laroque got to them.

Dreading what she would see, Emily carefully edged open the door.

Chapter 12

22:37 *Zulu. Tuesday, November 12.*
Rebel camp. Northern Ubasi jungle

She froze, heart thudding, waiting for the sound of voices. None came. The night sounds were cloaking her movements.

Emily carefully directed her flashlight into the shack. A black-and-yellow striped snake the length of a fishing rod slithered along the dirt floor, trying to escape her beam. She counted her breaths, waiting for it to leave, and then she slowly panned the inside of the tiny building with her light.

She could make out four men huddled against one another in the corner. They were so beaten and bloodied she could barely distinguish features or race. Her stomach tightened, and she moved rapidly forward.

She crouched down in front of one man. His eyes were swollen shut. She touched his arm gently and he groaned, trying to shrink back. "Shh, it's okay," she whispered. "You can trust me." His skin was burning hot. He was running a raging fever. She figured this was one of the Nigerian nationals. She quickly scanned the others with her beam of light. They were in no better condition. They *were* more fair. One looked like his hair might once have been blond under the dirt and blood; the other two were brown-haired.

She couldn't find the fifth man.

Then she saw black boots sticking out from under a pile of old sacks. She touched the pile and flies rose in a cloud. Her stomach lurched.

What had they done to these men?

"Are you American?" she whispered to one as she carefully tried to removed the ragged cloth that gagged him.

He groaned, nodded slightly.

"They tortured you?"

He nodded, unable to speak.

"Did…did Jean-Charles Laroque do any of this to you?" She *had* to know.

He appeared confused. These men were all dying and Emily didn't know how to help.

"Le Diable," she whispered. "Did *he* hurt you?"

The man murmured something through his swollen lips, and nodded.

Inexplicable disappointment sunk through Emily. She leaned closer. "I can get help for you. Can you tell me who you are?"

His hand gripped hers suddenly, fingers digging with desperation into her skin. "Promise…" He groaned in pain. "Promise me…"

Emily leaned closer, urgency nipping at her. "Promise *what?*" she whispered.

"My…son. I…told him I'd be home…Thanksgiving. Must promise me, please…get home to…my boy for Thanksgiving."

Her heart buckled. "Where's home?"

"Oklahoma…home—" he croaked, blood leaking from the corner of his cracked mouth "—that's my…home."

Emily closed her eyes for a moment, holding back a shudder of emotion. There was no way in hell this man was ever going to see home again. She knelt closer, smoothed his hair back from his feverish forehead. "Tell me," she whispered. "Tell me why they brought you here."

14:00 Zulu. Thursday, November 14.
Ubasi jungle

"What's going to happen to the hostages?" Emily had to shout over the whine of the Jeep.

He continued to ignore her as he floored the gas, hitting a pothole with bone-jarring force. Emily ducked as vines whipped past her face. He'd been driving like this—belligerently and recklessly—for the past twenty-fours, and it was sending her clean over the edge.

"Dammit, Jean!" she yelled in frustration. "You dragged me all this way! The *least* you can do is *say* something!"

He slammed on the brakes suddenly and she flew forward, striking the dashboard with such force it knocked the air from her.

He whirled to face her, eyes glinting with green fire. "Do you think I don't know you went in there, Emma?"

She felt her jaw drop.

"You sneaked in behind my back to see those captives, didn't you?"

Her chest tightened. She was suddenly afraid to speak, threatened by the hawkish glint in his eyes. She edged her hand slowly along the side of the Jeep, ready to find purchase if she needed to scramble out and run for her life into the forest, knowing at the same time she'd never survive a night on her own in this place.

"Do you think I don't know what those men told you?"

She tried to moisten her bone-dry mouth. "You... spied on me?"

He barked a harsh laugh. *"Spy!* What the hell do you think *you* were doing if not *spying?"*

Her cheeks went hot. "You set me up. You specifically waited for me to go there."

He lowered his voice further, glacial eyes cleaving

into hers. "Why did you do it, Emma? Why are you spying on me?" His voice was dangerously level, quiet.

She glanced away, trying to gather herself, scrambling for words. She'd so desperately wanted to believe everything he'd told her, but after seeing those men, she couldn't. And it had *broken* something inside her, to think he'd done that to innocent men with families back home. It had hardened her resolve to fulfill her mission, but it had also filled her heart with pain.

"*Why,* Emma?"

She turned slowly to face him, her eyes moistening. "Because…they're my fellow citizens, Jean," she said. "I couldn't just sit there and do nothing. I *had* to see them. I…" She looked down at her hands. "They're hurt, Jean." Her eyes flashed up. "*You* hurt them."

His eyes burned into her, and a small muscle pulsed rapidly at his jaw. "You're lying to me, Emma."

She swallowed. "It's the truth."

"Give me the knife."

Her eyes flickered. "What…knife?"

"The knife in your boot, dammit. *My* knife."

She sat motionless. He waited, his eyes locked onto hers. She slowly extracted the hunting blade she'd taken and held it out to him.

He took it, unsheathed it, held the gleaming hooked tip in front of her face. Emily stared at it, adrenaline surging into her blood, the fight or flight impulses warring inside her. She couldn't breathe.

"And what were you doing with *this?*"

She didn't dare swallow, let alone speak, for fear he'd kill her.

"What *else* have you taken from me, Emma?"

The blade glinted, catching light as he twisted it, and his eyes lanced hers. In them she could read not only rage, but disappointment, pain. And that hurt Emily more than anything. He seemed to be fighting with his emotions, struggling against something. He pulled back suddenly and thrust the knife into a pocket of the door with a hard thud.

Her eyes watered with relief and she covered her throat with her hands, heart slamming wildly.

He glared at the dirt track ahead. "Whatever those men told you, Emma, they lied."

The residual effects of adrenaline made her begin to shake. She wanted to cry. She was so damn conflicted she didn't know what to do. "Those men weren't lying, Jean." Her voice came out hoarse, wobbly. "They were *beyond* lying. One man is a father. He just wants to get home to his family for Thanksgiving. He works security for a mine in Nigeria, and he was due to go home when your men took them. I have no idea why you wanted them, but whoever you thought they were…they're innocent."

He laughed dryly.

Anger began to pull at Emily's mouth. She tried to control herself, tried to tell herself to shut up, but she had virtually nothing to lose now. The FDS and Souleyman's men would be storming the castle in less than ten hours, and Jean would be dead.

"Those men have been hurt," she said quietly. "They need help. They are not going to survive more than a day or so in this climate with wounds like that. They'll be dead before tomorrow, if they aren't already."

He whipped his eyes to hers. "You actually believe *them* over me?"

Her jaw tightened. "Tell me why you took them, Jean."

"Why should I?"

So that I can pick a damn side!

She dropped her face into her hands. It was no use. She had no idea what to believe anymore.

"They knew the game, Emma."

She looked up sharply. "What do you mean?"

"They went in knowing the risks. Do *you* know the risks?"

She felt the blood drain from her face. "What are you implying?"

He started the Jeep, shunted it into gear and began to drive. Frustration exploded in her. "You're no better than Souleyman, you know that!"

He slammed on the brakes and spun round, ice in his eyes. "Don't you *ever* compare me to that man," he growled through clenched teeth, stark white against the dark anger in his face.

"Why *not?*" she said, holding his gaze. "Why is it right for you to hurt innocent people like those hostages? How is that any different from Souleyman hurting your sister for his own political gain?"

"Those men," he said, "are not oil workers.

They're mercenaries. They signed up for this. My sister *didn't*. Those men don't give a damn who they kill, or what they destroy, because when they pick up guns, they do it solely for the cash."

"Mercenaries?"

He watched her struggle with the notion. "Yes, and they lied to you, Emma, because they thought the lies might save them."

"I…who're they working for, then? What…what did they do? Why did you take them?"

"They killed those four American geologists."

The CIA agents?

Her jaw dropped. "What?"

"That's right. Do you feel so sorry for them now?"

"I…don't believe you."

He snorted as if she was no longer worth wasting precious time on. Slamming the Jeep back into gear, he hit the gas and they swerved forward into red mud.

Emily literally shook with adrenaline. Could it possibly be true? Did Jean actually *know* the geologists were CIA agents? Had his suspicions—that someone paid mercenaries to kill the agents in a way that would set Jean up to take the fall—been right all along?

And here she was, part of Washington's initiative—a pawn sent to destroy him, her own people backing Souleyman.

The cloak and daggers of this game were confounding.

She felt sick.

She had to get word to Jacques. This could change everything.

She stared at Laroque's rugged profile, and her heart swelled with pain and emotion. He looked so alone. And she didn't know if she should believe him—and help him.

She had no idea what side to step down on, yet the clock was ticking fast. If she did nothing, he would be killed in under ten hours.

Tension ratcheted in her stomach. Even if she wanted to help him, the only way to do it now would be to come clean, tell him who she worked for, so that he'd allow her to access her communications systems.

That would mean losing him—forever. This was not the kind of man to take betrayal lightly.

She'd seen what happened to the soldier who'd deceived him.

And coming clean would mean blowing a Pentagon-CIA initiative. She had to be *damn* sure that what her gut was telling her was right.

Laroque swerved into the castle courtyard and screeched to a halt, his heart racing. Under torture, the so-called hostages had confessed they were freelance fighters contracted by a covert arm of the Chinese government. This covert and renegade faction of the ruling Chinese communist party had tried to frame Laroque and force him into a deadly confrontation with Washington. In the meantime, the

Chinese were backing Souleyman in a bid to over-throw Laroque and take Ubasi, and Souleyman's men were mobilizing for attack this very minute.

Laroque did not have a moment to lose if he wanted to save his country.

In return for military aid and substantial funding, Souleyman had promised the Chinese sole access to the Ubasi oil reserves. The Chinese also wanted to nip Laroque's oil cartel in the bud.

Laroque's sole intent now was to find out who Emma Sanford was working for—the Chinese or someone else—and her computer was going to tell him.

Almost immediately, he saw Mano motioning urgently to him from the far end of the courtyard. Laroque raised two fingers in acknowledgment as he swung his legs over the side of the Jeep.

Emma scrambled out, hesitated, uncertainty in her eyes. "Jean—"

"Make sure she goes directly to her room," he commanded his guards, cutting her off. "Bolt her in."

Shock and fear rippled over her features as his men took her by the arms.

"Jean, wait!"

"Take her. Now."

He watched them go. He saw the determination in the set of her shoulders, then, suddenly, a flash of vulnerability. He clenched his fists. He could use a woman like her on his side. He *wanted* her at his side. He wanted her in his bed. He simply wanted her.

But she wasn't Emma. And she stood against him...he *couldn't* let her get in his way.

Then, before he even knew what he was doing, he yelled after her. "I didn't touch them!"

She stopped and slowly turned round, the sun catching her eyes.

"I did not touch those hostages, Emma."

She held his eyes for a long beat, guards waiting on either side. Then she spun away and entered his castle, his guards escorting her.

Laroque palmed off his beret and dragged his hand over his hair. He didn't know what the hell had compelled him to say that. *Especially* with his men watching.

But he needed her to know that he hadn't beaten those men himself.

His mouth turned bitter.

One of these days his men were going to call him on this sort of thing. They were going to see that his bark was worse than his bite, that he didn't physically have it in him to kill a man—or woman—who wasn't fighting him squarely back on even terms.

Laroque liked a challenge. But he was not an abuser of power.

He liked to win fair.

The trouble was, if he wanted to hold on to his power and keep the respect of his army—especially men like those rebels in the north—he was going to need to be seen meting out swift punishment to those who committed treason, or betrayal.

And that included Emma.

Whether she was working for the Chinese or someone else, he was going to have to act. And ruthlessly so.

Justice in this land tended to be harsh. It's what people expected, because the land itself was harsh.

As she disappeared up the castle stairs, flanked by his guards, her hair catching the last rays of the evening sun, Mano approached him.

"We've set her up, Jean."

He nodded.

"All she has to do is start typing."

"Let's do it, then," he said. "We have no time to waste."

But as Laroque marched across the courtyard, he found himself praying that somehow, he'd still find her innocent.

That he wouldn't be put to the test.

17:03 Zulu. Thursday, November 14.
Ubasi Palace

The guards unlocked the door to her suite, and Emily stepped in—and stilled instantly.

Her computer lay on the bed.

She stared at it, anxiety ripping through her. The bolt slid into place behind her, and she waited until the echo of the guards' boots faded down the corridor before walking slowly over to the bed to examine the laptop.

It was definitely her system.

Sweat prickled over her skin.

Jean was on to her. She'd felt it as they'd headed into the jungle. Known it for certain when she'd badgered him about the hostages. Now this. What game was he playing now?

Emily rubbed her hand over her brow as she stared at the computer—her only link to the outside world.

She glanced up at the clock. Jacques's men would be moving in less than nine hours.

She began to pace the room, trying to think.

Jean obviously didn't know *exactly* who she was, because he would have done something about it. He must, however, have found solid reason to mistrust her—in her computer. And now he was setting her up.

Emily swore softly, sat on the bed, picked up her laptop and turned it over, trying to see if he'd tampered with it.

She could just forget the damn computer. Do nothing.

She'd be okay in the castle. Jacques's men would find her here. She pushed a lock of damp hair off her face. The FDS would storm the palace with Souley-man's men. They'd take Jean down. Kill him.

She jerked to her feet, began to pace again.

Ubasi would be a dead zone under Souleyman. She couldn't let that happen. And she could *not* let them assassinate Jean-Charles Laroque—not if he was innocent of killing those CIA agents, not if what he'd said about forming a cartel was true. It would be plain wrong.

Never mind her own attraction to Jean.

And in spite of what Washington or the other superpowers of the world might want, she believed a cartel that saw oil profits benefit the indigenous populations would be a good thing.

If the United States was using her and the FDS as pawns in a bid to stop a cartel forming in the Gulf of Guinea, she had to take a stand against it.

Who would she be if she didn't?

She pressed her hand against her stomach, trying to quell the nerves.

She'd seen what Jean was trying to protect, to build in this country. The more she thought about it, the more she believed he was telling the truth.

She didn't yet understand how the hostages fitted in, or who might have paid them to kill the CIA agents, but it was her duty to inform Jacques about what she'd seen and heard. Jacques's men *needed* to know what they were up against, that things were not what they seemed in Ubasi.

And regardless of her personal feelings, her mission was to deliver a psychological assessment of *Le Diable*.

She *had* to use the computer.

Emily stared at it, anxiety and adrenaline warring in her body, sweat totally drenching her shirt.

She pulled her hair back with both hands. If she risked using the laptop, and Jean was monitoring her, she'd tip him off to Jacques's men. She could be placing her own FDS colleagues directly in the line of fire.

She could be endangering their lives and her own

while single-handedly scuttling a CIA-Pentagon initiative.

But if she *didn't* take action, and he was killed, and his dream of an independent Ubasi was destroyed, she'd be tormented for the rest of her life over her decision. She'd be liable for perpetuating foreign policies she could no longer believe in.

Whose lives weighed more? And who the hell was she to judge?

God, she was in an impossible bind.

Emily plunked herself down onto the bed and buried her face in her hands. She had to trust her heart, that's all she could do.

And her heart was telling her that she'd been falling in love with Jean-Charles Laroque every step of the way.

And that she was compelled to save him—and his dream.

But if she touched that computer, she was going to lose him forever. He would see firsthand that she had betrayed him in the most intimate fashion.

But if she didn't touch it…emotion burned in her chest.

Emily's eyes flicked toward the clock, and the belt of tension tightened another notch over her stomach. She was running out of time.

She had to do it. Now. Suffer any consequence. And if she ever got out of this alive, Emily vowed she would not look back. Ever. She'd just let go of Jean and all the mistakes she'd ever made. She'd move forward, make some serious changes in her life and work toward something positive. Something fresh.

She sucked in a deep breath, opened the laptop, closed her eyes for a second, steadying her mind, then started it up, typing in the code that would activate the signal and relay her words directly to the monitors on São Diogo Island.

17:20 Zulu. Thursday, November 14.
Communications room. FDS Base, São Diogo Island

The monitor flashed a steady alert signal, then crackled softly to life. Code started to move rapidly across the screen. April Ngomo's heart slammed against her rib cage. She lurched across the desk, hit the button that sounded the alarm in Jacques's office.

Relief gushed through Jacques as he raced to the communications room. Damn, he'd been worried about Emily Carlin. He flung open the door just in time to see her first sentence appearing on the large LCD screen above April's desk.

"Been to see hostages. Four still alive. Need medical attention ASAP. Laroque claims they are mercenaries responsible for CIA deaths. Being held in rebel camp in Purple foothills just west of laptop GPS coordinates. I'm safe, being held at palace..."

Jacques glanced quickly at the green GPS signal on the other monitor. It had moved within the palace for the first time in days. He whipped his eyes back to the main screen, conscious of Hunter entering the room behind him.

"Laroque would not make cooperative captive in my assessment. Capture would ensure martyrdom status. But situ—" The screen suddenly went dead.

Jacques's heart plummeted.

Everyone in the room sat silent for a moment, staring at the blank screen.

Jacques shot a look at April. "What happened?"

"Someone cut her off!" said April, spinning back to her keyboard and quickly entering a series of codes. "She didn't sign out. Someone's tracking *us*..." She rapidly hit more keys. "Damn, I can't track back."

"What do you mean?" asked Jacques, moving quickly to her side.

"I mean, they've hacked into her system! They saw what we just saw up on that monitor." She pointed. "They're on to us. They're on to her. She's in trouble!"

"We move. Now." Jacques spun round. "Give the orders to mobilize ASAP. Code Green."

That was the code to assassinate Laroque at first opportunity.

"You sure, Jacques?" Hunter sounded skeptical.

"As sure as I can be."

Hunter stepped forward, kept his voice low. "There's a *'but'* in that message. It looked as though Carlin was going to add some sort of qualifier."

"It doesn't matter," said Jacques. "We don't have time to second-guess her. Carlin's job was to make that one assessment. She has. And she's given us the coordinates for the mercs."

"That's not part of *our* job."

"No. It's not. But she said it herself, those hostages are mercs and could be linked to the CIA deaths. It's consistent with what we dug up on them. Something else is going down here, and like it or not, we've been engaged. We're going after those prisoners—and Laroque."

17:20 Zulu. Thursday, November 14.
Communications room. Ubasi Palace

Mano shot his hand into the air. "She's in!"

Laroque spun to face the monitor. A grave silence filled the room.

Code began to appear on the screen. Mano motioned quickly for his techs to start triangulating. Seconds clicked on the clock. She needed to stay on her system for twenty seconds minimum to get an accurate reading on the coordinates.

Laroque's eyes locked onto the letters as they appeared. She began to type fast, and his chest tightened.

"Been to see hostages. Four still alive. Need..."

He flicked his eyes briefly to the clock, back to the text.

"...medical attention ASAP. Laroque claims they are mercenaries responsible for CIA deaths. Being held in rebel camp in Purple foothills just west of laptop GPS coordinates. I'm safe, being held at palace..."

The bitter taste of betrayal leached up the back of his throat.

"Laroque would not make cooperative captive in my assessment…"

His hands fisted. It was so damned personal. A desecration.

"…Capture would ensure martyrdom…"

"Got it! We got a GPS reading!"

"Kill it!" Laroque barked to the techs.

"…status. But the situ—"

"Now, goddammit! Stop that thing!"

The screen went blank. He was breathing hard. Sweating. Shaking inside.

"Where are they?" he said, his neck muscles bunched so tight he could barely squeeze the words out.

Mano rapidly hit a few keys, and the global positioning coordinates came up. A map enlarged, crosshairs zeroing in to a small island.

"There!" Mano pointed. "São Diogo Island, off the Angolan coast."

Laroque stared blindly at the blatant proof of her deceit mocking him from the screen, ripping him apart from the inside out. His nails bit into his palms as he clenched his fists in a struggle to restrain the rawness of his emotion, to digest what she'd done to him.

This was it.

He *had* to face the test.

He knew that every man in the room had their eyes trained on him at this very moment. He was their leader. And they waited to see what he'd do to the woman who'd come to destroy their country.

The woman who had made love to him with such tenderness in her eyes that he had dared dream of a future.

Now she was taking it all. And he'd made it possible by allowing himself to be played for a fool.

He could not let her win. He would *not* let her take him down.

He clenched his teeth, spun on his heels and barked a command to his men.

They reached for their weapons and followed him down the corridor, toward her room.

17:20 Zulu. Thursday, November 14.
Guest suite. Ubasi Palace

Emily froze as the screen suddenly went stone-cold dead.

Her heart started to thud. She quickly tried to reboot, reenter her code, type again. Nothing worked.

Panic shot through her as she heard several sets of boots thundering down the corridor toward her room. She heard a barked command.

Laroque's voice!

Her bedroom door smashed open and cracked back against the wall.

Laroque filled the door frame, fury twisting his features, the agony of betrayal burning in his eyes.

Chapter 13

Laroque stepped up to her, toe-to-toe, forcing her to look up and expose the smooth column of her neck. His men guarded the door with their rifles and bayonets.

"Who *are* you?" he asked.

Her eyes flicked to the guards, the weapons. Her features were taut with distress, perspiration drenching her shirt.

"Jean, please…I can explain. I—"

He raised his hand to silence her. "I want your name, your *real* name." It was the only question he wanted answered.

Laroque had a burning need to know who he had fallen for, who had betrayed him in this most intimate fashion, cracking through his emotional armor, exposing the intensely personal and private part of his heart.

Who was this woman who'd come so very close to destroying his dream for Ubasi?

She swallowed, and tears filled her eyes. "Emily," she said, very softly. "My name is Dr. Emily Carlin."

Laroque's chest burned as he looked into those glistening violet eyes. "You *are* a doctor?"

She nodded. "A psychologist."

A strange wave of relief surged through Laroque. He couldn't explain why. Perhaps it was because her name was so close to her alias. Perhaps it was because parts of her *were* real. But it was small comfort.

"Who are you working for?"

"The Force du Sable."

He swore. The mercenary world was an incredibly small one. The FDS was a known outfit based off the coast of Angola. Her information jibed with coordinates Mano had just triangulated. "Who are *they* working for?" he demanded.

She looked away sharply.

Aware that his men were watching, he grabbed her chin, twisting her head back to face him. "Answer me. And don't try to lie to me, Dr. Carlin. It won't help you," he said, holding her chin firmly.

"Jean, please—"

"*Who!*"

She swallowed. "The United States."

His stomach muscles tightened. "You've made contact with your people. What is their plan now?"

"I…I'm so sorry, Jean." The moisture escaped her eyes and trickled down her cheeks.

He swore bitterly. "Don't feed me that line. At least do me *that* justice. Tell me what to expect."

Emily closed her eyes, and inhaled a shuddering breath. "They'll attack," she said, looking slowly back up at him. "They'll be mobilizing now. They're backing Souleyman."

Disappointment smacked hard. "A coup?"

She nodded.

"Fools!" He spat the word at her. "You thought you were doing me in, didn't you?" He backed away from her. "But you're just screwing yourselves, do you know that?"

She winced. "It wasn't like that, Jean."

"What the hell was it, then? Jesus, Emma, you made me *care!*"

"Emily," she whispered.

"Right. I fell for someone who doesn't exist." He fingered the knife hilt in the sheath at his hip, and her eyes nervously tracked his movement.

"If your FDS friends and the Pentagon are backing Souleyman, they're in for one hell of a rude awakening, Dr. Carlin."

"Why?" she asked softly.

He snorted. "Because he's a two-timing, double-crossing sonofabitch, that's why. He's in bed with someone else already."

Her eyes flared. "*Who* else?" she whispered.

"Those mercenaries you so desperately wanted to

save? They were hired by a Chinese organization linked all the way up to Beijing. You see, *Emily,* it's not only the United States who wants access to Ubasi oil. The Chinese want it, too. And they've backed Souleyman to the hilt in a deal to get it—all of it—because they sure as hell knew they weren't going to get it from me. *They* paid those mercenaries to slaughter and gut your CIA agents."

Blood drained from her face. *"Oh my God."*

"That surprises you, does it, Dr. Carlin? Those dead CIA agents discovered that this covert arm of the Beijing government had been working behind the scenes to undermine U.S. interests in the Gulf, and the Chinese couldn't afford to let that secret out. Not while Beijing is in sensitive trade negotiations with Washington and playing all nice at the diplomatic table. They had to get rid of those agents fast, and make it look like someone else did it, or they were going to have a nice neo-Cold War on their hands."

"So they framed you."

"Why not? Everyone else thinks I'm the bad guy. Their hope was that when Souleyman finally killed me off, their secret would die with me, and the U.S. would come looking no further. My death would end the cartel that would have restricted China's oil access."

He barked a harsh laugh. "Bet they didn't count on *your* friends actually helping give Souleyman a leg up. He's going to turn around and stab your FDS buddies in the back as soon as he has my head on a stick."

"How…how do you *know* this?"

"That dead man you saw in that shack? The other hostages didn't want to end up like him. They spilled their guts to my men. Those mercs hold no allegiance to anything other than cash. They weren't going to die for a secret Chinese organization."

"Jean…I…I had no idea—"

He came up close to her, bent his head low, bringing his mouth alongside her ear so that his men couldn't hear. "I should have known better than hope you were for real, Emily Carlin," he whispered against her ear. "I thought I could love you." She shuddered, and her tear-filled eyes flashed wide to his. Her lips were so close to his that he felt the familiar, deceptive jolt to the groin. He clenched his jaw. "You are the worst kind of enemy, you know that?" he murmured through gritted teeth, almost touching her cheek with his lips.

Then he jerked back sharply and turned to his guards.

"Take her to the dungeons!"

The guards stepped in and grabbed her by the arms. She strained against them. *"Jean!"* But he turned away, he couldn't bear to look at her. He couldn't bear the pain.

"Wait, Jean!"

He walked toward the door.

"Wait, please, for God's sake. Just listen to me! They *will* kill you!"

He stopped in the doorway, then turned slowly to face her. "That was your plan, wasn't it? To assess whether I was worthy of capture, or death?"

"No…yes…I mean—"

He left.

"Jean, dammit! Wait!"

He kept on walking down the passage.

"Jean! I can help you! I…I can save you if you just let me speak to the FDS. Jean! I *believe* in you. I…I *care* for you, too, dammit! What we shared—that was *real!*"

He stood stone-still. His hands fisted at his sides. He swallowed, forcing himself not to look back.

He did not want to hear another word from her traitorous mouth. The desperation was from fear for herself and her own team now. This was a calculating woman who'd slept with him in order to get into his mind. She was not above saying this now, of hurting him in the deepest way possible. If only she knew just how much he'd wished for her to be someone else.

He inhaled sharply, shoring his anger, and he walked away without looking. He didn't have a moment to lose now. He was at war.

"Evacuate the palace!" he ordered his men as he stalked down the passage. "Go to ground. Plan delta."

"What about the woman?"

He hesitated briefly. "The safest place is the dungeons. It's designed as a bomb shelter."

He saw the quick exchange of glances. He knew his men wanted her executed, and soon. She was a curse to them. To their country. *To him.* And they were going to see his failure to swiftly deal with her as a weakness.

But as deeply as Emily Carlin had hurt him, as close as she'd come to bringing him and his country down, it wasn't in Laroque to hurt the woman he loved.

Even if her betrayal could be his downfall.

Emily huddled in the corner of her dank cell. There were no windows or electricity down in the dungeons. Rusting manacles still hung from chains bolted to the stone walls, thick with mold and years of grime. This place had been built at the time of the Crusades and had not changed since.

But she didn't give a damn about herself now. She had to find a way to warn Jacques about Souleyman and the Chinese, and she had to do it soon.

His men would be mobilizing, sparked by her prematurely truncated message. And they'd have gotten the wrong idea about Jean.

She'd been about to type that although Jean was not a good candidate for capture, she believed he was doing good, and that the coup must be stopped.

God, if only he'd let her type long enough he would have seen for himself that she was on his side now. She was on both sides. Jean *had* to see that. The FDS could be his best ally now. She could be his only hope.

Emily stood on tiptoe and tried to peer through the bars of the iron door on her cell. She could make out a guard standing near a torch farther along the dark corridor. "Hey! Hello there! Hey!" she yelled as she banged on the door, trying to get the guard's attention.

He glanced her way and her heart raced.

"Help me, please!" She banged on the door in desperation. "Please!"

He didn't move, but she could see that she'd snared his interest.

"Please, come here. You *must* listen to me. Laroque—Le Diable—your leader, he is in danger. His *life* is in danger!"

Desperation choked Emily. Her eyes filled with hot emotion. *"Please."*

He must have heard the sheer anguish in her voice, because he edged closer, curious.

"Look, just come here and listen to me. I can't do anything to you. But *you* could do something. You could save Le Diable. You could save Ubasi. Just hear me out, please."

He hesitated, then swung his AK round in front of him, and walked over to her cell, stopping a short distance away.

"Ask him to come down here, please. I have information that will enable him to stop the attack on Ubasi. But it can't wait. I must speak to him now. In a few more minutes it will be too late."

The guard studied her, suspicion in his eyes.

She tried to steady her voice as she gripped tighter on the bars. "It can do no harm for him to come, can it?" she said softly, tears starting to spill down her cheeks. "But it would save his life. I promise you that."

Hesitation rippled through the young man's features. He didn't like her, Emily could see that. But she had to count on the fact that this soldier revered his leader. Without Laroque, he was not going to have a future in Ubasi.

"You could be a hero," she said softly. "For your country."

His eyes narrowed sharply, then he turned and walked away.

Emily sank down into a limp pile behind the iron door and buried her head against her knees. She rocked her body, tears streaming silently down her face.

She'd failed.

Chapter 14

"I apologize if I am wrong, but I thought it best I alert you, sir."

Laroque studied the earnest young guard's face and he couldn't help thinking of himself at that age, fighting his father's brutal wars. It was not something he'd wish on anyone. This man still had a chance. It was young men like him who were Ubasi's future. Laroque owed it to him not to ignore any hope at peaceful resolution. No matter how small.

He went down to her cell.

He heard her out without looking at her even once, and then he'd had her brought in handcuffs up to the communications room. He still could not look at her.

He motioned to Mano to take over. "Take the cuffs off. Give her whatever she needs."

Mano quickly set up a communications link with Jacques Sauvage at the FDS base, and offered Emily a seat in front of the terminal.

Laroque would have left her to it, but he had to hear what she said to the FDS. He needed to be in a position to stop her if he suspected foul play.

But just being in the same room as her was painful.

"Jean?" she said, before taking her seat in front of the terminal. The soft hesitation, the broken spirit in her voice, ripped through him, but he forced himself to remain cold. But inside he burned—with betrayal, with unspent passion for her.

"Jean, I…I meant what I said. When I—"

"Just contact your damn people," he growled through clenched teeth. "Then leave me the hell alone."

23:58 Zulu. Thursday, November 14.
FDS Base, São Diogo Island

Jacques signed off. Carlin's news worked through his brain, all the little disjointed pieces that had been nagging at him slotting fast and cleanly into place.

He trusted she was not speaking under duress. They had code for that. And what she had just told him about Souleyman, while shattering, added up. They had to move fast now. Blake Weston was not going to like this, but he'd change his mind pretty damn quick when he learned about the alleged Chinese involvement.

If Beijing really was behind the scenes, the U.S. could be facing a neo-Cold War era—especially given China's recently demonstrated antisatellite capabilities. This could shape up to be a race not only to secure world energy resources and control of space but global military domination, especially given the recent strengthening of Sino-Russian ties.

Jacques reached for the communications console and flicked a switch. "Change of plan. Call off Code Green. I repeat, terminate Code Green…." Then he barked a series of orders to his men with his classic machine-gun precision.

00:02 Zulu. Friday, November 15.
Communications room, Ubasi Palace

Emily rubbed her wrists where the handcuffs had chafed her skin, but it was a different kind of pain she needed to assuage. She ached to touch Jean just one more time, just to have him look her in the eyes again. But he'd shut her out.

He stood like a towering hunk of cold granite, his back to her, waiting for her to leave the room.

"Jean, please look at me."

He stood silent for a long time, and then walked slowly from the room, leaving a hollow in her stomach.

He didn't close the door. He didn't say not to follow him, either. It was almost as if he needed to see that she would dare come after him now that her job here was done.

She did.

She found him in his private quarters, which commanded a startling view of the jungle canopy all the way to the Purple Mountains. But dawn was still hours away and the night was dark and oppressive, the air charged with the pressure and electricity of a coming storm. Emily could hear choppers, faint in the distance, cutting over the black canopy from Cameroon—Jacques's men coming to get her. The tall palms outside rattled their leaves in the gusts of hot, mounting wind.

He stood staring out the arched stone windows into the blackness as the breeze billowed over his cotton shirt and lifted his hair. Emily approached softly behind him.

She hesitated, unsure of what to say, how close to go. She reached out to touch him, almost finding words, but she was so conflicted and confused about where to go from here that she was virtually paralyzed. She dropped her hand back to her side.

He broke the silence, speaking into the distance.

"She said a woman with eyes the same color as the hills out there would be my downfall."

Surprise shimmered through her. "Who said that?"

"The Ubasi high priestess," he said, without looking at her. "I never listened, didn't even remember her words, until my men reminded me." He remained silent a long time. "I should have listened."

"You don't believe in that stuff, Jean."

"I don't. But my people do. Souleyman used your

arrival as a sign. He started the rumor that you were the temptress of the prophecy, and when Souleyman said I was growing weak because of you, that's when I felt something change in my men." He paused. "Or maybe it was me that changed. Because you *did* make me weak. I allowed your hold over me to jeopardize my dream." He snorted softly, still refusing to look at her. "Maybe it *is* true. Maybe there are such things." He was silent. "Maybe it's over."

A strange chill brushed her skin "What exactly did the priestess say?"

"That I would hold power until a woman with eyes the color of the Purple Mountains arrived and changed everything."

"She didn't say you'd lose power."

"Doesn't matter. I never wanted to rule. I did this job for the king, and for my sister. I did it for my country." He paused. "And it is my country. It's become my home."

"The king?"

"He hired me to take Ubasi. He paid me in oil exploration blocks."

"Where is he?" she asked, bewildered.

"Doesn't matter. Not to you."

Hurt pinged through her. "Change doesn't mean downfall, Jean. Change—the end of something—usually signals rebirth."

He was quiet for a moment. "I'd like you to leave."

She touched his shoulder and he tensed like wire under her fingertips. "I meant what I said, Jean.

I...I don't think I've ever felt this way about another man. I—"

He whipped around, cold ice in his eyes. "You *used* me. You probed right into my head. Into my memories, my past, my dreams, my heart. You got me to say things I have never said to another human being. Ever." He fisted his hand and knocked it against his chest. "I opened up, here. I let you in, *Emily.*" His faced darkened. "How do you think that makes me feel, *doctor?* What does the shrink have to say about *that?*"

Heat flushed her cheeks. "The very fact you did let me in saved you, Jean."

His eyes burned into her, into every little crevice of her brain and body. "Well, thank you, doctor, for coming to my rescue."

"You showed me that you are not what the rest of the world believes you to be, Jean. You are nowhere near evil." She hesitated. "Nothing like your father."

Emotion slashed over his features, then was gone. "That's your *professional* assessment, Dr. Carlin?" Cold anger clipped his words.

"It's personal, Jean. Every damn thing about this mission has been personal. Too personal. That's my problem. That's—" she glanced away "—a serious problem," she said, barely audibly.

"Well, you better sort yourself out before you take another job and start sleeping with your next target."

She winced inwardly and emotion burned into her eyes. "If it matters at all to you what I think, you're like your mother, Jean. You have her empathy and her elegance without her fragility." She looked up into his eyes. "And you're like your sister. She was a soldier. She burned with the same fire and determination as you. She also marched to her own drum. She was brave. Bold."

Emotion tore through into his features again, lingering in the glint in his eyes.

Her throat tightened at the rawness she saw in his face. "You're a damn fine person, Jean. Larger than life, bolder than most men could ever dream to be, and more honorable…and…" She looked down at her hands. "And more than most women could ever hope to have known," she said softly.

He didn't speak.

She lifted her eyes slowly, met his, and the memories of their intimacy surged between them, alive like a separate pulsing entity, crackling with the same electricity and pressure as the mounting storm.

"Is it true," he said quietly, "what you told me about your own father? Or was that just another ploy to get me to open up so you could pick at my brain?"

"It's true. Not his profession. He's not a fire chief—"

He turned sharply away.

"It's not the little details that mattered, Jean! I couldn't tell you those without blowing my cover, but the rest of it was all real. My father is a retired U.S. Army general. His name is Tom Carlin."

His back stiffened.

She had a desperate need to tell him the truth, all of it, give him as many facts as he could check. She wanted his trust. She wanted some small sense of reconnection before those choppers she could hear in the distance landed and took her away.

"And yes, I do blame him for my mother's death. And yes, I still love my dad. I don't *like* him, but some sad part of me has always needed him. Like my mother, I have always craved his approval, his affection. I joined the army to win his respect, on his own turf, but he was a hard man to please. I studied the psychology of alpha males and their codependents to better understand him and my mother. I left the army, got my doctorate and went on to become a specialist in tyrannical pathology. And while I enjoy some global renown in highly academic circles for my expertise, while I'm an independent adult with my own means, some sick part of me still seeks the approval of my father for every damn thing I do in my life …" Her voice grew small, almost indistinct. "Which scares the hell out of me."

She paused. "And you can check it. All of it. It's who I am."

He turned slowly to face her. "And you think this makes you somehow weak?"

She nodded.

"You're not weak."

"I am. And I screwed up. I keep screwing up because of this problem I can't seem to get out of my system."

He studied her intensely. "What do you mean?"

The beat of the choppers in the humid air grew louder, closer. Urgency rustled through her. "It's not just my father, Jean. I am habitually attracted to domineering men. Just as my mom was attracted to my dad. And then just when my relationships start getting serious, I think I subconsciously find ways to sabotage them. And I flee, I run, as if for my life, and I try to pretend it's the guy's fault, that he's trying to control my life, that's he's somehow *wrong*." She swallowed, the sound of the helicopters drawing closer, tension winding tighter. "What's wrong is *me,* Jean. I'm stuck in a pathological loop. I seriously screwed up back home, and I should have faced things. Instead I came here, and I fell for you. There. You have it. All of it. And I let it get in the way of my job."

She sucked in a shaky breath. "I've never told a soul. Not straight up like this. I…I never even admitted it to myself. And…" Her voice faltered. "And I'm sorry. I'm supposed to be a therapist," she muttered.

He studied her with cool, probing eyes. "Everything else is true?"

"What we had was real. That was true."

And now it was gone.

He nodded curtly and turned away. As if his need had been satisfied and she'd been dismissed for good.

Her heart bottomed out.

"You…you do understand, don't you?" she said.

He said nothing.

She could see the helicopter lights now, coming

over the black shape of the jungle canopy. The sound of the blades filled the air. Desperation surged in her. "If you'd just have let me finish typing you'd have seen that I believe you."

"Prove it," he said suddenly.

"What?"

He spun round to face her.

"If it's all true, Emily, prove it to me. Stay."

Confusion washed through her. "I don't underst—"

"Stay here in Ubasi. Help me through this. Help me win this war. Help me make it safe enough to bring back the royal family. Help *us* bring democracy to Ubasi." He stepped close, his voice growing low, seductive, aggressive with longing. "If you truly mean what you've just said, use the contacts you have and help me achieve my sister's dream for my people. For me. Right here at my side. *Show* me, Emily, that what we had really was true."

Her heart swooped up in a wild and dizzying roller-coaster lurch, and then plunged right back down the other side in a terrifying free fall.

He wanted commitment from her.

He was forcing her to choose between his life and hers. It was either his cause in Ubasi or her life in Manhattan.

Why did it always have to be like that?

There was no middle ground for this man, and she knew there would never be. He was too strong. Too dominant. Too determined.

And she was suddenly inexplicably terrified.

She jerked back in shock as an explosion rocked the ground just beyond the palace walls. The choppers closed in, filling the air with sound and hot vibration.

A barrage of gunfire peppered the sky.

"They're getting closer," she whispered. "Jacques's men, fighting with Souleyman."

"They've come to take you," he said, eyes not budging from hers.

Another shell hit, the impact reverberating through the stone walls. Panic tightened her throat. The heat and pressure was overwhelming. Another explosion pulsed through the dense air, and she heard the choppers coming in to land in the palace grounds.

Yelling broke out down in the courtyard, Laroque's men pulling back gates, letting FDS soldiers in as they fought back insurgents. She could hear boots clapping up the stairs, pounding down the corridor, growing louder. Wind began to whip fat drops in through the open window as the storm closed in.

His eyes never wavered. "Make your choice, Emily."

The doors swung open. "Carlin! You okay?"

She couldn't speak. Couldn't move.

"We've got orders to get you out ASAP, back to São Diogo. Chopper's waiting!"

One hovered right outside the window, searchlights illuminating the castle walls and grounds, the *thuck thuck thuck* sound pounding through the humid air, slamming through her head.

His eyes lanced hers, not even bothering to look

at the two FDS soldiers who'd burst into his room. Slowly he extended his hand to her. An offer. A bridge. A connection. Steady. Strong. A different life.

She stared at it, heart racing, perspiration prickling over her forehead, trickling down between her breasts.

"*Carlin!* You coming? Pilot needs to move before the storm closes in."

"Jean…I…I need to go back to São Diogo for de-briefing. I…I can return. We can see if—"

"It's now or never, Emily." His hand remained steady, palm up. A test.

Indecision immobilized her. Shots rang out again. The sound of the helicopter outside grew deafening. She couldn't think. Her head began to buzz. Suddenly she was completely out of her depth and shaken by everything. Shaken to her foundations as if she was a little girl again.

"Carlin, we need to move ASAP! The storm is closing in!"

"Jean…I *must*…"

He dropped his hand, spun abruptly away from her. He stared out the window, rigid as a stone sculpture, an image of both power and desperate solitude.

It was how he'd lived all his life. Unbearable compassion washed over her, sorrow for what she had done to him. She was so conflicted she felt ill. She loved him. Yes she truly loved this larger-than-life man, in an absurd larger-than-life way. Yet she was still afraid of him. Of *herself.* Of what she could allow him to become in her life, of losing her autonomy, of turning into her mother. She just couldn't make a huge all-or-nothing decision like this. Not in a few seconds.

"Jean?" she whispered, tears filling her eyes.

"Go!"

The single word slammed into her chest like a bullet. She sagged slightly.

Jacques's men took her arm, urging her away gently.

Tears began to stream down Emily's cheeks, and she let Jacques's men take her away.

Forever.

Chapter 15

One week later. CIA director's home.
Washington, D.C.

CIA director Blake Weston stared out his living room window into the dark night sky. Things had gone sideways in Ubasi, and the White House wanted answers ASAP.

It could cost him his job.

Blake had needed Laroque dead, and Souleyman in power. If Laroque had been assassinated in a coup, Washington might have believed that Laroque had discovered the CIA agents' identities on his own, and killed them all as a warning to the West to stay out of his country.

Instead, Souleyman had died in the fighting, and Blake was now faced with Laroque looking like the good guy, along with allegations that a covert faction of the ruling Chinese communist party had killed the agents.

But there was no proof such a Chinese faction even existed. All they had was Laroque's word and the word of his rebels. Blake needed to keep it that way, for reasons of his own.

However, once the so-called mercenaries Laroque's rebels had abducted from Nigeria were interrogated by U.S. forces, proof might indeed surface that they had been contracted by the Chinese to kill the CIA agents. It would also then become apparent that someone *inside* the CIA must have leaked the identities of those agents to the Chinese faction.

That meant serious trouble for Blake. Washington would see it for what it was—a mole somewhere deep within his agency.

Blake had to be seen to be moving swiftly to exorcise this informant. But if he failed to deliver the mole, he was damn well going to need another plan if he was to keep his post as CIA chief.

Blake turned as he heard his wife Shan enter the living room.

"You okay, honey?" she asked, handing him his drink, her long dark hair shimmering in the firelight.

Blake's chest tightened.

Shan had a way of changing his world when she

walked into a room. There was little he wouldn't do for his wife, and little he wouldn't share with her.

"I'm okay." He smiled wryly. "Just hassled about the Sino-African issue."

She touched his face, her exotic almond eyes luminous. "You'll be fine," she said. "You always are. You just have to make sure those captives *don't* talk."

Eleven months later. Late October.
Manhattan

A dense shroud of fog closed in around Manhattan's skyscrapers, socking the city in, making the world even more gray in the early twilight.

Rain flicked against the misted windows of the small café where Emily waited in line for her coffee as she halfheartedly watched the news on the television set above the counter. It was Friday evening, and she was going home to work. Again.

She took her latte from the barista, eyes suddenly glued to the news as coverage segued to a reporter in Ubasi covering the country's first-ever democratic elections.

Her pulse quickened. Coffee in hand, Emily moved closer to the set, riveted by the images of the hot country being transported right into her cold, gray, autumn world.

"The final tallies are now in," said the reporter, holding her ear and speaking into the microphone over the noise of jubilant crowds. Behind her, people were waving banners, chanting, ululating—the same haunting sounds that had assaulted Emily in the dusty streets of Basaroutou on that first day of her mission. The day she'd first laid eyes on Jean-Charles Laroque.

"Mangosutu Mephetwe has been elected the first president of Ubasi in a landslide victory in this small, oil-rich nation's first democratic elections," said the reporter. "The election was marked by long lines that sometimes stretched for miles as people waited patiently at polling booths around the country. Many had traveled for days from interior jungle villages to reach the polling stations, but it was a day unmarked by the violence that has plagued this country for the last three decades, one that will go down in history for the people of this war-torn country."

Goose bumps chased over Emily's skin, and moisture filled her eyes. He'd done it. He'd really done it. She smiled at the television as tears threatened to spill down her cheeks. *"Good for you, Jean,"* she whispered softly to herself. "Good for Ubasi."

She dug into her coat pocket for a tissue, and blew her nose. Then she pulled her coat closed, and stepped out into the cold evening, feeling more alone than she could ever remember. As she walked down the pavement, rain dampening her hair, she reminded herself she'd vowed not to look back, not to regret.

But it was hard not to.

More than anything, it was the irony that got to her. She'd made a habit of sabotaging her relationships with the alpha males she was habitually attracted to—because of her fear that she'd end up like her mom. And then Anthony had brought it all to a head by making a mockery of her pathology, hurting and humiliating Emily in the deepest way. So she'd fled. She'd *run* from her issues again. This time running right out of the country, slap-bang into the biggest Alpha Dog of them all.

And he'd trapped her for good.

Jean-Charles Laroque had made it impossible to run again. And in falling for Le Diable, Emily had been forced to finally confront her fear. For the first time in her life, she'd been able to fully articulate what she'd been doing to herself, and why.

As a therapist Emily knew what kind of catharsis that brought for her patients. Finally recognizing what it was that troubled them was often enough to make the problem go away, or at least give the clients tools to deal appropriately with their issues.

It had been no different for her. The catharsis she'd found in confronting Jean—a walking, breathing image of her fears—and articulating to him what she was truly afraid of, had finally freed her.

But she'd lost him in the process.

That's what ate at her.

Emily knew now that Jean was no tyrant. Yes, he was a potently powerful alpha. But he was a warrior, not an abuser. Jean had not been able to hurt her under the most extreme circumstances of betrayal and war—even though his men had *expected* it of him—and *that* told Emily he would never hurt her like her father had hurt her mother.

She stopped at a traffic light, still clutching her untouched coffee, the world around her a blur of cars and cabs and throngs of pedestrians, horns blaring and tires crackling on rain-smeared streets.

Emily could see now that much of Jean's power came from the mind, not violence. He was a master chess player, a shrewd manipulator. And when he did fight, the battle was always fair, and he sought to win on equal terms. The analyst in Emily could see all this in retrospect—Jean-Charles Laroque lived for challenge, not exploitation of the weak. He supported the disenfranchised in the same way he upheld his sister's dream and fought for the Ubasi people and their king.

She'd seen it in the way Jean had shown his love for those villagers, and for his land.

Her eyes misted again as she neared her apartment, the wind tugging at her hair and nipping at her cheeks. She'd lost a rare man.

She'd lost him because he'd asked her to commit so suddenly, under such extreme pressure, right in the middle of a war zone. It had been impossible for her to do it at that moment—it would have been wrong.

Yet he was such an all-or-nothing, larger-than-life guy—you were either with him or not. He'd been under stress, too. She'd hurt him badly, and she couldn't hold his impetuousness against him.

She nodded at her doorman as she entered her

building and made her way to the elevators, but he stopped her.

"Emily, someone was here for you."

She turned round, puzzled. She'd been so involved in her work she'd virtually become a recluse these past months. She'd thought she'd be happy this way, but in reality, her work was all she had now. "Who?" she asked, frowning.

"He wouldn't leave his name. Said he'd come back. He's already been by three times. Keeps driving past in a limo."

Emily's heart kicked. No. *It couldn't be.* Why should she even think it?

Her mouth went dry. She handed her coffee cup to the doorman. "Here, can you hold this?" Without thinking, she stepped back out into the rain, eyes searching the street for a limousine.

But there was nothing.

She was being ridiculous. Why would he even come to Manhattan? There was no way he'd be in New York, especially today, when the first president was being elected in his country.

Her heart felt flat, her hair damp. She drew her coat closer against the biting cold and turned to reenter her building. That's when she caught sight of a long black limousine coming around the corner.

Emily froze.

The rain-covered limo pulled up on the opposite curb, and her chest tensed as the door slowly opened.

He climbed out, stood to his full height and

stared at her from across the street. His hair was pulled back in elegant dreadlocks, his dark features exotic among the sea of urbane faces that suddenly looked soft and bland juxtaposed alongside his towering strength.

Jean-Charles Laroque literally telegraphed power and an easy physical confidence. It was no different here in New York than seeing him sitting on the back of that Jeep in Basaroutou. And once again, his eyes were trained directly on her, and on her alone.

He smiled, a slash of piratical white against mocha skin, and he raised his hand in a bold salute.

Wild emotion tore through her body with such force it brought tears to Emily's eyes and rooted her to the spot.

He stepped off the curb and came toward her, his coat billowing out behind him, rain glistening on his dark hair, closing the distance between them without breaking eye contact.

And she braced herself, as if for a bullet headed her way.

"Emily—" He reached for her hands as he neared, his voice the low, resonant African base tinged with French that melted her from the inside out.

"Jean...what...what are you doing here?" Her words came out hoarse. "I...I saw the news. The election. You...you did it, Jean!"

He nodded, satisfaction gleaming in his pale green eyes, a sense of power rolling over him in waves. "*We* did it, Emily," he said, taking her hands in his and drawing her close.

"Why aren't you there? Why didn't *you* run for election like they were all pressing you to?"

"I've done my bit, and it was never my goal to govern." A twinkle of unspeakable mischief sparked in his eyes. "I'm not a tyrant, you see, Dr. Carlin."

She smiled. "Point taken. But I thought you'd want to be there today, with King Douala and the new president. You have a lot to celebrate."

His eyes turned serious. "I came for something that is more important to me now. I came for you."

She swallowed, almost afraid to say anything that might make this moment evaporate in front of her eyes.

"Do you think we might go inside, get out of the rain, perhaps?"

"I…oh, yes, I, of course." She felt nervous, excited, energized, and the cocktail of explosive emotion rocketing through her was affecting her ability to speak. "Would…you like to come up to my apartment?"

His gaze was clear and direct. "I'd like that. Very much."

She hesitated. "What about the car—"

He hooked his arm over her shoulder. "Come. My driver will take care of it. He's got Shaka in there. Shaka needs a walk anyway." Jean raised his hand, made a sign to the driver, and the limo pulled out into the traffic.

"You brought *Shaka?*"

"I'm here to stay awhile."

"In *New York?*"

He tipped his head. "Yes, in New York."

Emily poured Jean a glass of single-malt scotch, and his eyes tracked her every movement in a way that made her limbs feel disjointed.

Their fingers connected as she handed him the tumbler, and heat jolted through her. Emily almost jerked back with surprise at the intensity of the sensation. Just one touch and this man could do things to her no other could. She stepped back slowly, heart racing, and sat opposite him, watching his eyes.

There was something different about him. She could see it in his eyes. There was a luminosity she hadn't noticed before. "You look relaxed, Jean. At peace." And even more beautiful.

"I am at peace," he said, his smile reaching right into his eyes in a way that made them twinkle—and her heart spasm. "And you, Emily? How are *you?*"

She glanced down at the whiskey in her glass. "I'm fine. Doing well. Working hard." What else was there to say—*missing you like hell?*

He leaned forward suddenly, his energy intense. "Do you want to know why I'm at peace?"

"Because you have achieved a dream few men could?"

"Because of *you.*"

She frowned.

"You helped show me something I needed to see more than anything else in this world."

"I...I don't understand."

"The therapist in you should." He paused. "We all know what my father did, Emily. He was a brutal murderer and sexual sadist. While he used the arena of war to disguise his crimes—to hide—he was no different from a serial killer in an urban environment."

"You're right," Emily said quietly, trying to read his eyes.

"Well, I am the offspring of that man, and as with the child of any serial killer, there's always the fear that the genetic echo of a murderer lurks deep within him, too." He swirled his whiskey, concentrating on the gold liquid as ice chinked softly against the crystal. "You worry that, given a certain set of circumstances, the killer in you will be set free, too." He looked up. "In essence, you live in fear of *yourself*. Every time you get heated, passionate, angry, you are terrified it might be happening. You don't know what the emotions are supposed to feel like. You don't know if it's normal." He took a deep sip of his drink.

"Well, you took me to the edge of my fear, Emily. You forced me to look right over into that abyss, and you know what?" He grinned, his teeth impossibly white against his skin. "The devil did not look back at me. You showed me that, when pushed to the most extreme circumstances, when faced with a most hurtful and intimate betrayal that almost cost my nation, I was still unable to hurt you. Or anyone. I can't hurt people like he did, and I never will. I know that now. And *that,* Emily, has brought me peace. For that I am extremely grateful."

"I never set out to hurt you, Jean."

"I know that."

She studied him for a long time, and he met her scrutiny. Silence consumed the room, the air growing thick, charged.

"And I know you don't have one ounce of Peter Laroque's evil in you, Jean," she said finally, setting her drink carefully on the coffee table between them. "There was a point I was afraid you did—that you might kill me when you discovered who I really was. But at the end, when you were interrogating me, I saw the way your hand went for your knife. I saw the way you hesitated—how you couldn't draw it from the sheath despite the rage in your eyes. I knew then that you could never hurt me. Even after what I had done to you."

His features turned grave. "I am sorry if I frightened you."

She nodded. "Psychological power, that's your strength, Jean."

"And does *that* worry you, Emily?'

"I… Why should it?"

"You told me about your fears. Your relationships, how you sabotaged them."

Adrenaline skittered through her stomach. "We… we don't have a relationship, Jean. There's no reason it should worry me."

"What if I told you I would like to start one?"

Emotion surged sharply though her chest, and her world shifted slightly. "Jean, I've worked through a lot of things over this past year. I've confronted my issues because of what we went through in Ubasi. I faced them, talked them out, and I've come out the other side a stronger person. But I can't get involved with you."

His features shifted, and so did his energy. "Why not?"

"It won't work, you and me. Our lives are literally worlds apart. My work is here, yours is—"

His eyes narrowed sharply. "What's the real reason, Emily?" His voice was gruff.

Her pulse quickened, and she looked at her hands. "It's not because of my old fears. I can't do it because…because I think I'm in love with you, and you will end up breaking my heart when you go back to your life."

"Emily." He surged to his feet, came round the coffee table and sat on the sofa beside her, grasping her shoulders. "Look at me, Emily."

She lifted her eyes slowly and met his.

"You *know* me. Better than anyone else in this world. You understand who I am—that I am a man of dreams. Big, bold, brash ones. Do you want to know what my next dream is?"

Uncertainty washed through her.

"I wasn't going to tell you the big picture, because I haven't figured out all the pieces yet, and I didn't want to scare you away." His eyes tunneled into hers. "I didn't want you to feel cornered, because you've been so honest in telling me your fears. But I *am* a big-picture guy, and my dream goes well beyond a fling, Emily."

"Jean, I—"

He raised his hand. "No, listen to me. *Then* you can turn me down. If you want, I will walk out that door and never come back, because the last thing in the world I want to do is to make you feel trapped, Emily." He paused. "Or to ask you to sacrifice your autonomy in any way whatsoever. Will you hear me out?"

She nodded, her mouth dry.

"A ranch—" he said, standing up to his full height, stretching out his hand, painting the vision in his mind. "Acres and acres of Ubasi land as far as your eye can see. And up there, on the hill—" he pointed to an imaginary space "—a house overlooking a sugar-white beach, surf rolling like thunder along the shore, throwing white spindrift into the wind." His eyes locked on hers, his energy visceral, magnetic. "And that house, Emily, is where I will bring my wife, where we will raise *our* children, in a free nation—a place I helped build with my own blood and sweat. A place to belong. A home." He lowered himself onto the sofa beside her. "A place, Emily, that you helped me build." He stilled, eyes lancing hers. "And I want you to be my wife."

Her mouth opened, and emotion flooded to her eyes.

"You see? I didn't want to tell you this. I wanted to go one day at a time. But I also want you to know that I don't want to go back to Ubasi without you."

Emily began to tremble inside. "Jean, I...I don't know what to say. I can't go. My work is here. Everything of mine is here."

Insecurity ripped through his eyes, and his mouth flattened. It was the first time Emily had glimpsed this unfamiliar emotion in him.

"I took an apartment in Manhattan," he said tonelessly. "I have business here—my offshore investments, my oil interests. I have United Nations meetings to attend—I accepted a temporary post as Ubasi ambassador to the U.N. until they find someone else. Until I know if you want to be with me."

"You did this all for me, Jean?"

He shrugged, a vulnerability in his eyes. "I'm afraid that scares you, Emily. I go hard for my dreams. But I want you to understand—" he said, cupping her face so tenderly "—that even though I fought *hard* for my country, it now stands free. That's how I see us—a hard-won union. Strong together, yet always free. Always together."

She brushed away the tear that had spilled onto her cheek. "You really do nothing in half measures, do you?"

His eyes suddenly turned fierce. "I do. I *can*. Watch me. One day at a time. Baby steps. How about it, Emily? Anytime you want to step away, anytime you feel closed in, you are free to walk, and I will let you. I promise you that. I would never, ever ask you to be where you don't want. But this must be *your* choice."

She bit her lip, her heart bursting with such a powerfully raw love she could barely restrain it. After this past year, after working through her problems, after missing him so damn badly, all she wanted to do was say yes, and be with him.

But she was afraid to make that mistake.

"Jean, what about my work? I can't just give it all up." But even as Emily mouthed the words, she was thinking about the offer Jacques Sauvage had made her last month. He needed a therapist on call full-time for his growing private army on São Diogo. He wanted someone who understood the mindset of a soldier—someone who could handle complex psychological debriefings when needed. This, Jacques had said, would be in addition to her regular FDS profiling contracts. Emily had been sorely tempted, but unsure about permanently relocating to that part of the world.

But Ubasi was close to São Diogo, an hour or two max by military chopper. Maybe it *was* a viable alternative. Maybe she should try this all on for size, like Jean said, one baby step at a time. An uncontainable excitement began to build in her.

She looked at him, unable to temper the animation in her eyes. This was a man who would fight to the death to defend her, yet never hurt her. He would protect her right to freedom, just as she'd seen him do for his country.

Jean was more man than a woman could ever hope for.

Emily had vowed she would do something fresh

in her life—something new and exciting—if she ever made it out of Ubasi alive. Perhaps this was it. She just hadn't thought she might return to Africa to fulfill that promise she'd made to herself. She told herself this was not about looking back. This was about going forward. Leaving all her old paranoia behind her while taking a step in a bold new direction.

With the man who had shown her how to do that.

Jean was watching her face intently. The hope etched into his features touched her heart.

She nodded, tears suddenly streaming down her cheeks, even as she smiled.

He closed his eyes, a barely perceptible shudder running through his muscular frame. When he opened them, his relief was clear, raw. Emily began to laugh and sob at the same time, and he grabbed her, kissing her deeply and hard and completely.

He broke away and tenderly wiped the tears from her cheeks. "We should celebrate. Where do you like to go in Manhattan on a Friday night?"

Emily realized with mild alarm that she hadn't been out in months. While her work and the writing of her new book were going great, she'd had such a pathetic excuse for a social life, she was at a complete loss as to where she'd like to go. "How about," she said, smiling, "I cook you dinner?"

"Here?"

"Right here, in my apartment."

His eyes twinkled. "You cook?"

"Very well, actually."

He looked into her eyes, a warm appreciation and wonder blooming in his own. "I know you so intimately," he said softly, his voice husky. "Yet there are so many more things to discover." He traced the line of her face with his fingers as he spoke, and the seduction in his tone snaked warm and slow through her. She swallowed, her body tingling deep inside.

"One day at a time, Jean," she whispered, leaning forward and brushing her mouth over his.

A soft moan escaped his chest as her lips feathered his. Jean wrapped his arms around her and threw back his head, closing his eyes tight as emotion swam sharp and sweet behind his lids. For the first time since he could remember, he felt the impulse to cry.

He had finally gotten everything he had searched for. A country where he belonged; a place he could call home.

And beyond all that, in his arms he held a woman he not only loved with every molecule in his body, but a woman he respected as his equal. One of the strongest women he had ever met.

A woman who knew him better than anyone in this world—one he hoped to one day start a family with. The thought filled his belly with hot pleasure. He tilted her chin up and kissed her. "One day at a time," he murmured, and that's how he was going to hold on to her.

Forever.

Epilogue

Eighteen months later.
Ubasi Palace grounds

Laroque slipped his arm around Emily's waist, drawing her to his side as they stood by the dark waters of the rockpool in the Ubasi Palace gardens, greeting guests.

King Douala was hosting a lavish royal engagement celebration for Laroque and Emily. The night was sultry and heady with tropical fragrance. Torches lit the palace gardens. Drums beat, and tribal dancers entertained guests under a brilliant starry sky.

Things had stabilized in Ubasi. The economy was on the upswing and the first democratic elections had been an unquestionable success. President Mangosutu Mephetwe—the headman and friend who'd warned Laroque about the high priestess's prophecy—had established a solid cabinet, and encouraged a healthy opposition.

In the meantime, Laroque and King Douala had managed to broker groundbreaking treaties with neighboring governments and multinational oil corporations, and dates had been set for the first-ever official Niger Delta talks with the new Africa Oil Cartel.

Dignitaries from those neighboring countries were in attendance tonight, as was President Mephetwe. The high priestess herself was at the party, along with key rebel leaders and FDS boss Jacques Sauvage and his wife, Olivia. Also on hand for the celebration was a crew from *Vanity Fair,* who were doing a glossy spread on the "Manhattan psychologist and her mercenary" to coincide with the release of Emily's new book.

Over the past eighteen months Laroque had worked closely with Emily on her book, which had evolved to focus on the key psychological indicators that determined who might become a diabolical despot versus a truly powerful leader—be it in politics, war, business or relationships. She'd used Le Diable and the Ubasi story as the primary case study, contrasting Laroque's unorthodox rule to the reigns of African despots who'd achieved less happy outcomes.

Laroque had agreed to pose, with Shaka, for the cover, his mesmerizing green eyes and strikingly

powerful dark features enticing—almost *daring*—
readers to pick up the timely hardcover, which hit a
readership hungry for a radical success story in the
current environment of economic downturn and
global bad news.

In many ways, the book had become Laroque's
public absolution. Emily herself was thrilled the
world could now see her fiancé for the sensitive and
peace-loving man he really was. Above all, Emily
hoped the phenomenal publicity they were getting
would help generate even more funding for the foundation she and Jean had started to support and rehabilitate child soldiers.

Her new clinic on their Ubasi ranch would serve
as a refuge for many of those young soldiers—mere
boys who had been driven into war in much the same
way Laroque had been at age thirteen. It was serious
work. Emily was also contracting to the FDS in a
therapeutic capacity for Jacques's mercenaries, who
suffered from varying degrees of PTSD, or who
needed professional debriefing in other ways. She
was ideally suited to this role, given her own military
background and her relationship to Jean.

But there was more than their love and Ubasi's
future to celebrate tonight. Emily was pregnant, and
Laroque could not have been more thrilled at the
prospect of having his child born right here in his
country—a symbol of the new era of hope, a bridge
over the chasm of African and Western ideology.

Both he and Emily had agreed that if the baby was a girl, her name would be Tamasha.

Jacques caught Emily's and Laroque's attention as they made their way through the garden, and he drew them aside for a moment. "Congratulations again on the engagement." He smiled.

"Thanks in part to you," said Laroque, grinning. "You sent her my way."

Jacques slapped Laroque on the back. "You did good by her. And it's always nice to make a new ally, *mon ami.*"

"Still no news on that alleged covert arm of the Beijing government?" Laroque asked as they walked up the lawn together.

Jacques stopped, glanced over his shoulder and lowered his voice. "Everything points to a force operating behind the scenes for the Chinese, and not just in Africa," he said. "But we have no *proof.* Not since the U.S. convoy transporting those mercs you captured came under attack. All evidence died with them."

"Do you have any idea who attacked them?" asked Emily.

"Not yet. It looked like renegades, but we assume it was Chinese-backed, and that they were tipped off about the convoy." He lowered his voice further. "Between us, we think there's a mole deep in the CIA itself. Someone is *still* feeding highly sensitive information directly to Beijing."

"What's Blake Weston doing about it?"

"He's done what he can," said Jacques. "There's been an inquiry. He fired a few people to appease Washington brass, and he kept his job. But otherwise, the leads have gone stone-cold. Until *now*." He paused, making doubly sure no one was eavesdropping. "Some very interesting information has just come out of Vancouver on Canada's west coast. Weston has asked us to look into it. He wants to appear completely hands-off on this, because he can't trust his own right now."

"So he's outsourced this to the FDS?" said Emily.

"Correct."

"What kind of information?" asked Laroque.

"Jessica Chan, a BBC foreign correspondent who used to be stationed in Shanghai, must know something because she appears to have been targeted by this organization. She's gone to ground, and we need to find her before they do."

"So this woman could provide proof that this organization exists?"

Jacques nodded. "*Oui.* And she could potentially lead us right to the mole. My key Pacific Rim operative, Luke Stone, has been dispatched to handle the case." He paused. "That proof—when and *if* Stone gets it—has the potential to change the world's political climate. If the Communist party really is working behind the scenes for global domination while pretending to play nice at international negotiation tables, we're looking at another Cold War scenario here."

Jacques slapped Laroque's shoulder. "But there is a time for everything, and tonight we must celebrate our achievements—and your happiness. Let's go back to the party. I hear King Douala has fireworks planned."

Jean winked at Emily, and she returned his smile as they linked hands and walked up the palace lawn to greet their guests in a land they had made their home.

* * * * *

*Mills & Boon® Intrigue brings you
a sneak preview of...*

Delores Fossen's Security Blanket

*Quinn "Lucky" Bacelli thought saving Marin Sheppard
would be the end of their dalliance. But then she asked
him for protection from her domineering parents. And
to pretend to be the father of her infant son...*

Don't miss this thrilling first story in the new
TEXAS PATERNITY: BOOTS AND BOOTIES
*mini-series available next month from
Mills & Boon® Intrigue.*

Security Blanket
by
Delores Fossen

The man was watching her.

Marin Sheppard was sure of it.

He wasn't staring, exactly. In fact, he hadn't even looked at her, though he'd been seated directly across from her in the lounge car of the train for the past fifteen minutes. He seemed to focus his attention on the wintry Texas landscape that zipped past the window. But several times Marin had met his gaze in the reflection of the glass.

Yes, he was watching her.

That kicked up her heart rate a couple of notches. A too-familiar nauseating tightness started to knot Marin's stomach.

Was it starting all over again?

Was he watching her, hoping that she'd lead him to her brother, Dexter? Or was this yet another attempt by her parents to insinuate themselves into her life?

It'd been over eight months since the last time this happened. A former "business associate" of her brother who was riled that he'd paid for a "product" that Dexter hadn't delivered. The man had followed her around Fort Worth for days. He hadn't been subtle about it, either, and that had made him seem all the more menacing. And she hadn't given birth to Noah yet then.

The stakes were so much higher now.

Marin hugged her sleeping son closer to her chest. He smelled like baby shampoo and the rice cereal he'd had for lunch. She brushed a kiss on his forehead and rocked gently. Not so much for him—Noah was sound asleep and might stay that way for the remaining hour of the trip to San Antonio. No, the rocking, the kiss and the snug embrace were more for her benefit, to help steady her nerves.

And it worked.

"Cute kid," she heard someone say. The man across from her. Who else? There were no other travelers in this particular section of the lounge car.

Marin lifted her gaze. Met his again. But this time it wasn't through the buffer of the glass, and she clearly saw his eyes, a blend of silver and smoke, framed with indecently long, dark eyelashes.

She studied him a moment, trying to decide if she knew him. He was on the lanky side. Midnight-colored hair. High cheekbones. A classically chiseled male jaw.

The only thing that saved him from being a total pretty boy was the one-inch scar angled across his right eyebrow, thin but noticeable. Not a precise surgeon's cut, a jagged, angry mark left from an old injury. It conjured images of barroom brawls, tattooed bikers and bashed beer bottles. Not that Marin had firsthand knowledge of such things.

But she would bet that he did.

He wore jeans that fit as if they'd been tailor-made for him, a dark blue pullover shirt that hugged his chest and a black leather bomber jacket. And snakeskin boots—specifically diamondback rattlesnake. Pricey and conspicuous footwear.

No, she didn't know him. Marin was certain she would have remembered him—a realization that bothered her because he was hot, and she was sorry she'd noticed.

He tipped his head toward Noah. "I meant your baby," he clarified. "Cute kid."

"Thank you." She looked away from the man, hoping it was the end of their brief conversation.

It wasn't.

"He's what…seven, eight months old?"

"Eight," she provided.

"He reminds me a little of my nephew," the man continued. "It must be hard, traveling alone with a baby."

That brought Marin's attention racing across the car. What had provoked that remark? She searched his face and his eyes almost frantically, trying to figure out if it was some sort of veiled threat.

He held up his hands, and a nervous laugh sounded from deep within his chest. "Sorry. Didn't mean to alarm you. It's just I noticed you're wearing a medical alert bracelet."

Marin glanced down at her left wrist. The almond-shaped metal disc was peeking out from the cuff of her sleeve. With its classic caduceus symbol engraved in crimson, it was like his boots—impossible to miss.

"I'm epileptic," she said.

"Oh." Concern dripped from the word.

"Don't worry," she countered. "I keep my seizures under control with meds. I haven't had one in over five years."

She immediately wondered why in the name of heaven she'd volunteered that personal information. Her medical history wasn't any of his business; it was a sore spot she didn't want to discuss.

"Is your epilepsy the reason you took the train?" he asked. "I mean, instead of driving?"

Marin frowned at him. "I thought the train would make the trip easier for my son."

He nodded, apparently satisfied with her answer to his intrusive question. When his attention strayed back in the general direction of her bracelet, Marin followed his gaze. Down to her hand. All the way to her bare ring finger.

Even though her former fiancé, Randall Davidson, had asked her to marry him, he'd never given her an engagement ring. It'd been an empty, bare gesture. A thought that riled her even now. Randall's betrayal had cut her to the bone.

Shifting Noah into the crook of her arm, she reached down to collect her diaper bag. "I think I'll go for a little walk and stretch my legs."

And change seats, she silently added.

Judging from the passengers she'd seen get on and off, the train wasn't crowded, so moving into coach seating shouldn't be a problem. In fact, she should have done it sooner.

"I'm sorry," he said. "I made you uncomfortable with my questions."

His words stopped her because they were sincere. Or at least he sounded that way. Of course, she'd been wrong before. It would take another lifetime or two for her to trust her instincts.

And that was the reason she reached for the bag again.

"Stay, *please*," he insisted. "It'll be easier for me to move." He got up, headed for the exit and then stopped, turning back around to face her. "I was hitting on you."

Marin blinked. "You…what?"

"Hitting on you," he clarified.

Oh.

That took her a few moments to process.

"Really?" Marin asked, sounding far more surprised than she wanted.

He chuckled, something low, husky and male. Something that trickled through her like expensive warm whiskey. "Really." But then, the lightheartedness faded from his eyes, and his jaw muscles started to stir. "I shouldn't have done it. Sorry."

Again, he seemed sincere. So maybe he wasn't watching her after all. Well, not for surveillance any way. Maybe he was watching her because she was a woman. Odd, that she'd forgotten all about basic human attraction and lust.

"You don't have to leave," Marin let him know. Because she suddenly didn't know what to do with her fidgety hands, she ran her fingers through Noah's dark blond curls. "Besides, it won't be long before we're in San Antonio."

He nodded, and it had an air of thankfulness to it. "I'm Quinn Bacelli. Most people though just call me Lucky."

She almost gave him a fake name. Old habits. But it was the truth that came out of her mouth. "Marin Sheppard."

He smiled. It was no doubt a lethal weapon in his arsenal of ways to get women to fall at his feet. Or into his bed. It bothered Marin to realize that she wasn't immune to it.

Good grief. Hadn't her time with Randall taught her anything?

"Well, Marin Sheppard," he said, taking his seat again. "No more hitting on you. Promise."

Good. She mentally repeated that several times, and then wondered why she felt mildly disappointed.

Noah stirred, sucked at a nonexistent bottle and then gave a pouty whimper when he realized it wasn't there. His eyelids fluttered open, and he blinked, focused and looked up at Marin with accusing blue-green eyes that were identical to her own. He made another whimper, probably to let her know that he wasn't pleased about having his nap interrupted.

Her son shifted and wriggled until he was in a sitting position in her lap, and the new surroundings immediately caught his attention. What was left of his whimpering expression evaporated. He examined his puppy socks, the window, the floor, the ceiling and the ruby-red exit sign. Even her garnet heart necklace. Then, his attention landed on the man seated across from him.

Noah grinned at him.

The man grinned back. "Did you have a good nap, buddy?"

Noah babbled a cordial response, something the two males must have understood, because they shared another smile.

Marin looked at Quinn "Lucky" Bacelli. Then, at her son. Their smiles seemed to freeze in place.

There was no warning.

A deafening blast ripped through the car.

One moment Marin was sitting on the seat with her son cradled in her arms, and the next she was flying across the narrow space right at Lucky.

Everything moved fast. So fast. And yet it happened in slow motion, too. It seemed part of some nightmarish dream where everything was tearing apart at the seams.

Debris spewed through the air. The diaper bag, the magazine she'd been reading, the very walls themselves. All of it, along with Noah and her.

Something slammed into her back and the left side of her head. It knocked the breath from her. The pain was instant—searing—and it sliced right through her, blurring her vision.

She and Noah landed in Lucky's arms, propelled against him. But he softened the fall. He turned, immediately, pushing them down against the seat and crawling over them so he could shelter them with his body.

⊚™ INTRIGUE

Coming next month

2-IN-1 ANTHOLOGY

SECURITY BLANKET by Delores Fossen

Lucky thought saving Marin would be the end of their affair.
But when she asks him to pretend to be the father of her
infant son, it's an offer he can't refuse...

HIS 7-DAY FIANCÉE by Gail Barrett

When Amanda is held at gunpoint in his casino it's up to Luke
to protect her – by pretending to be her fiancé! Yet could their
fake engagement put them in danger too?

2-IN-1 ANTHOLOGY

THE BODYGUARD'S PROMISE by Carla Cassidy

Clay West isn't happy about his latest bodyguard assignment,
protecting a Hollywood child star from an unknown menace...
until he meets the tiny starlet's sexy mum!

THE MISSING MILLIONAIRE by Dani Sinclair

Harrison's shocked to discover beautiful Jamie's his new
bodyguard. And Jamie's ready to risk everything to
protect him – even losing her heart.

SINGLE TITLE

THE VAMPIRE'S QUEST by Vivi Anna

Nocturne™

Vampire Kellen has come to the city of Nouveau Monde
to save himself. But fiery Sophie is about to cause
him even more trouble!

On sale 18th December 2009

Available at WHSmith, Tesco, ASDA, Eason and all good bookshops.
For full Mills & Boon range including eBooks visit
www.millsandboon.co.uk

INTRIGUE

Coming next month

2-IN-1 ANTHOLOGY

HIS BEST FRIEND'S BABY by Mallory Kane

When ex-air-force man Matt's dead best friend's tiny son goes missing he is determined to save the child. But he didn't expect his attraction to widow Aimee.

THE NIGHT SERPENT by Anna Leonard

Lily is an ordinary girl. Until she's caught up in a murder investigation led by Special Agent Jon Patrick and learns she is being stalked by the Night Serpent.

SINGLE TITLE

MATCHMAKING WITH A MISSION
by BJ Daniels

McKenna can't keep her mind off brooding bad boy Nate. He's come back to town to bury his past – but McKenna is determined to get him back at the ranch by her side.

SINGLE TITLE

CAVANAUGH HEAT
by Marie Ferrarella

It's been years since top cop Brian Cavanaugh has seen his former partner Lila, but he's surprised to discover their chemistry is as hot as ever!

On sale 1st January 2010

⊚ MILLS & BOON

are proud to present our...

Book of the Month

Snowbound: Miracle Marriage
by Sarah Morgan from
Mills & Boon® Medical™

Confirmed bachelor Dr Daniel Buchannan is
babysitting his brother's children and needs help!
Stella, his ex-fiancée, reluctantly rescues him and,
snowbound with his makeshift family, Daniel
realises he can never let Stella go again...

Enjoy double the romance in this
great-value 2-in-1!
Snowbound: Miracle Marriage
&
Christmas Eve: Doorstep Delivery
by Sarah Morgan

Mills & Boon® Medical™
Available 4th December 2009

Something to say about our
Book of the Month?
Tell us what you think!
millsandboon.co.uk/community

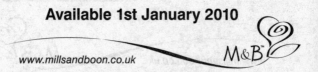

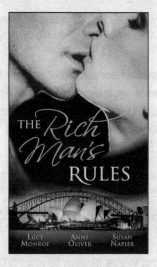

millsandboon.co.uk Community

Join Us!

The Community is the perfect place to meet and chat to kindred spirits who love books and reading as much as you do, but it's also the place to:

- Get the inside scoop from authors about their latest books
- Learn how to write a romance book with advice from our editors
- Help us to continue publishing the best in women's fiction
- Share your thoughts on the books we publish
- Befriend other users

Forums: Interact with each other as well as authors, editors and a whole host of other users worldwide.

Blogs: Every registered community member has their own blog to tell the world what they're up to and what's on their mind.

Book Challenge: We're aiming to read 5,000 books and have joined forces with The Reading Agency in our inaugural Book Challenge.

Profile Page: Showcase yourself and keep a record of your recent community activity.

Social Networking: We've added buttons at the end of every post to share via digg, Facebook, Google, Yahoo, technorati and de.licio.us.

www.millsandboon.co.uk

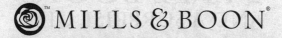

2 FREE BOOKS
AND A SURPRISE GIFT

We would like to take this opportunity to thank you for reading this Mills & Boon® book by offering you the chance to take TWO more specially selected books from the Intrigue series absolutely FREE! We're also making this offer to introduce you to the benefits of the Mills & Boon® Book Club™—

- **FREE home delivery**
- **FREE gifts and competitions**
- **FREE monthly Newsletter**
- **Exclusive Mills & Boon Book Club offers**
- **Books available before they're in the shops**

Accepting these FREE books and gift places you under no obligation to buy, you may cancel at any time, even after receiving your free books. Simply complete your details below and return the entire page to the address below. You don't even need a stamp!

YES Please send me 2 free Intrigue books and a surprise gift. I understand that unless you hear from me, I will receive 5 superb new stories every month, including two 2-in-1 books priced at £4.99 each and a single book priced at £3.19, postage and packing free. I am under no obligation to purchase any books and may cancel my subscription at any time. The free books and gift will be mine to keep in any case.

Ms/Mrs/Miss/Mr _____ Initials _____

_____

Surname _____

Address _____

_____

_____ Postcode _____

Send this whole page to: Mills & Boon Book Club, Free Book Offer, FREEPOST NAT 10298, Richmond, TW9 1BR